image

IMAGE COMICS PRESENTS

FOR LUIS R. RODRIGUEZ, MY GRANDFATHER,
WITH LOVE. 1925-2013 R.I.P.
-FJB

FOR MY FATHER, THOMAS P. MOONEYHAM.
MISS YOU EVERY DAY.
-CTM

ISSUE SIX ART & COVER BY GARRY BROWN
"MOTH" PIN UP, COVER 7 COLORS, &
LOST COASTLINES MAP BY S.M. VIDAURRI
BOOK PRODUCTION BY ADDISON DUKE
VARIANT COVERS BY:
JOE BOWEN
PAOLO RIVERA
RILEY ROSSMO
ROB GUILLORY

FIVE GHOSTS CREATED BY
BARBIERE & MOONEYHAM

IMAGE COMICS, INC.
Robert Kirkman – Chief Operating Officer
Erik Larsen – Chief Financial Officer
Todd McFarlane – President
Marc Silvestri – Chief Executive Officer
Jim Valentino – Vice-President

Eric Stephenson – Publisher
Corey Murphy – Director of Sales
Jeremy Sullivan – Director of Digital Sales
Kat Salazar – Director of PR & Marketing
Emily Miller – Director of Operations
Branwyn Bigglestone – Senior Accounts Manager
Sarah Mello – Accounts Manager
Drew Gill – Art Director
Jonathan Chan – Production Manager
Meredith Wallace – Print Manager
Randy Okamura – Marketing Production Designer
David Brothers – Branding Manager
Ally Power – Content Manager
Addison Duke – Production Artist
Vincent Kukua – Production Artist
Sasha Head – Production Artist
Tricia Ramos – Production Artist
Emilio Bautista – Sales Assistant
Chloe Ramos-Peterson – Administrative Assistant
IMAGECOMICS.COM

FIVE GHOSTS

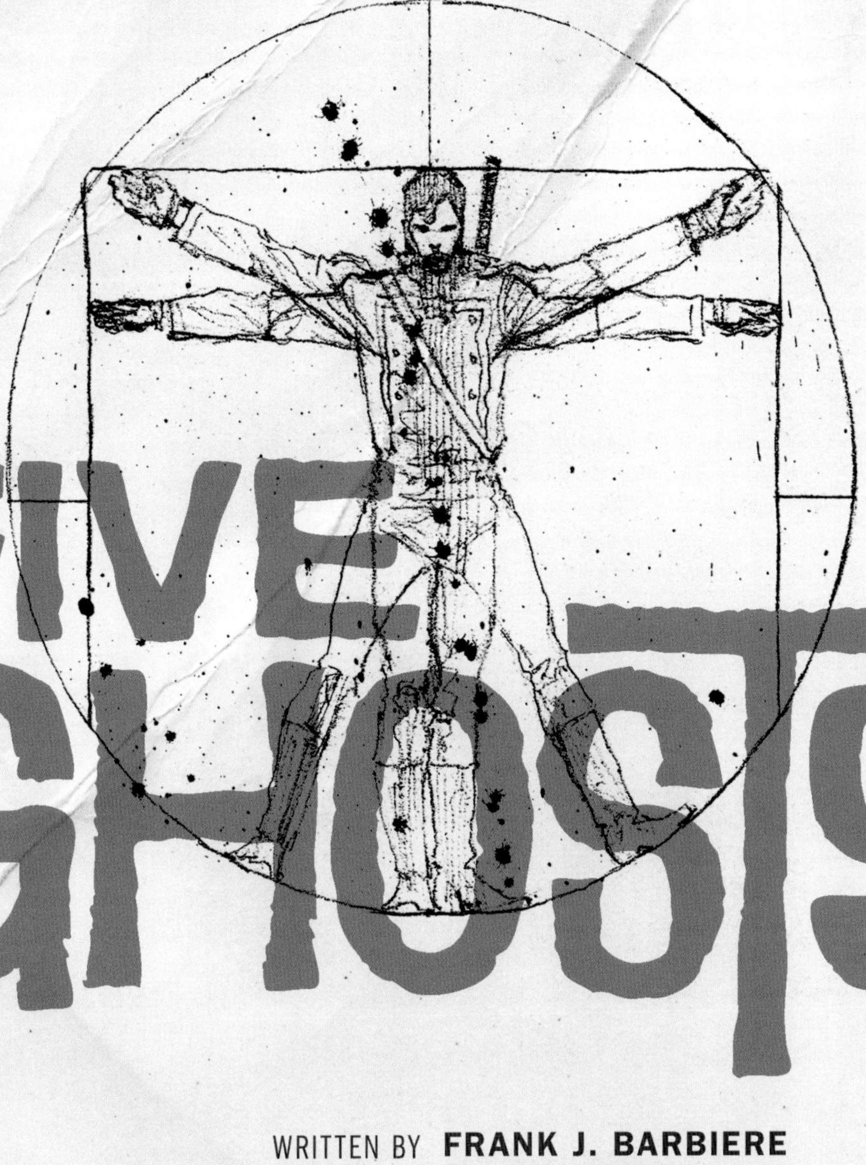

WRITTEN BY **FRANK J. BARBIERE**
ART BY **CHRIS MOONEYHAM**
COLORS BY **LAUREN AFFE**
LOGO AND GRAPHIC DESIGN BY **DYLAN TODD**

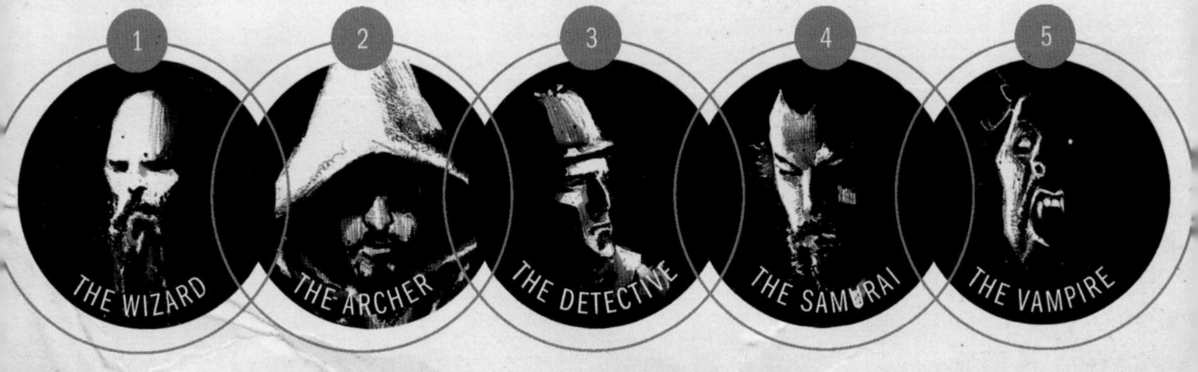
1
THE WIZARD
2
THE ARCHER
3
THE DETECTIVE
4
THE SAMURAI
5
THE VAMPIRE

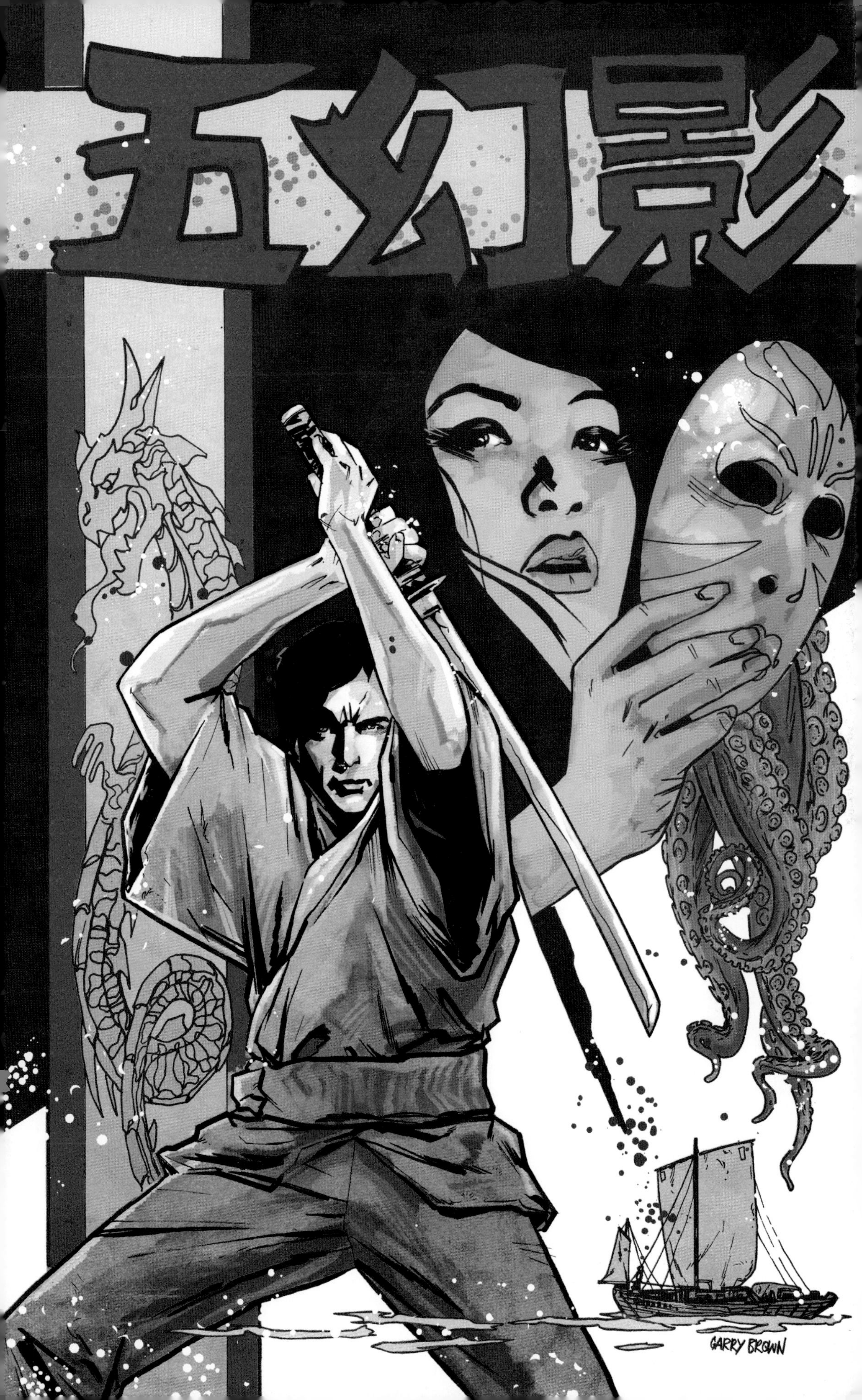
五幻影
GARRY BROWN

PLATE No. 3

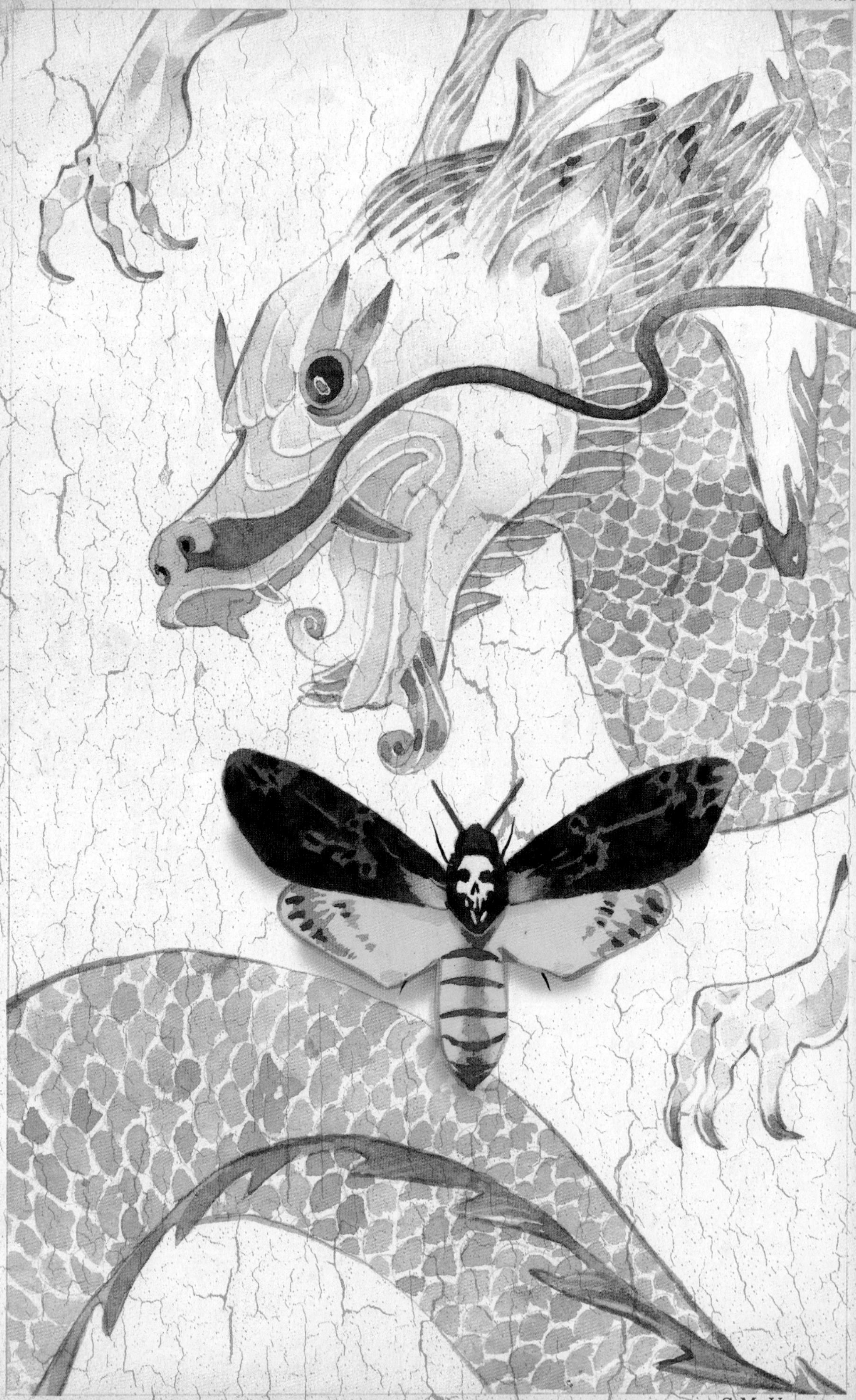

S.M. Vidaurri

"WHAT A STRANGE THING!

TO BE ALIVE

BENEATH CHERRY BLOSSOMS."

-KOBAYASHI ISSA, *POEMS*

"IF I GOT RID OF MY DEMONS,

I'D LOSE MY ANGELS."

-TENNESSEE WILLIAMS

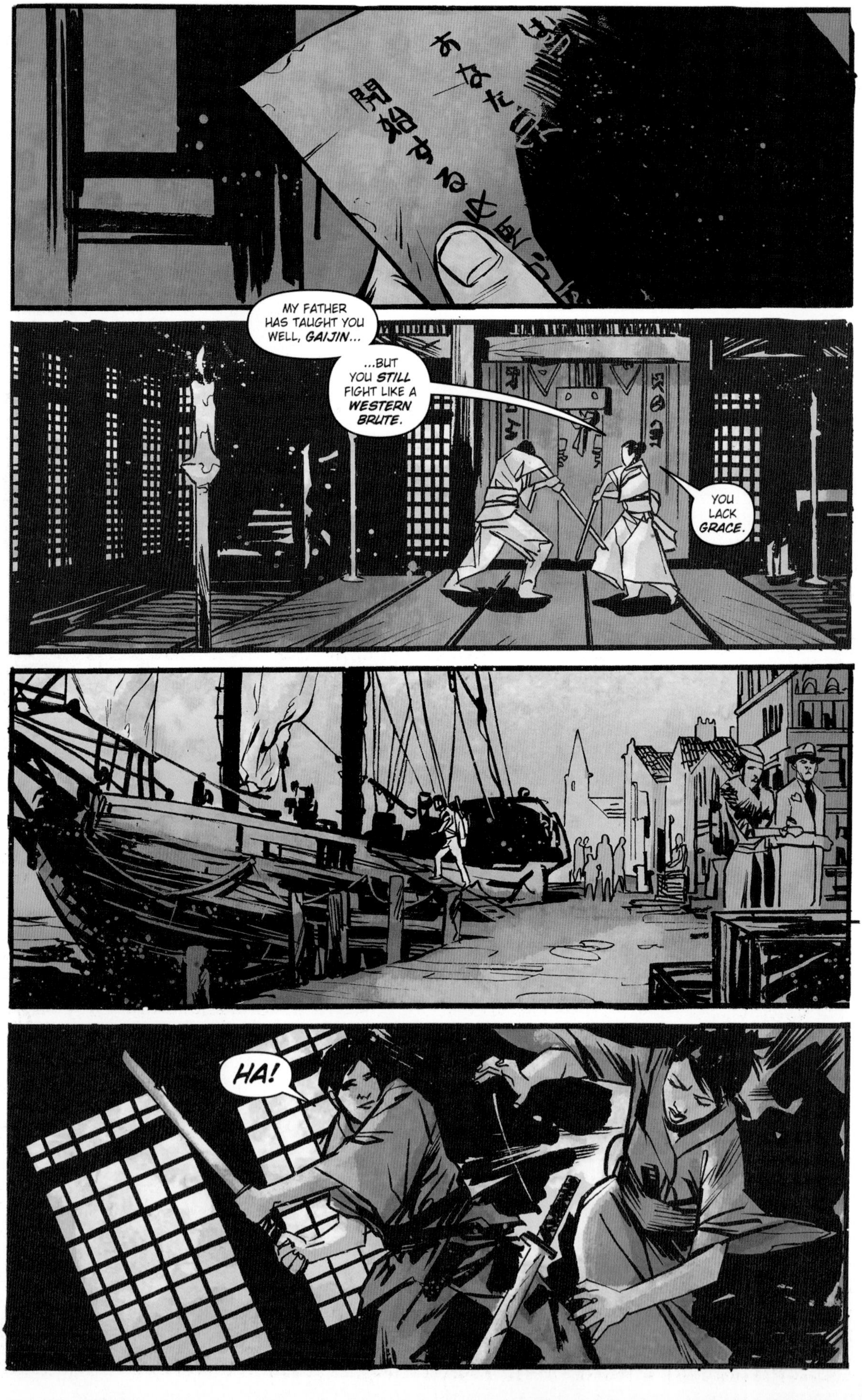
あなた
開始する
MY FATHER HAS TAUGHT YOU WELL, GAIJIN...
...BUT YOU STILL FIGHT LIKE A WESTERN BRUTE.
YOU LACK GRACE.
HA!

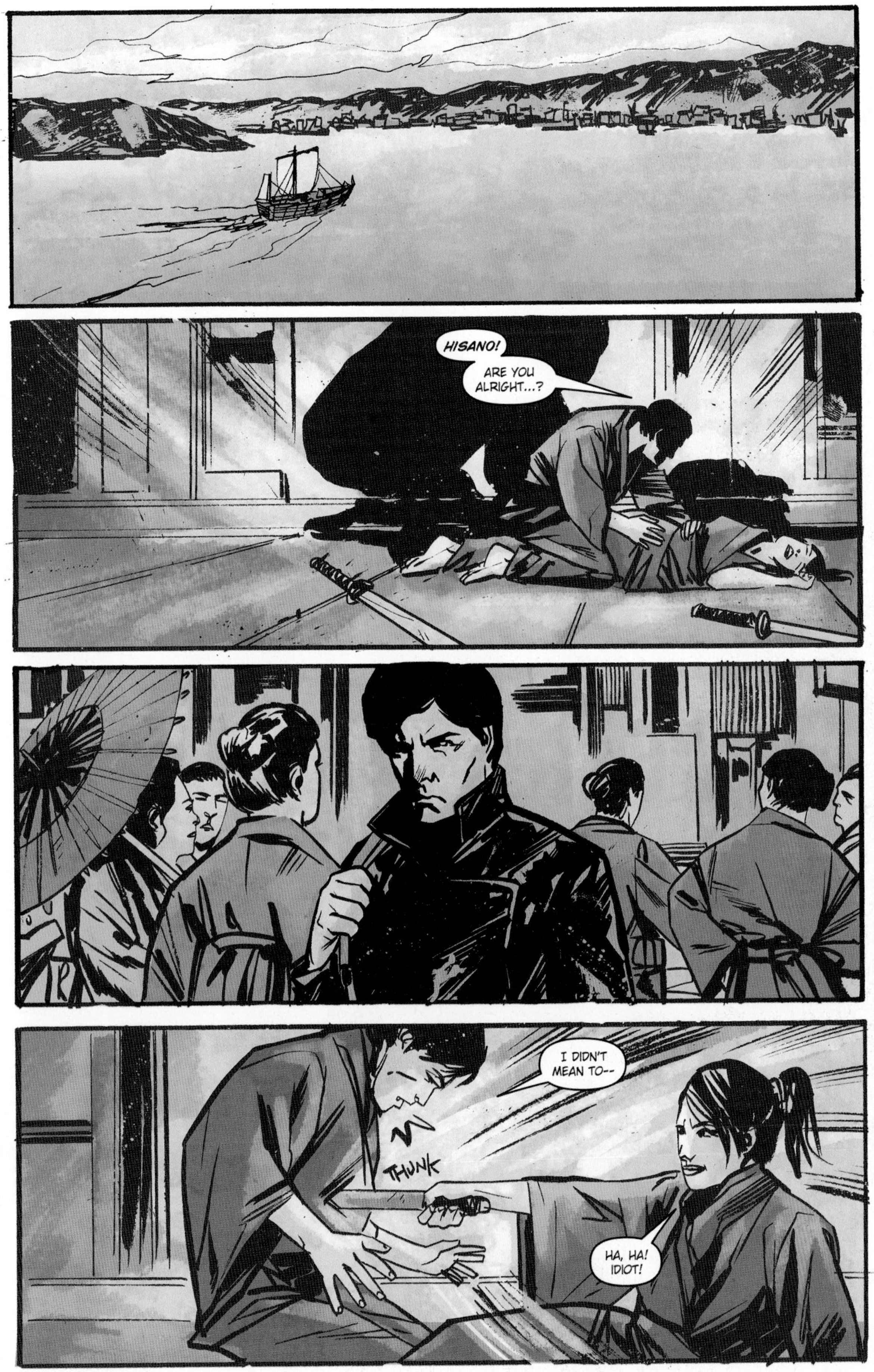
HISANO!
ARE YOU ALRIGHT...?
I DIDN'T MEAN TO--
THUNK
HA, HA! IDIOT!

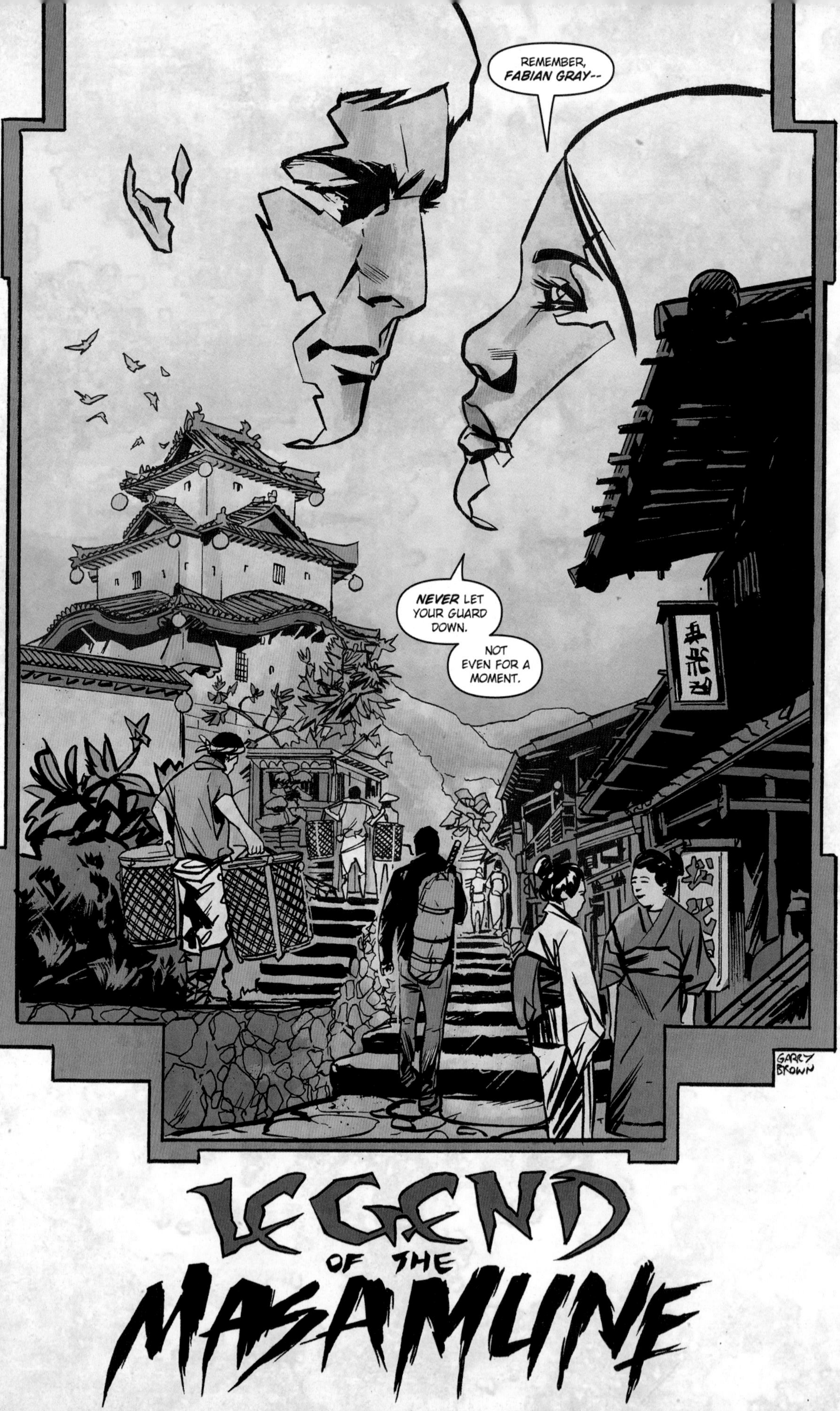
REMEMBER, FABIAN GRAY--
NEVER LET YOUR GUARD DOWN.
NOT EVEN FOR A MOMENT.
GARRY BROWN

LEGEND OF THE MASAMUNE

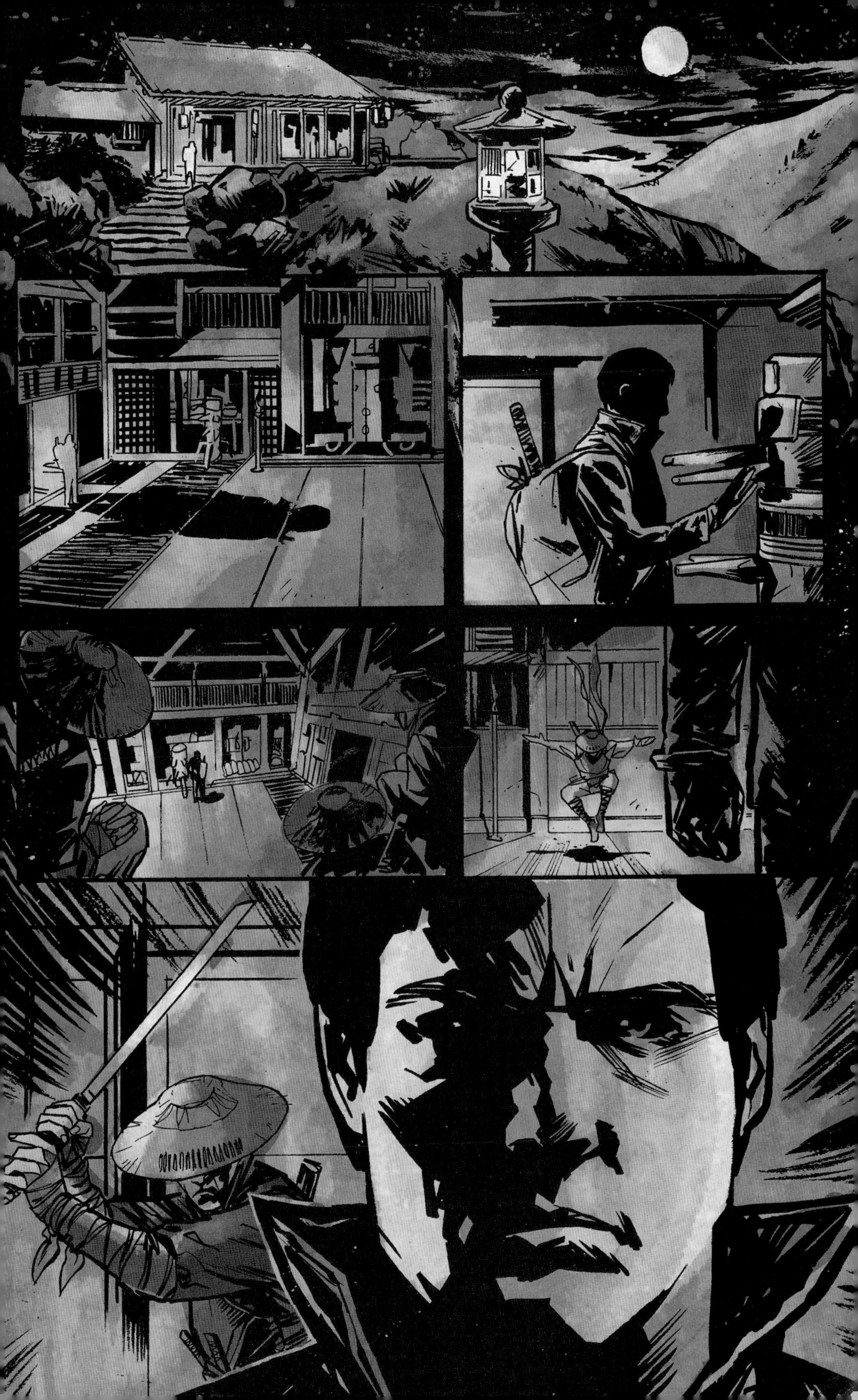

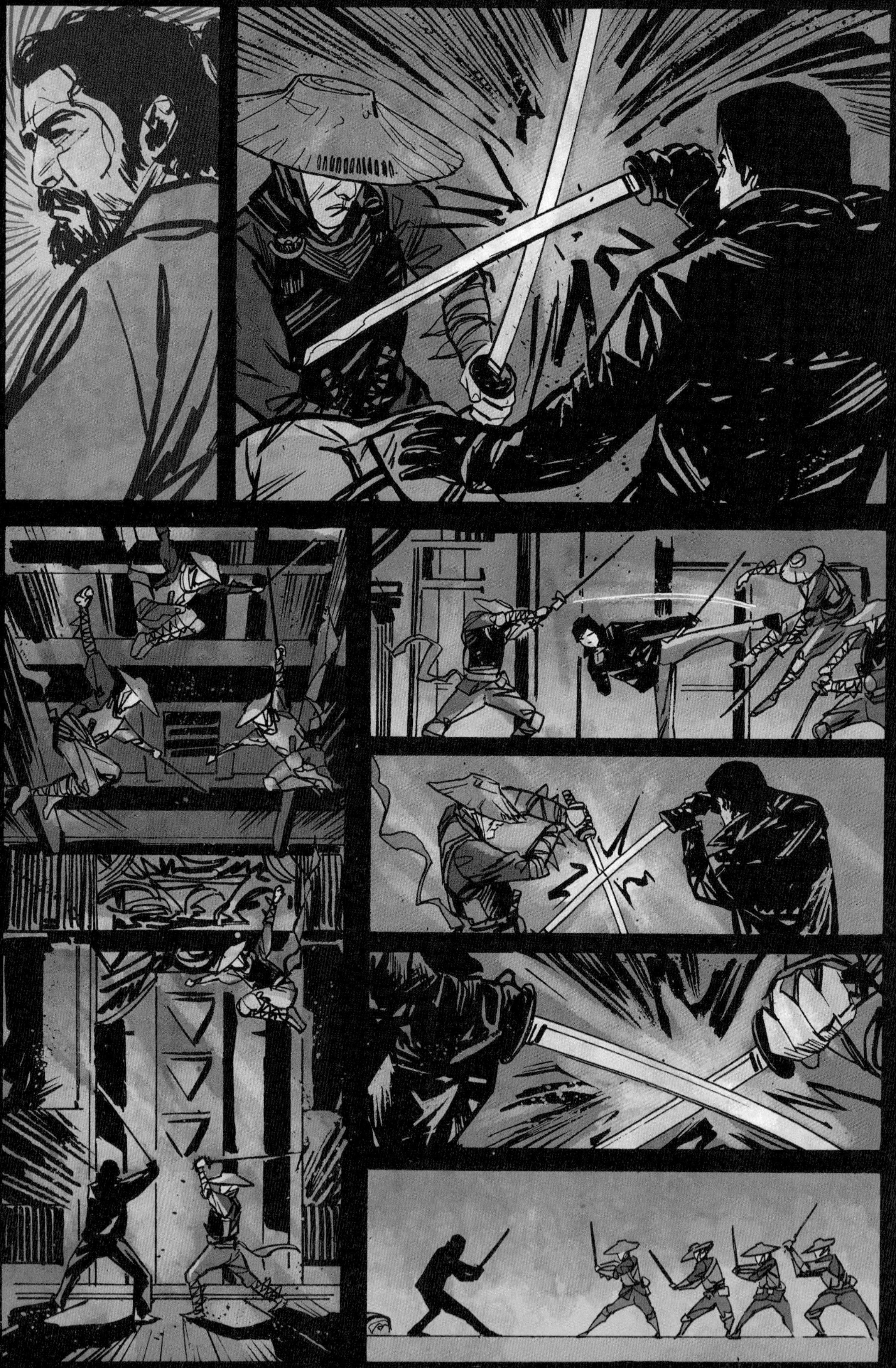

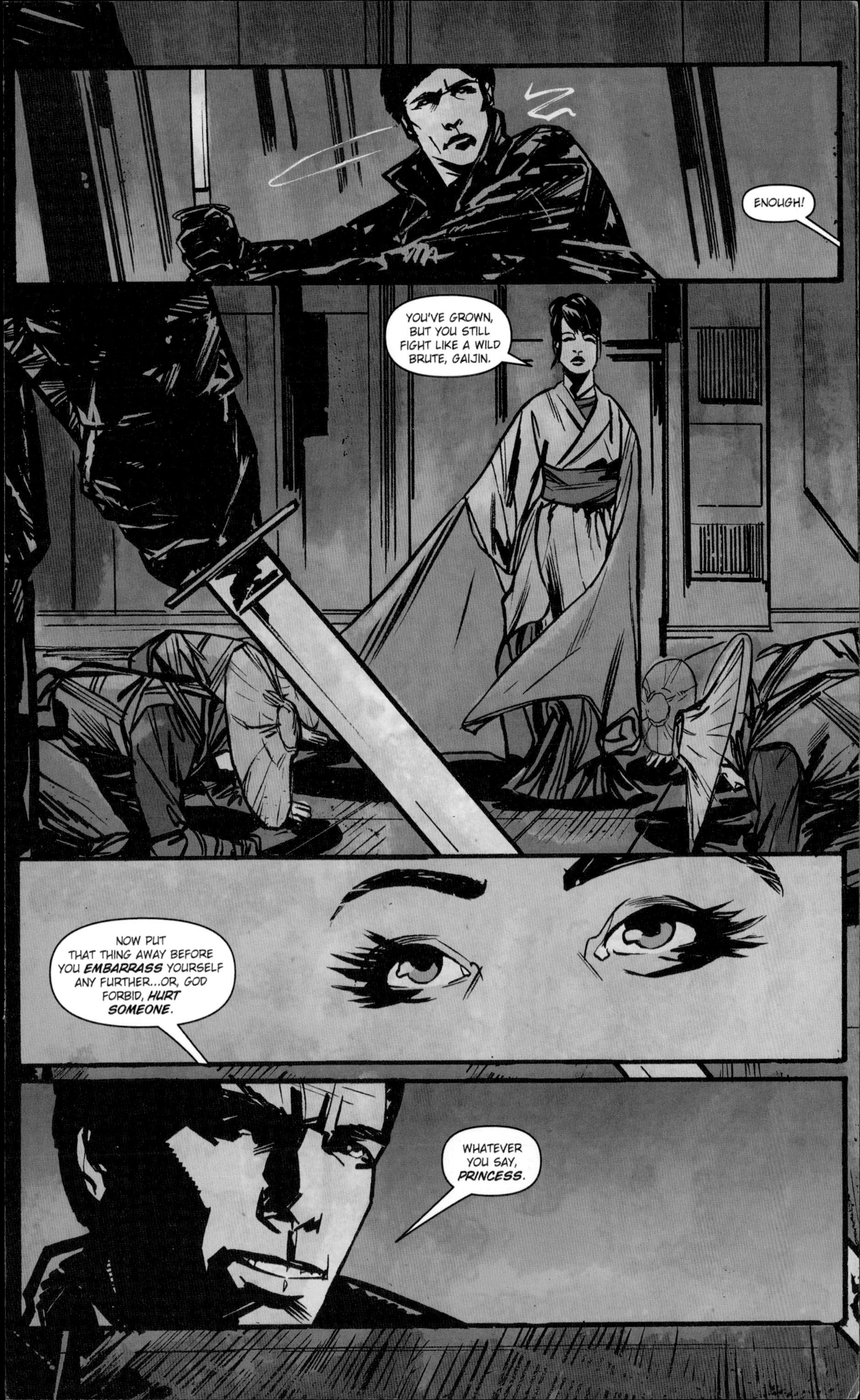
ENOUGH!
YOU'VE GROWN, BUT YOU STILL FIGHT LIKE A WILD BRUTE, GAIJIN.
NOW PUT THAT THING AWAY BEFORE YOU **EMBARRASS** YOURSELF ANY FURTHER...OR, GOD FORBID, ***HURT SOMEONE***.
WHATEVER YOU SAY, ***PRINCESS***.

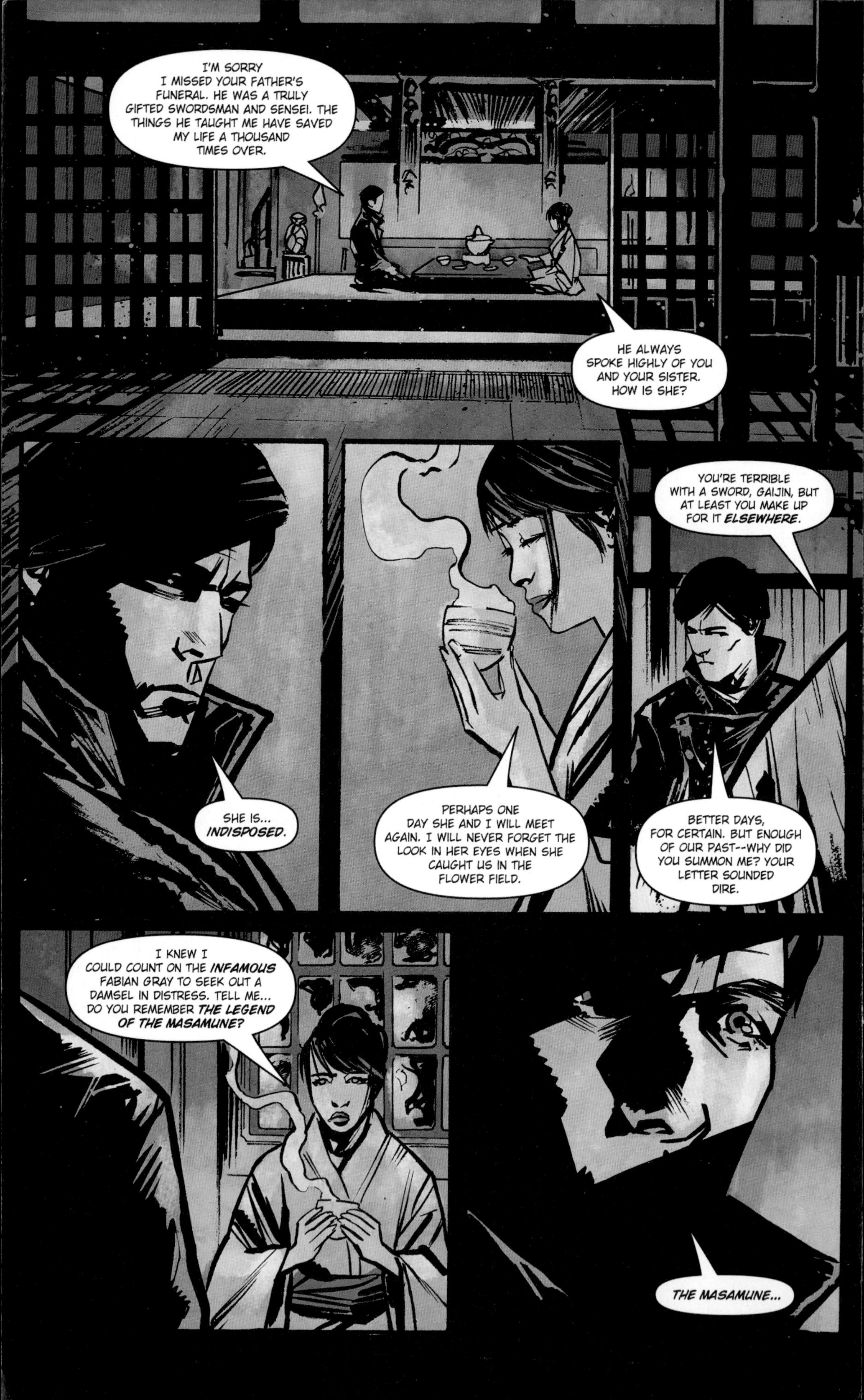
I'M SORRY I MISSED YOUR FATHER'S FUNERAL. HE WAS A TRULY GIFTED SWORDSMAN AND SENSEI. THE THINGS HE TAUGHT ME HAVE SAVED MY LIFE A THOUSAND TIMES OVER.
HE ALWAYS SPOKE HIGHLY OF YOU AND YOUR SISTER. HOW IS SHE?
SHE IS... *INDISPOSED*.
PERHAPS ONE DAY SHE AND I WILL MEET AGAIN. I WILL NEVER FORGET THE LOOK IN HER EYES WHEN SHE CAUGHT US IN THE FLOWER FIELD.
YOU'RE TERRIBLE WITH A SWORD, GAIJIN, BUT AT LEAST YOU MAKE UP FOR IT *ELSEWHERE*.
BETTER DAYS, FOR CERTAIN. BUT ENOUGH OF OUR PAST--WHY DID YOU SUMMON ME? YOUR LETTER SOUNDED DIRE.
I KNEW I COULD COUNT ON THE *INFAMOUS* FABIAN GRAY TO SEEK OUT A DAMSEL IN DISTRESS. TELL ME... DO YOU REMEMBER *THE LEGEND OF THE MASAMUNE?*
THE MASAMUNE...

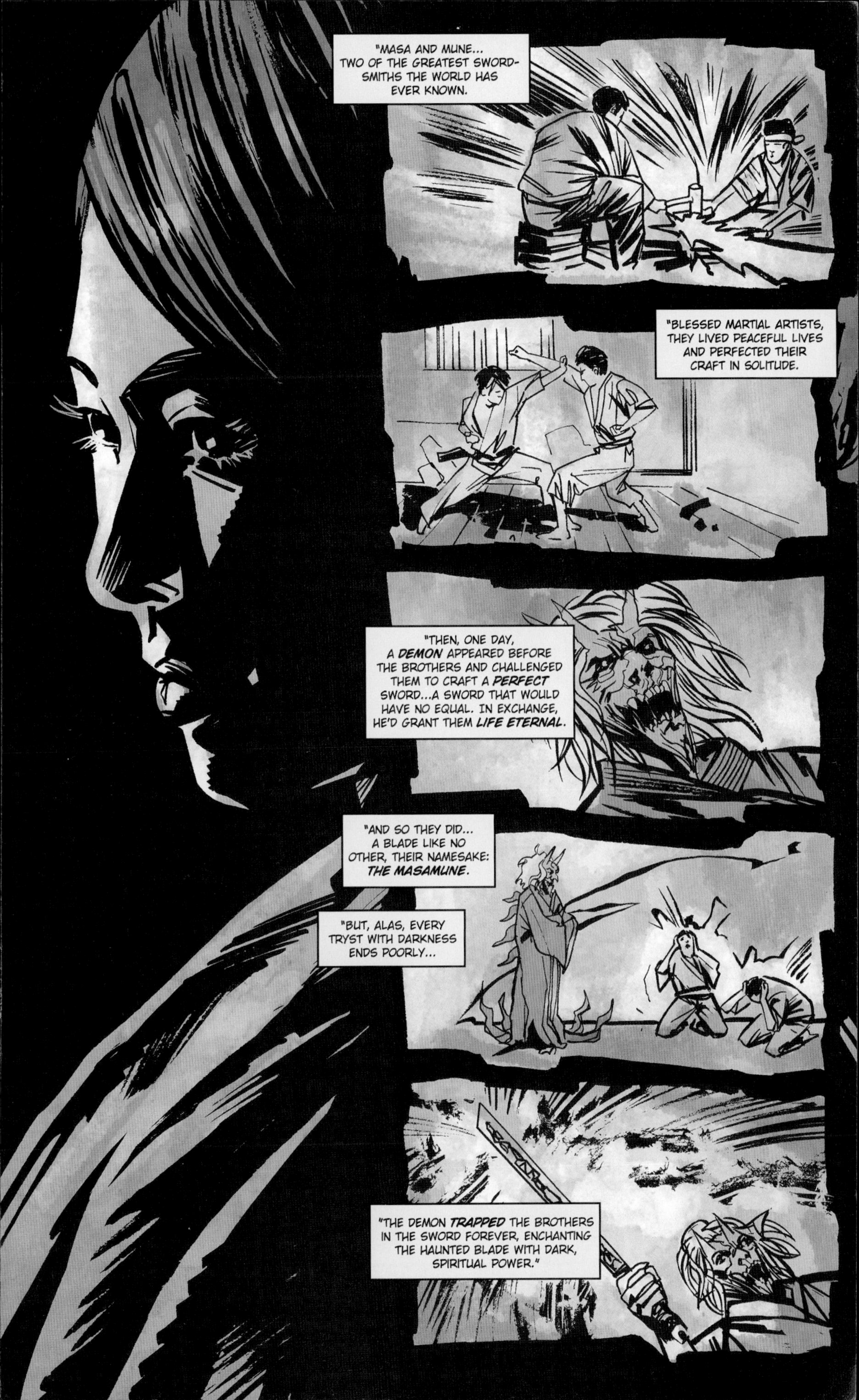
"MASA AND MUNE... TWO OF THE GREATEST SWORD-SMITHS THE WORLD HAS EVER KNOWN.
"BLESSED MARTIAL ARTISTS, THEY LIVED PEACEFUL LIVES AND PERFECTED THEIR CRAFT IN SOLITUDE.
"THEN, ONE DAY, A DEMON APPEARED BEFORE THE BROTHERS AND CHALLENGED THEM TO CRAFT A PERFECT SWORD...A SWORD THAT WOULD HAVE NO EQUAL. IN EXCHANGE, HE'D GRANT THEM LIFE ETERNAL.
"AND SO THEY DID... A BLADE LIKE NO OTHER, THEIR NAMESAKE: THE MASAMUNE.
"BUT, ALAS, EVERY TRYST WITH DARKNESS ENDS POORLY...
"THE DEMON TRAPPED THE BROTHERS IN THE SWORD FOREVER, ENCHANTING THE HAUNTED BLADE WITH DARK, SPIRITUAL POWER."

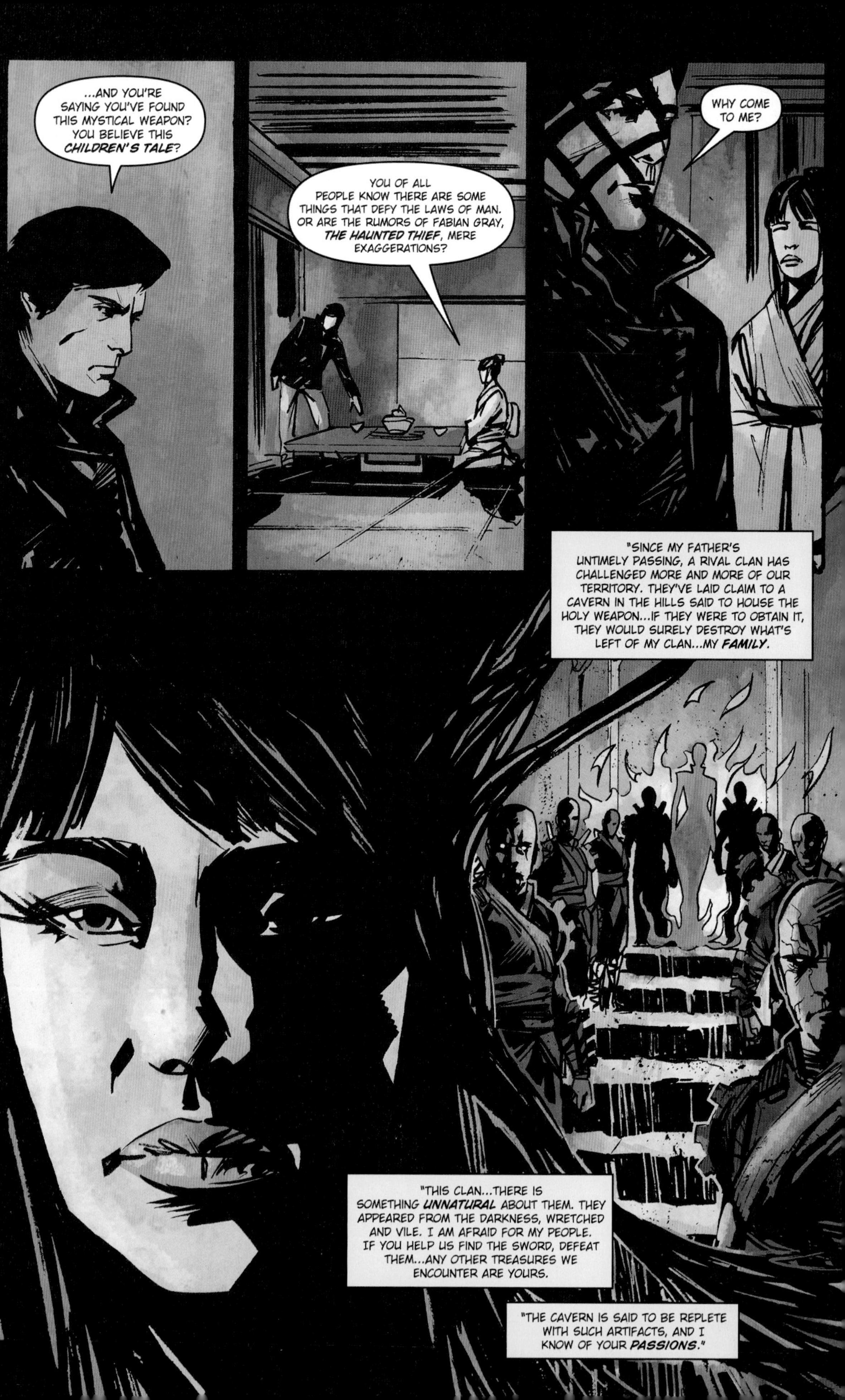
...AND YOU'RE SAYING YOU'VE FOUND THIS MYSTICAL WEAPON? YOU BELIEVE THIS CHILDREN'S TALE?
YOU OF ALL PEOPLE KNOW THERE ARE SOME THINGS THAT DEFY THE LAWS OF MAN. OR ARE THE RUMORS OF FABIAN GRAY, THE HAUNTED THIEF, MERE EXAGGERATIONS?
WHY COME TO ME?
"SINCE MY FATHER'S UNTIMELY PASSING, A RIVAL CLAN HAS CHALLENGED MORE AND MORE OF OUR TERRITORY. THEY'VE LAID CLAIM TO A CAVERN IN THE HILLS SAID TO HOUSE THE HOLY WEAPON...IF THEY WERE TO OBTAIN IT, THEY WOULD SURELY DESTROY WHAT'S LEFT OF MY CLAN...MY FAMILY.
"THIS CLAN...THERE IS SOMETHING UNNATURAL ABOUT THEM. THEY APPEARED FROM THE DARKNESS, WRETCHED AND VILE. I AM AFRAID FOR MY PEOPLE. IF YOU HELP US FIND THE SWORD, DEFEAT THEM...ANY OTHER TREASURES WE ENCOUNTER ARE YOURS.
"THE CAVERN IS SAID TO BE REPLETE WITH SUCH ARTIFACTS, AND I KNOW OF YOUR PASSIONS."

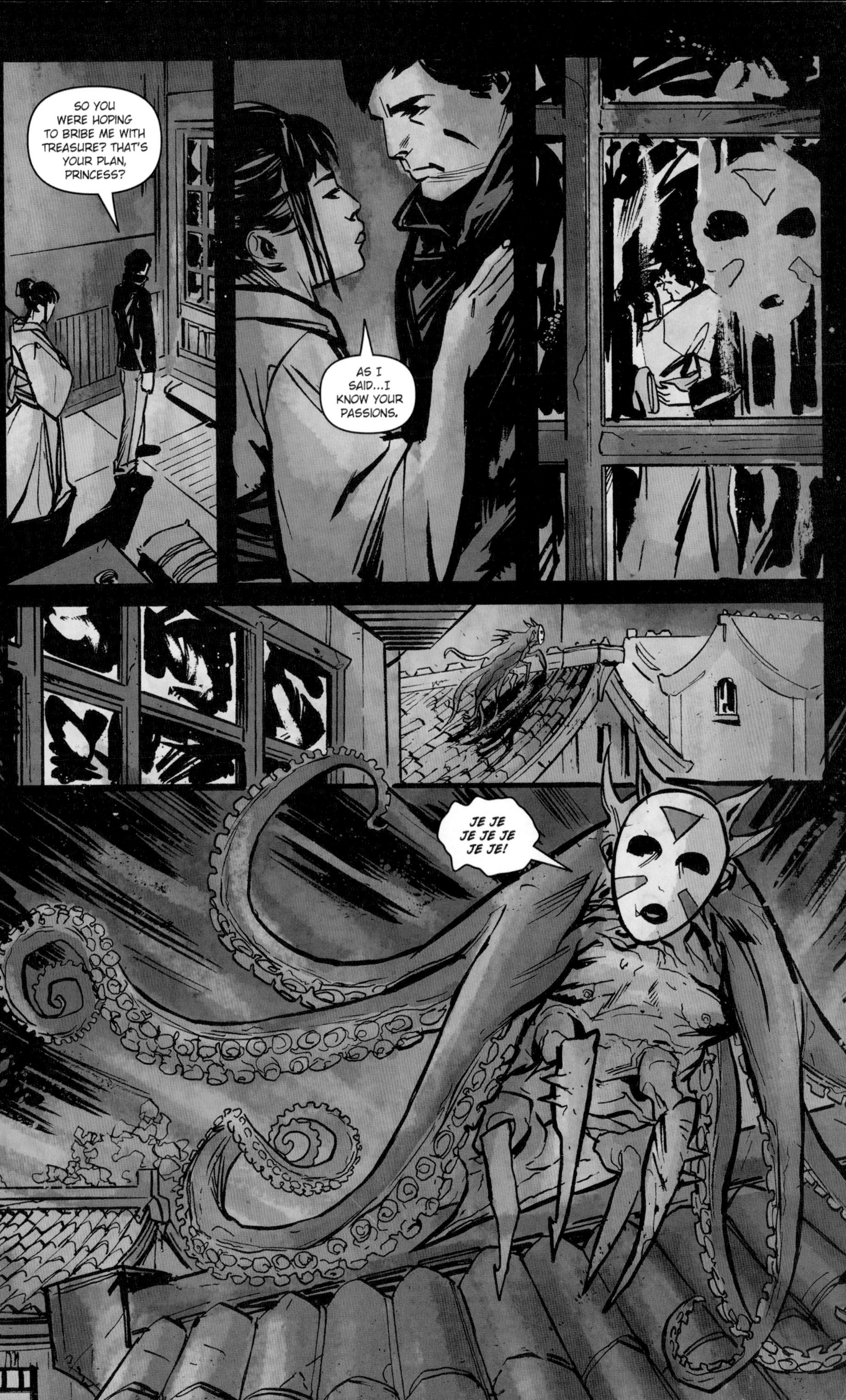
SO YOU WERE HOPING TO BRIBE ME WITH TREASURE? THAT'S YOUR PLAN, PRINCESS?
AS I SAID...I KNOW YOUR PASSIONS.
JE JE JE JE JE JE JE!

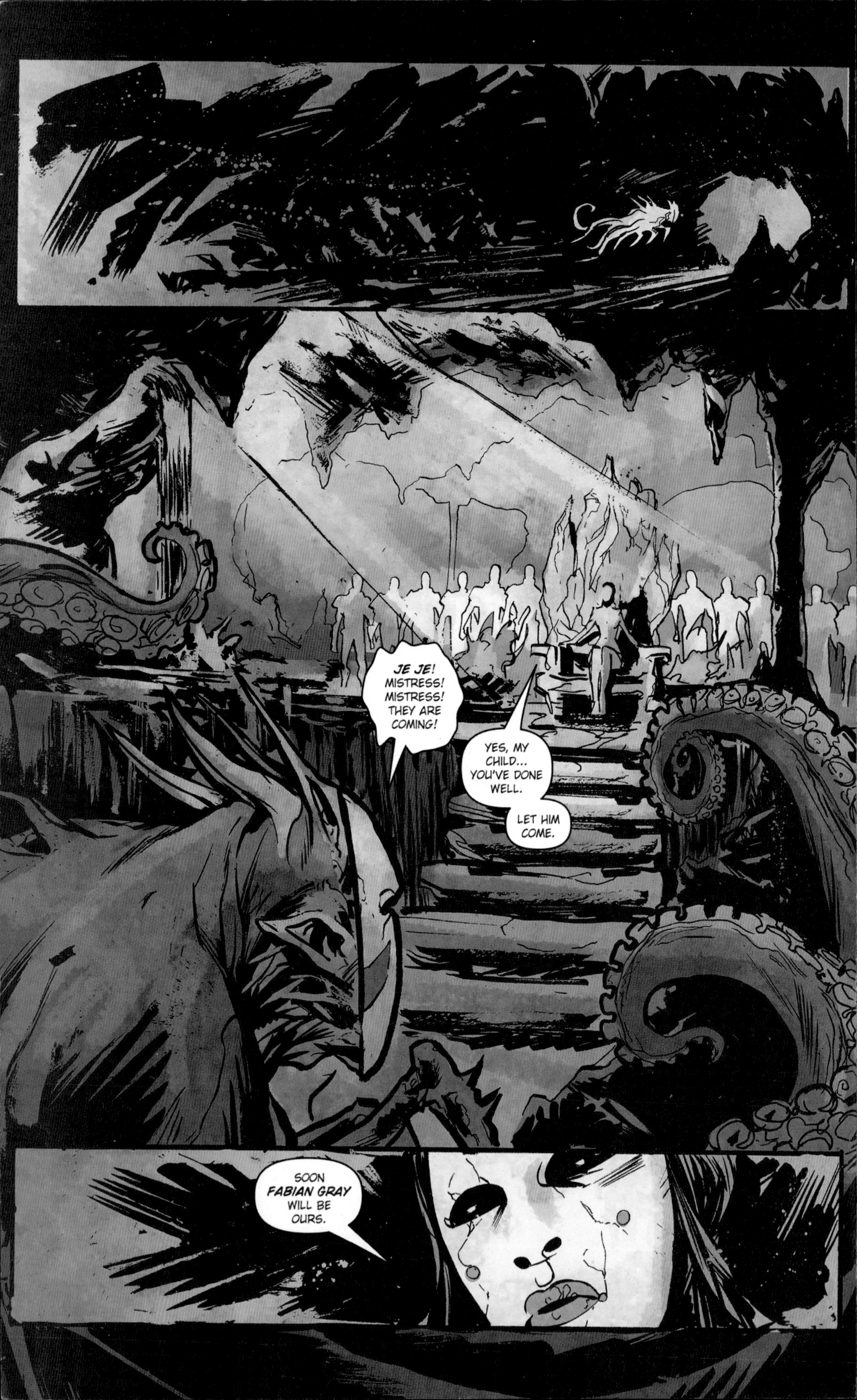

JE JE! MISTRESS! MISTRESS! THEY ARE COMING!
YES, MY CHILD... YOU'VE DONE WELL.
LET HIM COME.
SOON FABIAN GRAY WILL BE OURS.

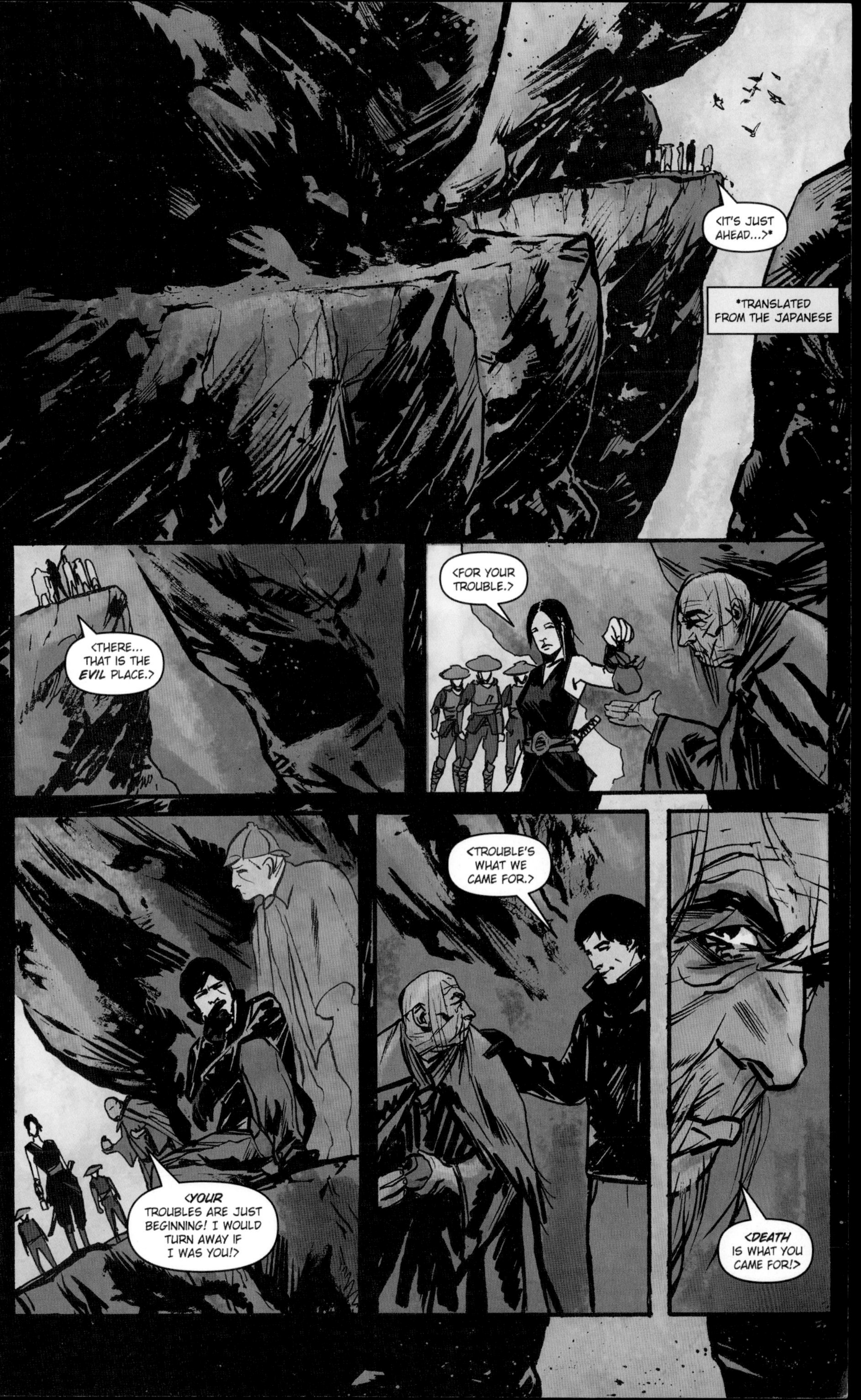
<IT'S JUST AHEAD...>*
*TRANSLATED FROM THE JAPANESE
<THERE... THAT IS THE EVIL PLACE.>
<FOR YOUR TROUBLE.>
<YOUR TROUBLES ARE JUST BEGINNING! I WOULD TURN AWAY IF I WAS YOU!>
<TROUBLE'S WHAT WE CAME FOR.>
<DEATH IS WHAT YOU CAME FOR!>

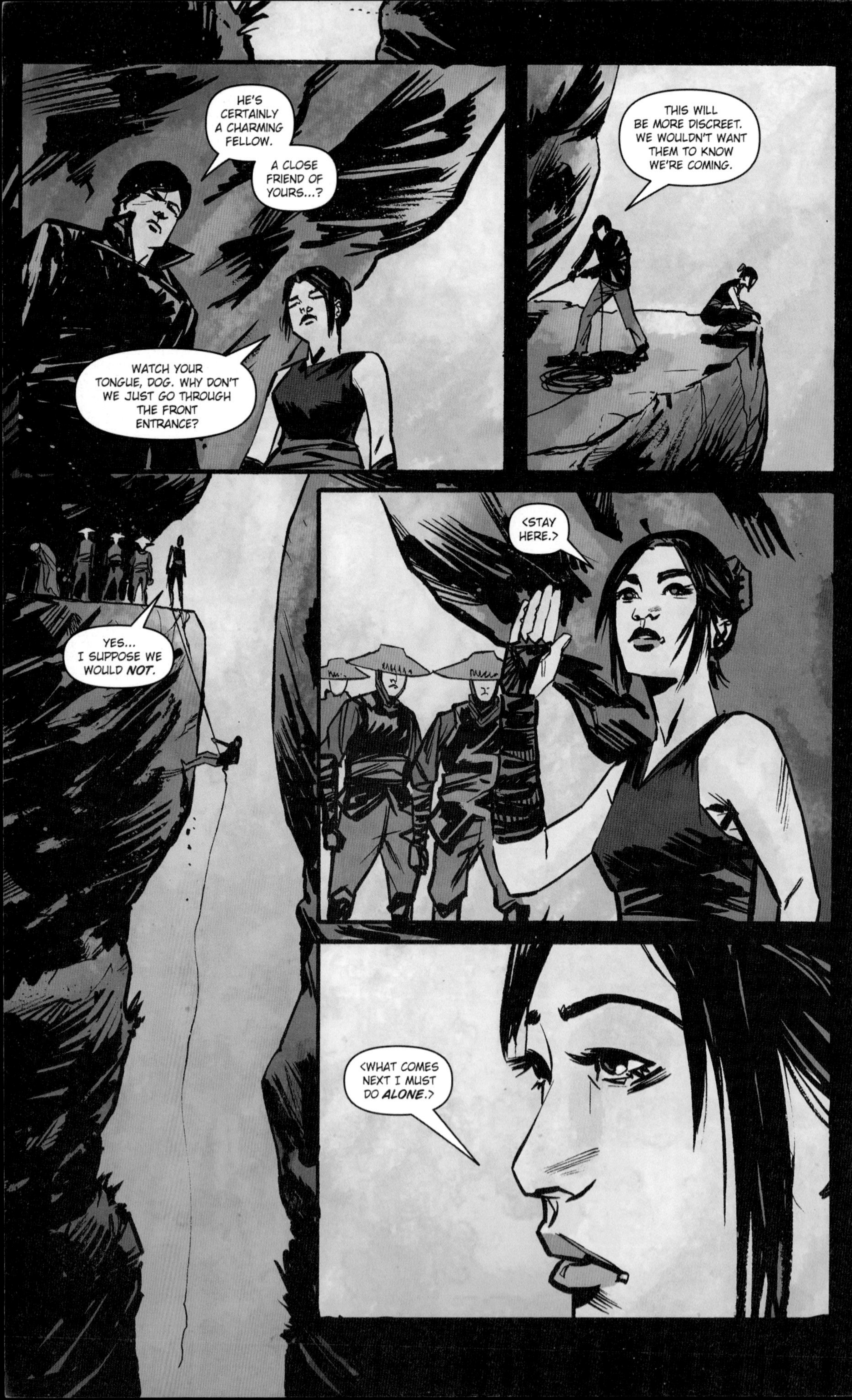
HE'S CERTAINLY A CHARMING FELLOW.
A CLOSE FRIEND OF YOURS...?
WATCH YOUR TONGUE, DOG. WHY DON'T WE JUST GO THROUGH THE FRONT ENTRANCE?
THIS WILL BE MORE DISCREET. WE WOULDN'T WANT THEM TO KNOW WE'RE COMING.
YES... I SUPPOSE WE WOULD ***NOT***.
<STAY HERE.>
<WHAT COMES NEXT I MUST DO ***ALONE***.>

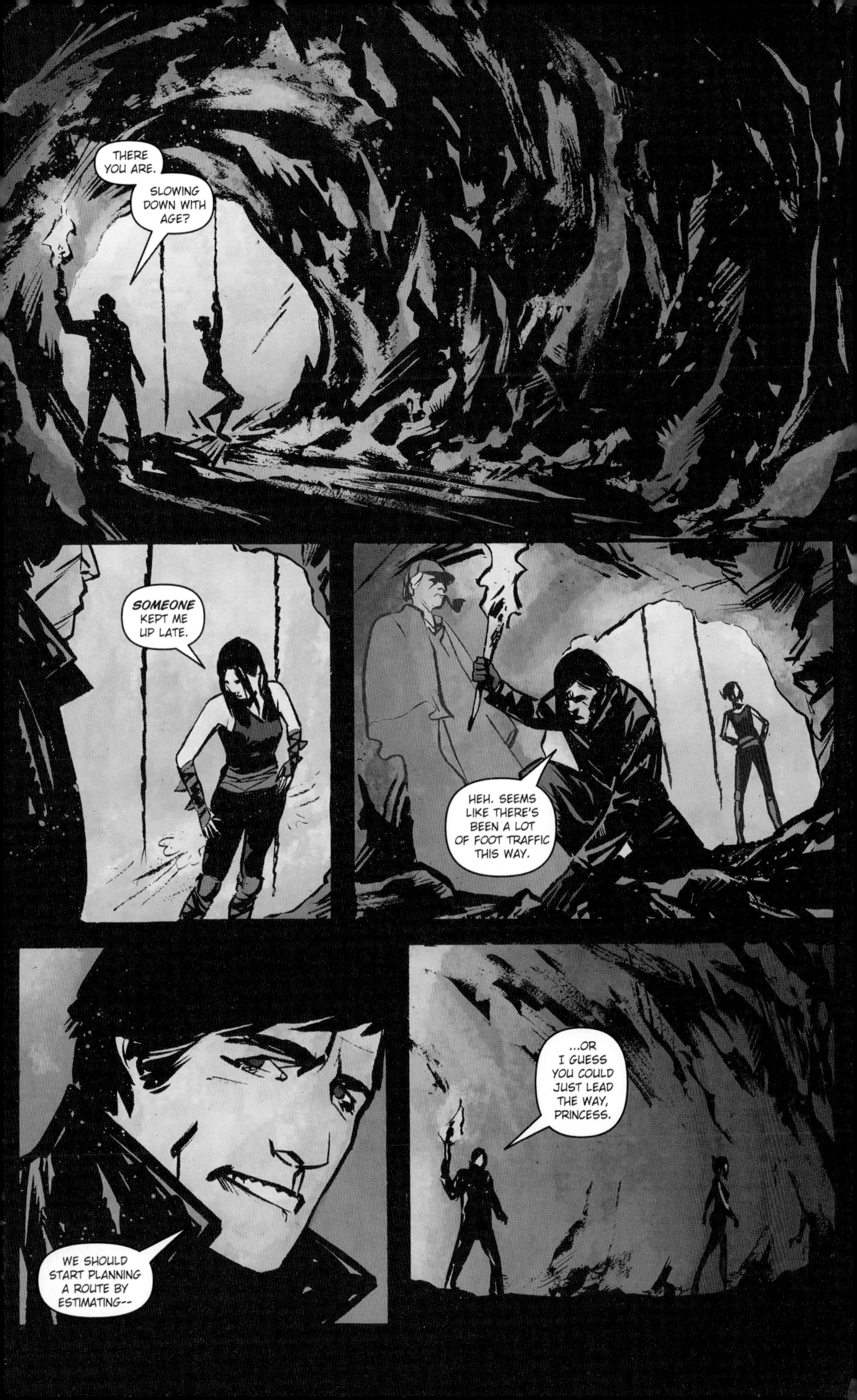
THERE YOU ARE.
SLOWING DOWN WITH AGE?
SOMEONE KEPT ME UP LATE.
HEH. SEEMS LIKE THERE'S BEEN A LOT OF FOOT TRAFFIC THIS WAY.
WE SHOULD START PLANNING A ROUTE BY ESTIMATING--
...OR I GUESS YOU COULD JUST LEAD THE WAY, PRINCESS.

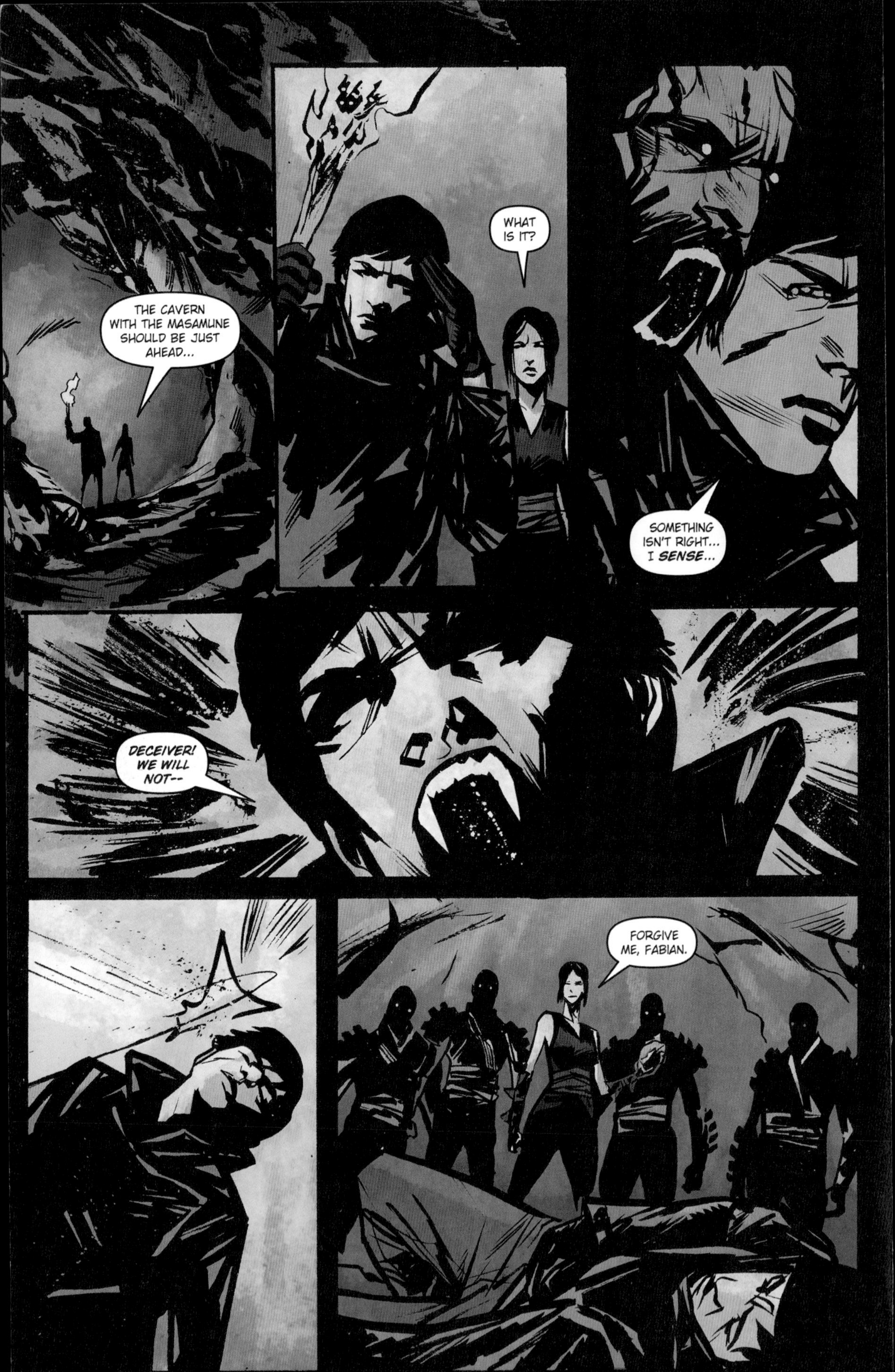
THE CAVERN WITH THE MASAMUNE SHOULD BE JUST AHEAD...
WHAT IS IT?
SOMETHING ISN'T RIGHT... I *SENSE*...
DECEIVER! WE WILL NOT--
FORGIVE ME, FABIAN.

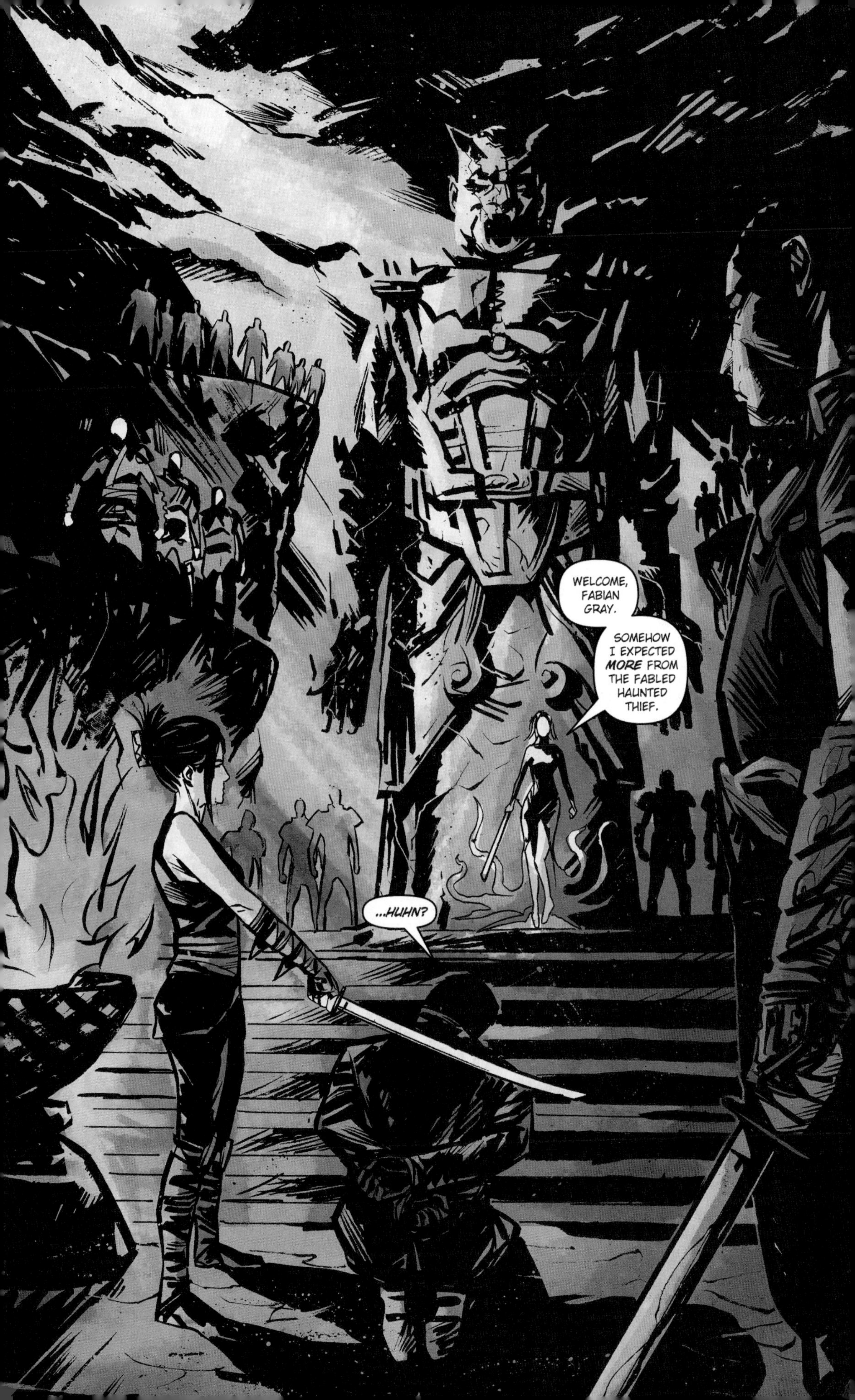
WELCOME, FABIAN GRAY.
SOMEHOW I EXPECTED MORE FROM THE FABLED HAUNTED THIEF.
...HUHN?

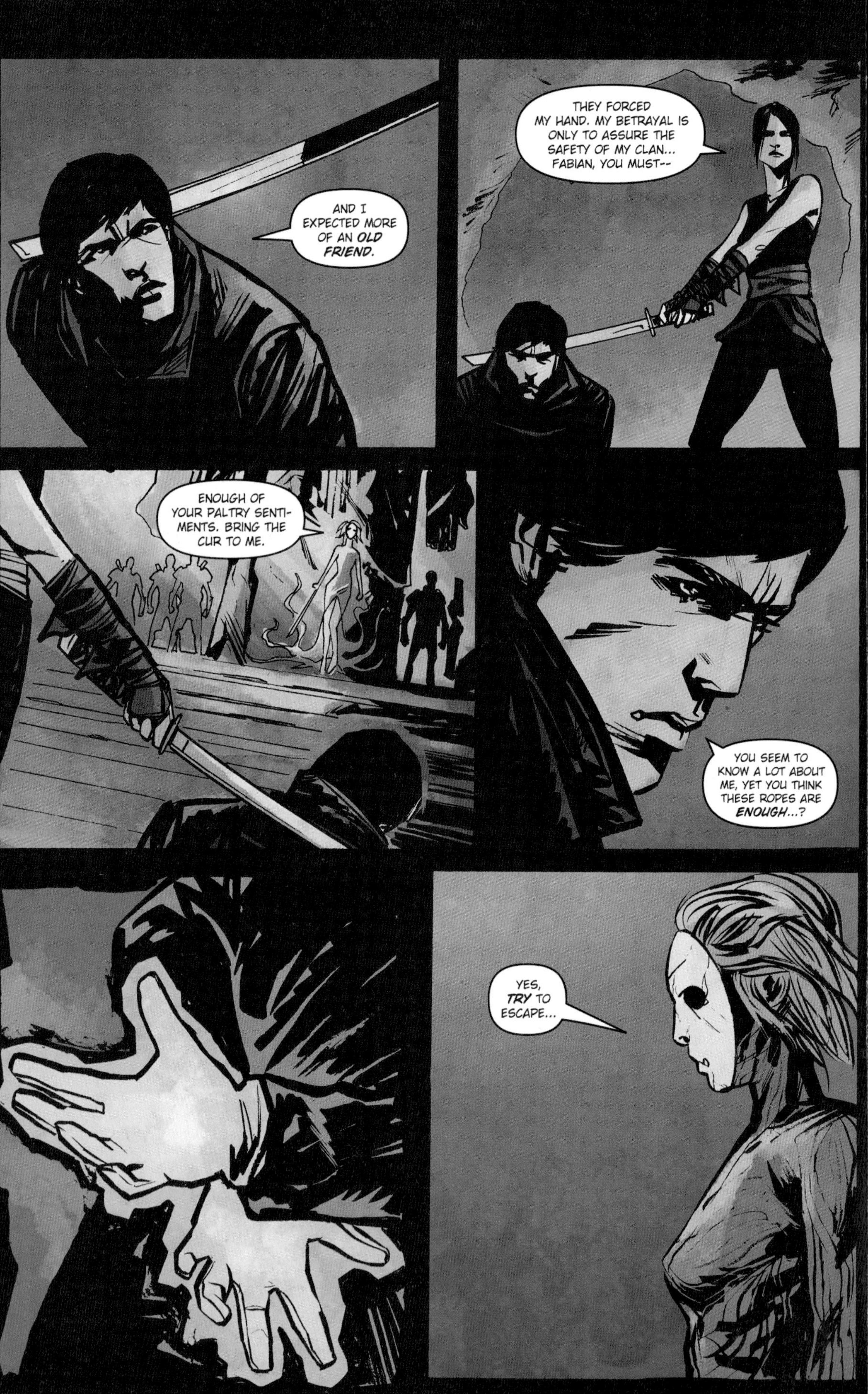

AND I EXPECTED MORE OF AN OLD FRIEND.
THEY FORCED MY HAND. MY BETRAYAL IS ONLY TO ASSURE THE SAFETY OF MY CLAN... FABIAN, YOU MUST--
ENOUGH OF YOUR PALTRY SENTI-MENTS. BRING THE CUR TO ME.
YOU SEEM TO KNOW A LOT ABOUT ME, YET YOU THINK THESE ROPES ARE ENOUGH...?
YES, TRY TO ESCAPE...

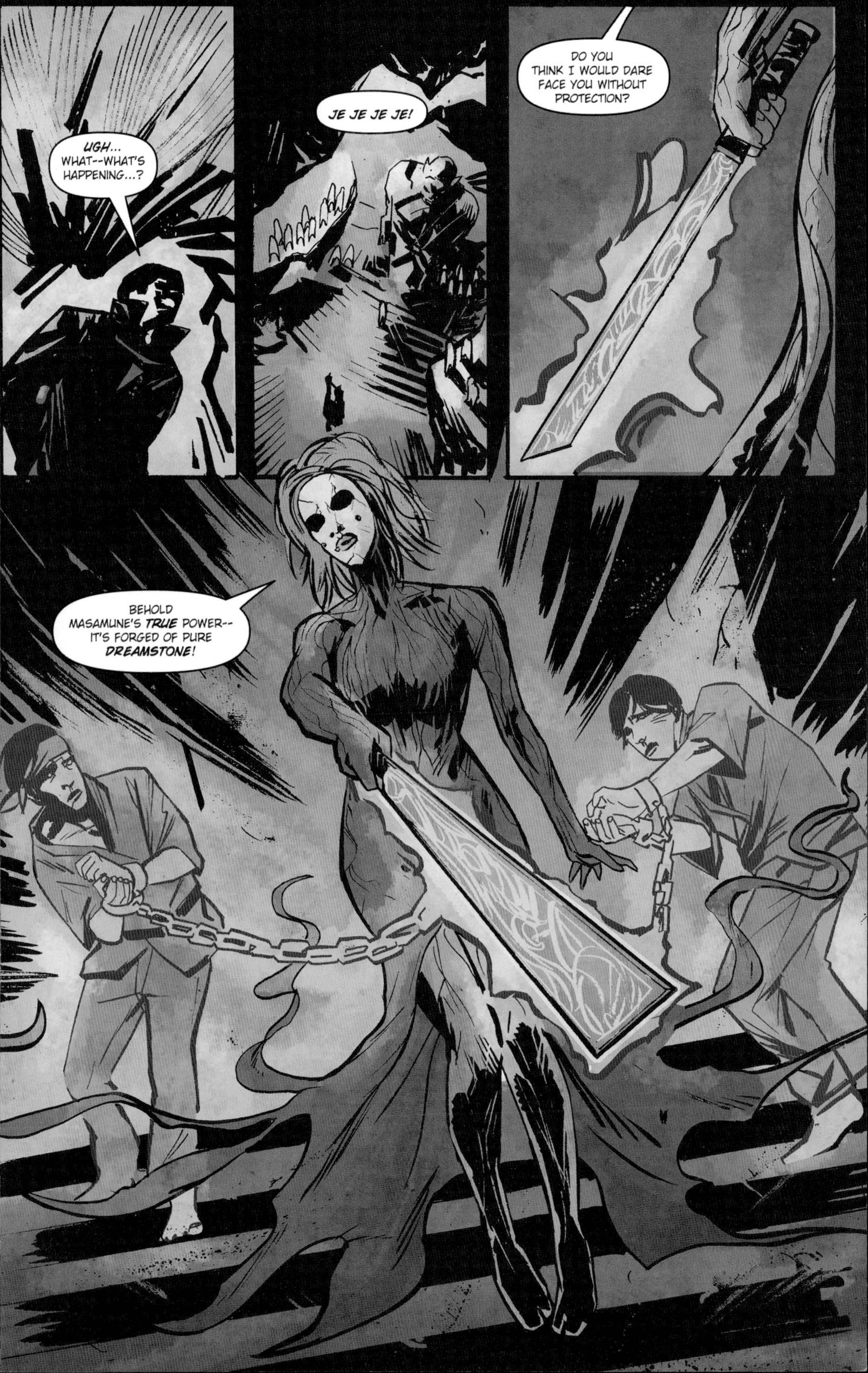
UGH... WHAT--WHAT'S HAPPENING...?
JE JE JE JE!
DO YOU THINK I WOULD DARE FACE YOU WITHOUT PROTECTION?
BEHOLD MASAMUNE'S TRUE POWER--IT'S FORGED OF PURE DREAMSTONE!

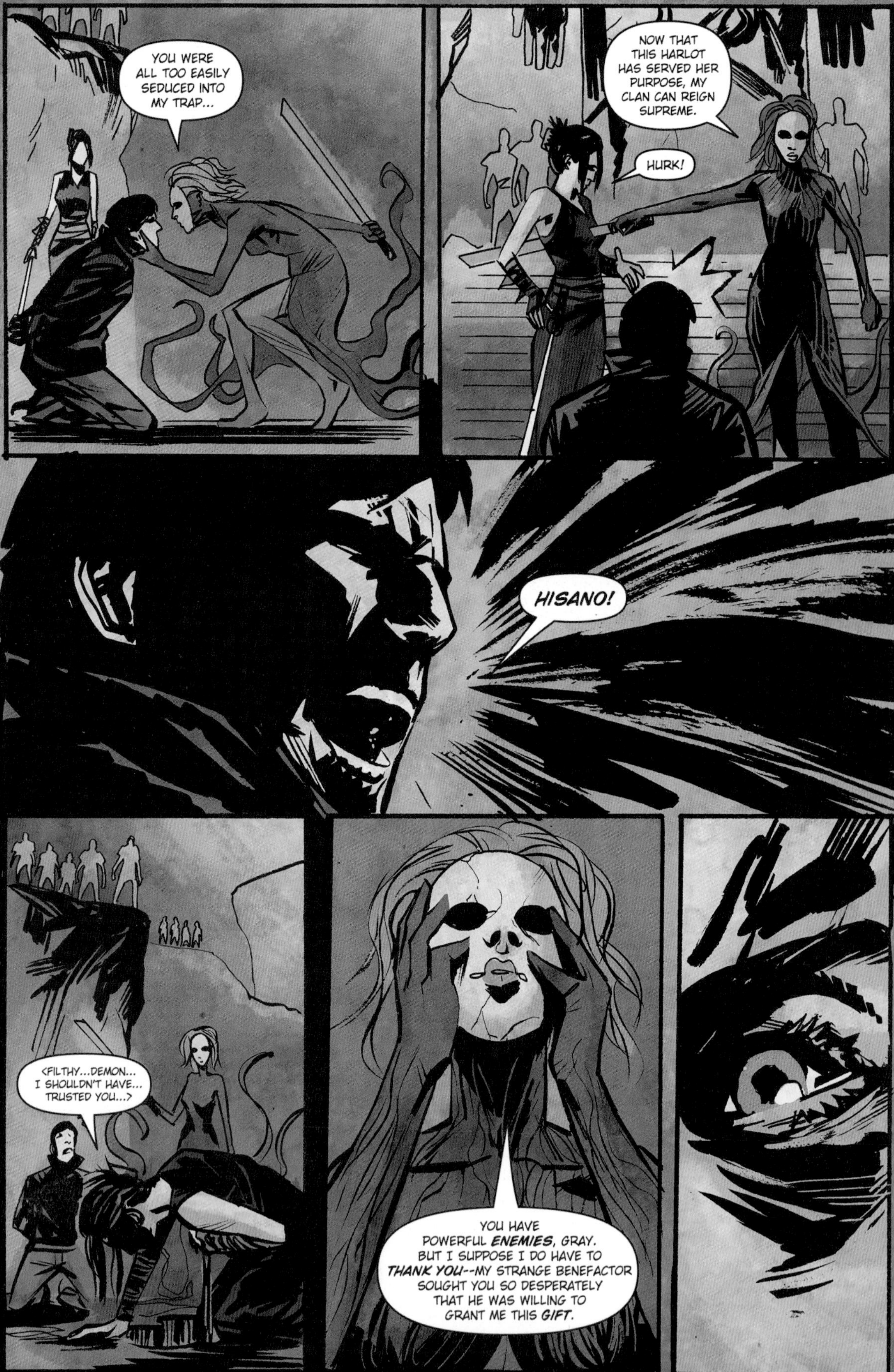
YOU WERE ALL TOO EASILY SEDUCED INTO MY TRAP...
NOW THAT THIS HARLOT HAS SERVED HER PURPOSE, MY CLAN CAN REIGN SUPREME.
HURK!
HISANO!
<FILTHY...DEMON... I SHOULDN'T HAVE... TRUSTED YOU...>
YOU HAVE POWERFUL ENEMIES, GRAY. BUT I SUPPOSE I DO HAVE TO THANK YOU--MY STRANGE BENEFACTOR SOUGHT YOU SO DESPERATELY THAT HE WAS WILLING TO GRANT ME THIS GIFT.

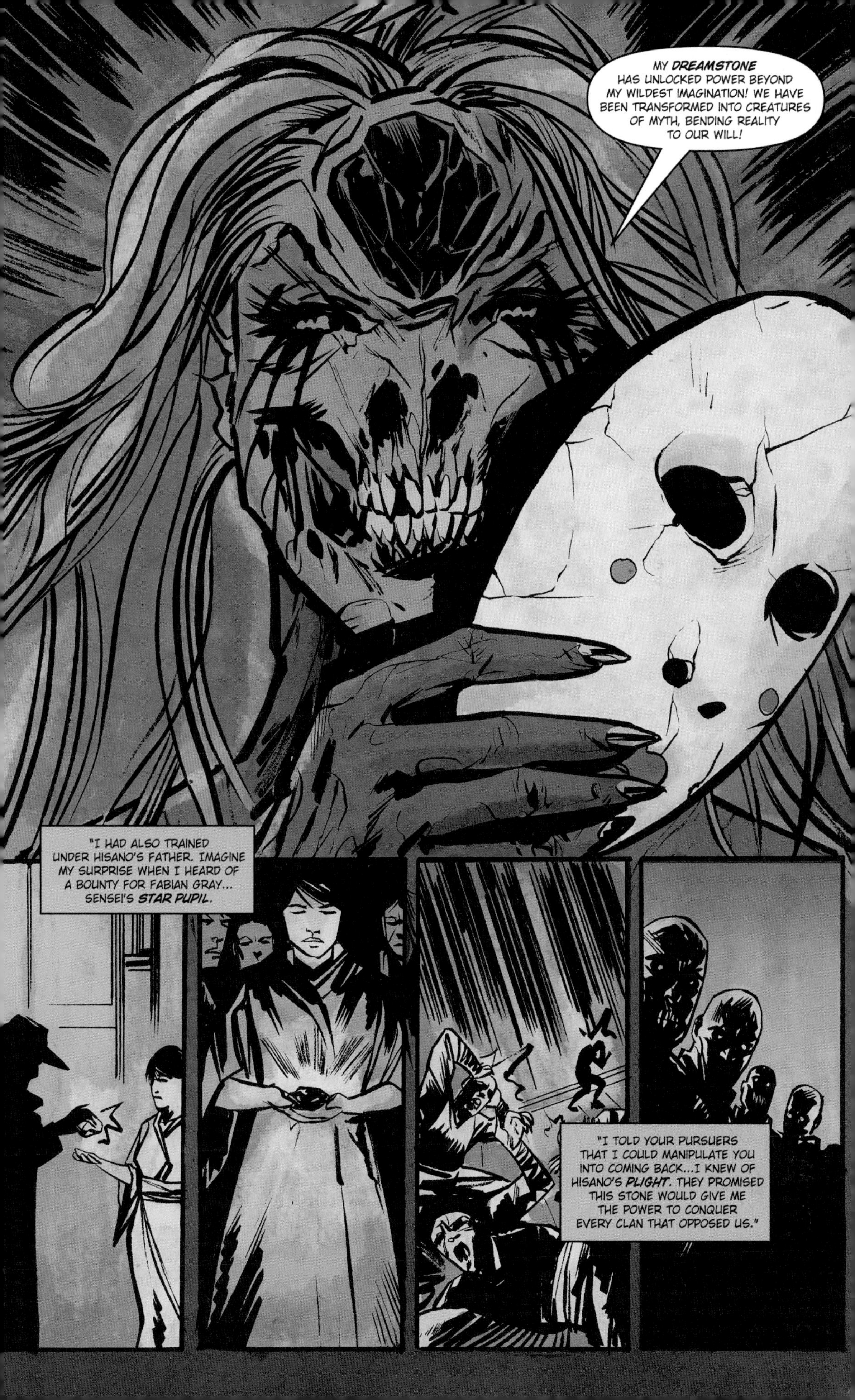
MY DREAMSTONE HAS UNLOCKED POWER BEYOND MY WILDEST IMAGINATION! WE HAVE BEEN TRANSFORMED INTO CREATURES OF MYTH, BENDING REALITY TO OUR WILL!
"I HAD ALSO TRAINED UNDER HISANO'S FATHER. IMAGINE MY SURPRISE WHEN I HEARD OF A BOUNTY FOR FABIAN GRAY... SENSEI'S STAR PUPIL.
"I TOLD YOUR PURSUERS THAT I COULD MANIPULATE YOU INTO COMING BACK...I KNEW OF HISANO'S PLIGHT. THEY PROMISED THIS STONE WOULD GIVE ME THE POWER TO CONQUER EVERY CLAN THAT OPPOSED US."

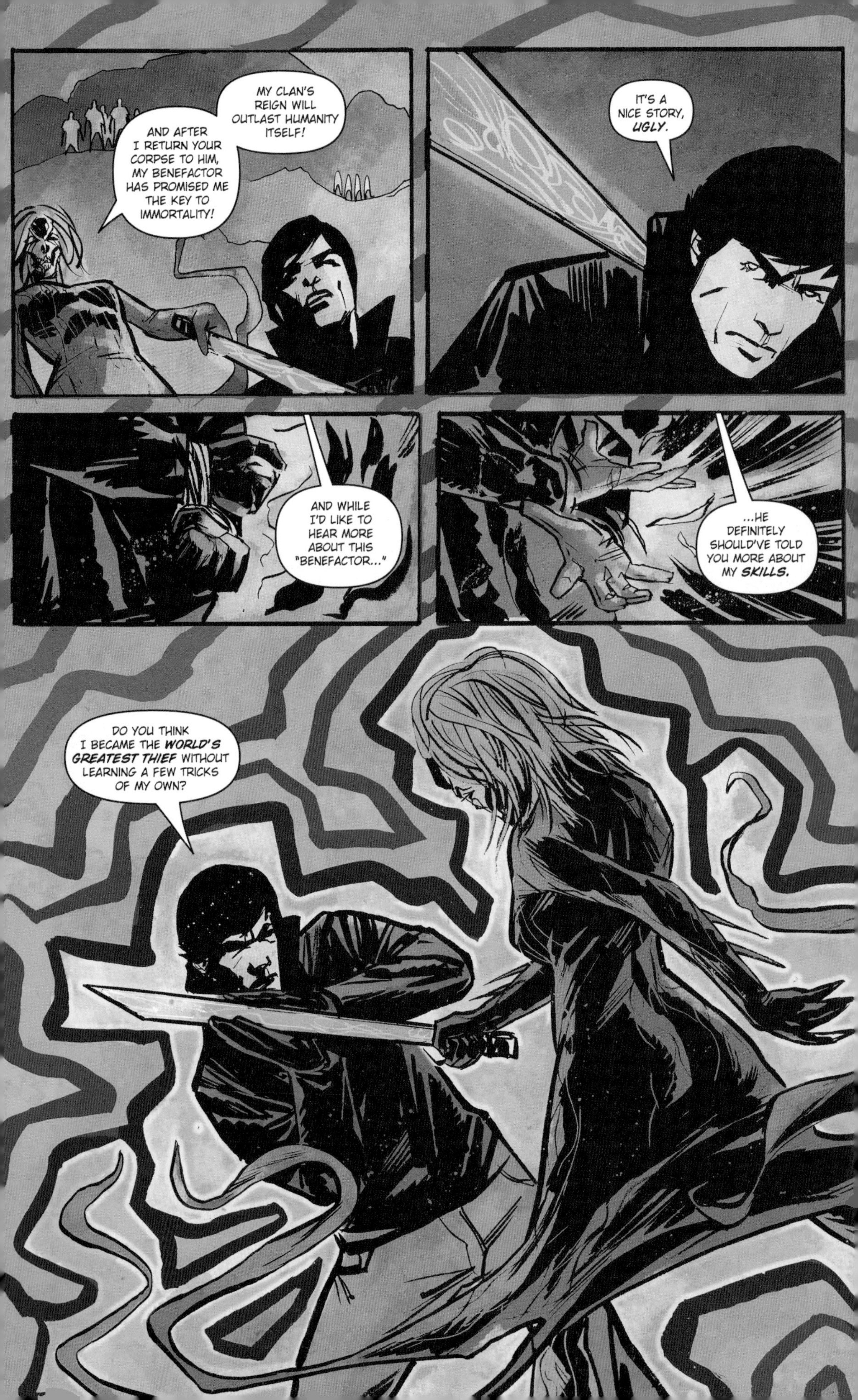
MY CLAN'S REIGN WILL OUTLAST HUMANITY ITSELF!
AND AFTER I RETURN YOUR CORPSE TO HIM, MY BENEFACTOR HAS PROMISED ME THE KEY TO IMMORTALITY!
IT'S A NICE STORY, UGLY.
AND WHILE I'D LIKE TO HEAR MORE ABOUT THIS "BENEFACTOR..."
...HE DEFINITELY SHOULD'VE TOLD YOU MORE ABOUT MY SKILLS.
DO YOU THINK I BECAME THE WORLD'S GREATEST THIEF WITHOUT LEARNING A FEW TRICKS OF MY OWN?

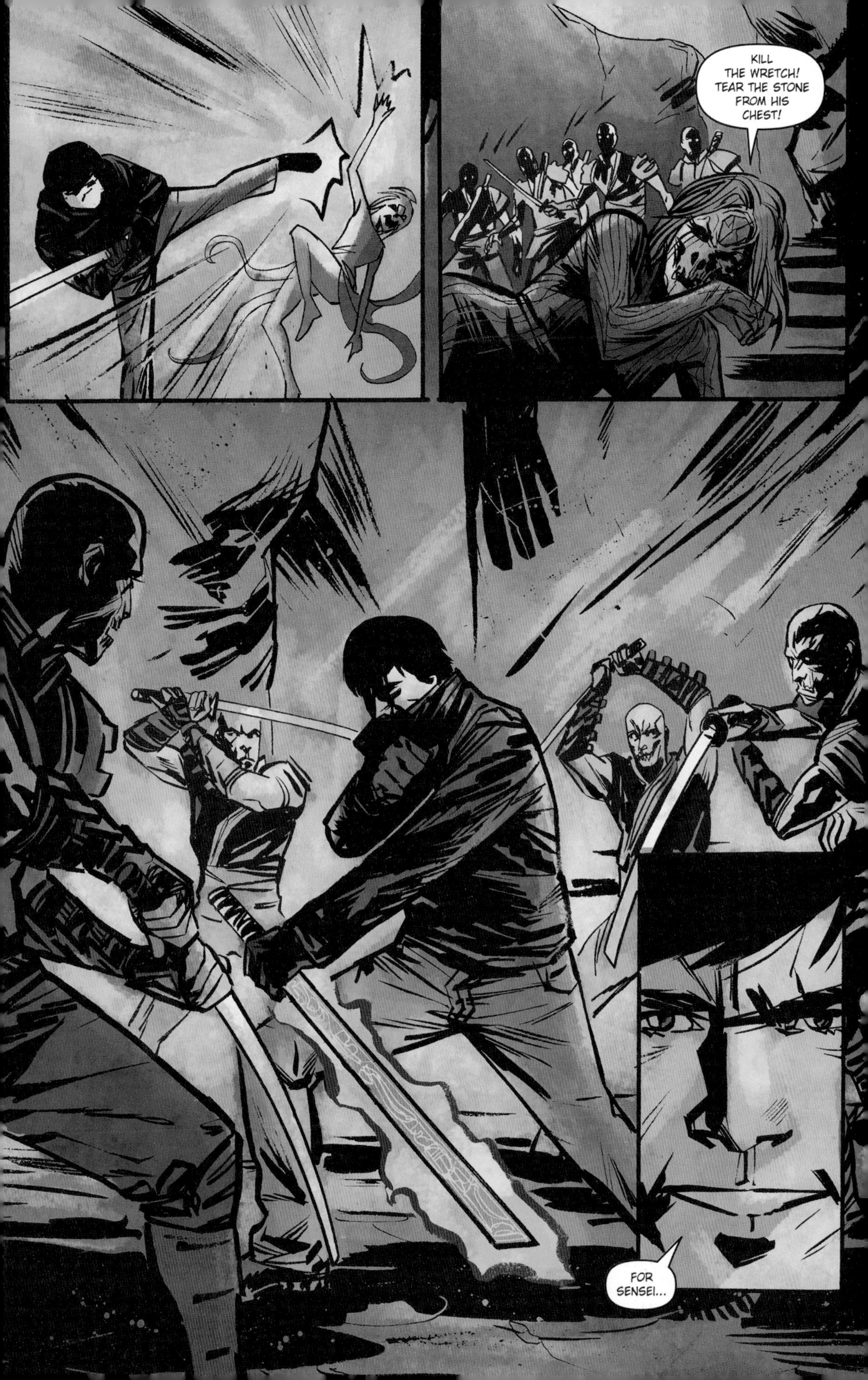
KILL THE WRETCH! TEAR THE STONE FROM HIS CHEST!
FOR SENSEI...

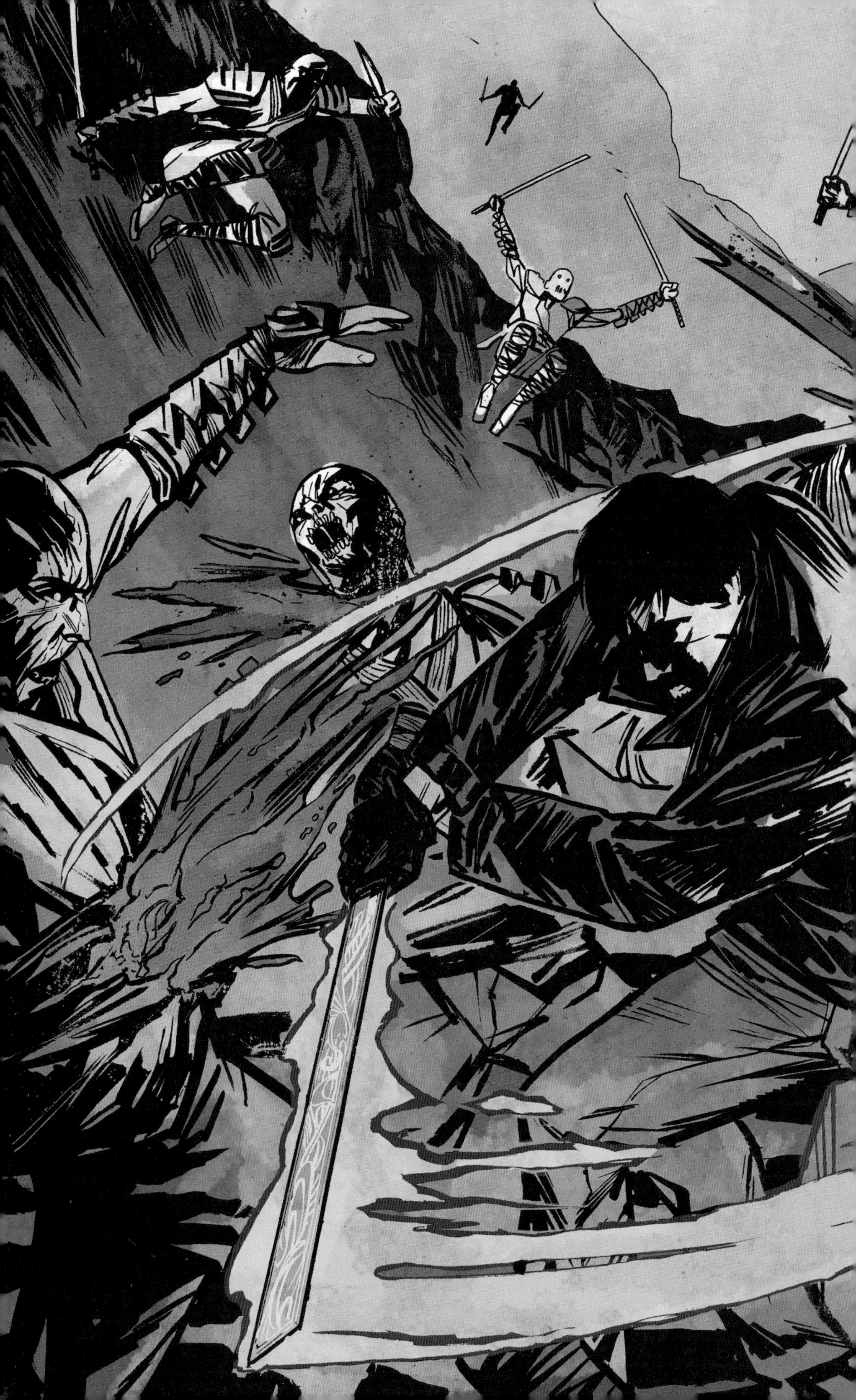

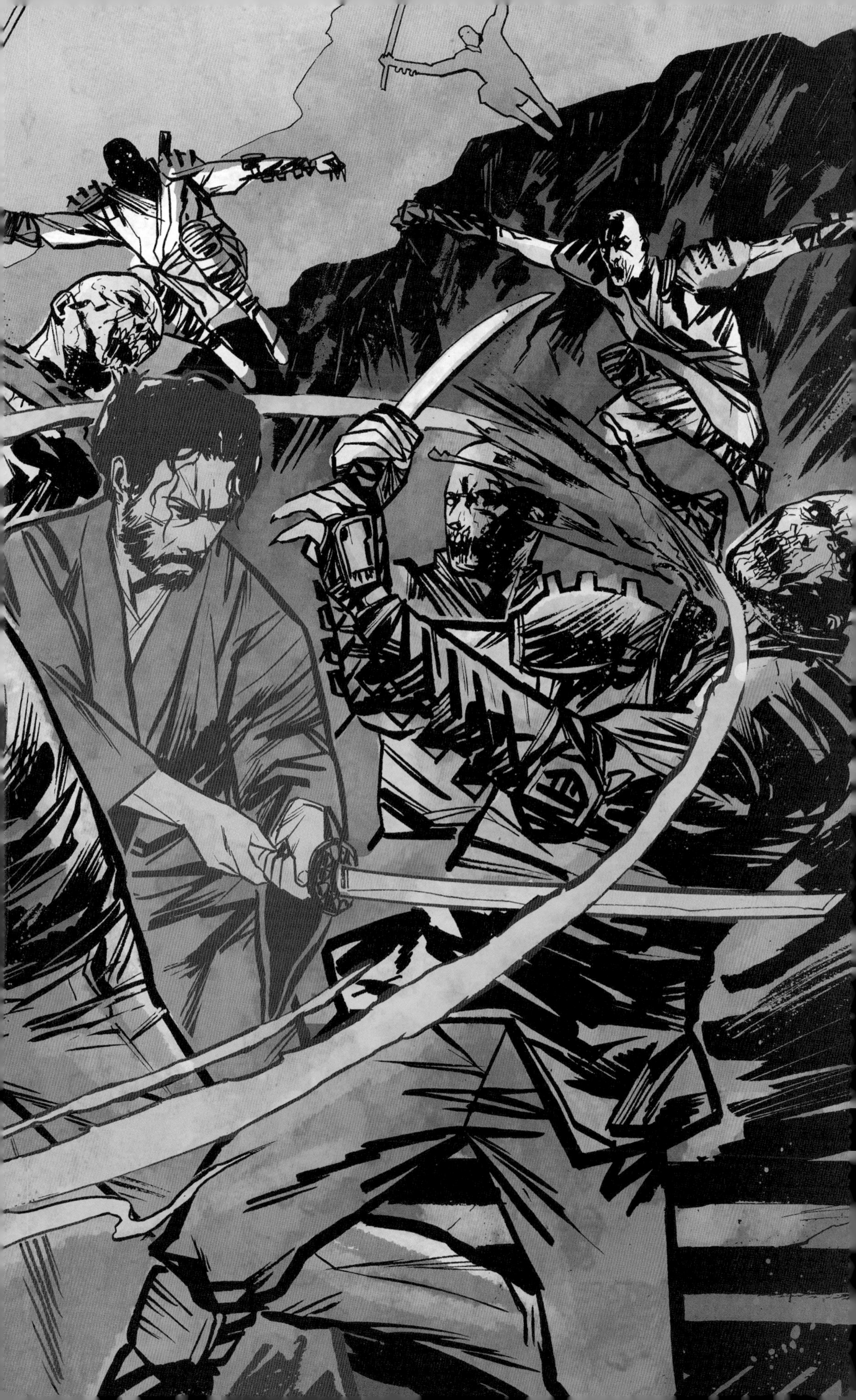

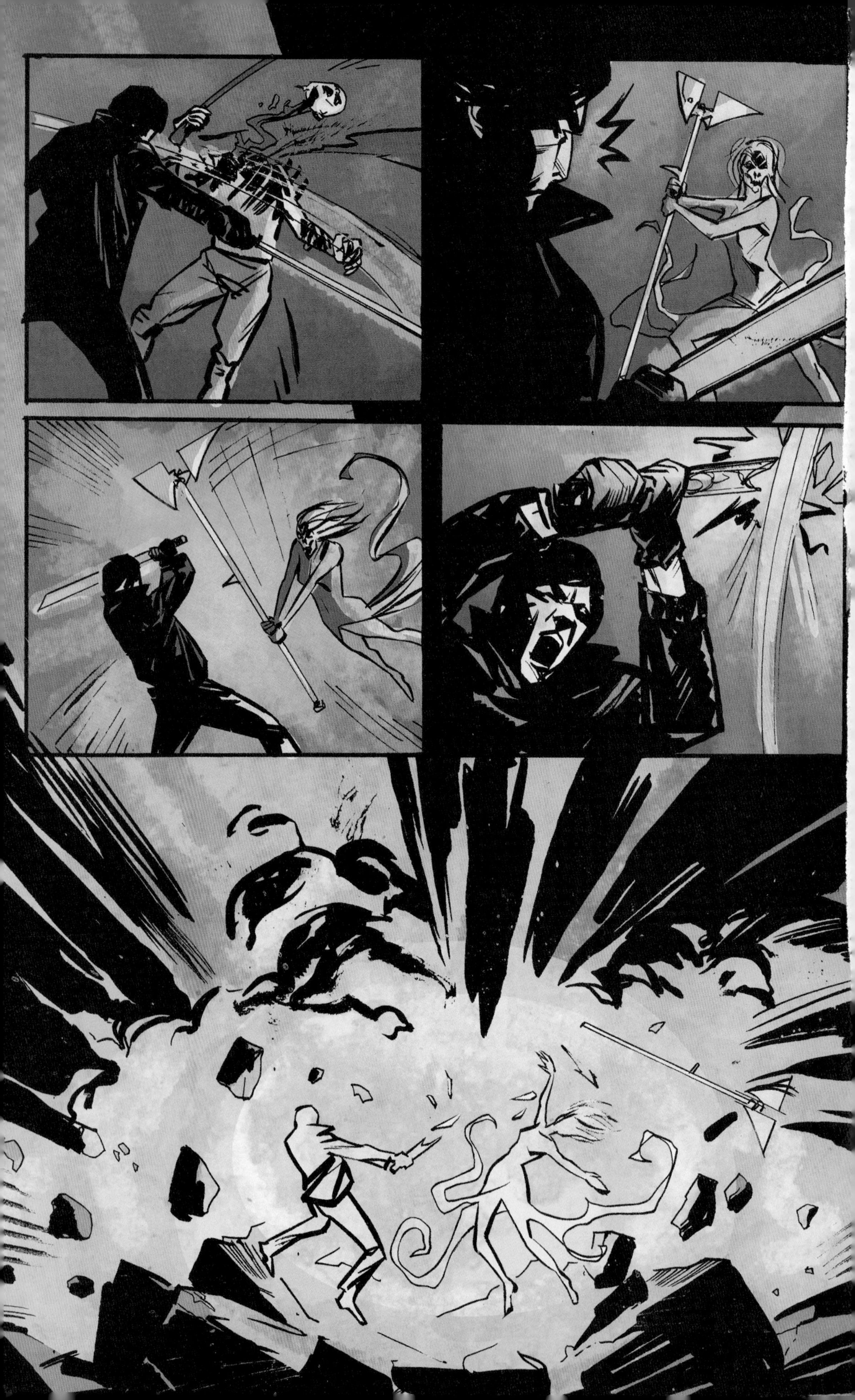

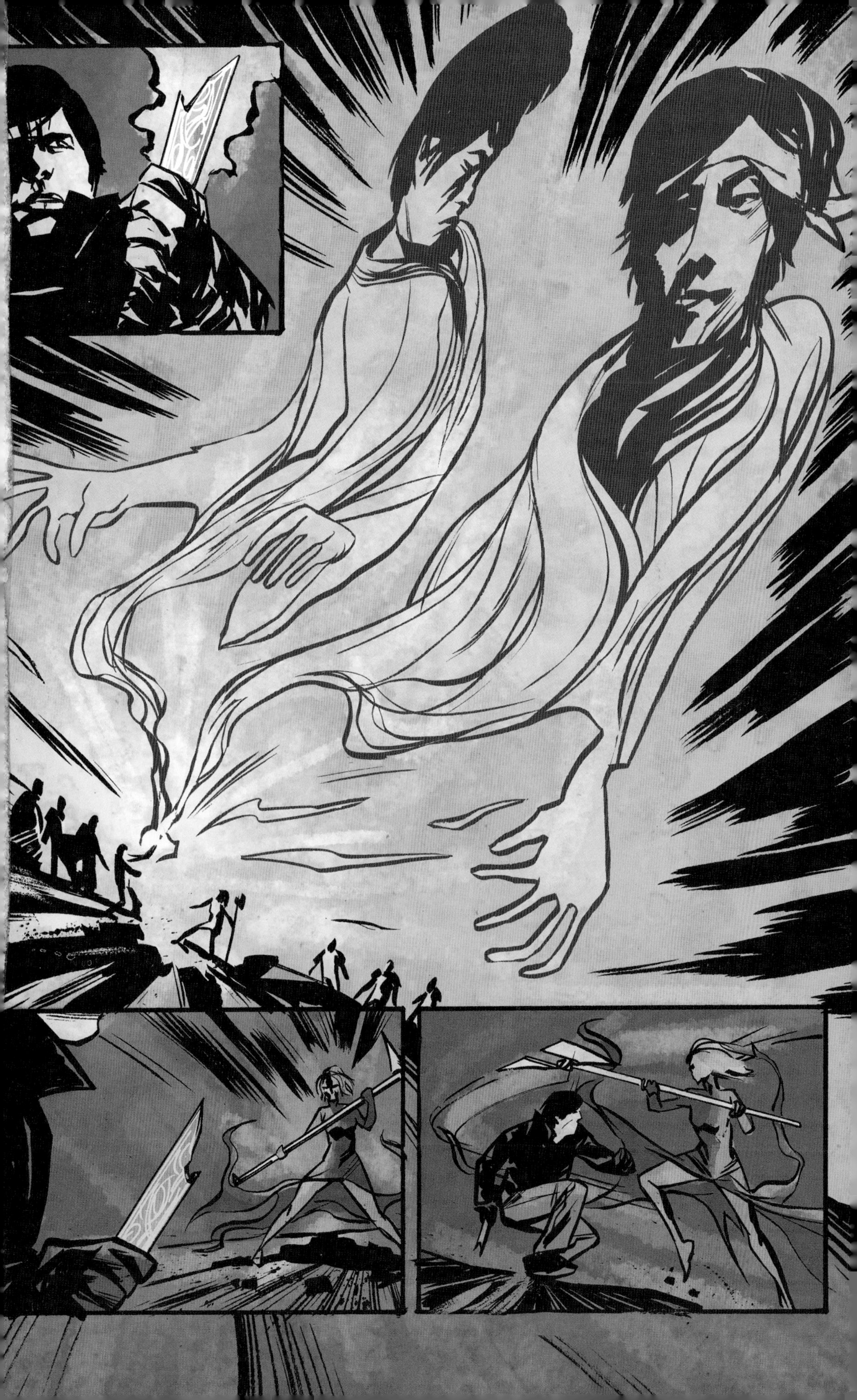

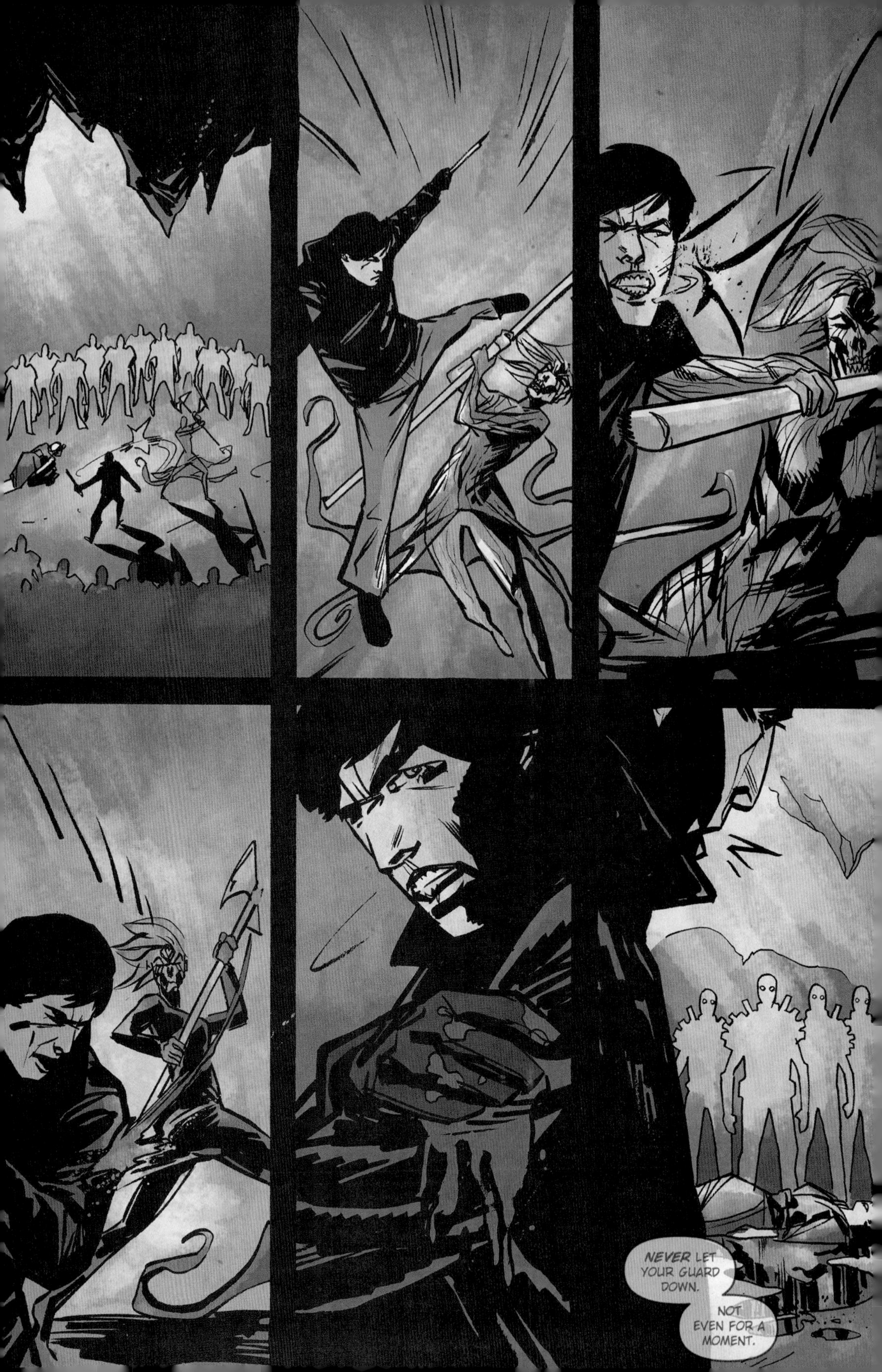
NEVER LET YOUR GUARD DOWN.
NOT EVEN FOR A MOMENT.

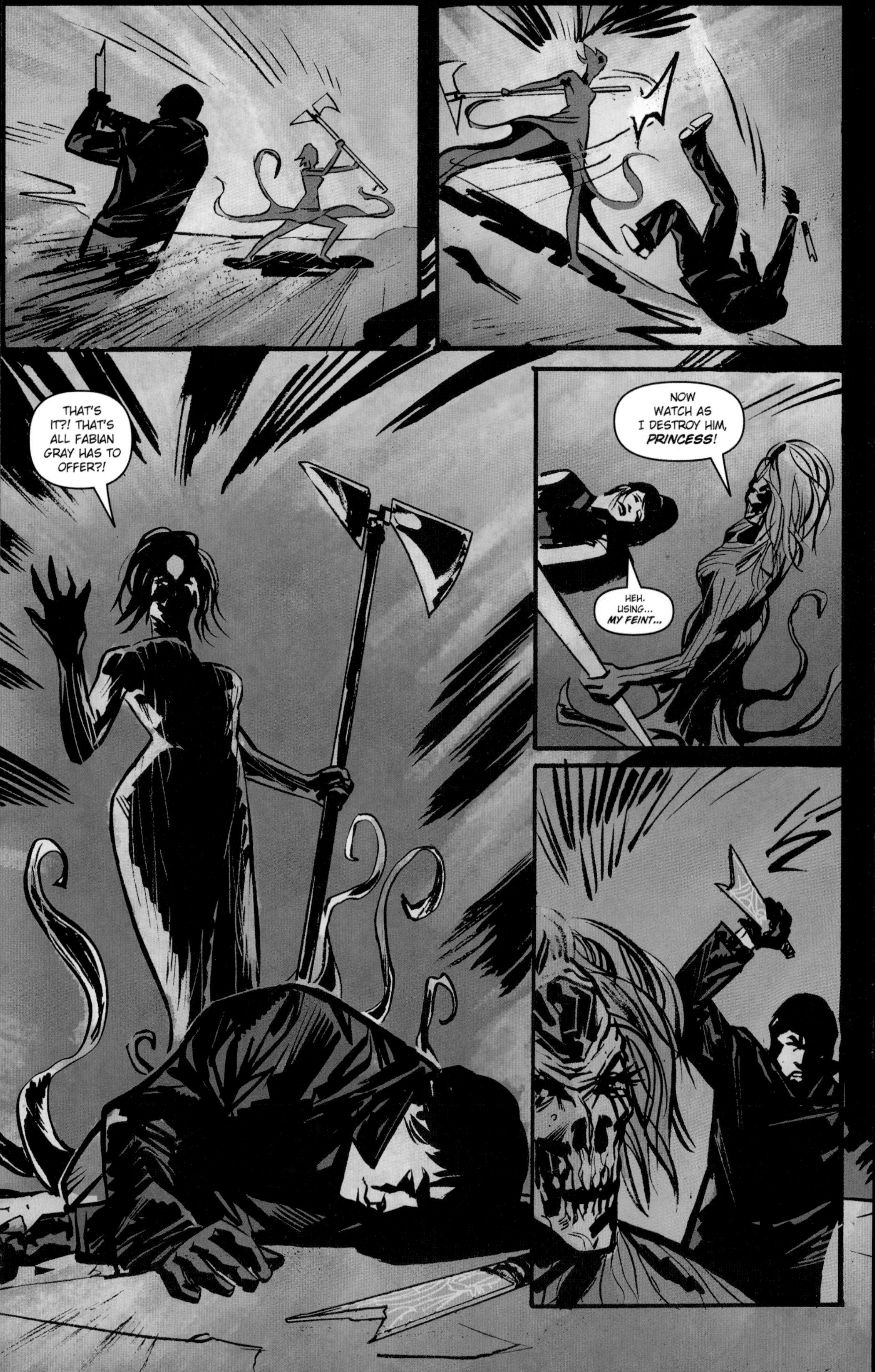
THAT'S IT?! THAT'S ALL FABIAN GRAY HAS TO OFFER?!
NOW WATCH AS I DESTROY HIM, *PRINCESS*!
HEH. USING... *MY FEINT*...

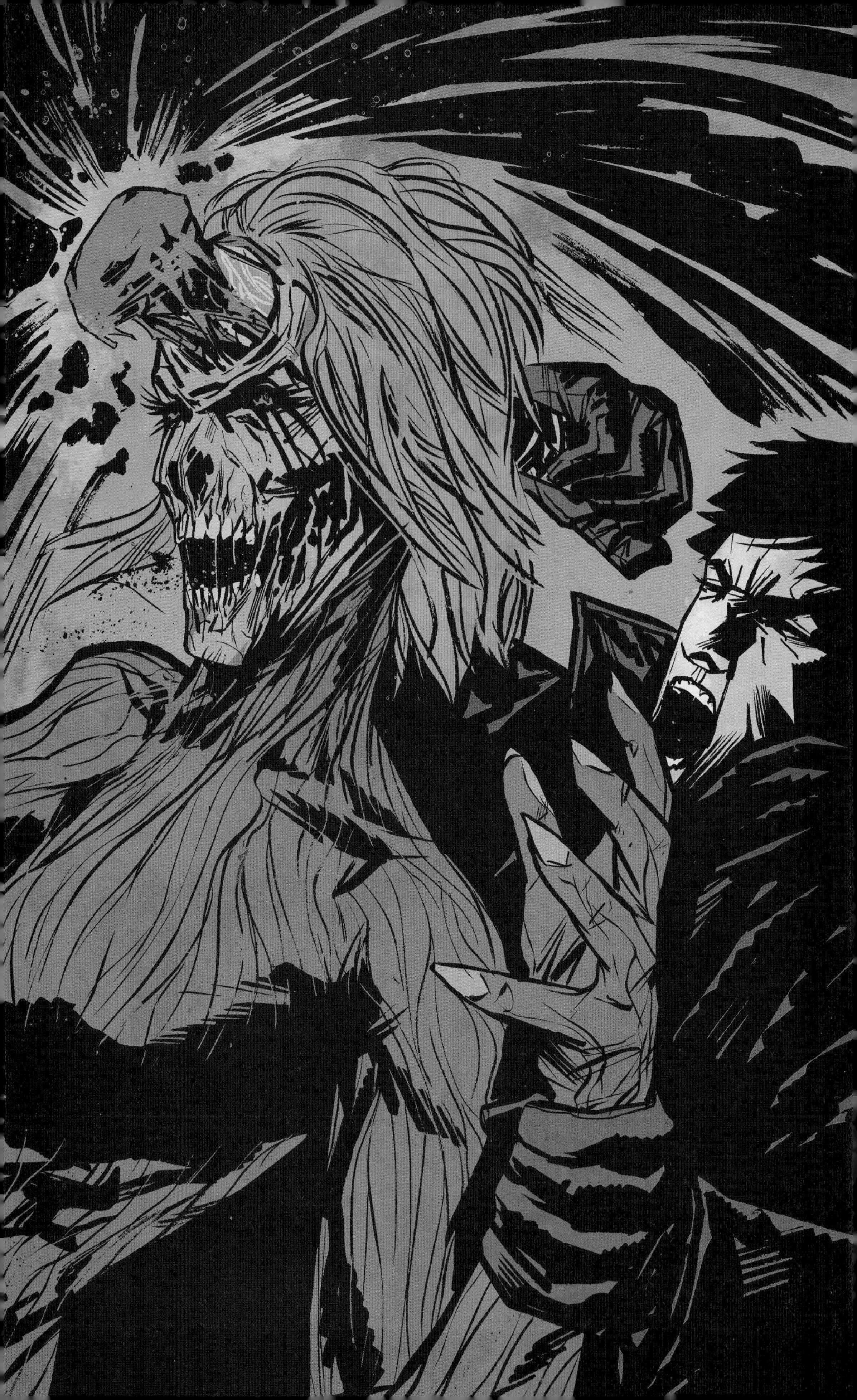

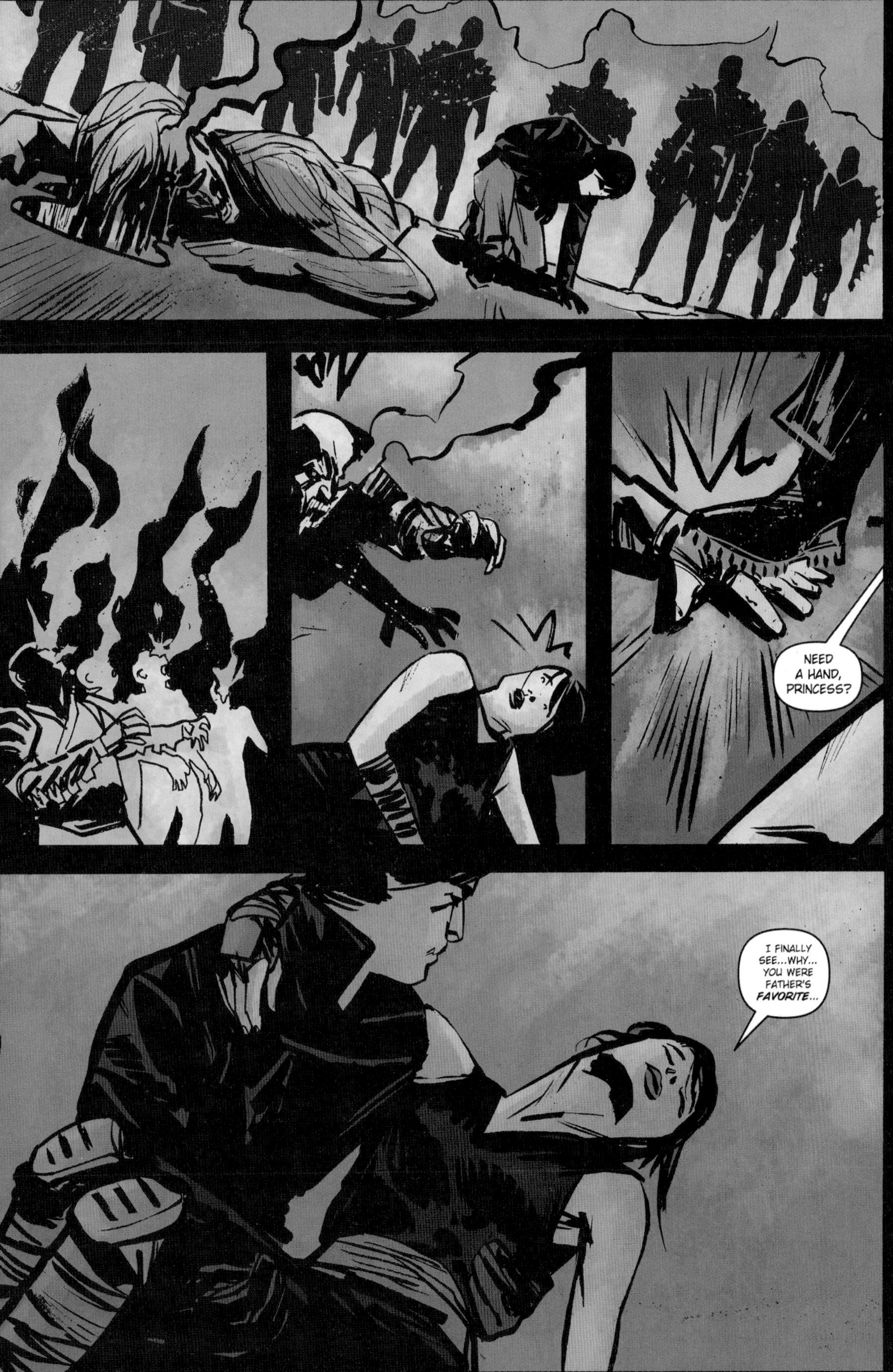
NEED A HAND, PRINCESS?
I FINALLY SEE...WHY... YOU WERE FATHER'S *FAVORITE*...

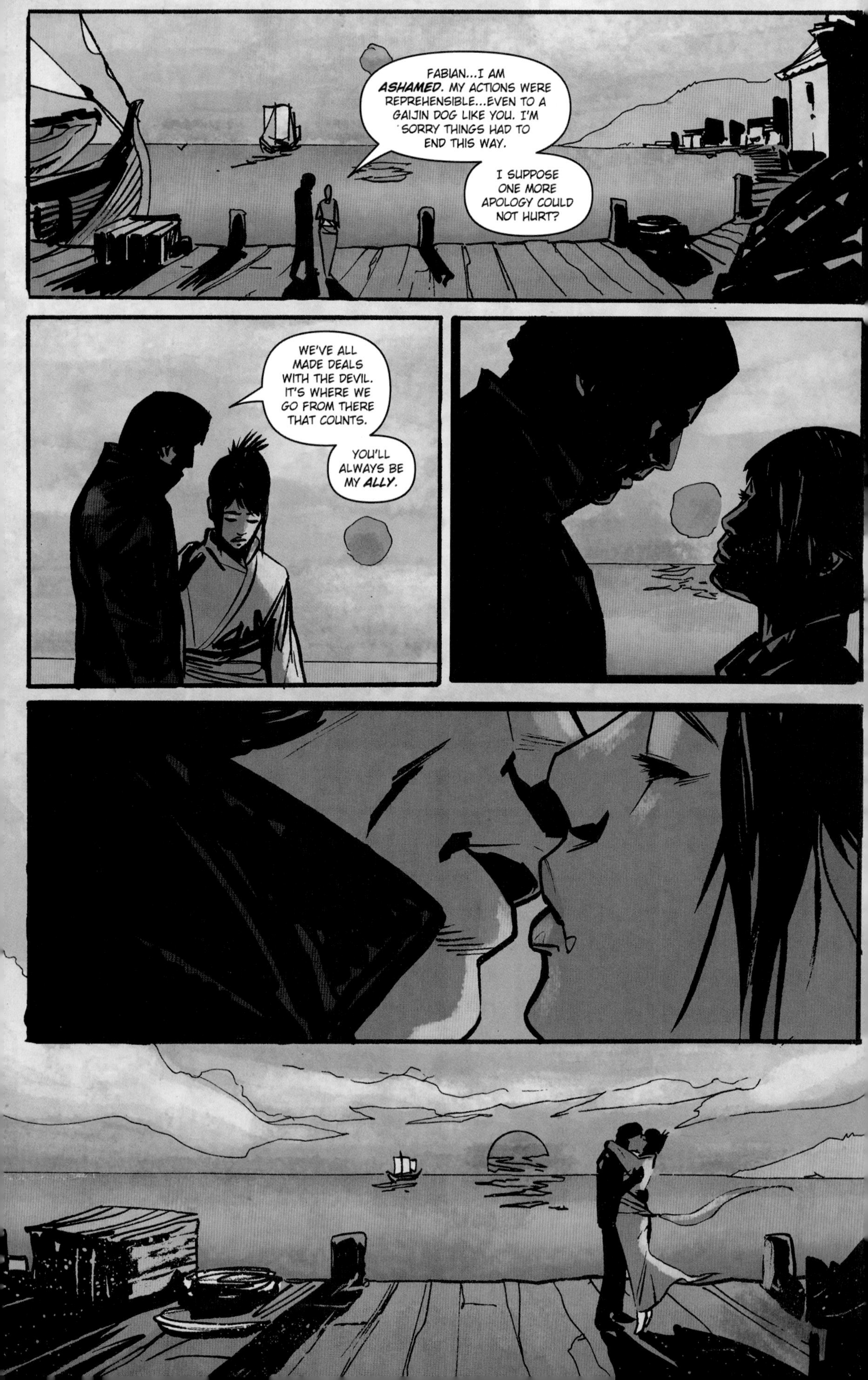
FABIAN...I AM ASHAMED. MY ACTIONS WERE REPREHENSIBLE...EVEN TO A GAIJIN DOG LIKE YOU. I'M SORRY THINGS HAD TO END THIS WAY.
I SUPPOSE ONE MORE APOLOGY COULD NOT HURT?
WE'VE ALL MADE DEALS WITH THE DEVIL. IT'S WHERE WE GO FROM THERE THAT COUNTS.
YOU'LL ALWAYS BE MY ALLY.

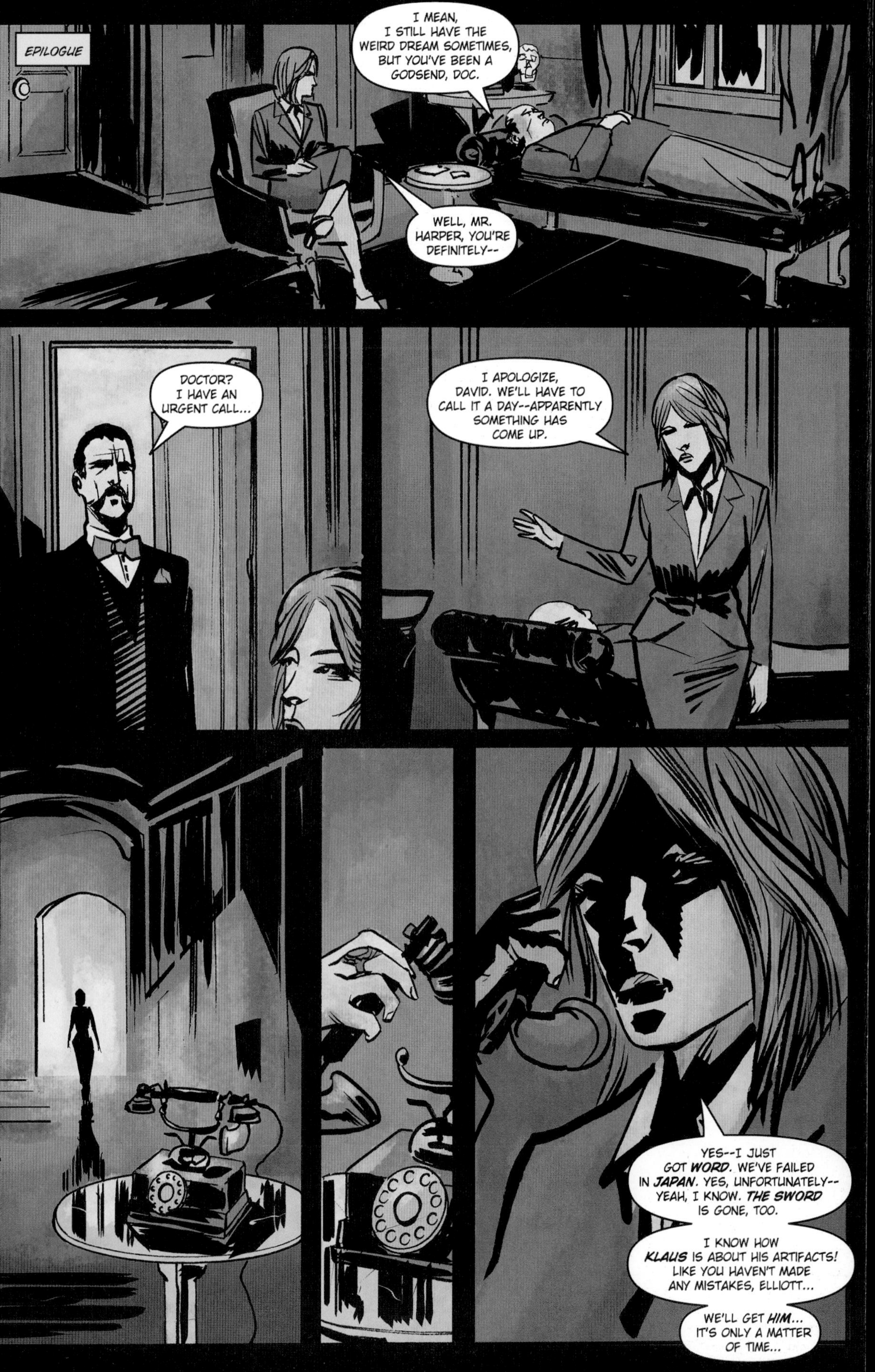
EPILOGUE
I MEAN, I STILL HAVE THE WEIRD DREAM SOMETIMES, BUT YOU'VE BEEN A GODSEND, DOC.
WELL, MR. HARPER, YOU'RE DEFINITELY--
DOCTOR? I HAVE AN URGENT CALL...
I APOLOGIZE, DAVID. WE'LL HAVE TO CALL IT A DAY--APPARENTLY SOMETHING HAS COME UP.
YES--I JUST GOT WORD. WE'VE FAILED IN JAPAN. YES, UNFORTUNATELY--YEAH, I KNOW. THE SWORD IS GONE, TOO.
I KNOW HOW KLAUS IS ABOUT HIS ARTIFACTS! LIKE YOU HAVEN'T MADE ANY MISTAKES, ELLIOTT...
WE'LL GET HIM... IT'S ONLY A MATTER OF TIME...

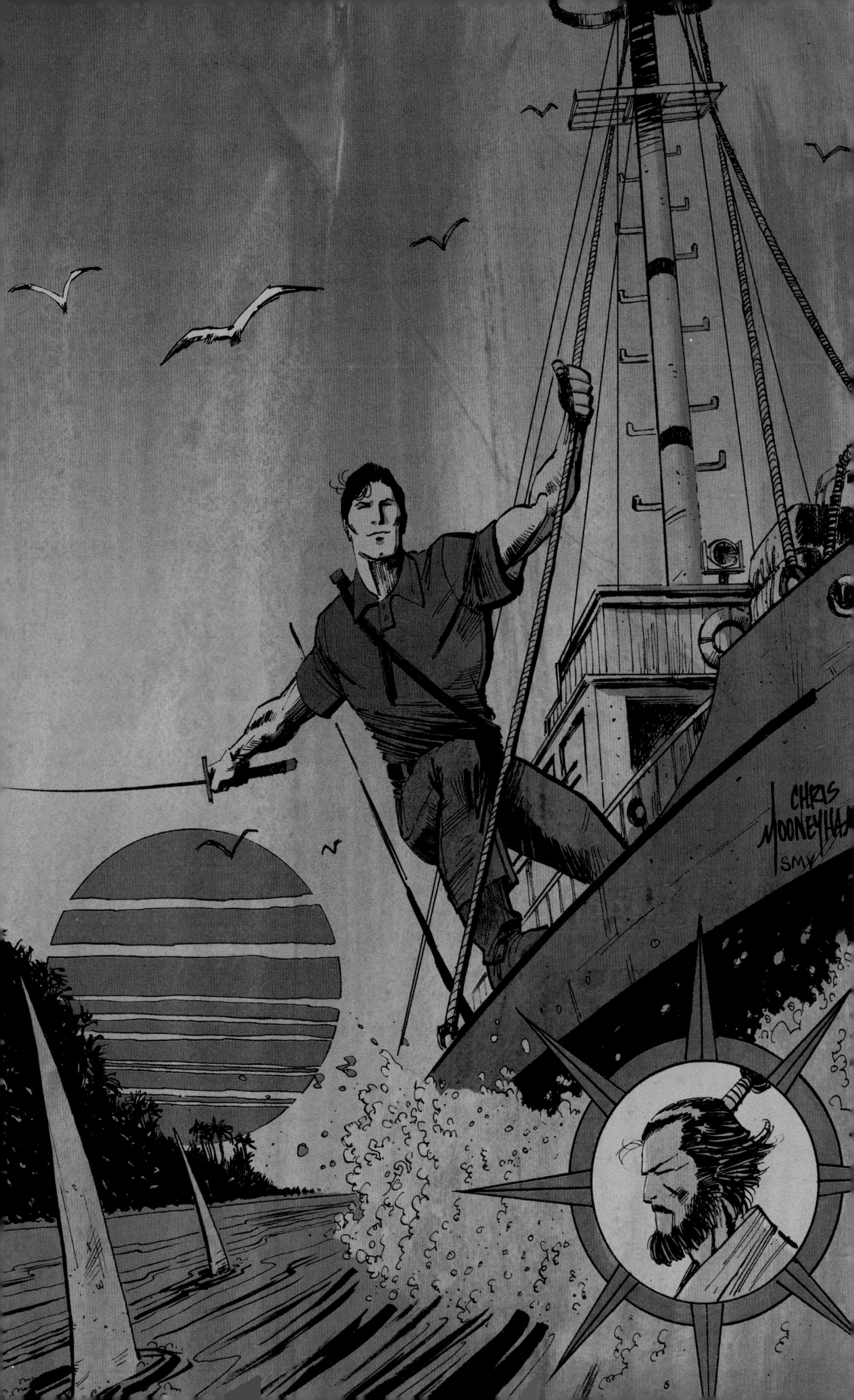
CHRIS
MOONEYHA
SMV

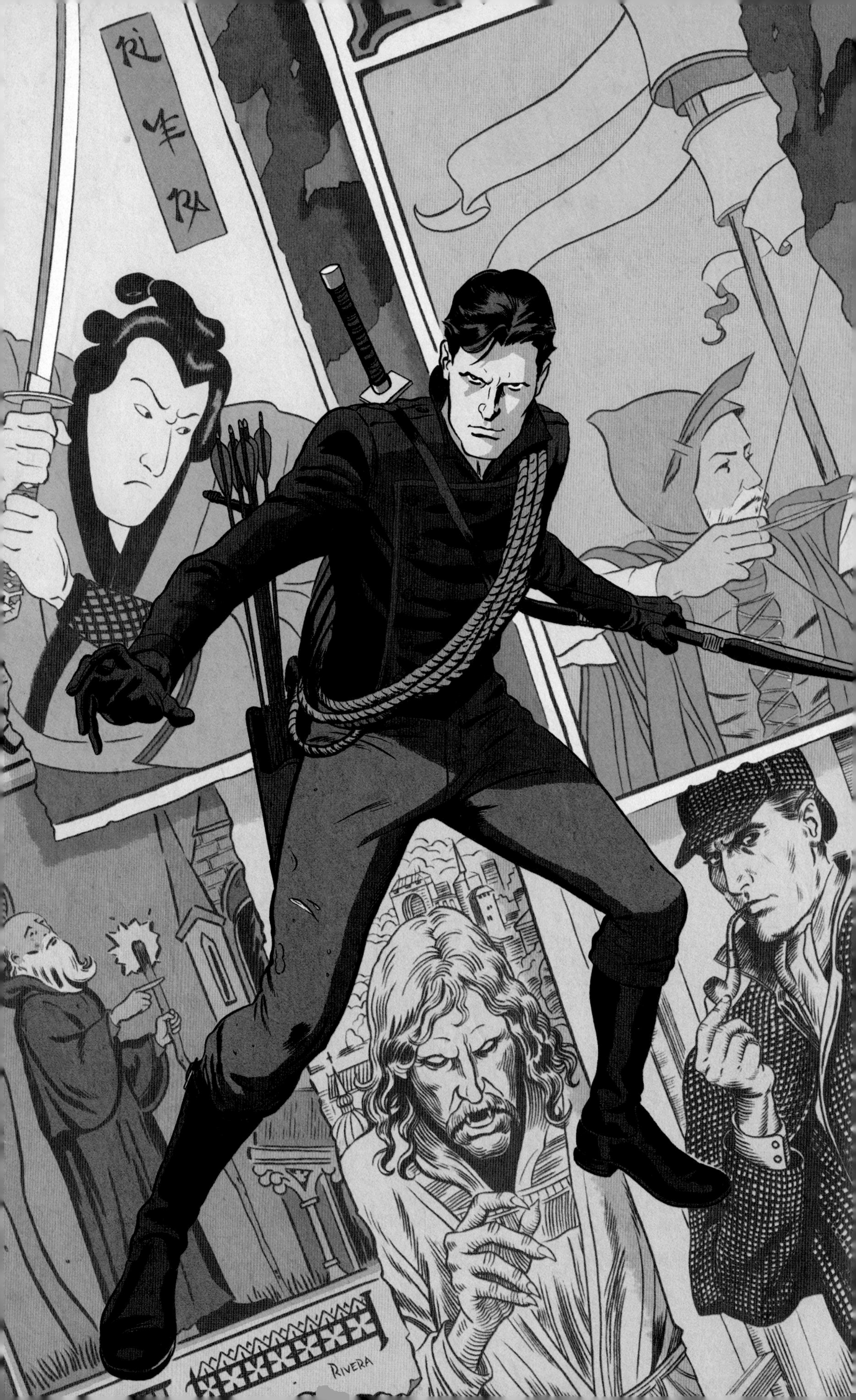
RIVERA

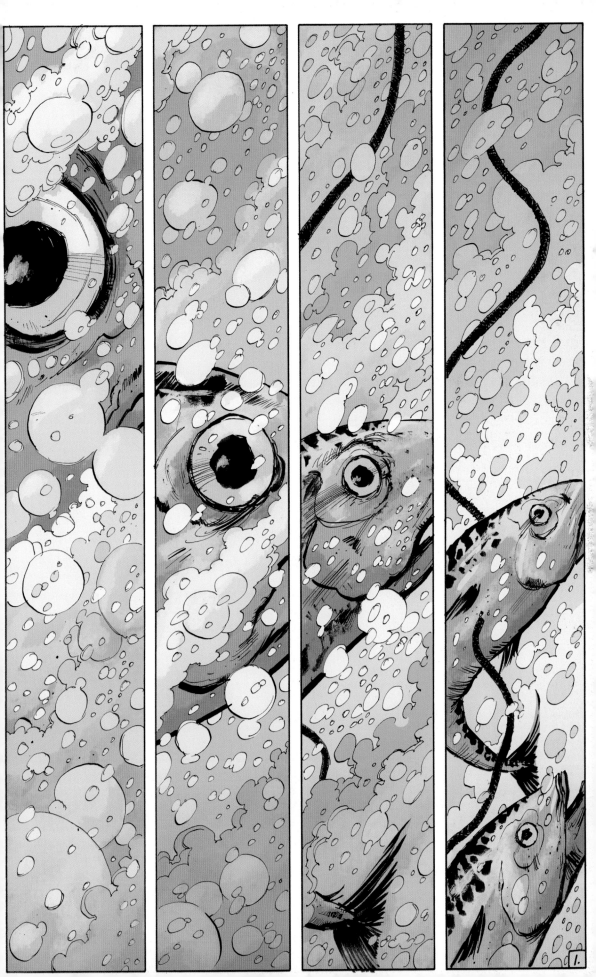

1.

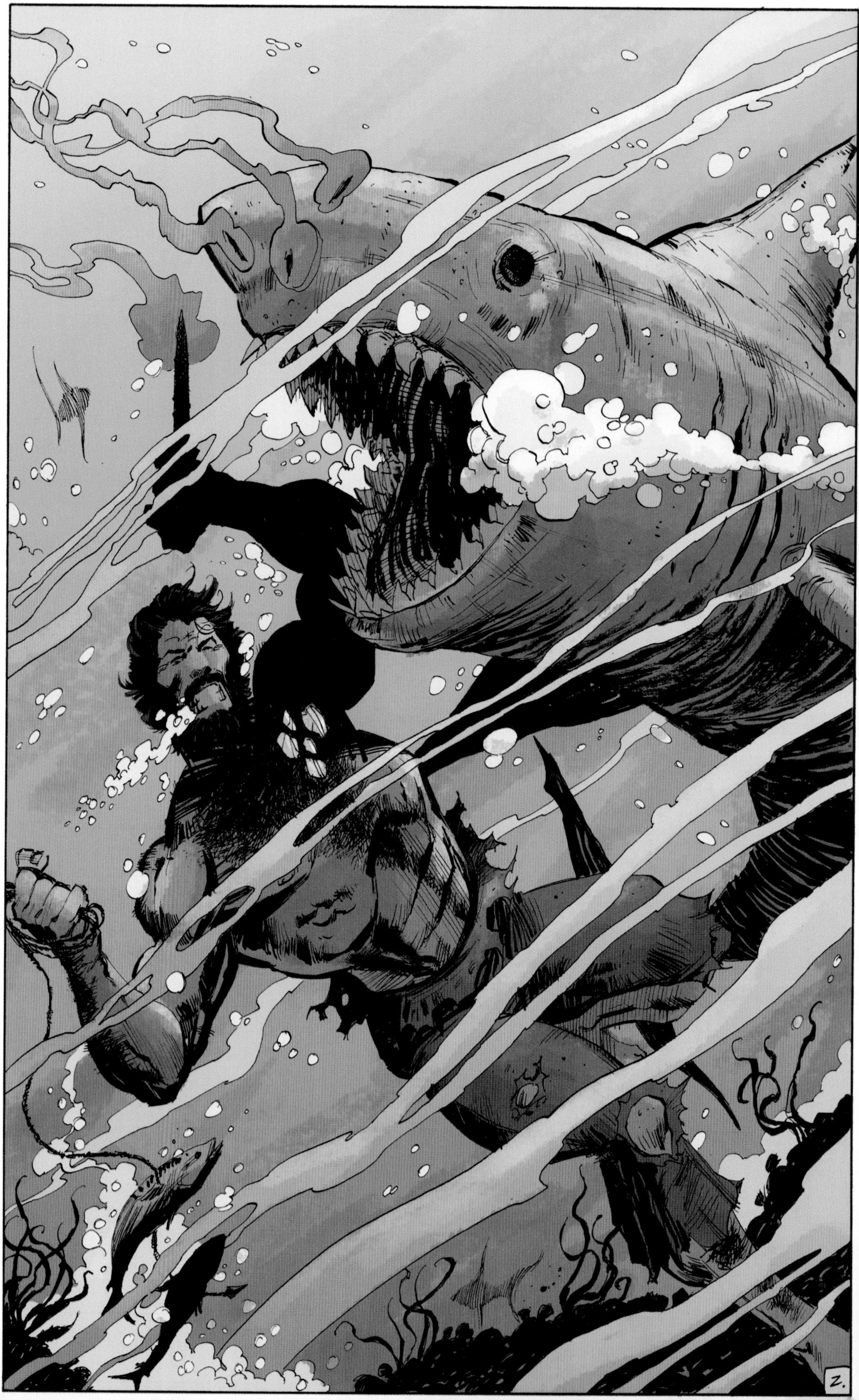

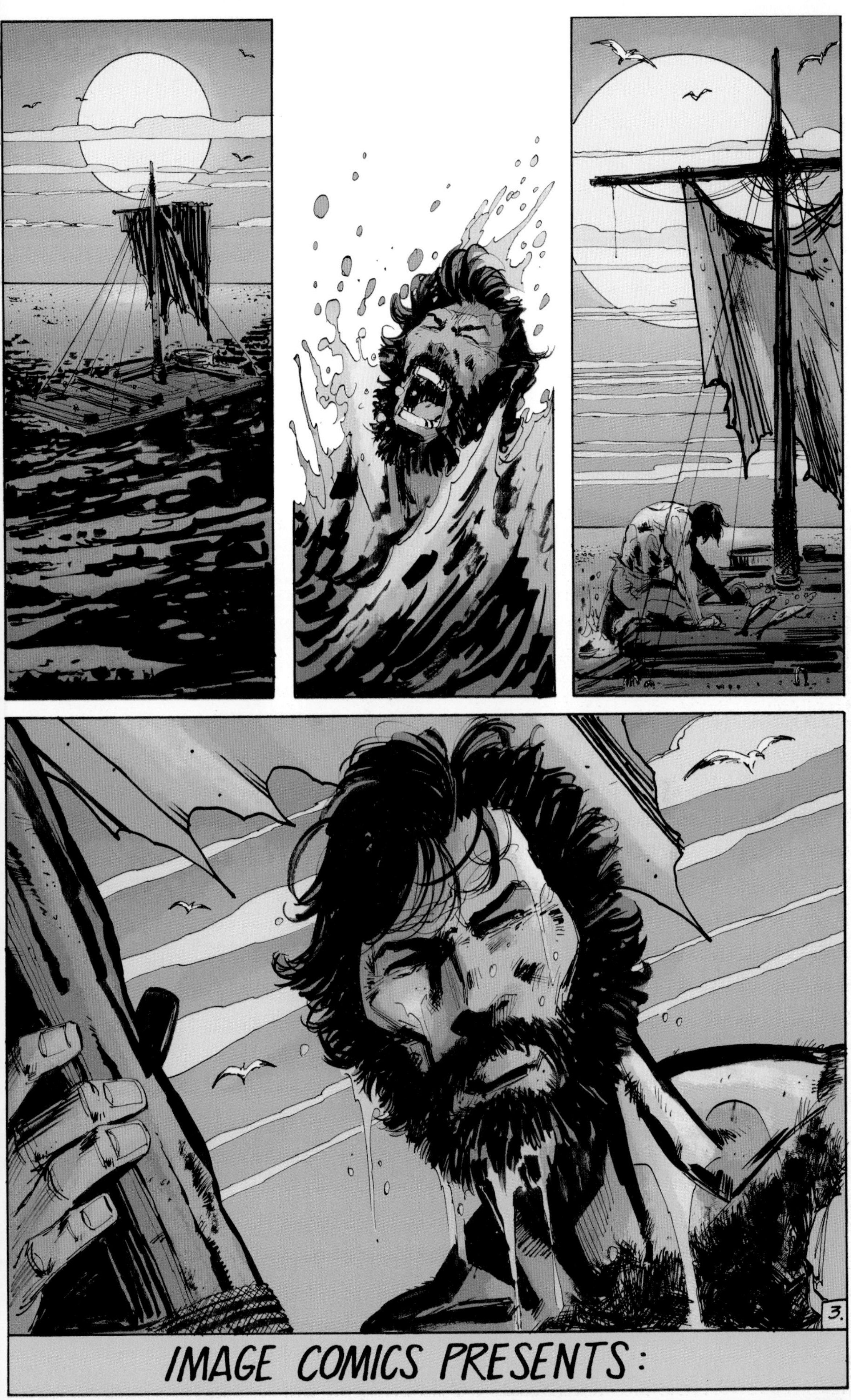
IMAGE COMICS PRESENTS:

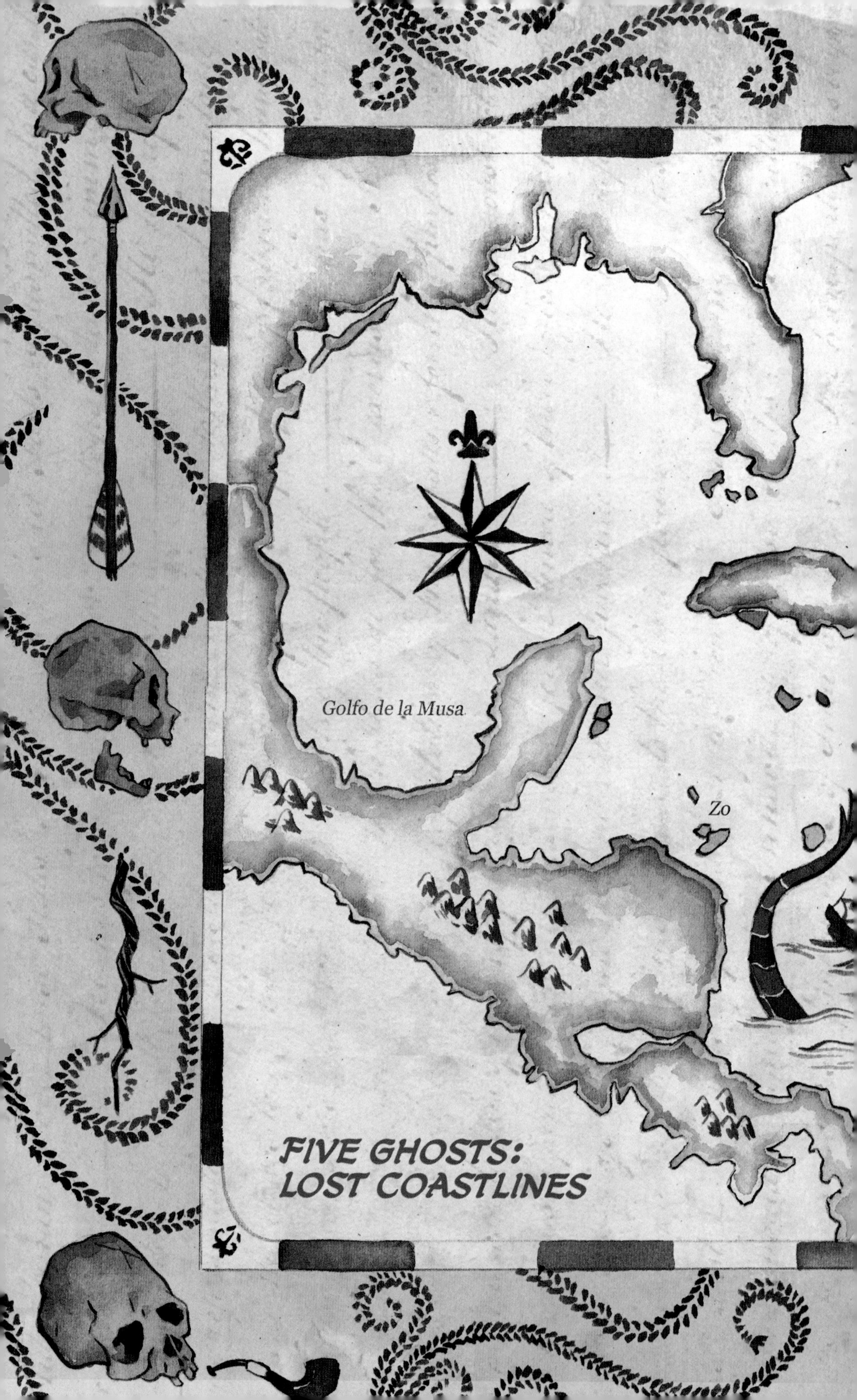
Golfo de la Musa
Zo

FIVE GHOSTS: LOST COASTLINES

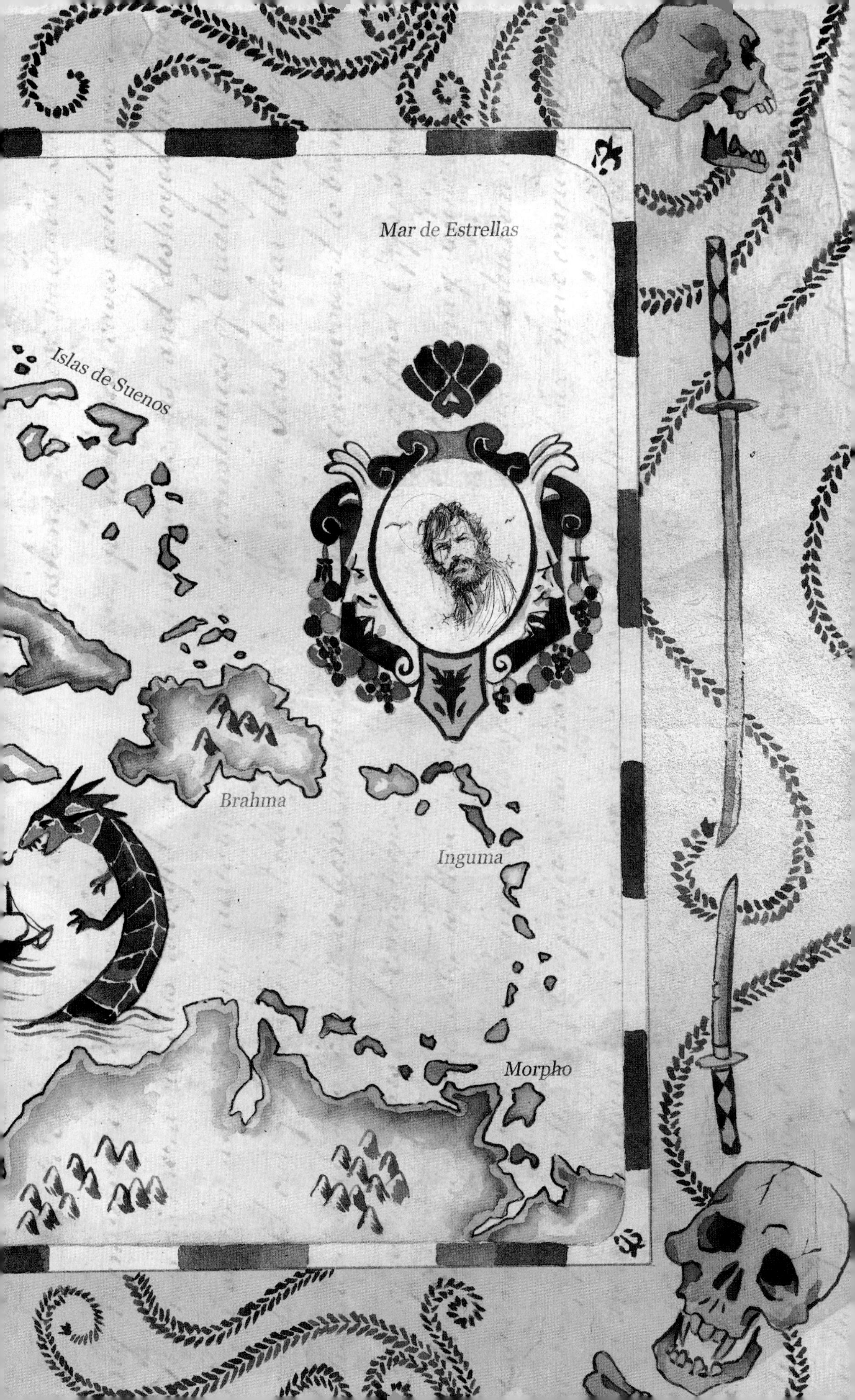
Mar de Estrellas
Islas de Suenos
Brahma
Inguma
Morpho

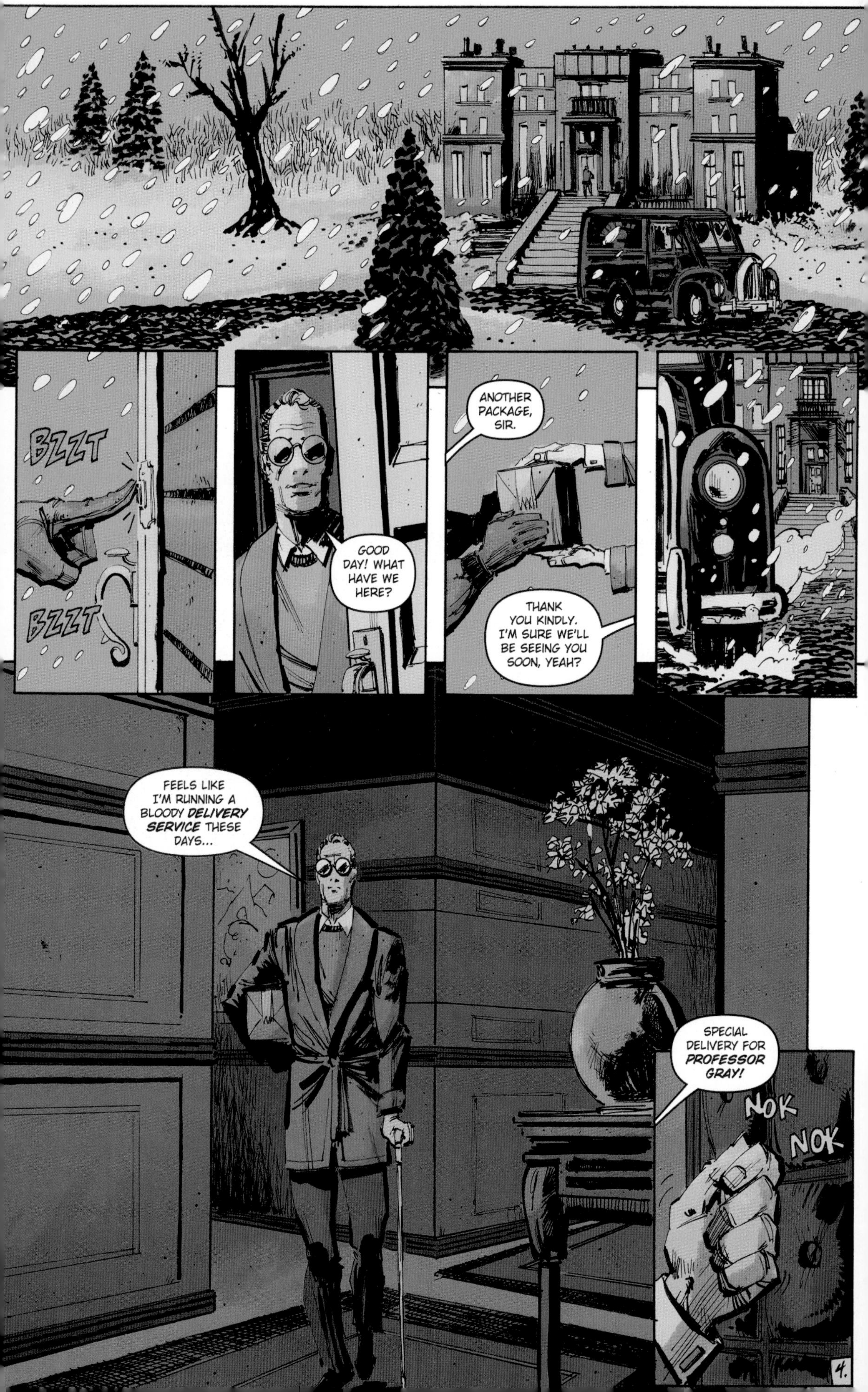
BZZT
BZZT
GOOD DAY! WHAT HAVE WE HERE?
ANOTHER PACKAGE, SIR.
THANK YOU KINDLY. I'M SURE WE'LL BE SEEING YOU SOON, YEAH?
FEELS LIKE I'M RUNNING A BLOODY DELIVERY SERVICE THESE DAYS...
SPECIAL DELIVERY FOR PROFESSOR GRAY!
NOK
NOK
4.

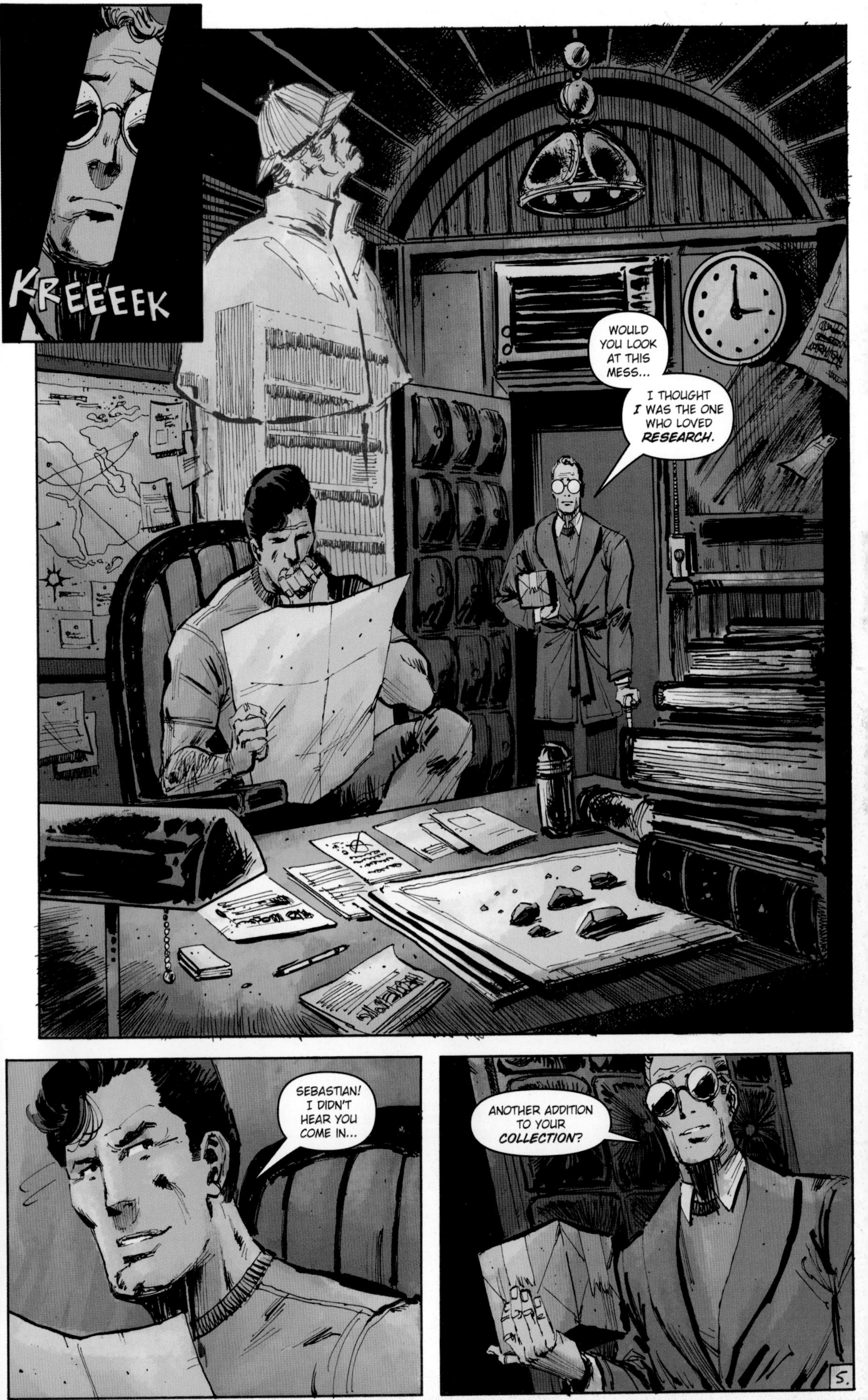
KREEEEK
WOULD YOU LOOK AT THIS MESS...
I THOUGHT I WAS THE ONE WHO LOVED RESEARCH.
SEBASTIAN! I DIDN'T HEAR YOU COME IN...
ANOTHER ADDITION TO YOUR COLLECTION?
5.

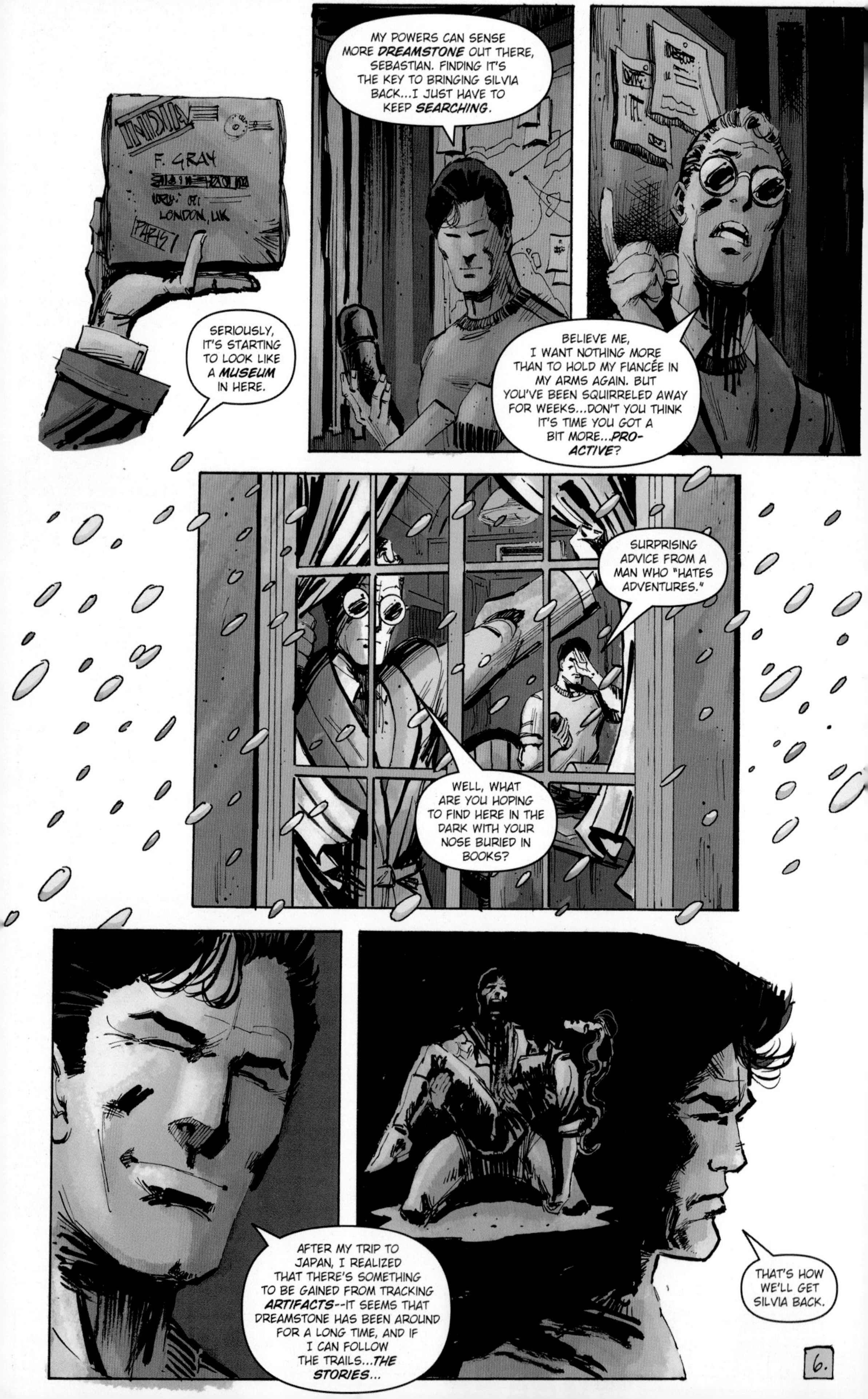
INDIA
F. GRAY
LONDON, UK
PARIS!
MY POWERS CAN SENSE MORE DREAMSTONE OUT THERE, SEBASTIAN. FINDING IT'S THE KEY TO BRINGING SILVIA BACK...I JUST HAVE TO KEEP SEARCHING.
SERIOUSLY, IT'S STARTING TO LOOK LIKE A MUSEUM IN HERE.
BELIEVE ME, I WANT NOTHING MORE THAN TO HOLD MY FIANCÉE IN MY ARMS AGAIN. BUT YOU'VE BEEN SQUIRRELED AWAY FOR WEEKS...DON'T YOU THINK IT'S TIME YOU GOT A BIT MORE...PRO-ACTIVE?
SURPRISING ADVICE FROM A MAN WHO "HATES ADVENTURES."
WELL, WHAT ARE YOU HOPING TO FIND HERE IN THE DARK WITH YOUR NOSE BURIED IN BOOKS?
AFTER MY TRIP TO JAPAN, I REALIZED THAT THERE'S SOMETHING TO BE GAINED FROM TRACKING ARTIFACTS--IT SEEMS THAT DREAMSTONE HAS BEEN AROUND FOR A LONG TIME, AND IF I CAN FOLLOW THE TRAILS...THE STORIES...
THAT'S HOW WE'LL GET SILVIA BACK.

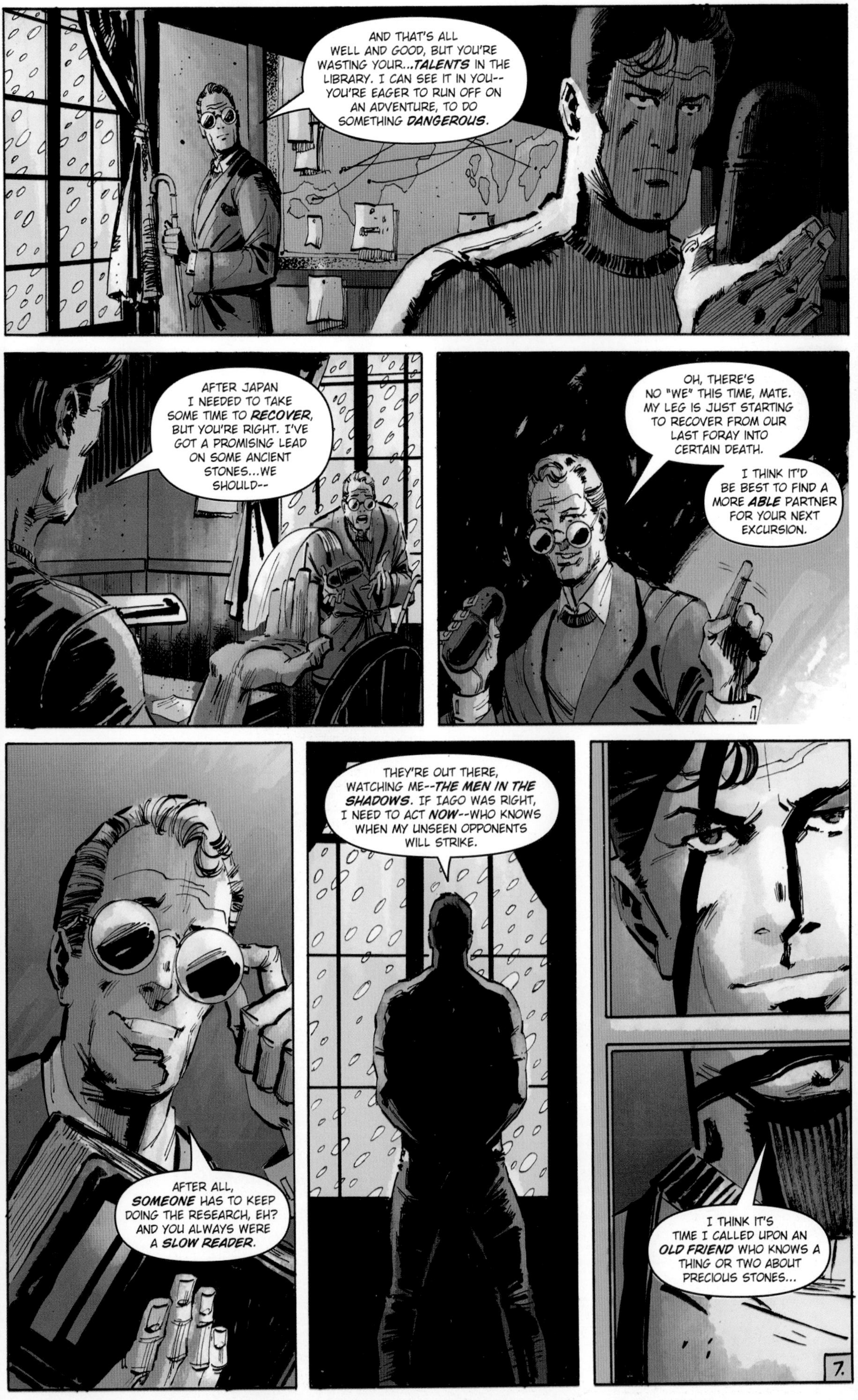

AND THAT'S ALL WELL AND GOOD, BUT YOU'RE WASTING YOUR...*TALENTS* IN THE LIBRARY. I CAN SEE IT IN YOU--YOU'RE EAGER TO RUN OFF ON AN ADVENTURE, TO DO SOMETHING *DANGEROUS*.
AFTER JAPAN I NEEDED TO TAKE SOME TIME TO *RECOVER*, BUT YOU'RE RIGHT. I'VE GOT A PROMISING LEAD ON SOME ANCIENT STONES...WE SHOULD--
OH, THERE'S NO "WE" THIS TIME, MATE. MY LEG IS JUST STARTING TO RECOVER FROM OUR LAST FORAY INTO CERTAIN DEATH.
I THINK IT'D BE BEST TO FIND A MORE *ABLE* PARTNER FOR YOUR NEXT EXCURSION.
AFTER ALL, *SOMEONE* HAS TO KEEP DOING THE RESEARCH, EH? AND YOU ALWAYS WERE A *SLOW READER*.
THEY'RE OUT THERE, WATCHING ME--*THE MEN IN THE SHADOWS*. IF IAGO WAS RIGHT, I NEED TO ACT *NOW*--WHO KNOWS WHEN MY UNSEEN OPPONENTS WILL STRIKE.
I THINK IT'S TIME I CALLED UPON AN *OLD FRIEND* WHO KNOWS A THING OR TWO ABOUT PRECIOUS STONES...

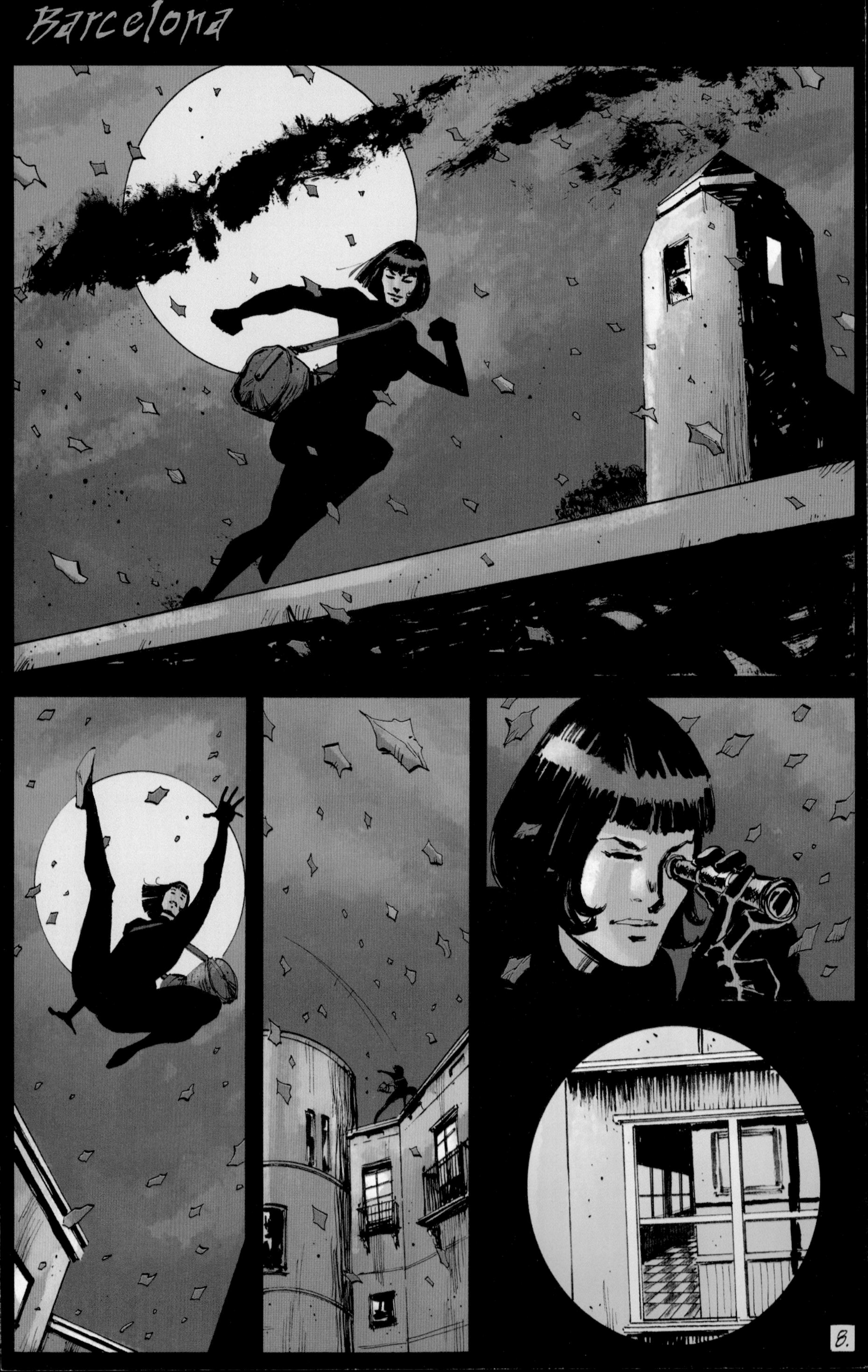
Barcelona

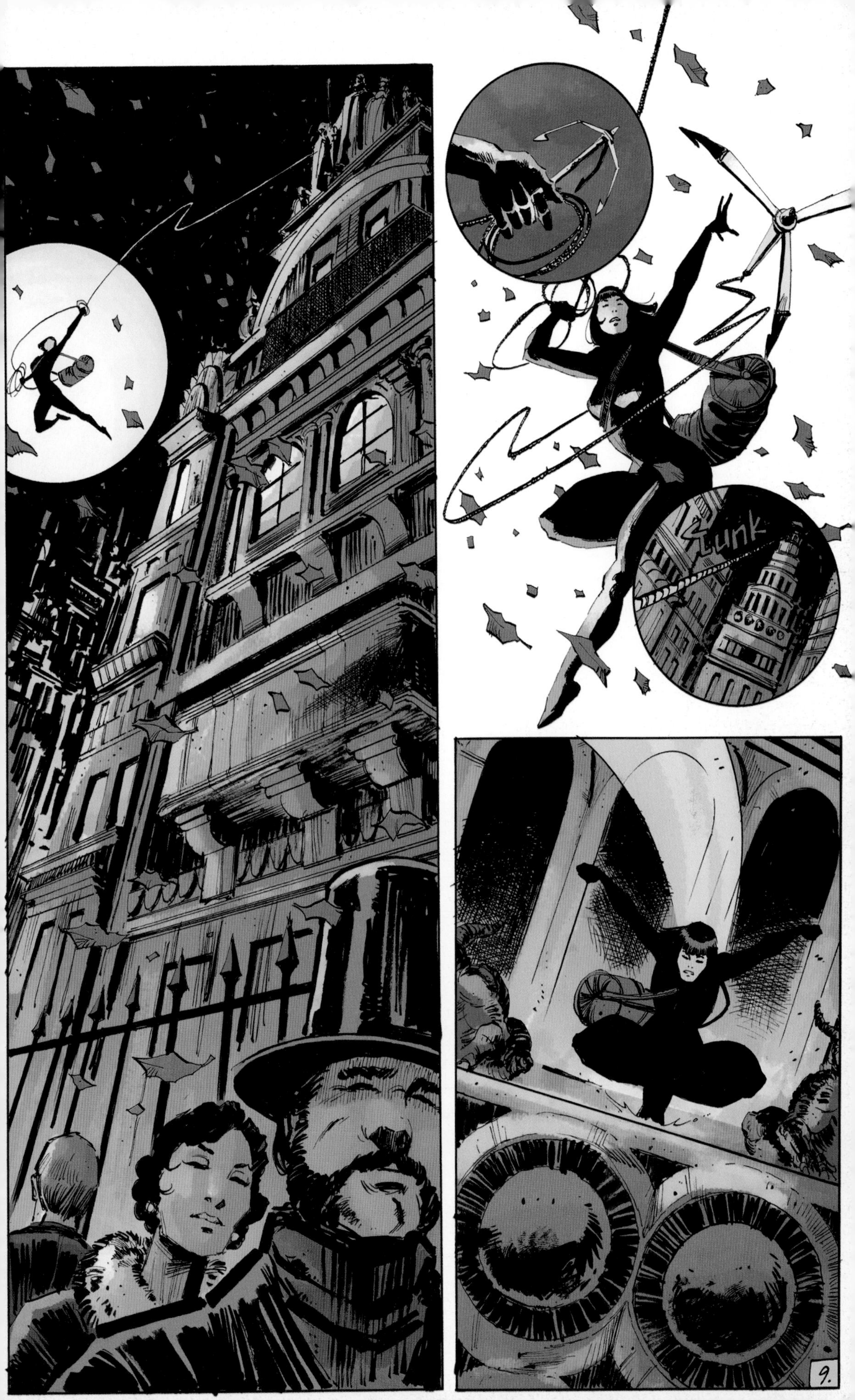
Lunk

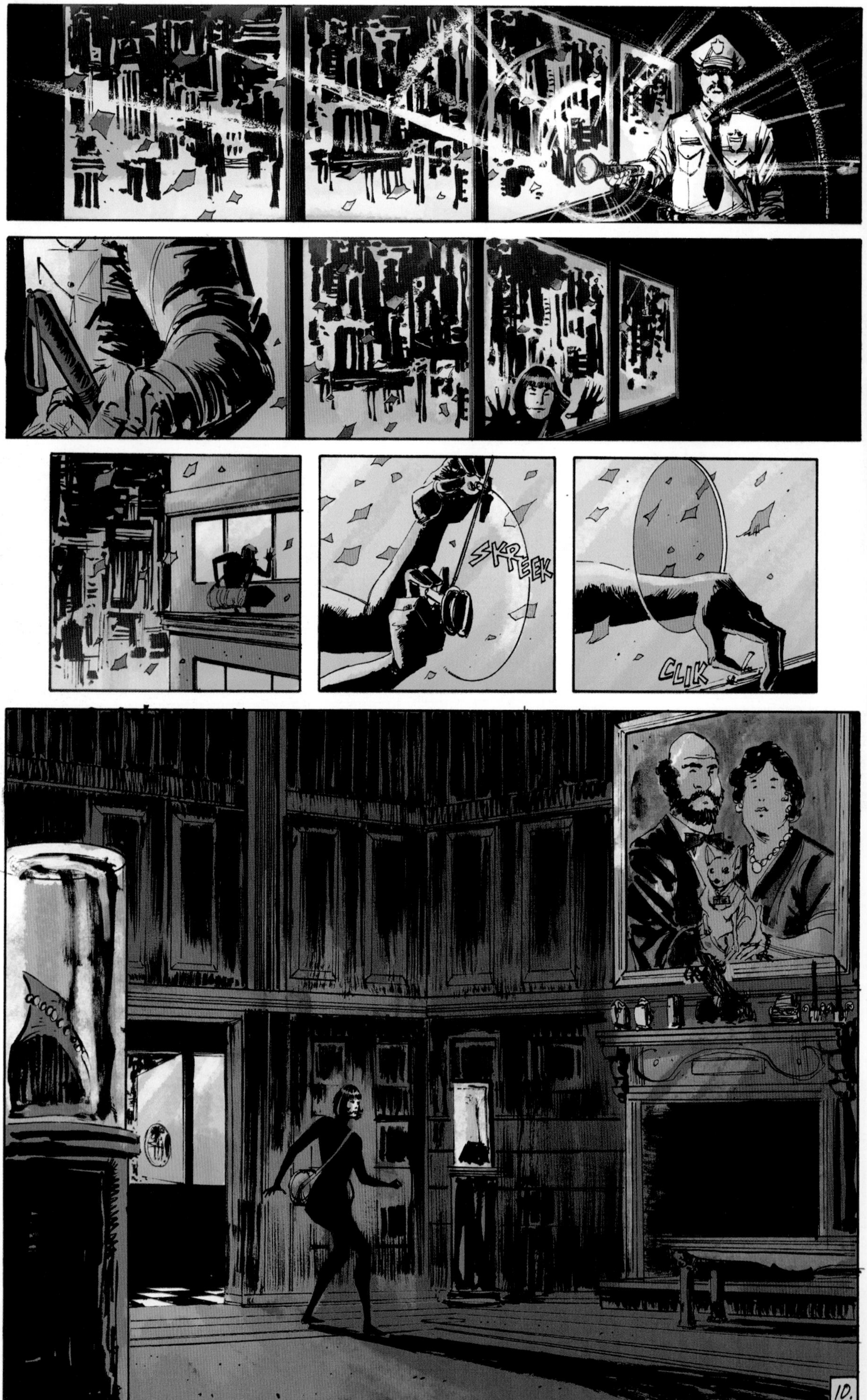
SKREEK
CLIK

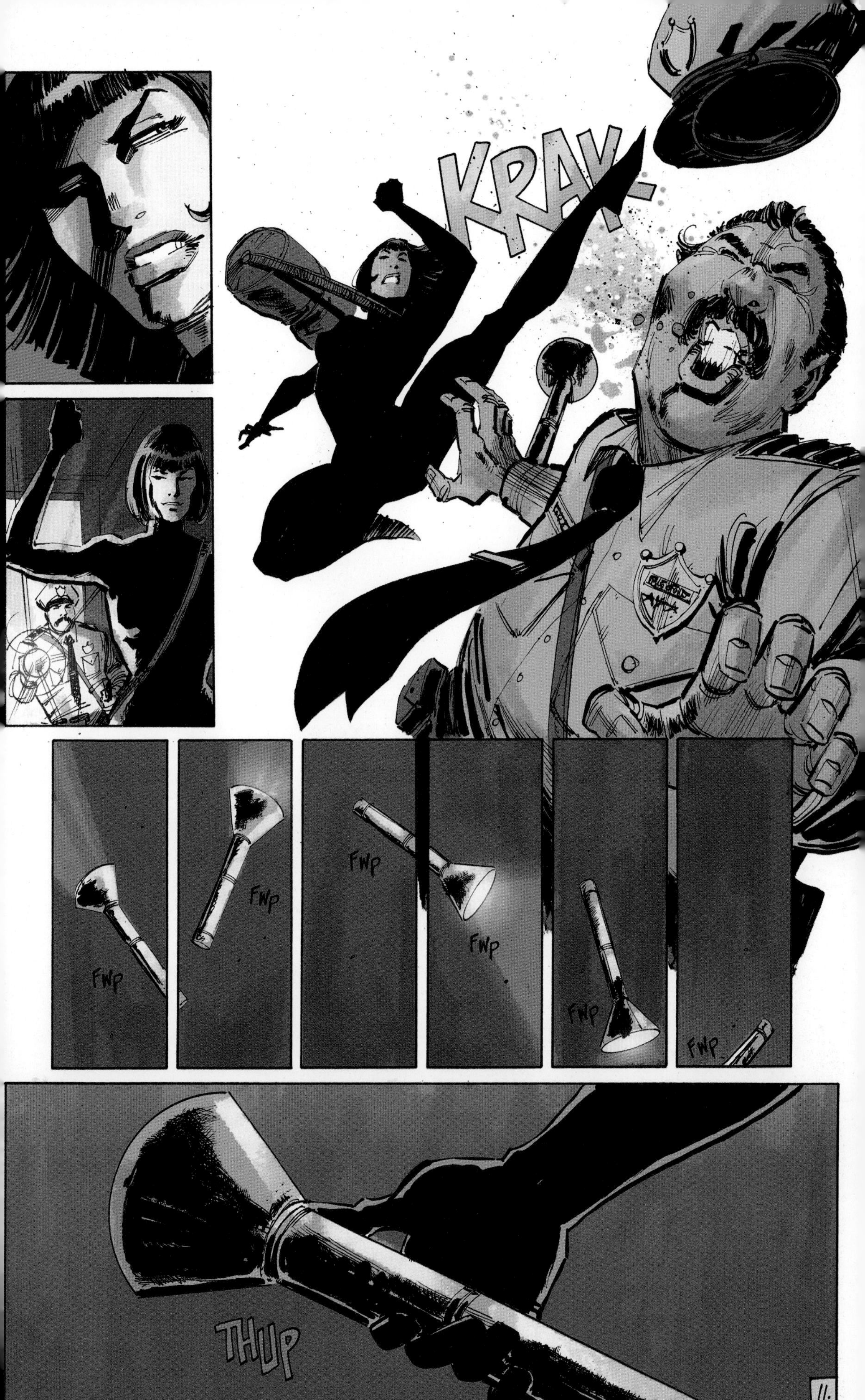
KRAK-
FWP
FWP
FWP
FWP
FWP
FWP
THUP

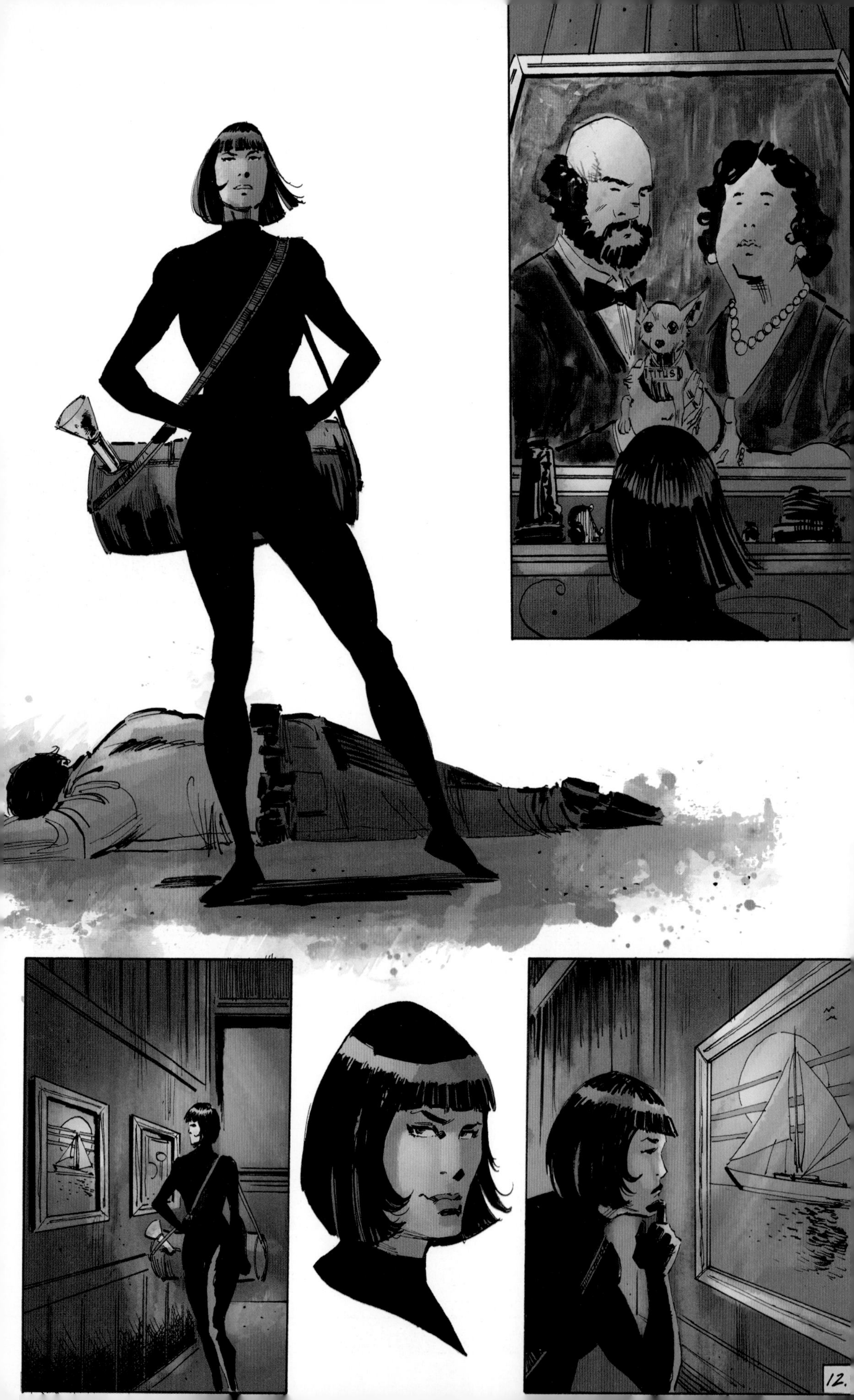
TITUS
12.

A A Z T K
B B A U L
C C B V M
TITUS
R G R S Q
T I T U S
V K V W U

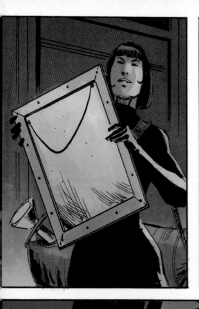

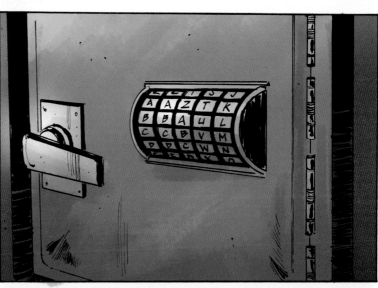

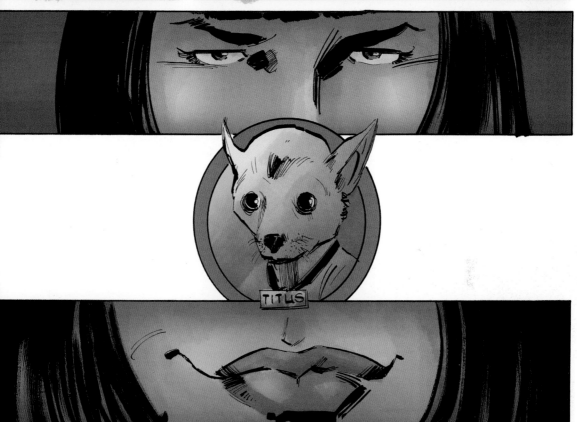

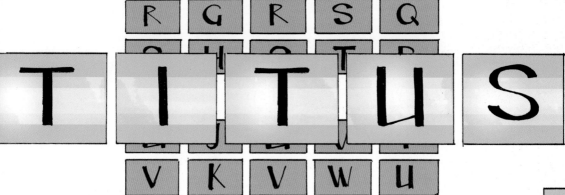

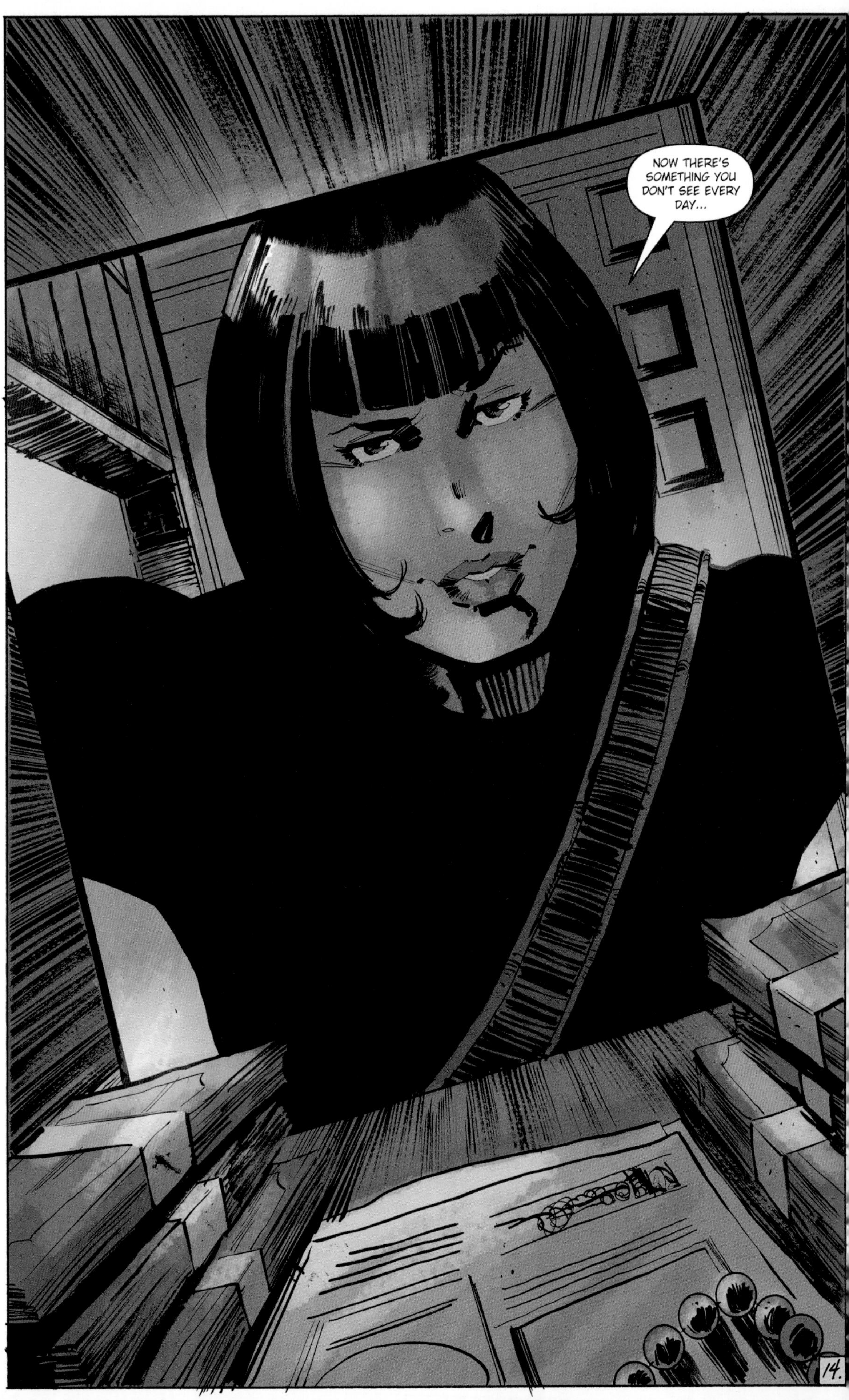
NOW THERE'S SOMETHING YOU DON'T SEE EVERY DAY...

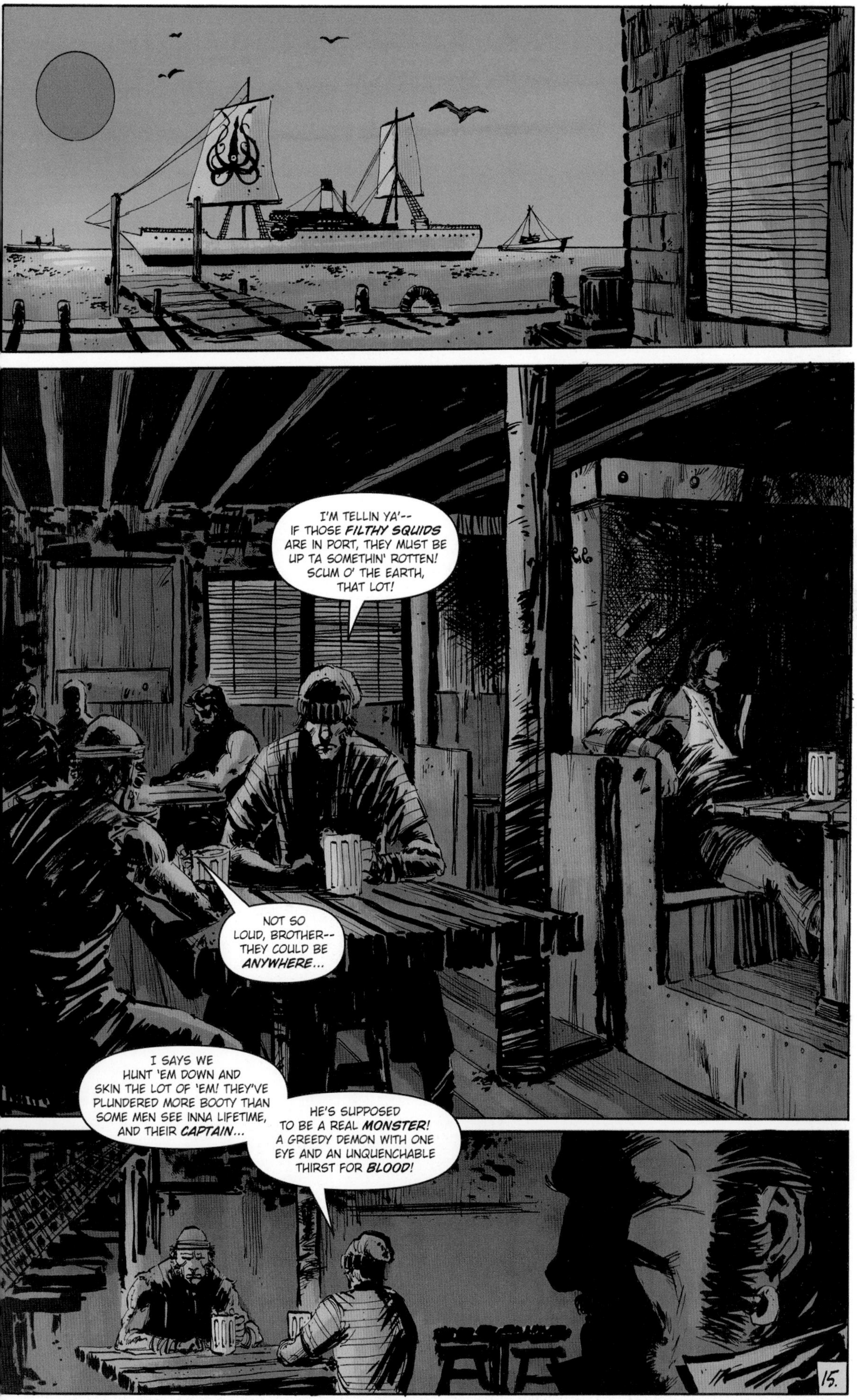
I'M TELLIN YA'-- IF THOSE FILTHY SQUIDS ARE IN PORT, THEY MUST BE UP TA SOMETHIN' ROTTEN! SCUM O' THE EARTH, THAT LOT!
NOT SO LOUD, BROTHER-- THEY COULD BE ANYWHERE...
I SAYS WE HUNT 'EM DOWN AND SKIN THE LOT OF 'EM! THEY'VE PLUNDERED MORE BOOTY THAN SOME MEN SEE INNA LIFETIME, AND THEIR CAPTAIN...
HE'S SUPPOSED TO BE A REAL MONSTER! A GREEDY DEMON WITH ONE EYE AND AN UNQUENCHABLE THIRST FOR BLOOD!

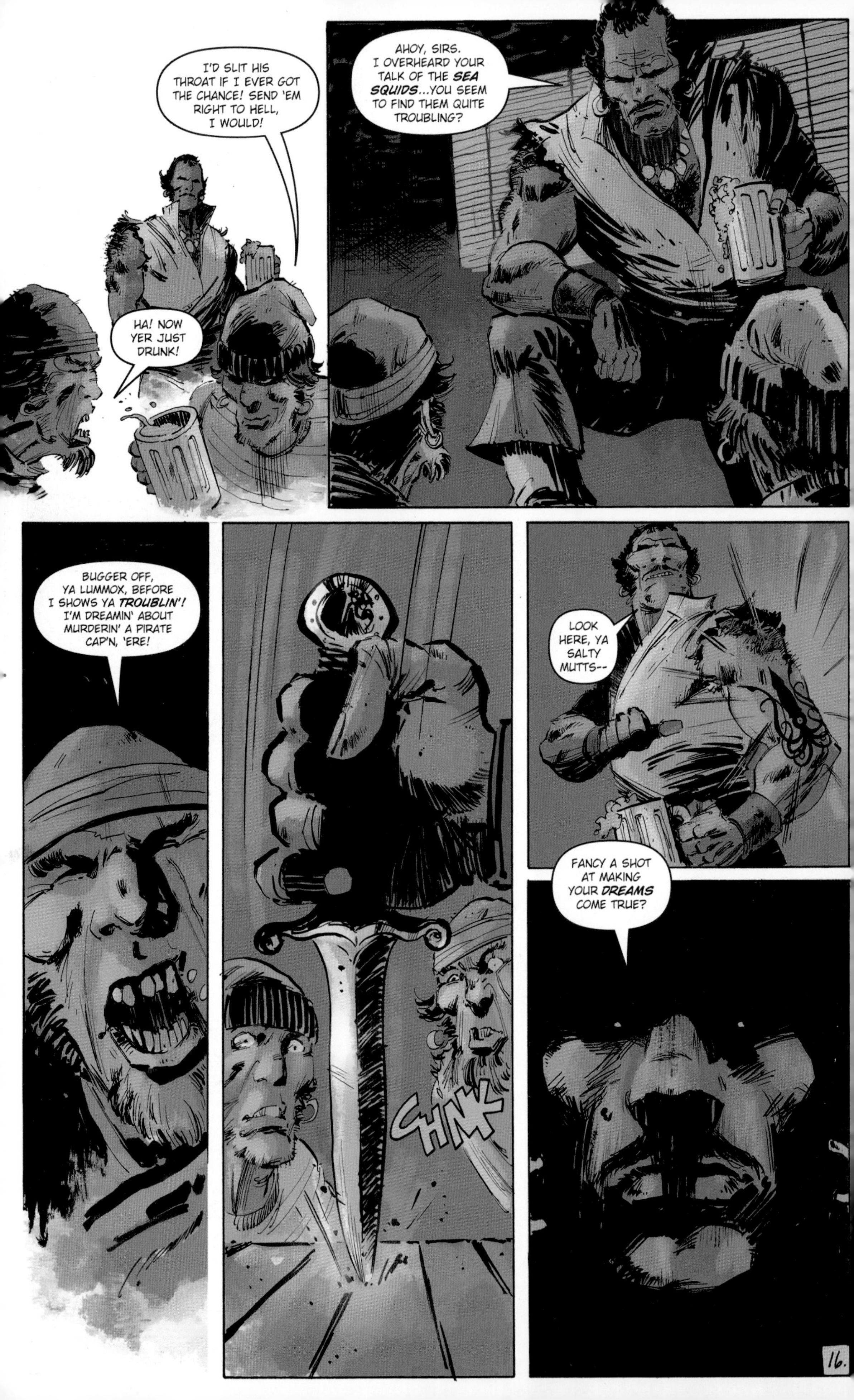
I'D SLIT HIS THROAT IF I EVER GOT THE CHANCE! SEND 'EM RIGHT TO HELL, I WOULD!
HA! NOW YER JUST DRUNK!
AHOY, SIRS. I OVERHEARD YOUR TALK OF THE SEA SQUIDS...YOU SEEM TO FIND THEM QUITE TROUBLING?
BUGGER OFF, YA LUMMOX, BEFORE I SHOWS YA TROUBLIN'! I'M DREAMIN' ABOUT MURDERIN' A PIRATE CAP'N, 'ERE!
CHNK
LOOK HERE, YA SALTY MUTTS--
FANCY A SHOT AT MAKING YOUR DREAMS COME TRUE?
16.

RUN FOR YER LIVES! IT'S HIM!!!

HEH. COWARDS.

ASIF QUINTANO... CAPTAIN OF THE SCREAMING SQUID....

MY MASTERS REQUIRE YOUR SERVICES.

YOU CAN GO STRAIGHT TO HELL, WEASEL. I'M NO MAN'S DOG.

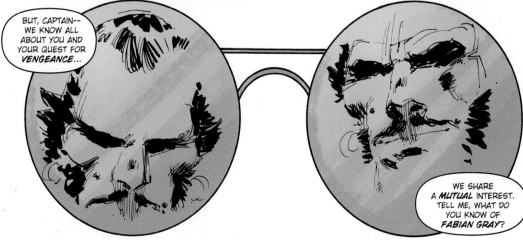

BUT, CAPTAIN-- WE KNOW ALL ABOUT YOU AND YOUR QUEST FOR VENGEANCE...

WE SHARE A MUTUAL INTEREST. TELL ME, WHAT DO YOU KNOW OF FABIAN GRAY?

17.

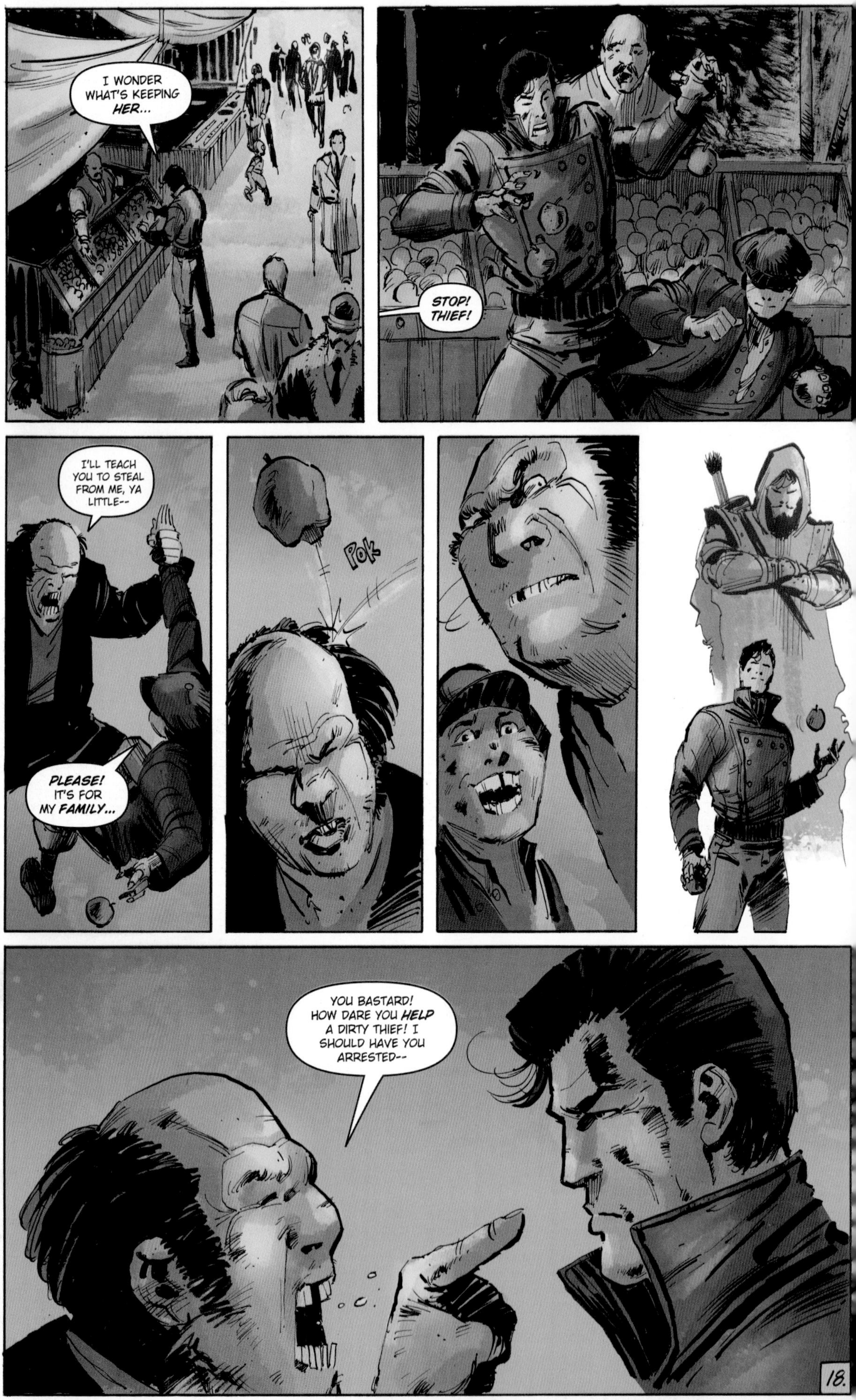
I WONDER WHAT'S KEEPING *HER*...
STOP! THIEF!
I'LL TEACH YOU TO STEAL FROM ME, YA LITTLE--
PLEASE! IT'S FOR MY *FAMILY*...
POK
YOU BASTARD! HOW DARE YOU *HELP* A DIRTY THIEF! I SHOULD HAVE YOU ARRESTED--

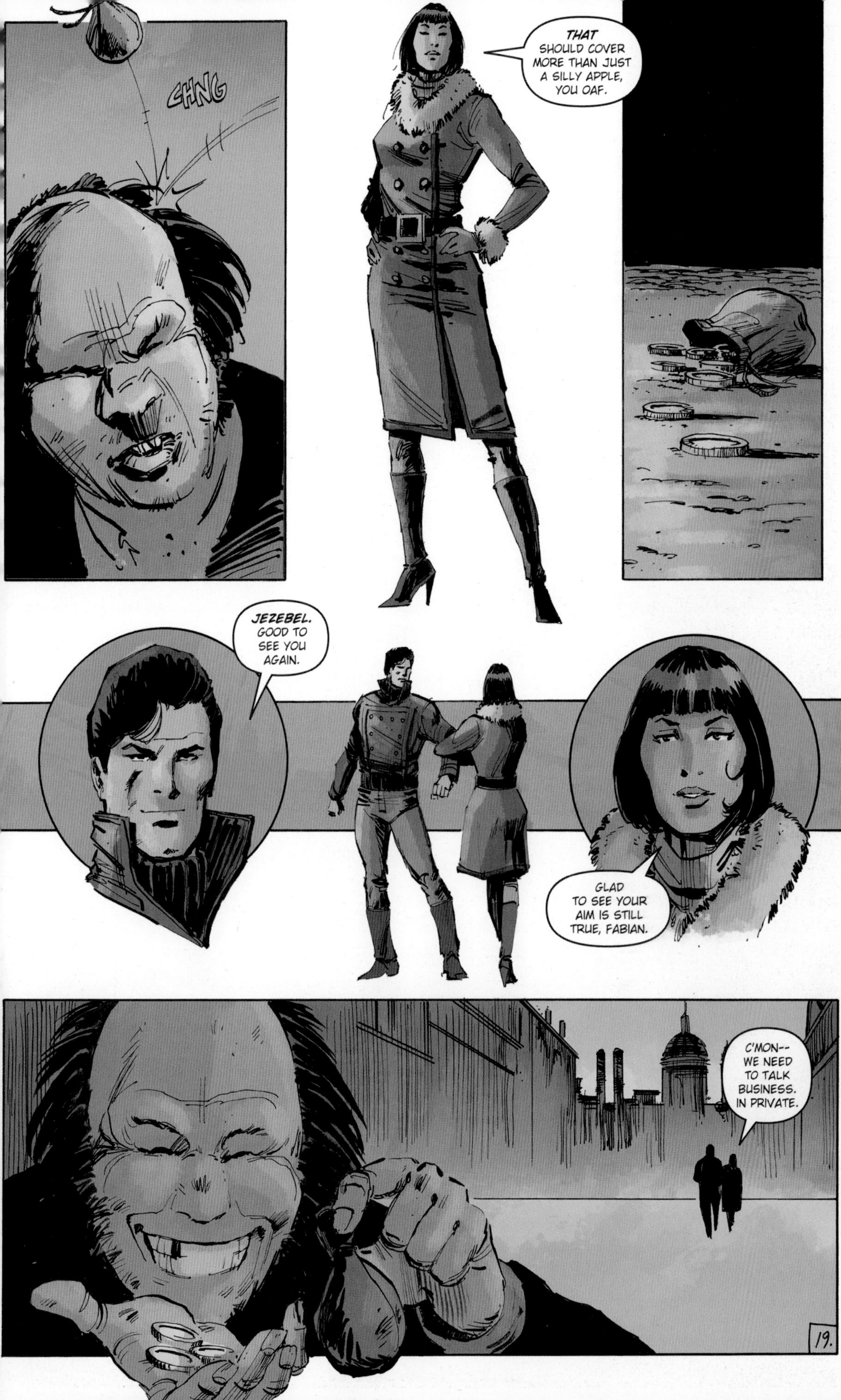
CHNG
THAT SHOULD COVER MORE THAN JUST A SILLY APPLE, YOU OAF.
JEZEBEL. GOOD TO SEE YOU AGAIN.
GLAD TO SEE YOUR AIM IS STILL TRUE, FABIAN.
C'MON-- WE NEED TO TALK BUSINESS. IN PRIVATE.

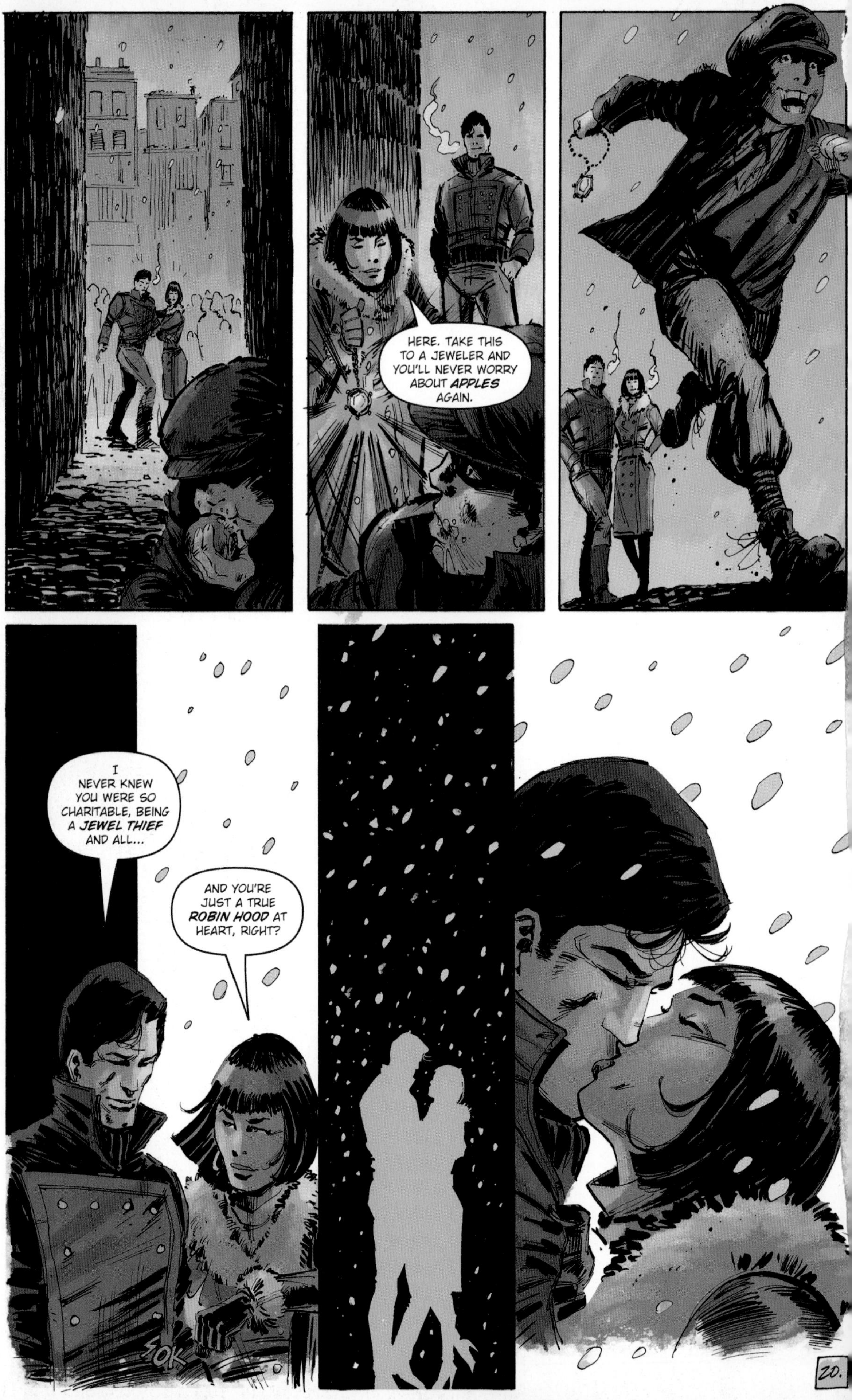
HERE. TAKE THIS TO A JEWELER AND YOU'LL NEVER WORRY ABOUT APPLES AGAIN.
I NEVER KNEW YOU WERE SO CHARITABLE, BEING A JEWEL THIEF AND ALL...
AND YOU'RE JUST A TRUE ROBIN HOOD AT HEART, RIGHT?
SOK
20.

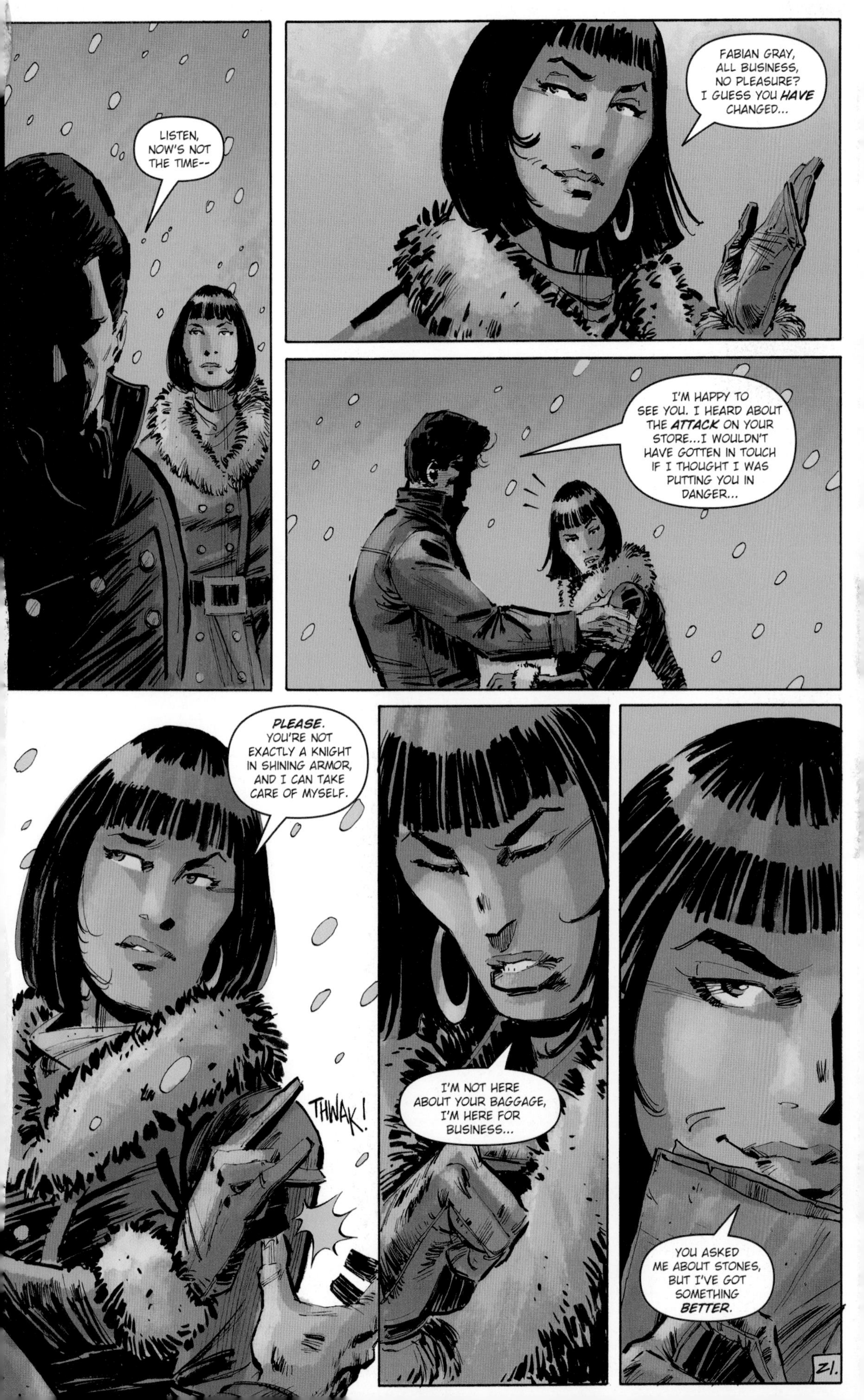
LISTEN, NOW'S NOT THE TIME--
FABIAN GRAY, ALL BUSINESS, NO PLEASURE? I GUESS YOU *HAVE* CHANGED...
I'M HAPPY TO SEE YOU. I HEARD ABOUT THE *ATTACK* ON YOUR STORE...I WOULDN'T HAVE GOTTEN IN TOUCH IF I THOUGHT I WAS PUTTING YOU IN DANGER...
PLEASE. YOU'RE NOT EXACTLY A KNIGHT IN SHINING ARMOR, AND I CAN TAKE CARE OF MYSELF.
THWAK!
I'M NOT HERE ABOUT YOUR BAGGAGE, I'M HERE FOR BUSINESS...
YOU ASKED ME ABOUT STONES, BUT I'VE GOT SOMETHING *BETTER*.
21.

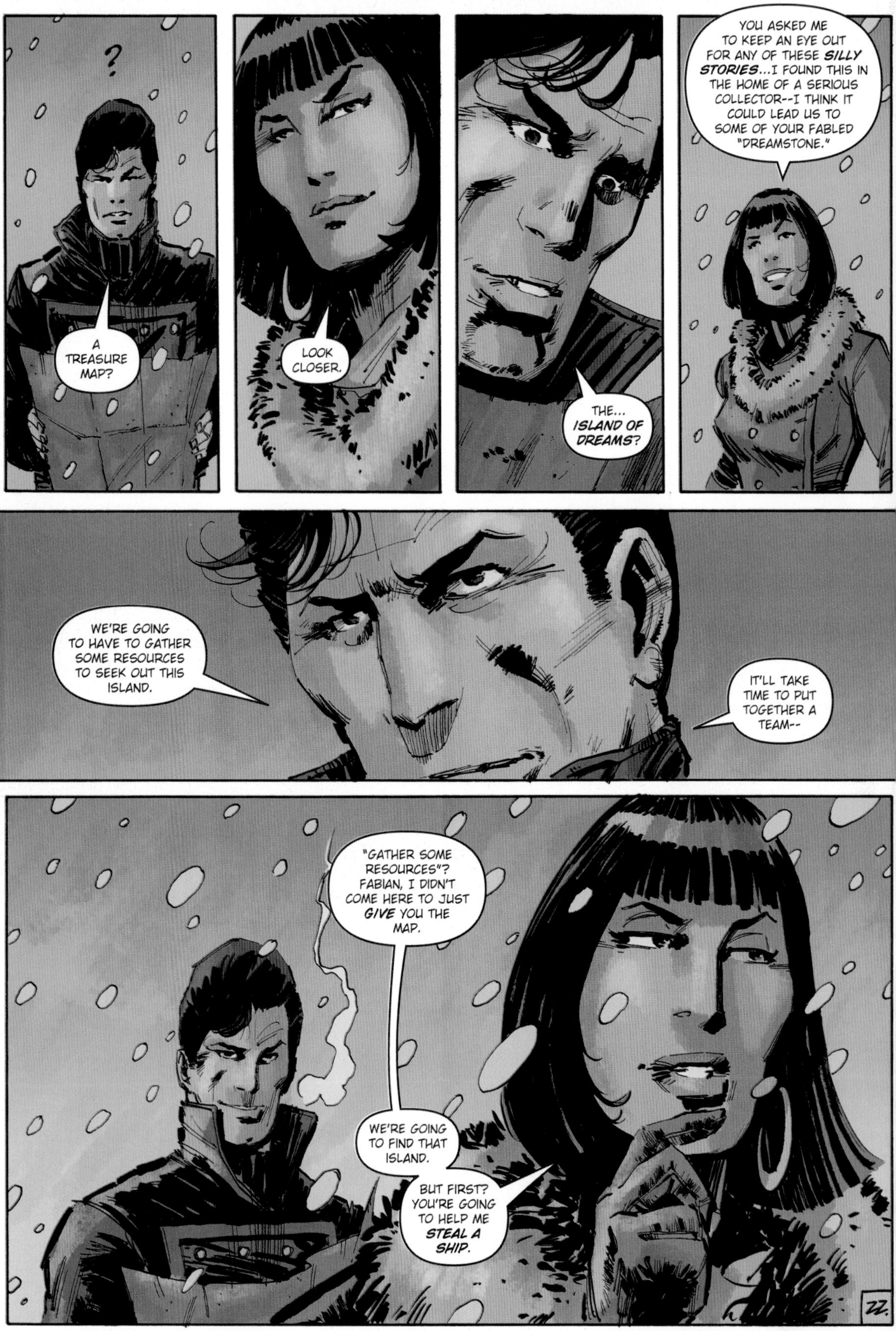
?
A TREASURE MAP?
LOOK CLOSER.
THE... ISLAND OF DREAMS?
YOU ASKED ME TO KEEP AN EYE OUT FOR ANY OF THESE SILLY STORIES...I FOUND THIS IN THE HOME OF A SERIOUS COLLECTOR--I THINK IT COULD LEAD US TO SOME OF YOUR FABLED "DREAMSTONE."
WE'RE GOING TO HAVE TO GATHER SOME RESOURCES TO SEEK OUT THIS ISLAND.
IT'LL TAKE TIME TO PUT TOGETHER A TEAM--
"GATHER SOME RESOURCES"? FABIAN, I DIDN'T COME HERE TO JUST GIVE YOU THE MAP.
WE'RE GOING TO FIND THAT ISLAND.
BUT FIRST? YOU'RE GOING TO HELP ME STEAL A SHIP.
ZZ.

NEXT: HONOR AMONGST THIEVES!

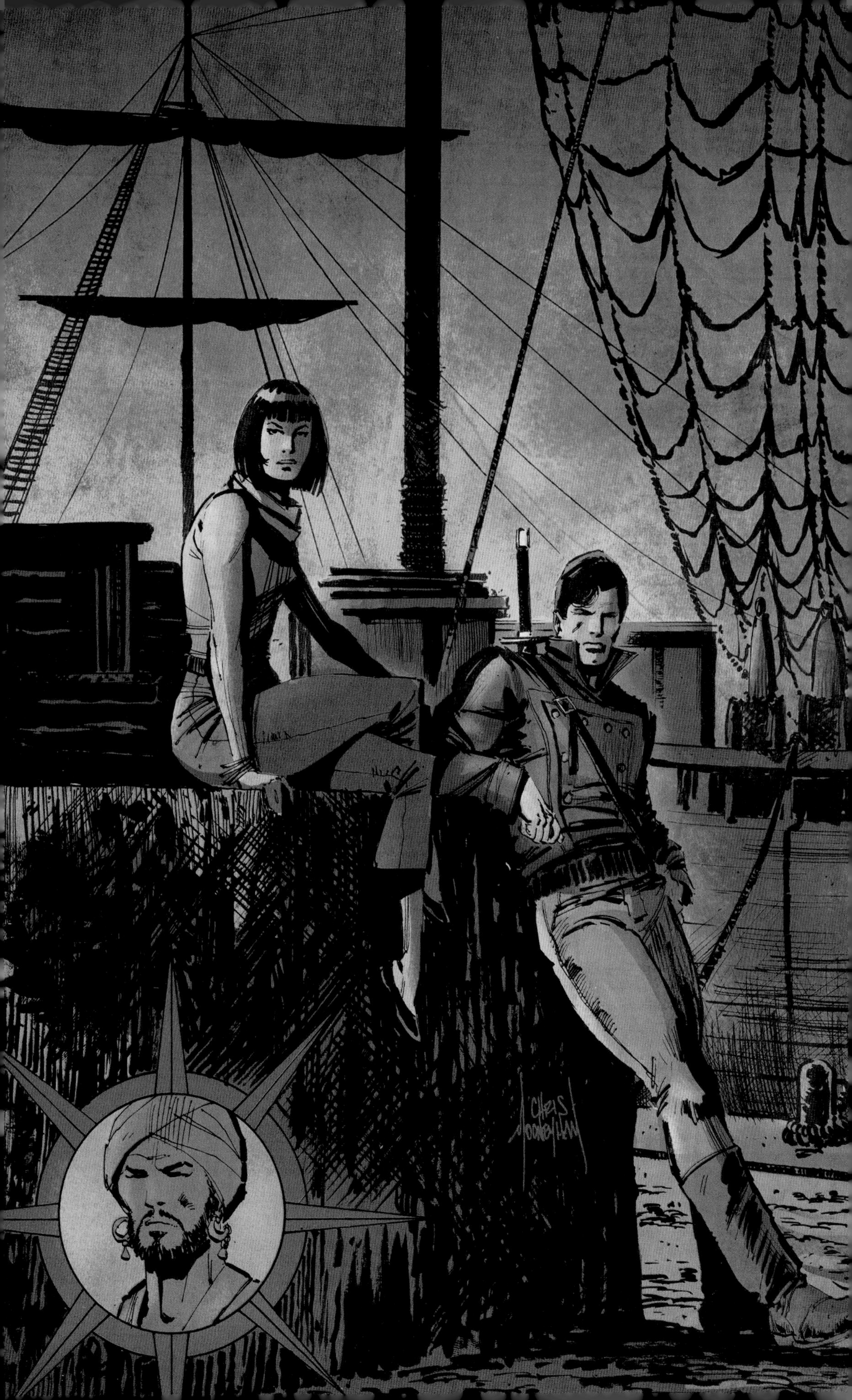

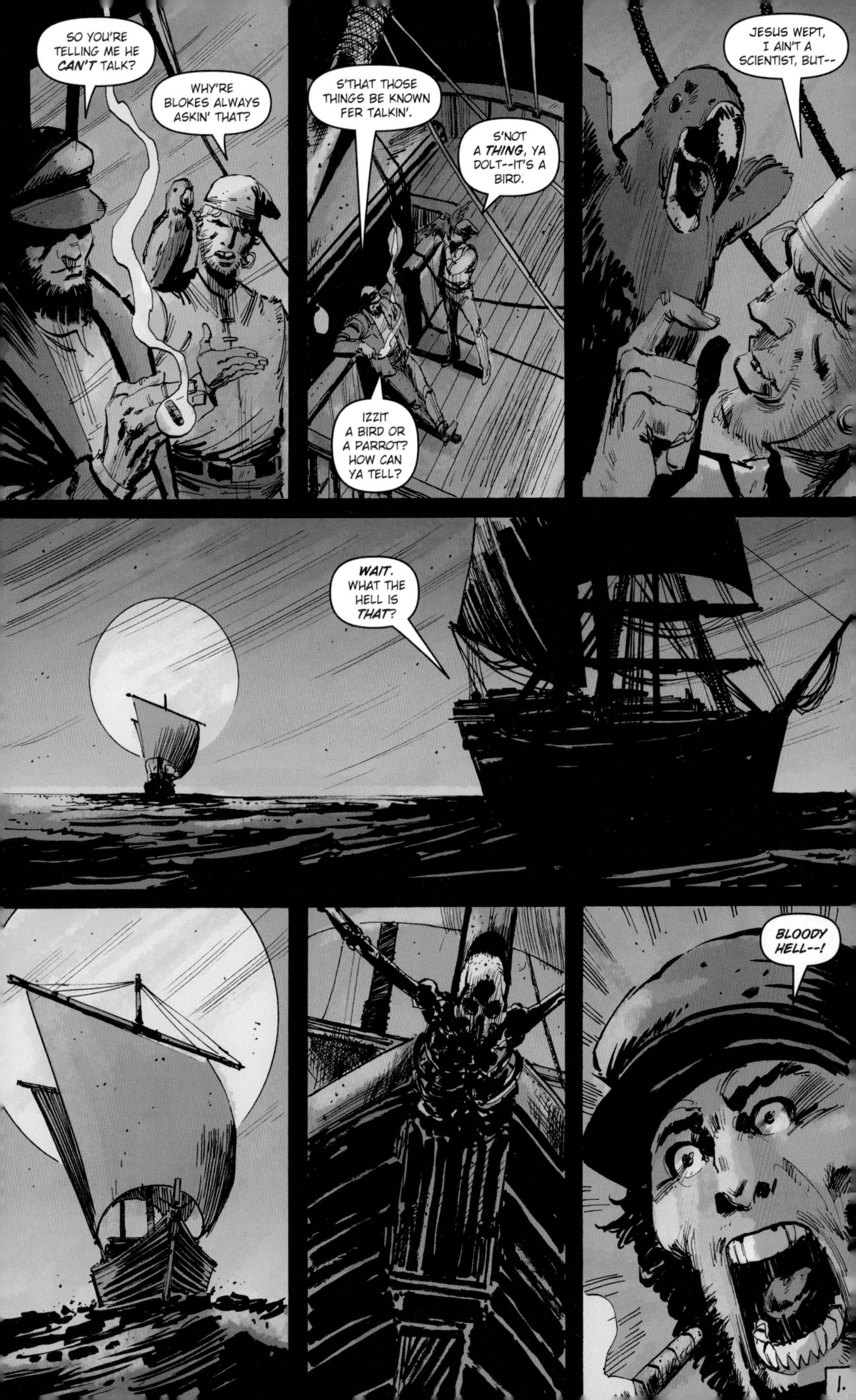
SO YOU'RE TELLING ME HE CAN'T TALK?
WHY'RE BLOKES ALWAYS ASKIN' THAT?
S'THAT THOSE THINGS BE KNOWN FER TALKIN'.
S'NOT A THING, YA DOLT--IT'S A BIRD.
IZZIT A BIRD OR A PARROT? HOW CAN YA TELL?
JESUS WEPT, I AIN'T A SCIENTIST, BUT--
WAIT. WHAT THE HELL IS THAT?
BLOODY HELL--!

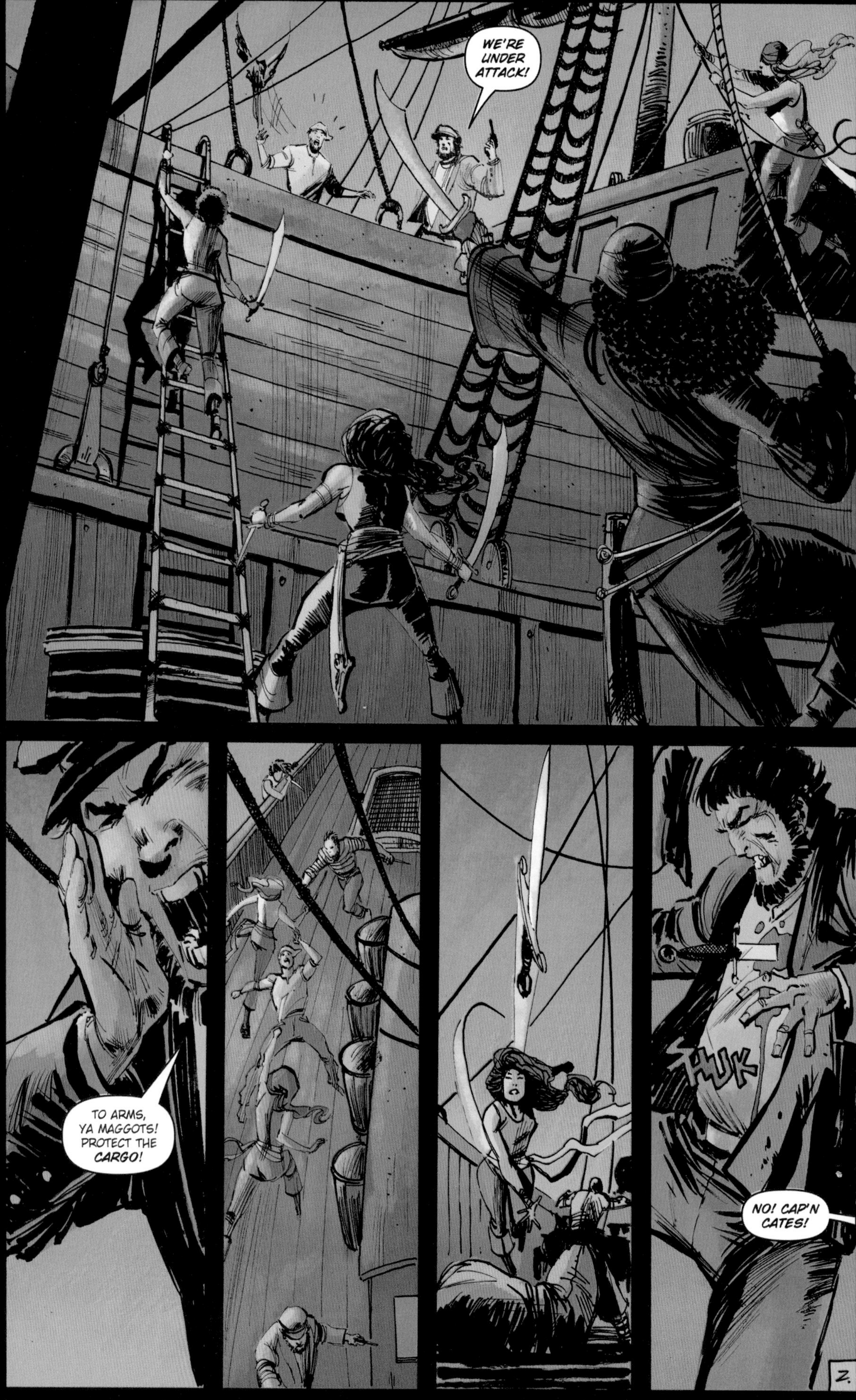
WE'RE UNDER ATTACK!
TO ARMS, YA MAGGOTS! PROTECT THE CARGO!
SHUK
NO! CAP'N CATES!

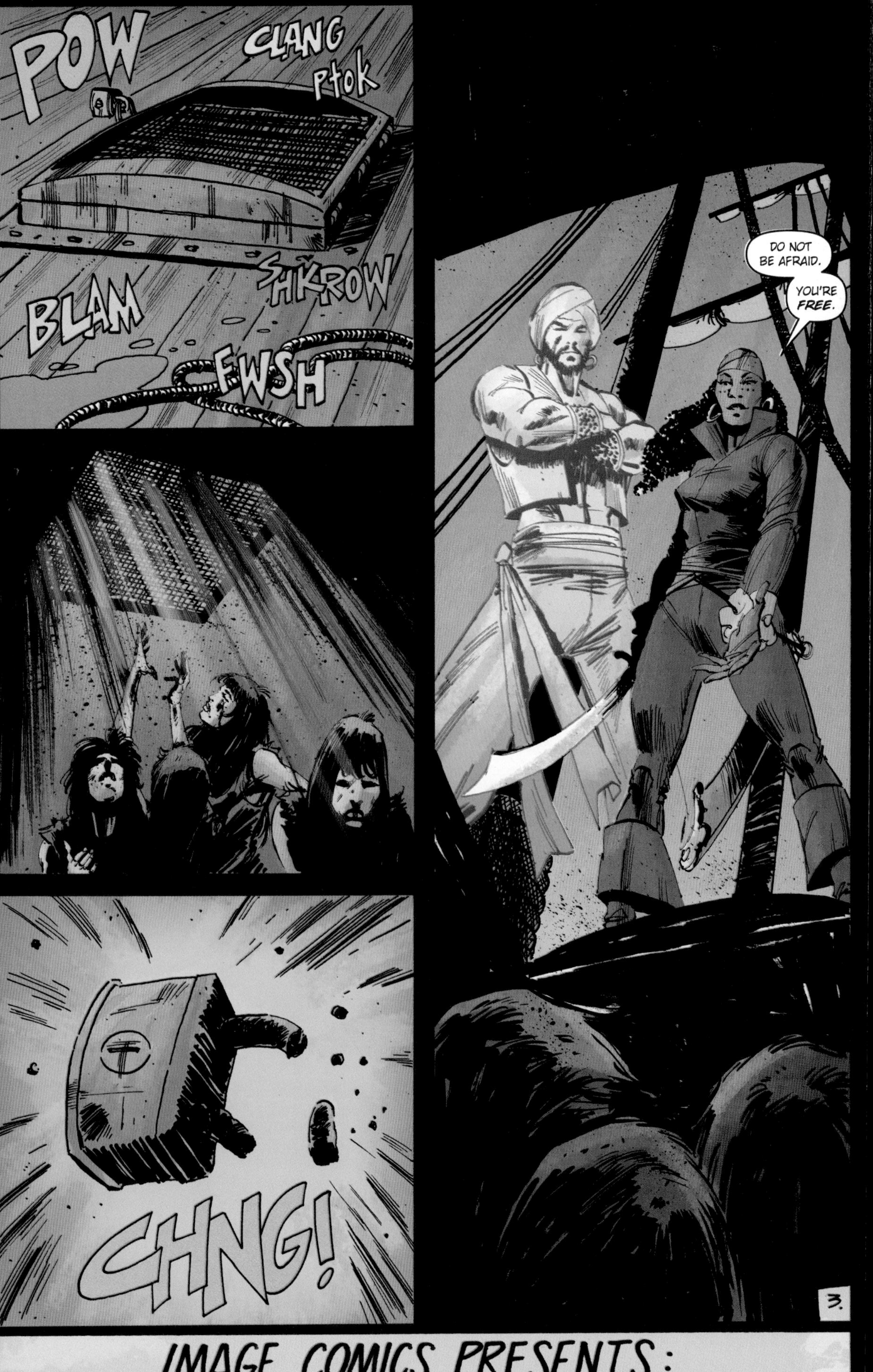
POW
CLANG
ptok
SHKROW
BLAM
FWSH
CHNG!
DO NOT BE AFRAID.
YOU'RE FREE.
3.

IMAGE COMICS PRESENTS:

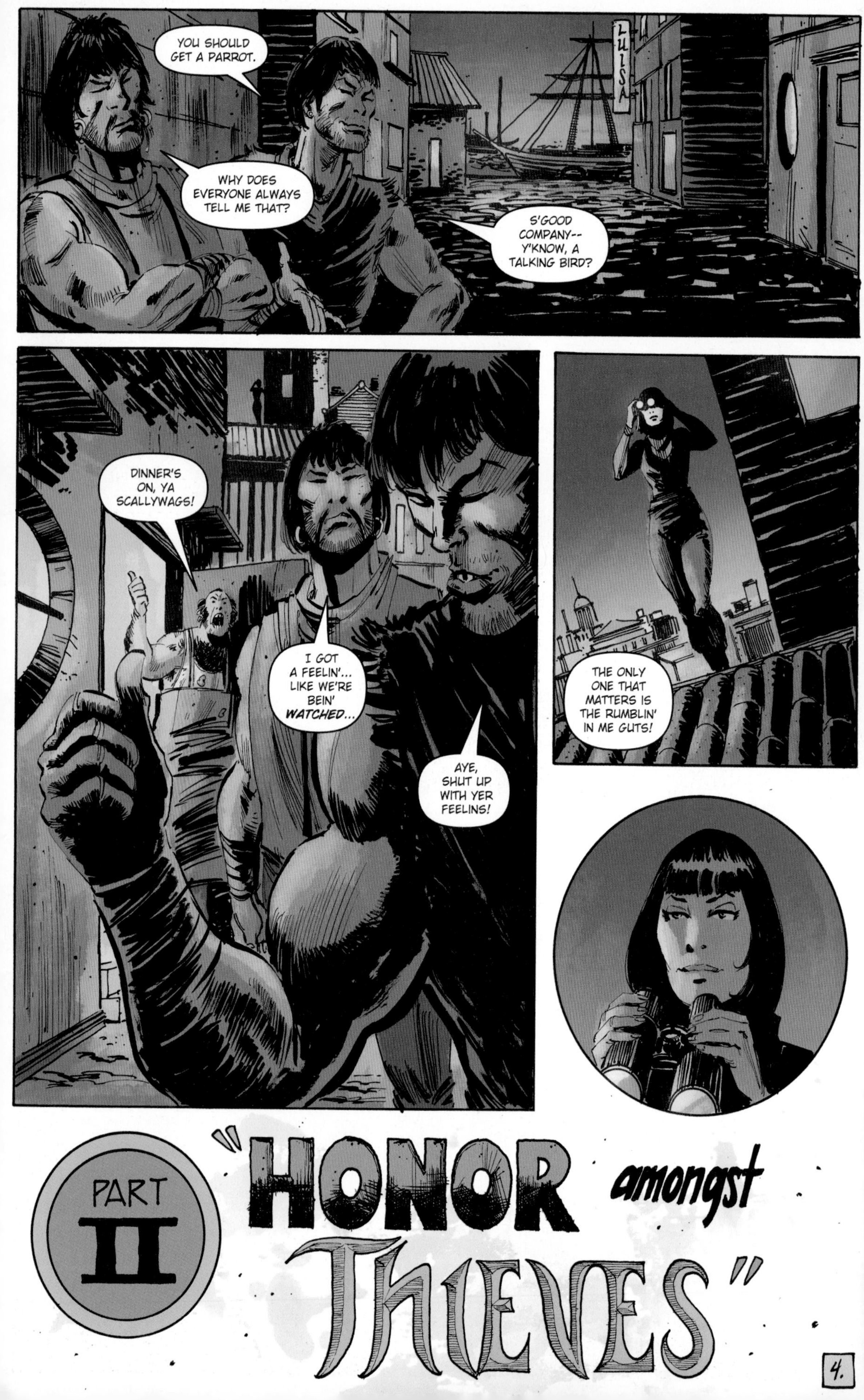

LUISA
YOU SHOULD GET A PARROT.
WHY DOES EVERYONE ALWAYS TELL ME THAT?
S'GOOD COMPANY-- Y'KNOW, A TALKING BIRD?
DINNER'S ON, YA SCALLYWAGS!
I GOT A FEELIN'... LIKE WE'RE BEIN' WATCHED...
AYE, SHUT UP WITH YER FEELINS!
THE ONLY ONE THAT MATTERS IS THE RUMBLIN' IN ME GUTS!

PART II "HONOR amongst THIEVES"

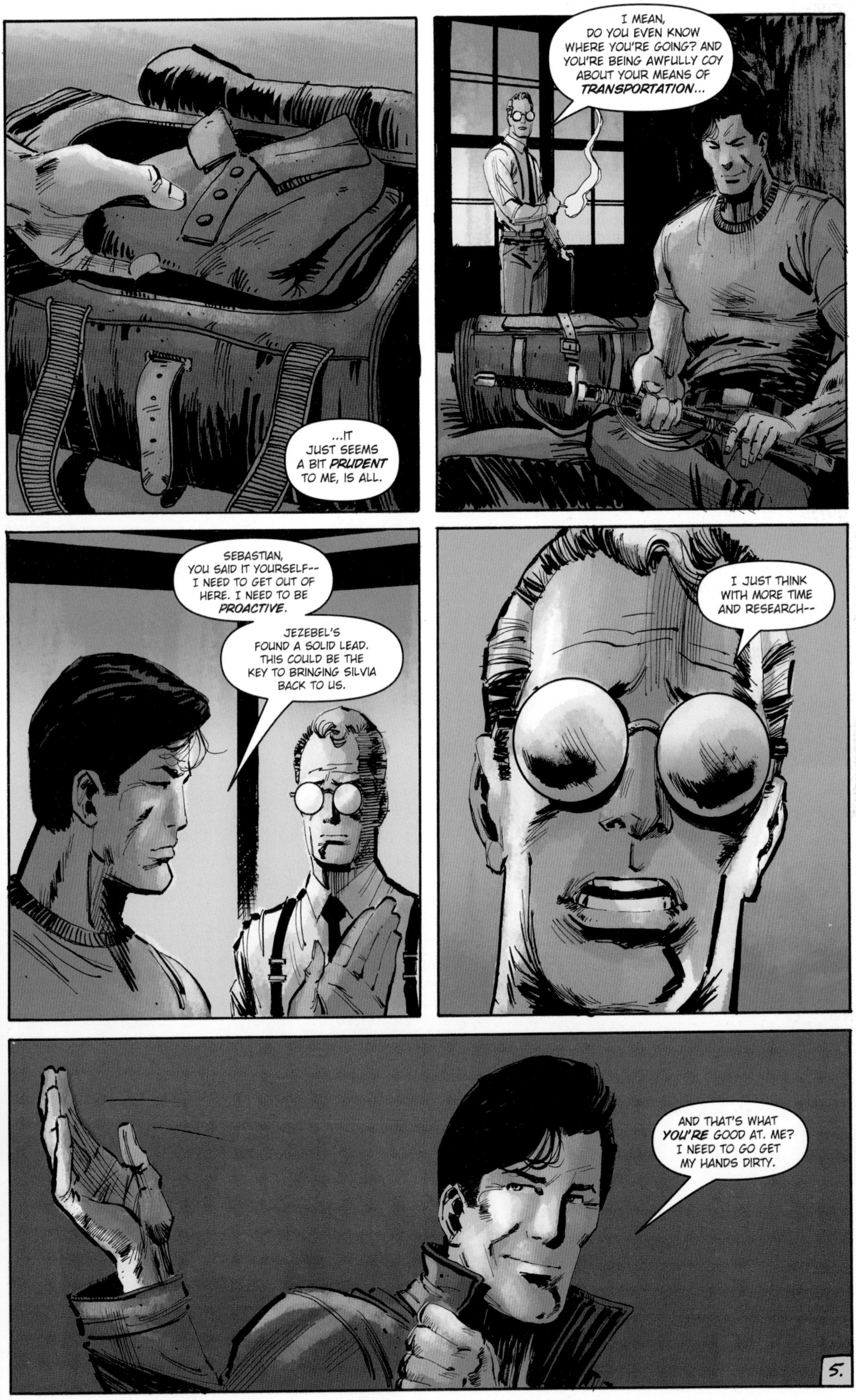
...IT JUST SEEMS A BIT PRUDENT TO ME, IS ALL.
I MEAN, DO YOU EVEN KNOW WHERE YOU'RE GOING? AND YOU'RE BEING AWFULLY COY ABOUT YOUR MEANS OF TRANSPORTATION...
SEBASTIAN, YOU SAID IT YOURSELF-- I NEED TO GET OUT OF HERE. I NEED TO BE PROACTIVE.
JEZEBEL'S FOUND A SOLID LEAD. THIS COULD BE THE KEY TO BRINGING SILVIA BACK TO US.
I JUST THINK WITH MORE TIME AND RESEARCH--
AND THAT'S WHAT YOU'RE GOOD AT. ME? I NEED TO GO GET MY HANDS DIRTY.
5.

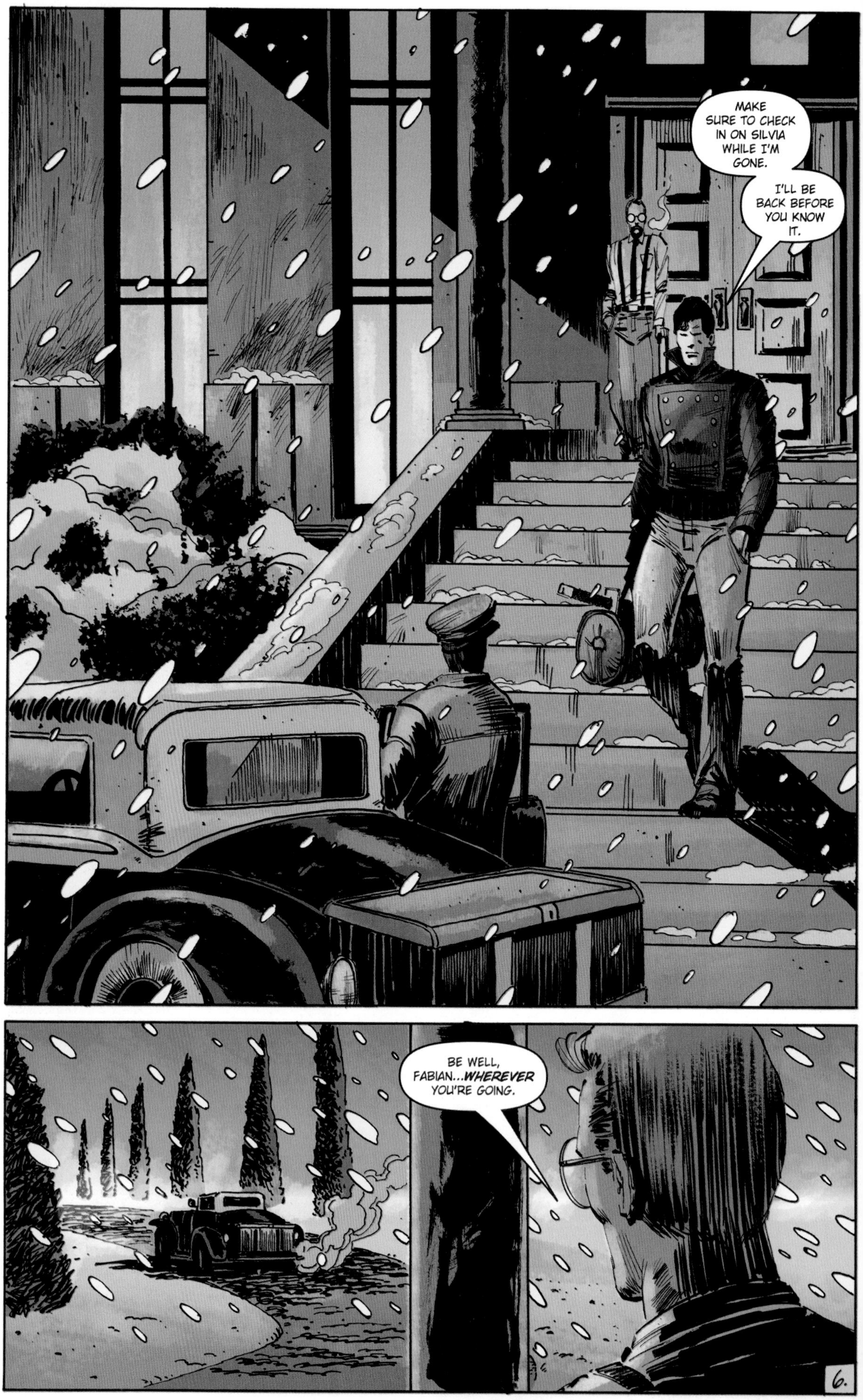
MAKE SURE TO CHECK IN ON SILVIA WHILE I'M GONE.
I'LL BE BACK BEFORE YOU KNOW IT.
BE WELL, FABIAN...*WHEREVER* YOU'RE GOING.
6.

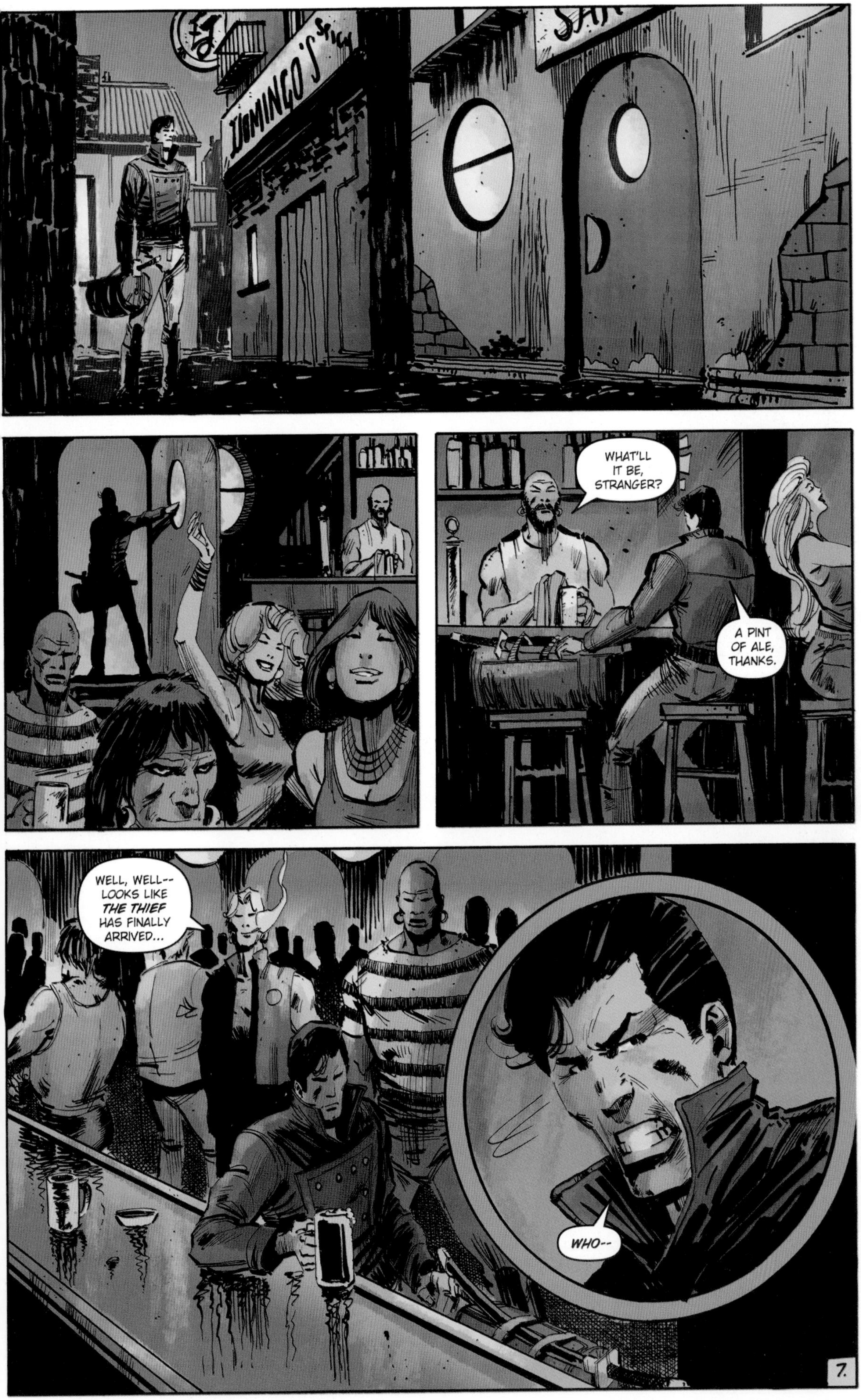
DOMINGO'S
WHAT'LL IT BE, STRANGER?
A PINT OF ALE, THANKS.
WELL, WELL-- LOOKS LIKE *THE THIEF* HAS FINALLY ARRIVED...
WHO--

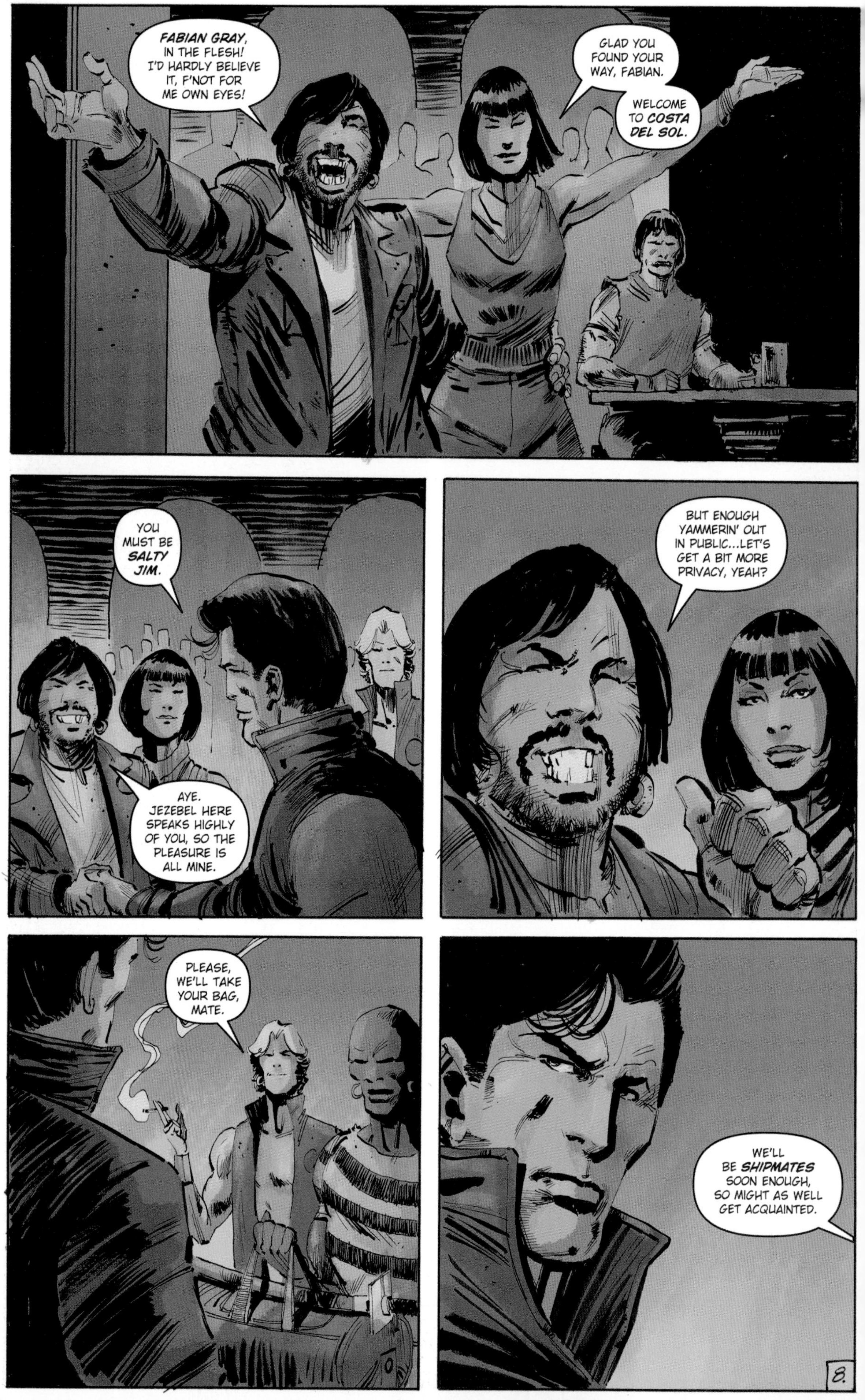
FABIAN GRAY, IN THE FLESH! I'D HARDLY BELIEVE IT, F'NOT FOR ME OWN EYES!
GLAD YOU FOUND YOUR WAY, FABIAN.
WELCOME TO COSTA DEL SOL.
YOU MUST BE SALTY JIM.
AYE. JEZEBEL HERE SPEAKS HIGHLY OF YOU, SO THE PLEASURE IS ALL MINE.
BUT ENOUGH YAMMERIN' OUT IN PUBLIC...LET'S GET A BIT MORE PRIVACY, YEAH?
PLEASE, WE'LL TAKE YOUR BAG, MATE.
WE'LL BE SHIPMATES SOON ENOUGH, SO MIGHT AS WELL GET ACQUAINTED.
8.

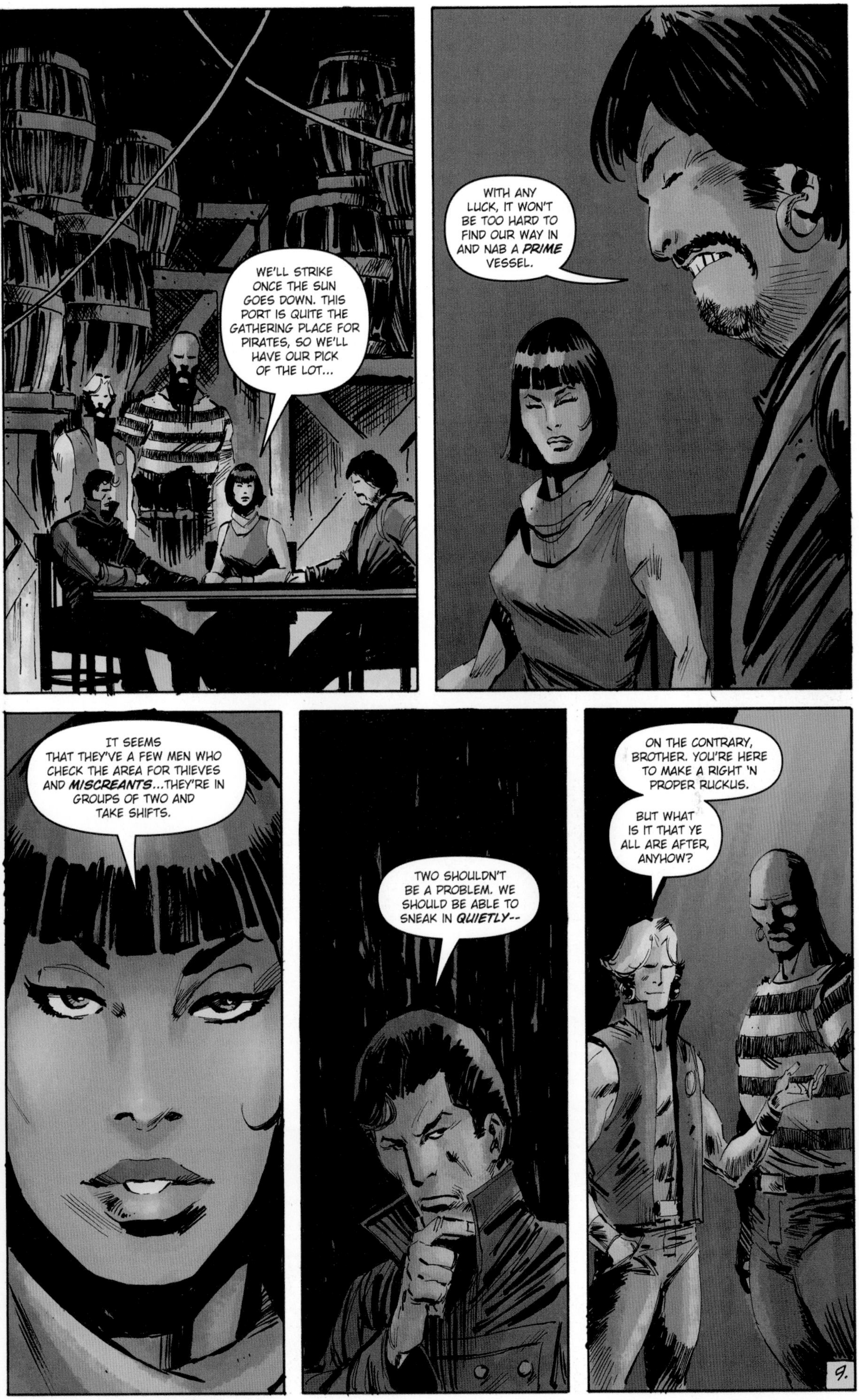
WE'LL STRIKE ONCE THE SUN GOES DOWN. THIS PORT IS QUITE THE GATHERING PLACE FOR PIRATES, SO WE'LL HAVE OUR PICK OF THE LOT...
WITH ANY LUCK, IT WON'T BE TOO HARD TO FIND OUR WAY IN AND NAB A PRIME VESSEL.
IT SEEMS THAT THEY'VE A FEW MEN WHO CHECK THE AREA FOR THIEVES AND MISCREANTS...THEY'RE IN GROUPS OF TWO AND TAKE SHIFTS.
TWO SHOULDN'T BE A PROBLEM. WE SHOULD BE ABLE TO SNEAK IN QUIETLY--
ON THE CONTRARY, BROTHER. YOU'RE HERE TO MAKE A RIGHT 'N PROPER RUCKUS.
BUT WHAT IS IT THAT YE ALL ARE AFTER, ANYHOW?
9.

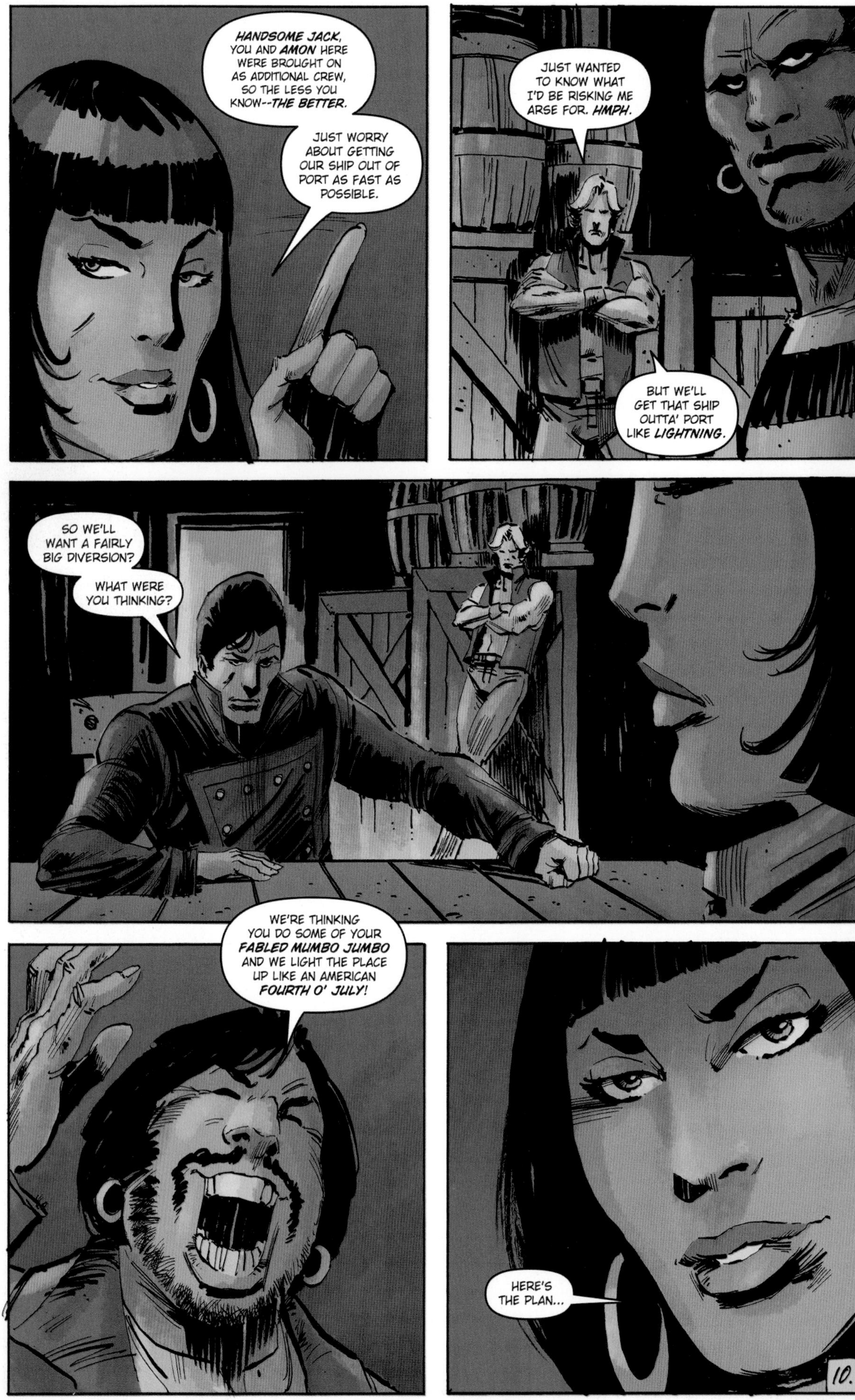
HANDSOME JACK, YOU AND AMON HERE WERE BROUGHT ON AS ADDITIONAL CREW, SO THE LESS YOU KNOW--THE BETTER.
JUST WORRY ABOUT GETTING OUR SHIP OUT OF PORT AS FAST AS POSSIBLE.
JUST WANTED TO KNOW WHAT I'D BE RISKING ME ARSE FOR. HMPH.
BUT WE'LL GET THAT SHIP OUTTA' PORT LIKE LIGHTNING.
SO WE'LL WANT A FAIRLY BIG DIVERSION?
WHAT WERE YOU THINKING?
WE'RE THINKING YOU DO SOME OF YOUR FABLED MUMBO JUMBO AND WE LIGHT THE PLACE UP LIKE AN AMERICAN FOURTH O' JULY!
HERE'S THE PLAN...
10.

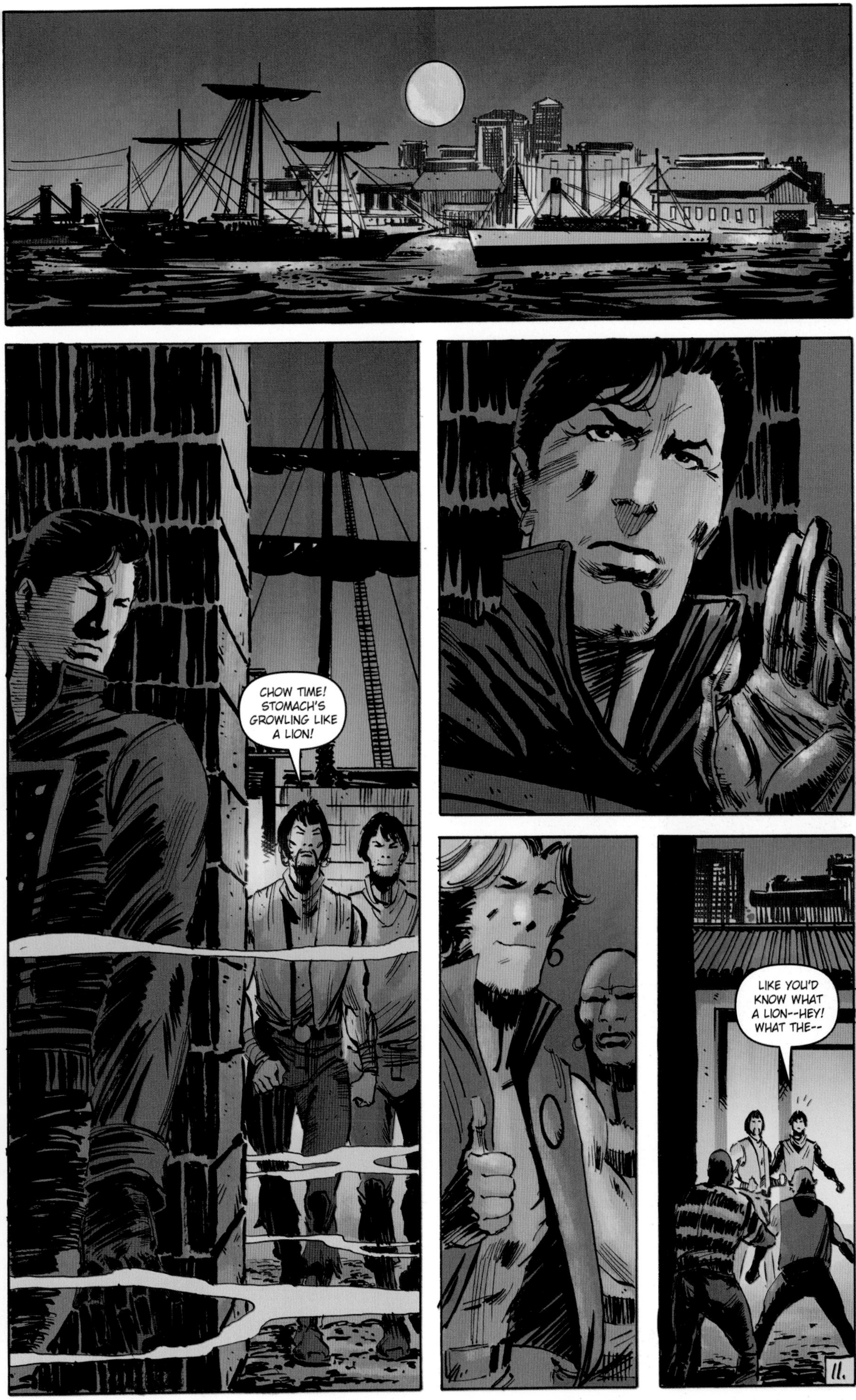
CHOW TIME! STOMACH'S GROWLING LIKE A LION!
LIKE YOU'D KNOW WHAT A LION--HEY! WHAT THE--

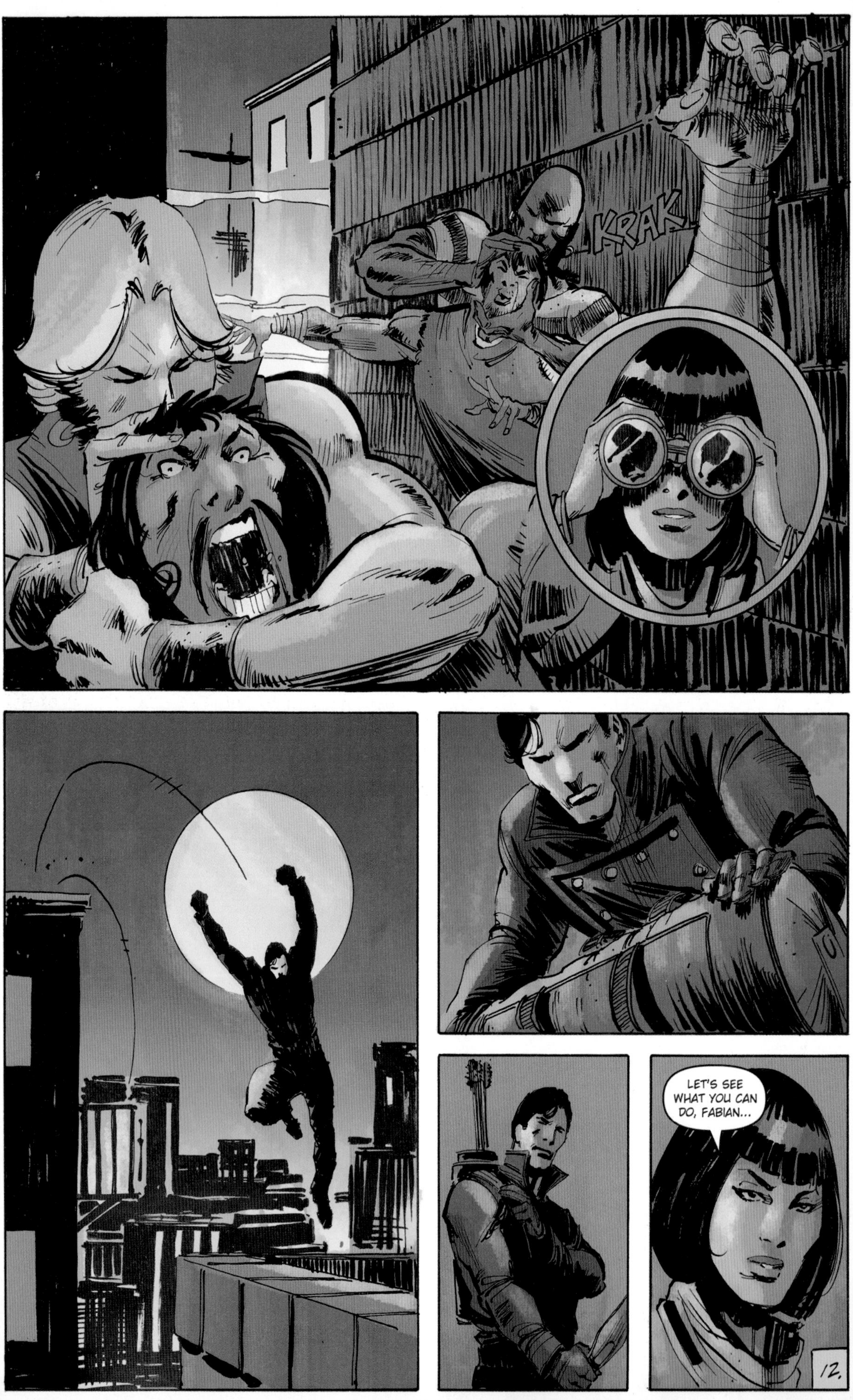
KRAK
LET'S SEE WHAT YOU CAN DO, FABIAN...
12.

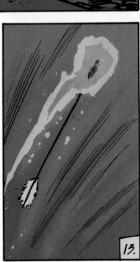

13.

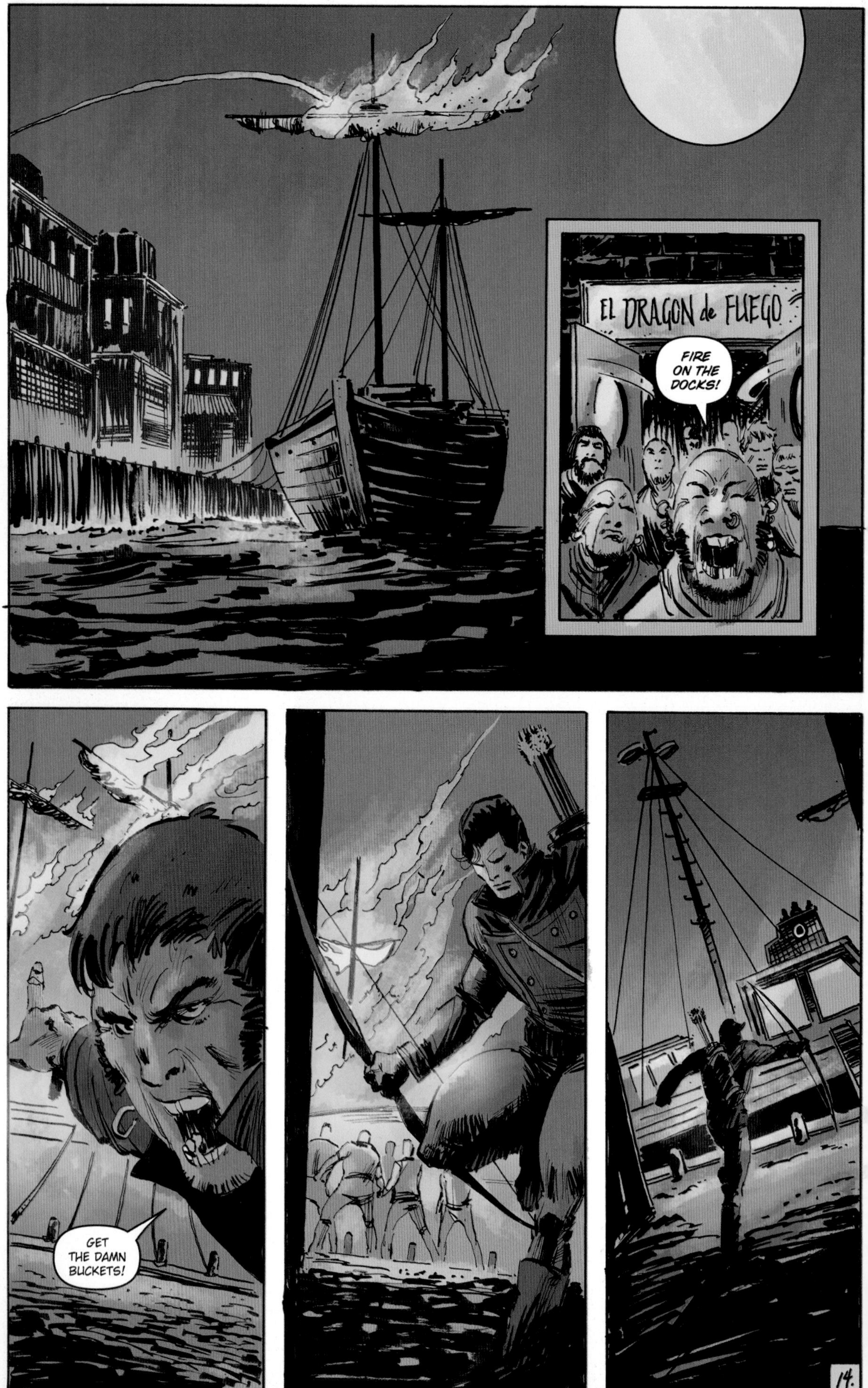
EL DRAGON de FUEGO
FIRE ON THE DOCKS!
GET THE DAMN BUCKETS!

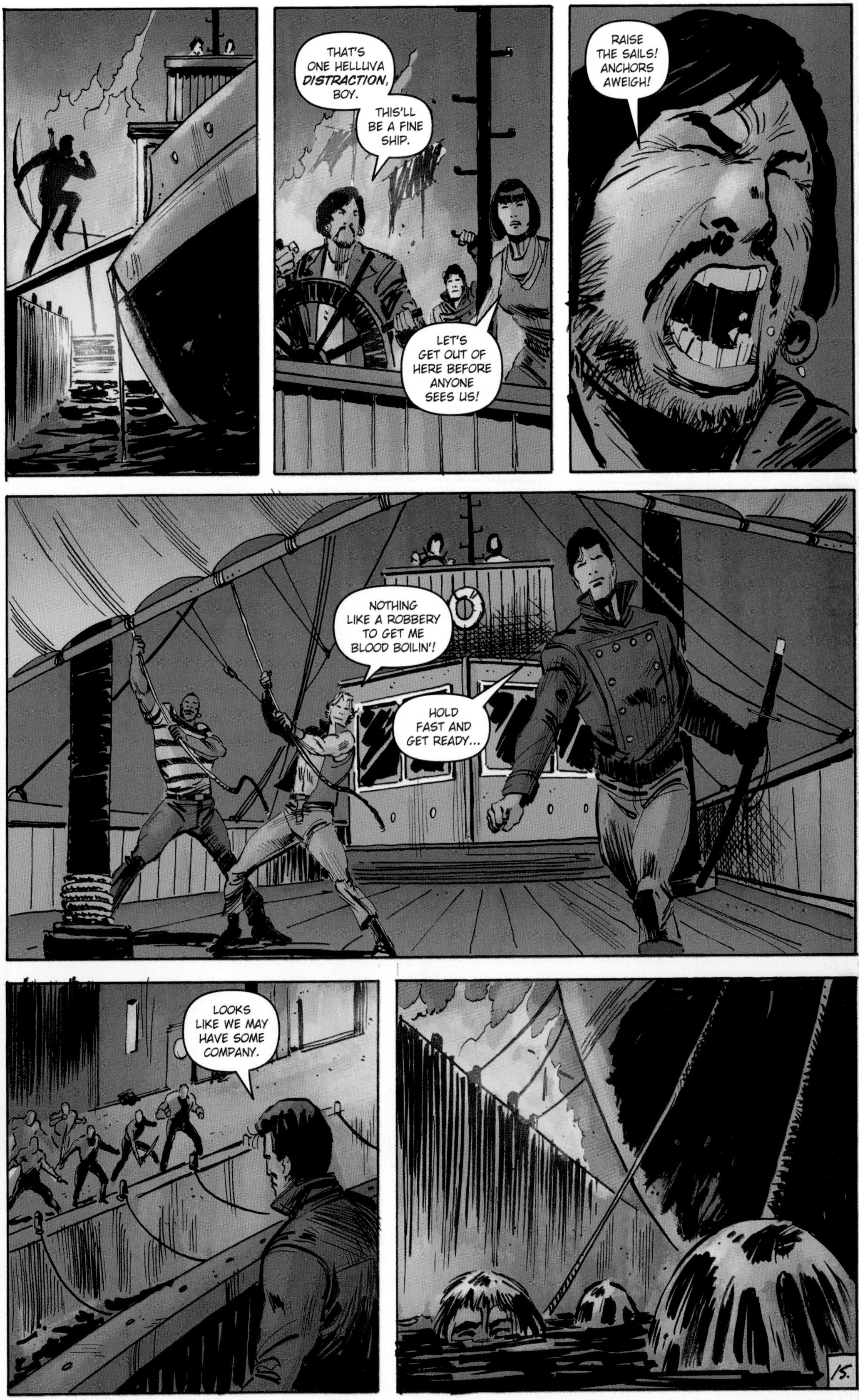
THAT'S ONE HELLUVA **DISTRACTION**, BOY.
THIS'LL BE A FINE SHIP.
LET'S GET OUT OF HERE BEFORE ANYONE SEES US!
RAISE THE SAILS! ANCHORS AWEIGH!
NOTHING LIKE A ROBBERY TO GET ME BLOOD BOILIN'!
HOLD FAST AND GET READY...
LOOKS LIKE WE MAY HAVE SOME COMPANY.
15.

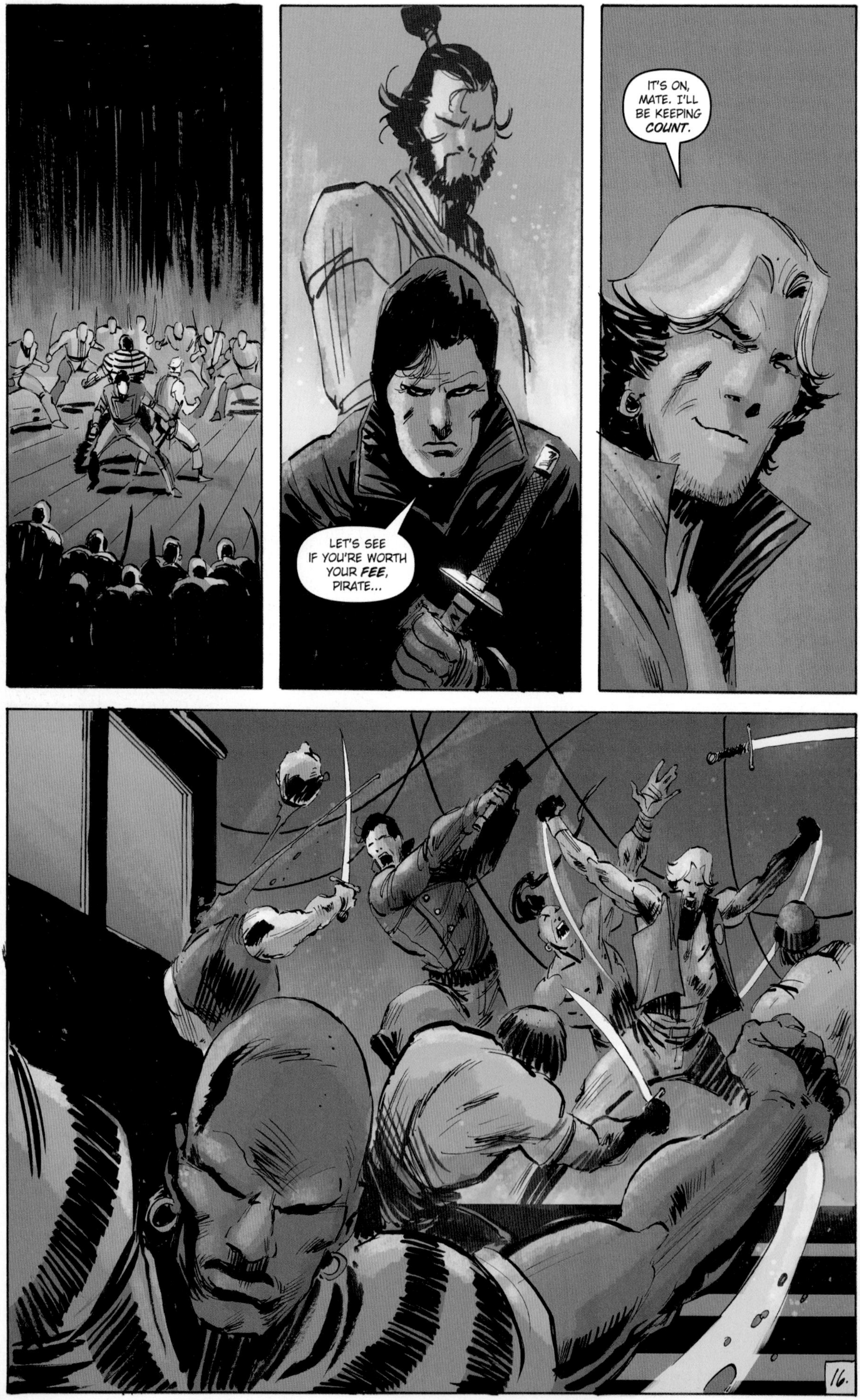
LET'S SEE IF YOU'RE WORTH YOUR FEE, PIRATE...
IT'S ON, MATE. I'LL BE KEEPING COUNT.

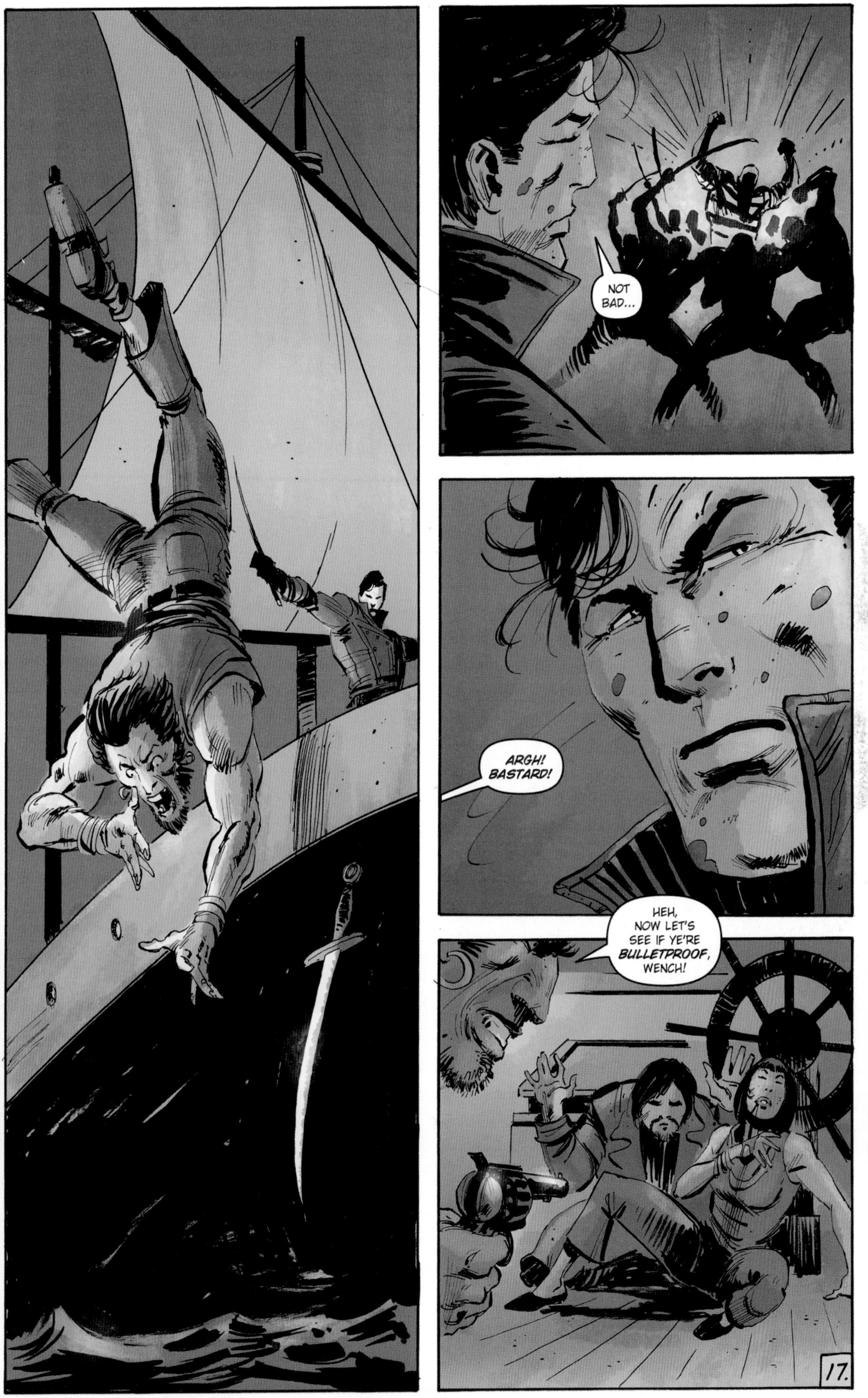
NOT BAD...
ARGH! BASTARD!
HEH, NOW LET'S SEE IF YE'RE BULLETPROOF, WENCH!

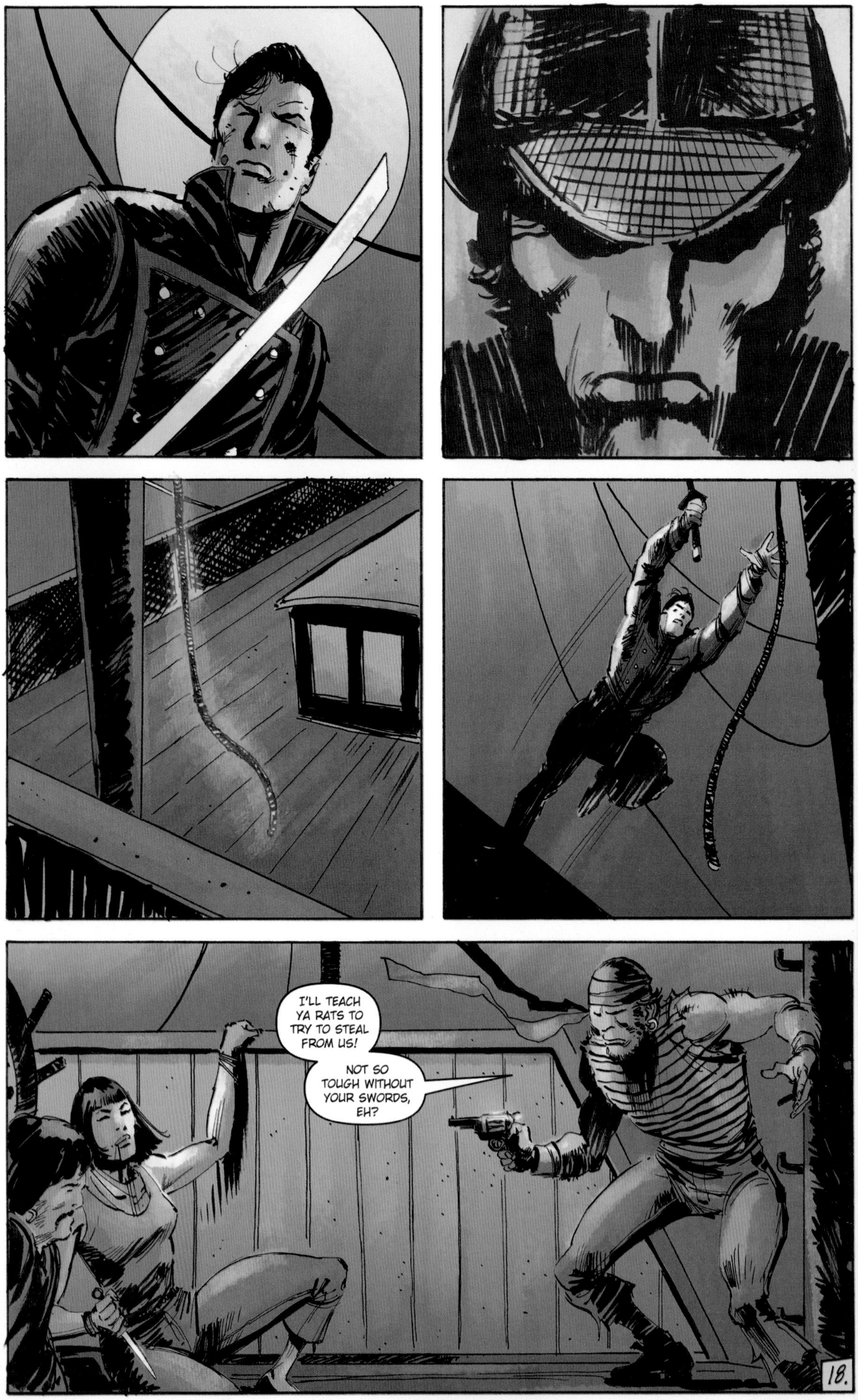
I'LL TEACH YA RATS TO TRY TO STEAL FROM US!
NOT SO TOUGH WITHOUT YOUR SWORDS, EH?
18.

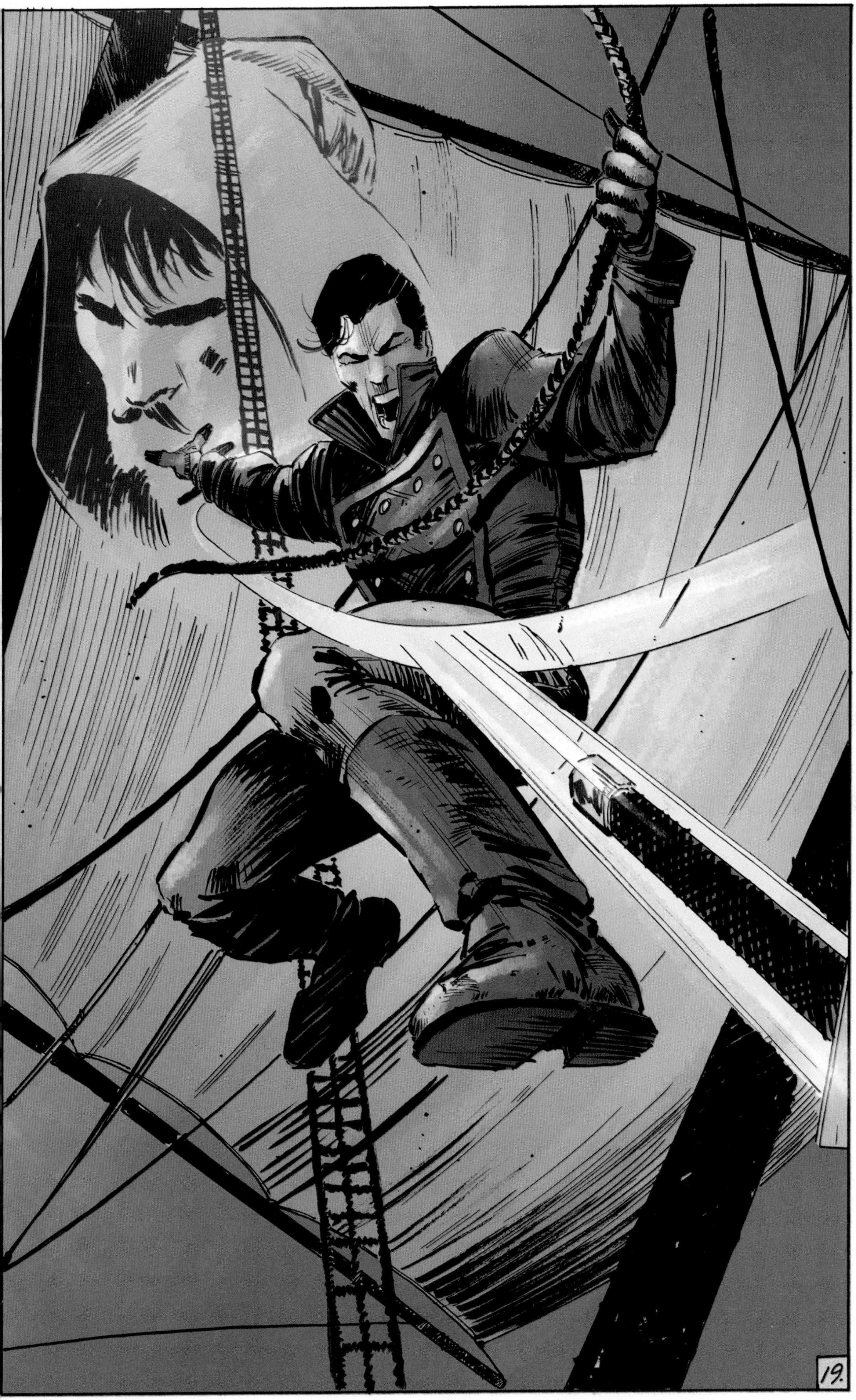

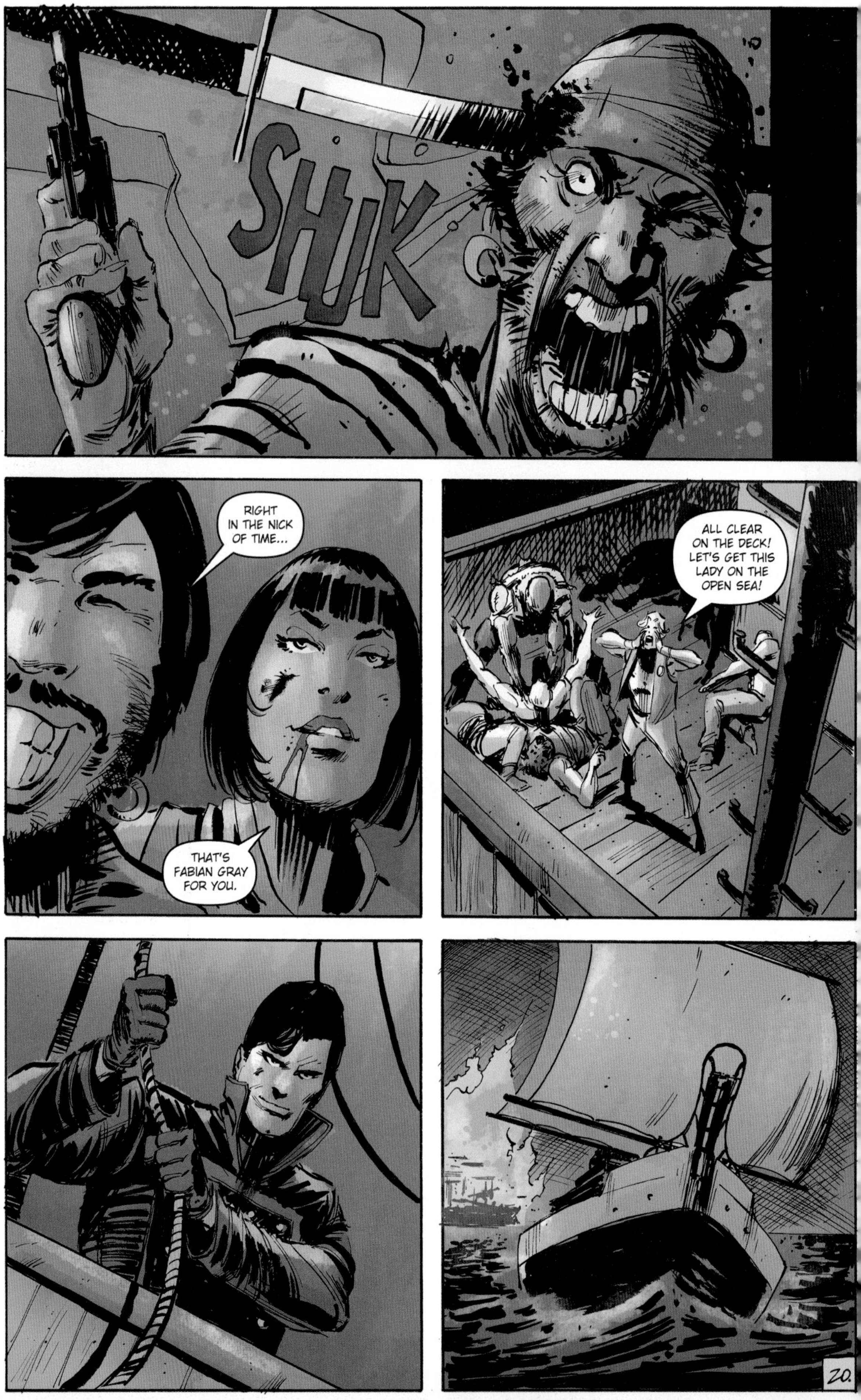
SHUK
RIGHT IN THE NICK OF TIME...
THAT'S FABIAN GRAY FOR YOU.
ALL CLEAR ON THE DECK! LET'S GET THIS LADY ON THE OPEN SEA!
20.

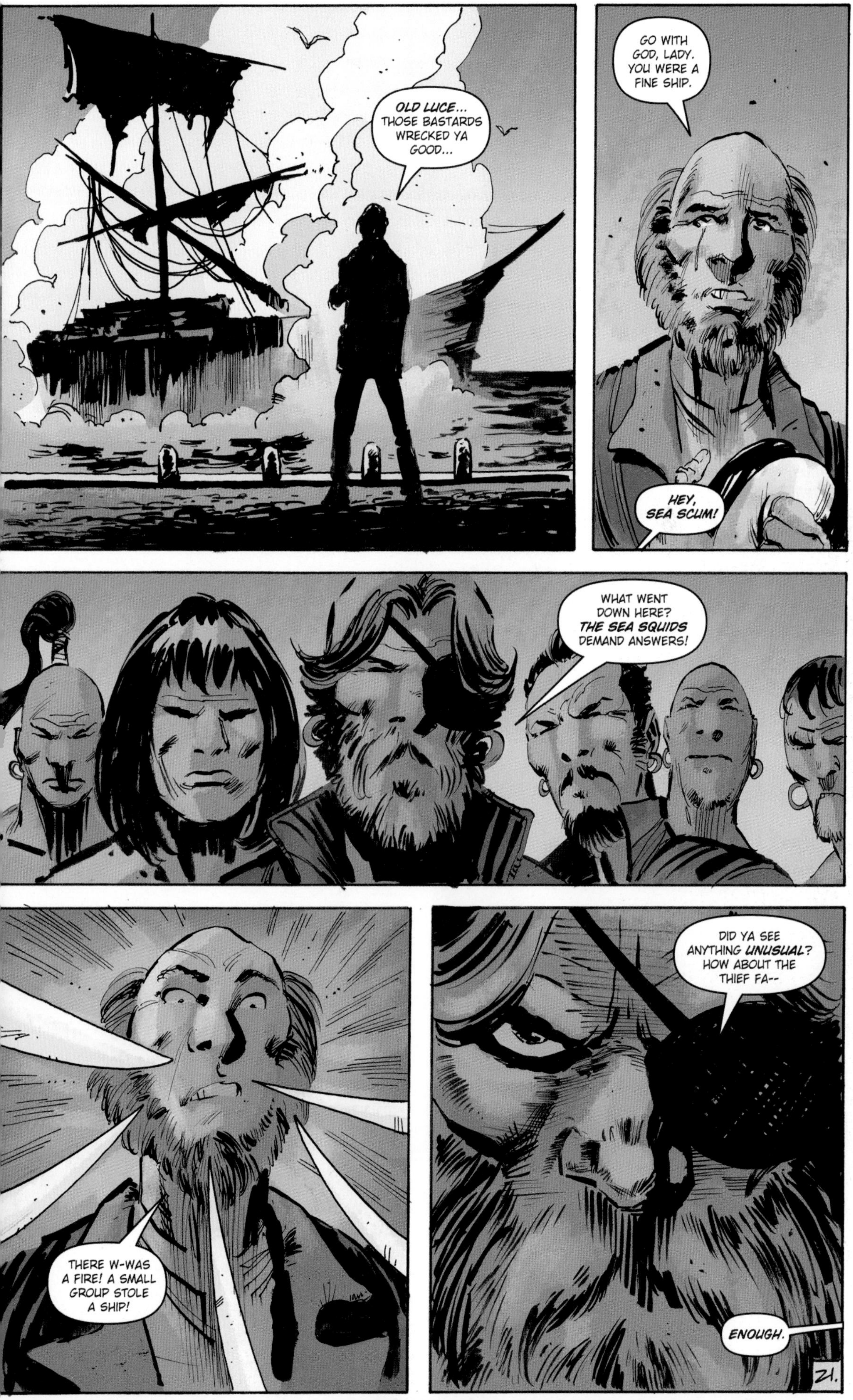
OLD LUCE... THOSE BASTARDS WRECKED YA GOOD...
GO WITH GOD, LADY. YOU WERE A FINE SHIP.
HEY, SEA SCUM!
WHAT WENT DOWN HERE? THE SEA SQUIDS DEMAND ANSWERS!
THERE W-WAS A FIRE! A SMALL GROUP STOLE A SHIP!
DID YA SEE ANYTHING UNUSUAL? HOW ABOUT THE THIEF FA--
ENOUGH.

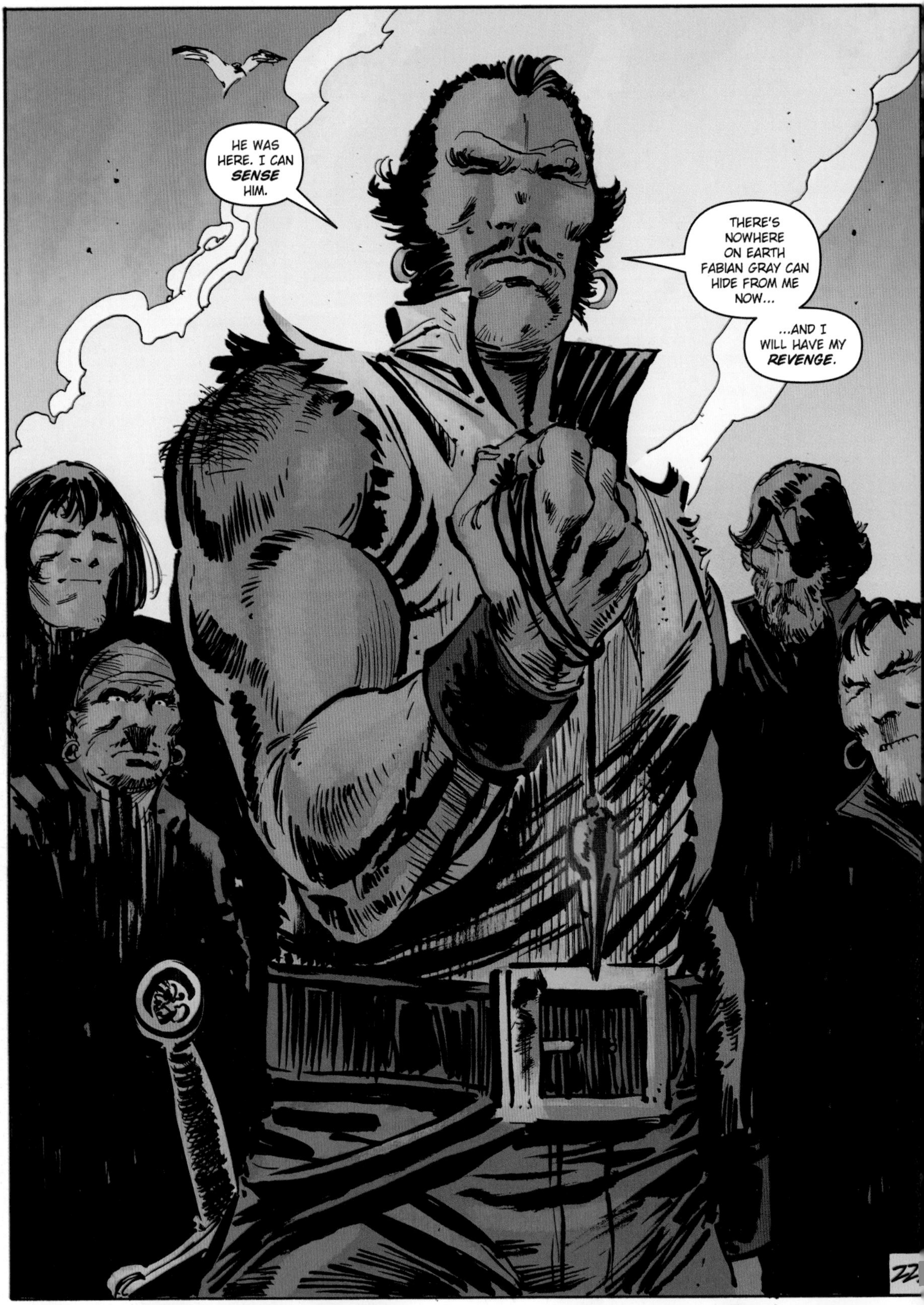
HE WAS HERE. I CAN SENSE HIM.
THERE'S NOWHERE ON EARTH FABIAN GRAY CAN HIDE FROM ME NOW...
...AND I WILL HAVE MY REVENGE.

NEXT SINS OF THE PAST

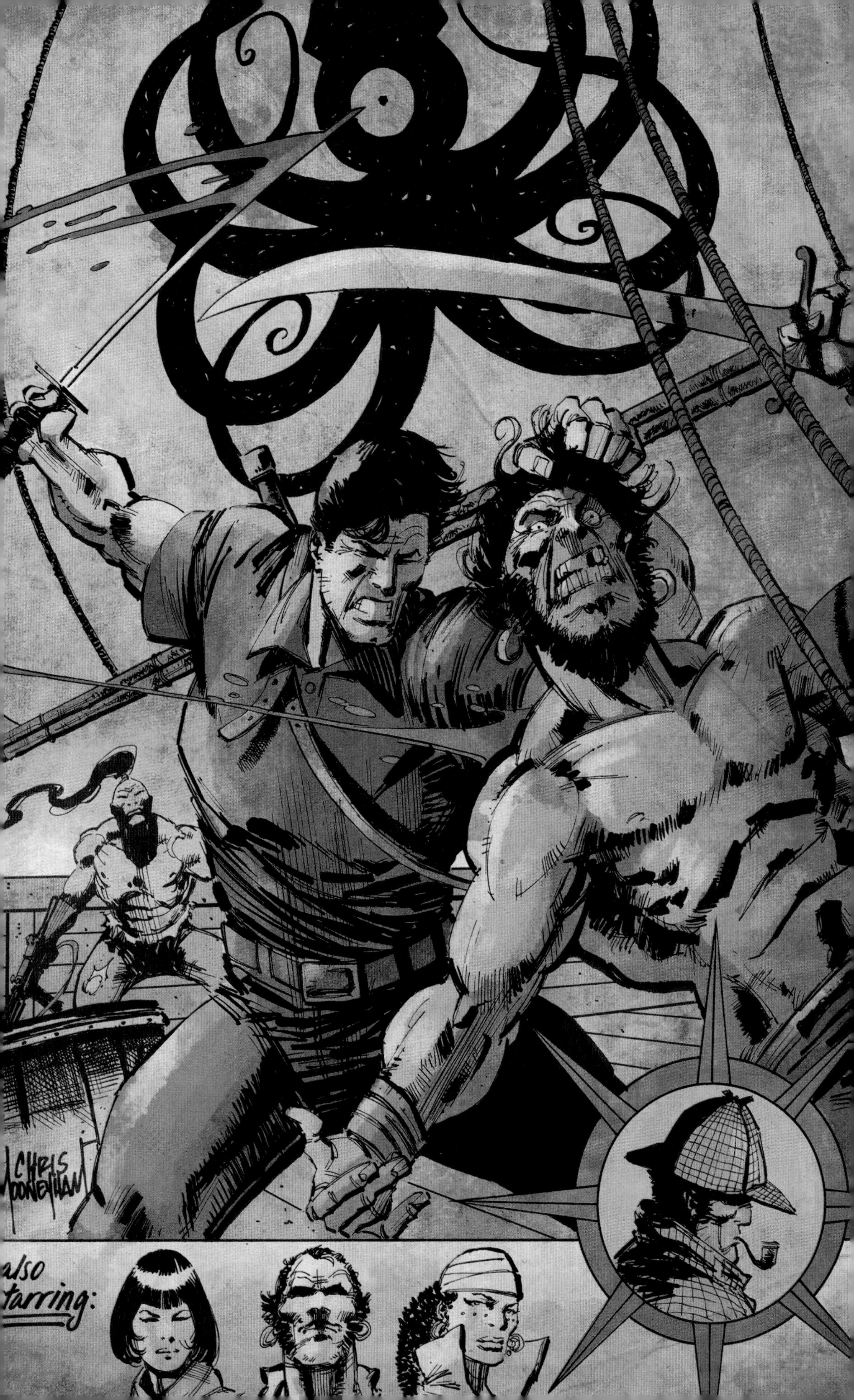
CHRIS MOONEYHAM
also starring:

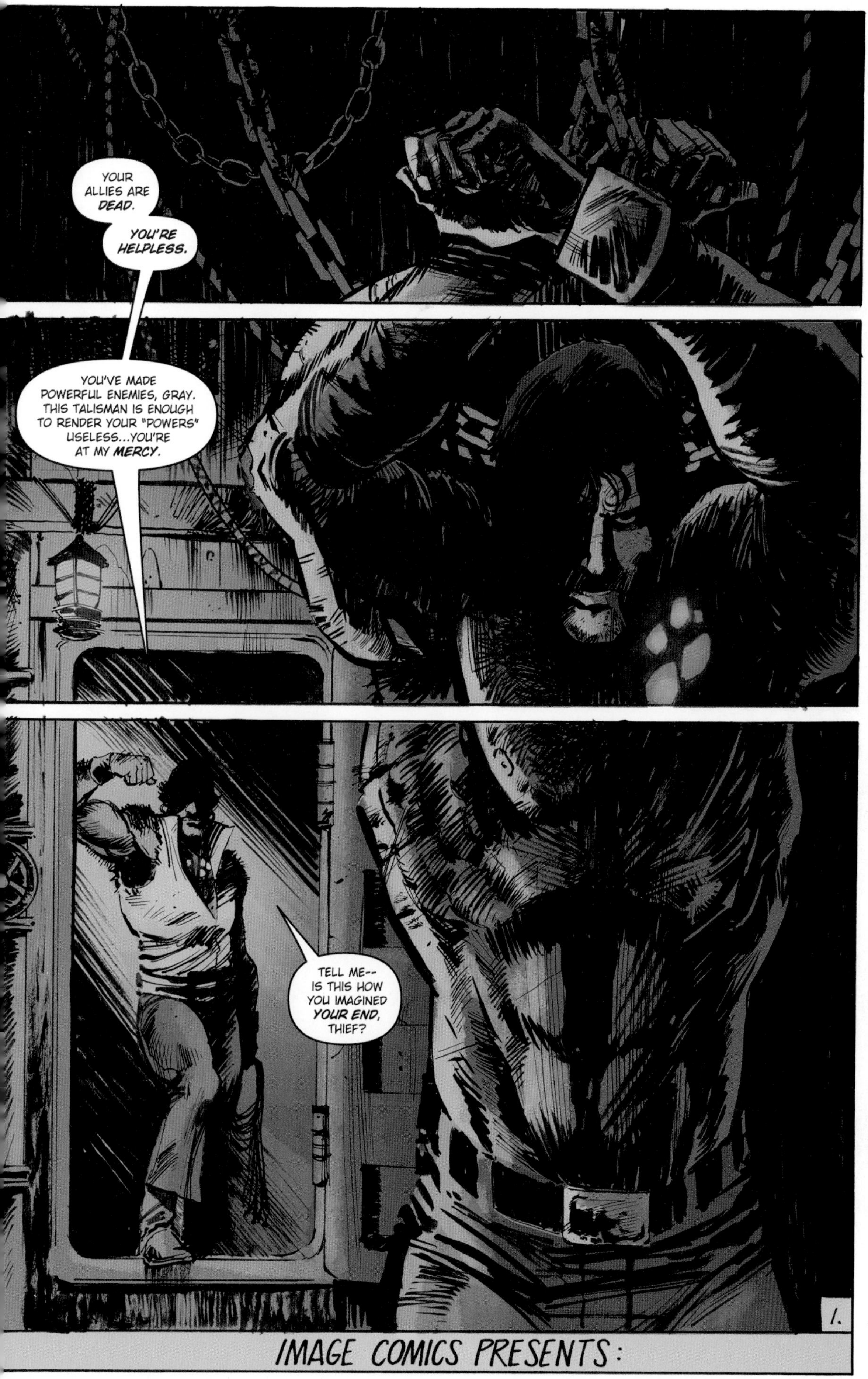
YOUR ALLIES ARE DEAD.
YOU'RE HELPLESS.
YOU'VE MADE POWERFUL ENEMIES, GRAY. THIS TALISMAN IS ENOUGH TO RENDER YOUR "POWERS" USELESS...YOU'RE AT MY MERCY.
TELL ME-- IS THIS HOW YOU IMAGINED YOUR END, THIEF?
1.
IMAGE COMICS PRESENTS:

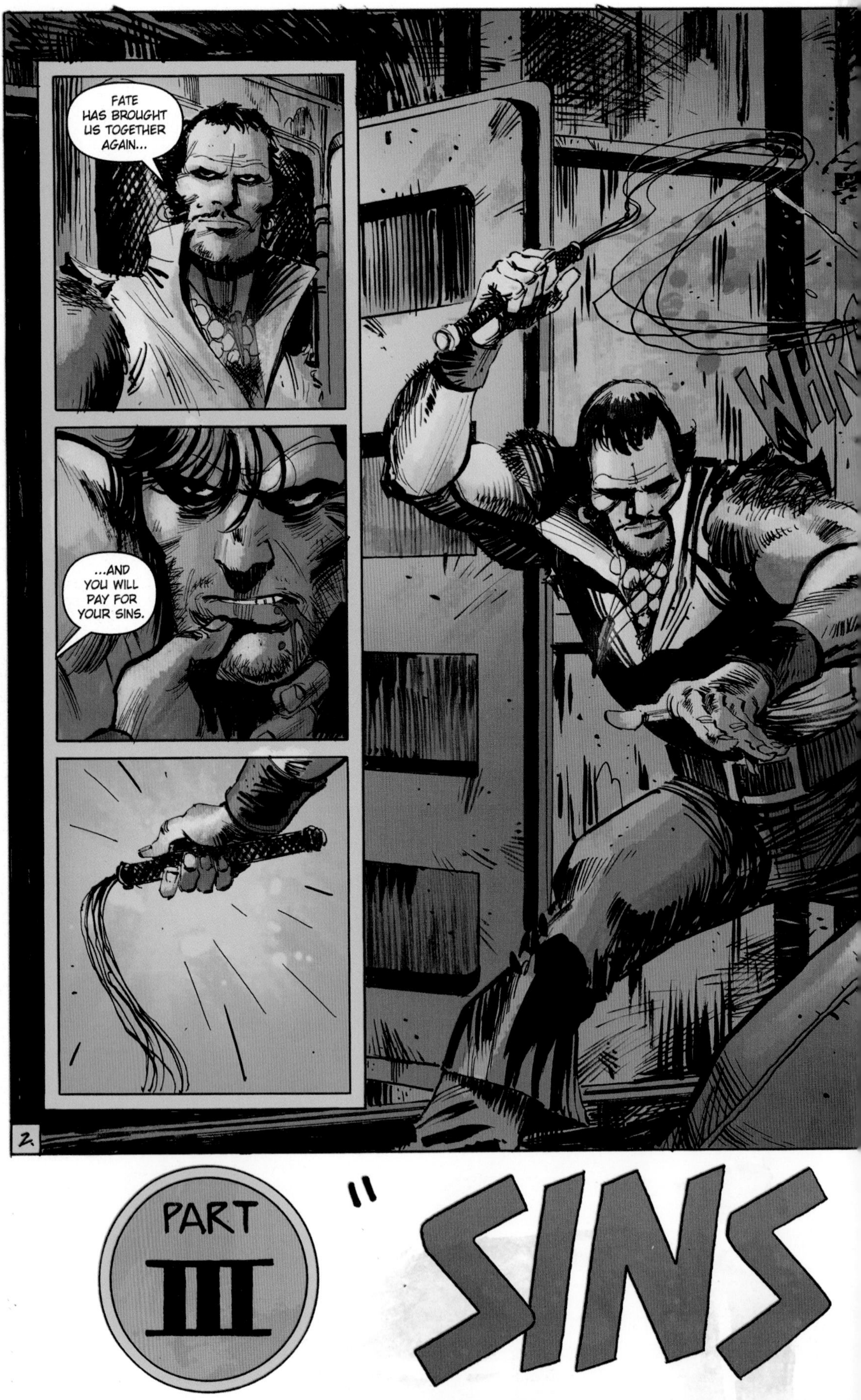
FATE HAS BROUGHT US TOGETHER AGAIN...
...AND YOU WILL PAY FOR YOUR SINS.
2.

PART III "SINS

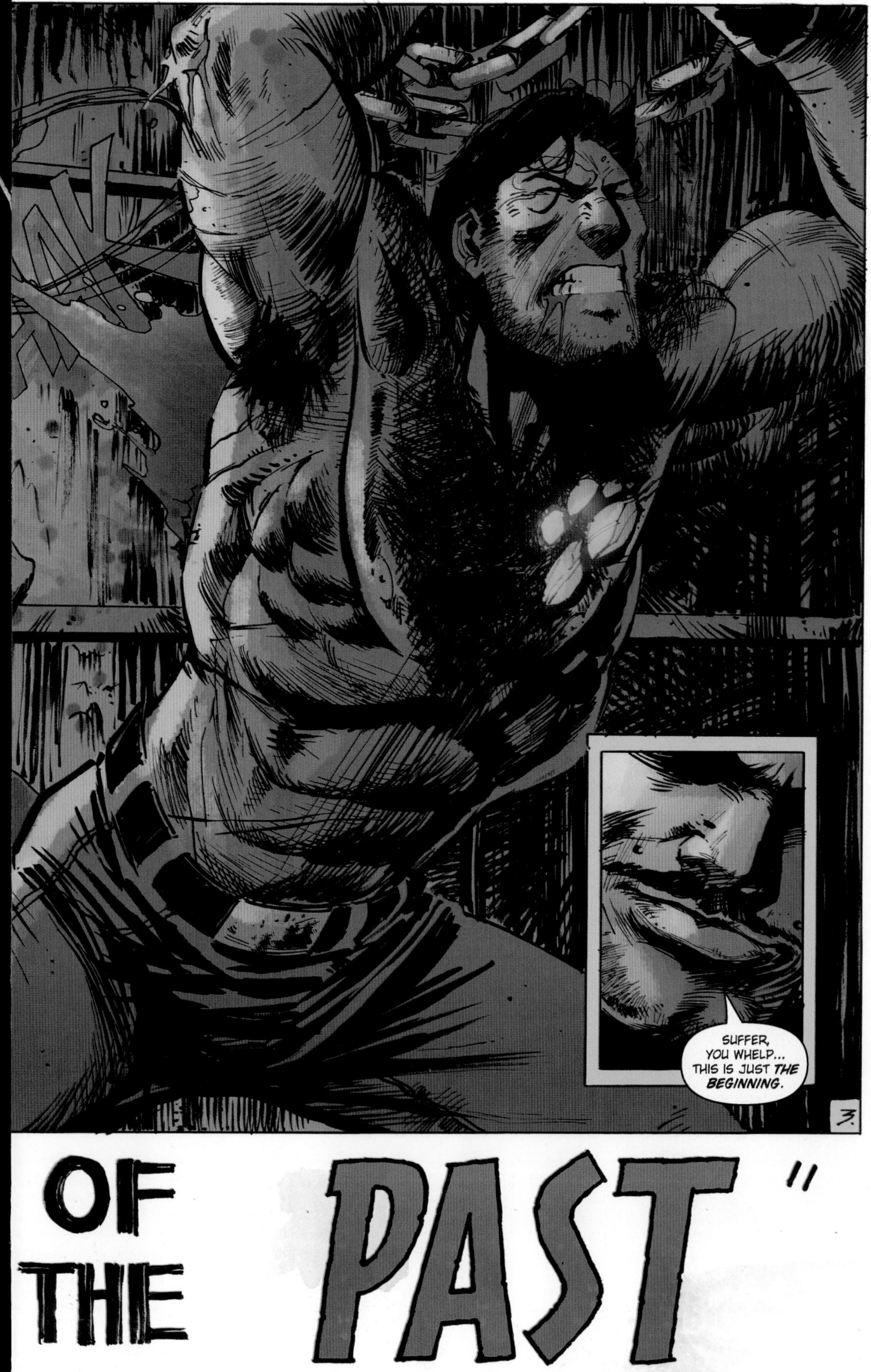
SUFFER, YOU WHELP... THIS IS JUST *THE BEGINNING*.

OF THE PAST"

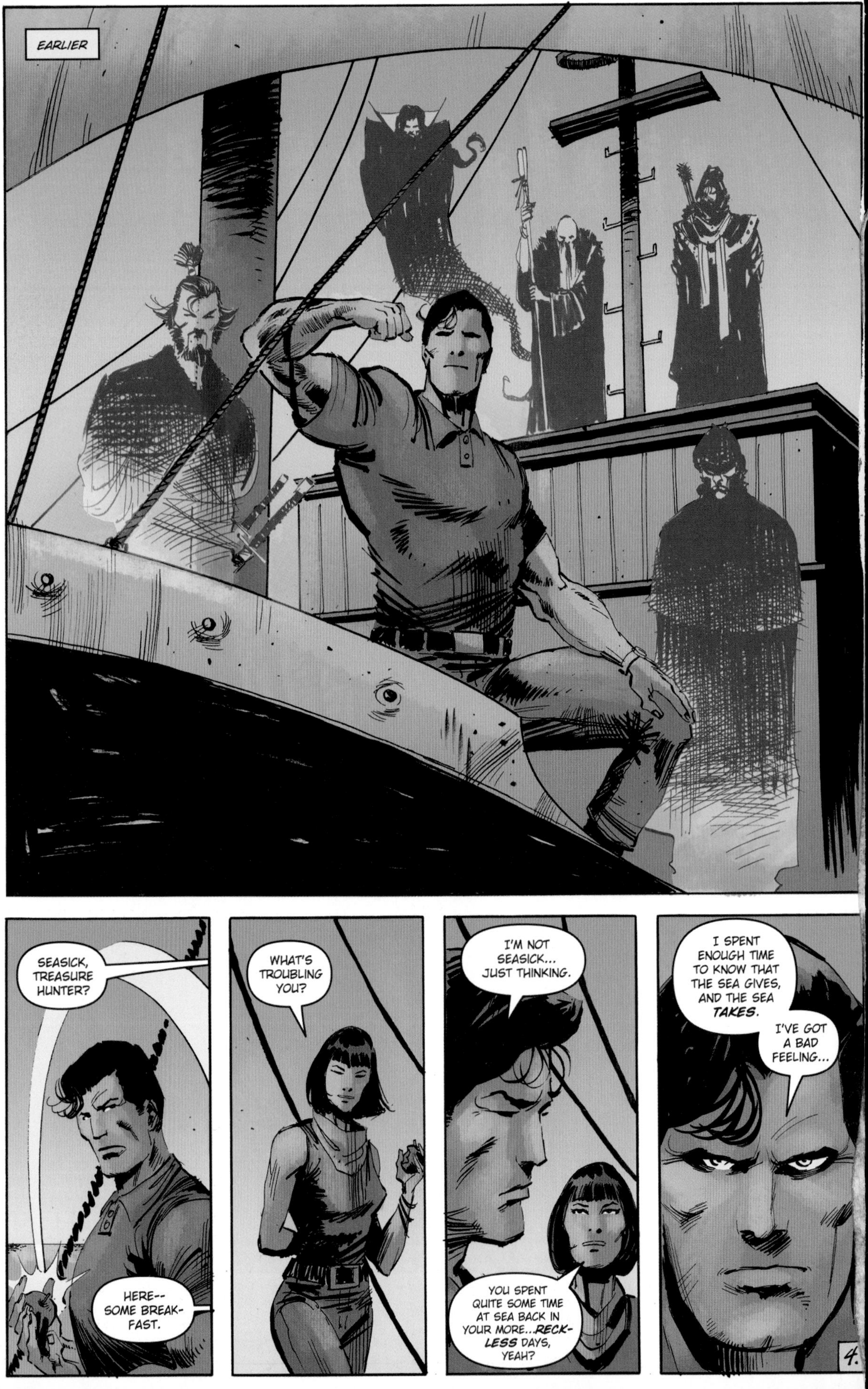
EARLIER
SEASICK, TREASURE HUNTER?
HERE-- SOME BREAK-FAST.
WHAT'S TROUBLING YOU?
I'M NOT SEASICK... JUST THINKING.
YOU SPENT QUITE SOME TIME AT SEA BACK IN YOUR MORE... RECK-LESS DAYS, YEAH?
I SPENT ENOUGH TIME TO KNOW THAT THE SEA GIVES, AND THE SEA TAKES.
I'VE GOT A BAD FEELING...
4.

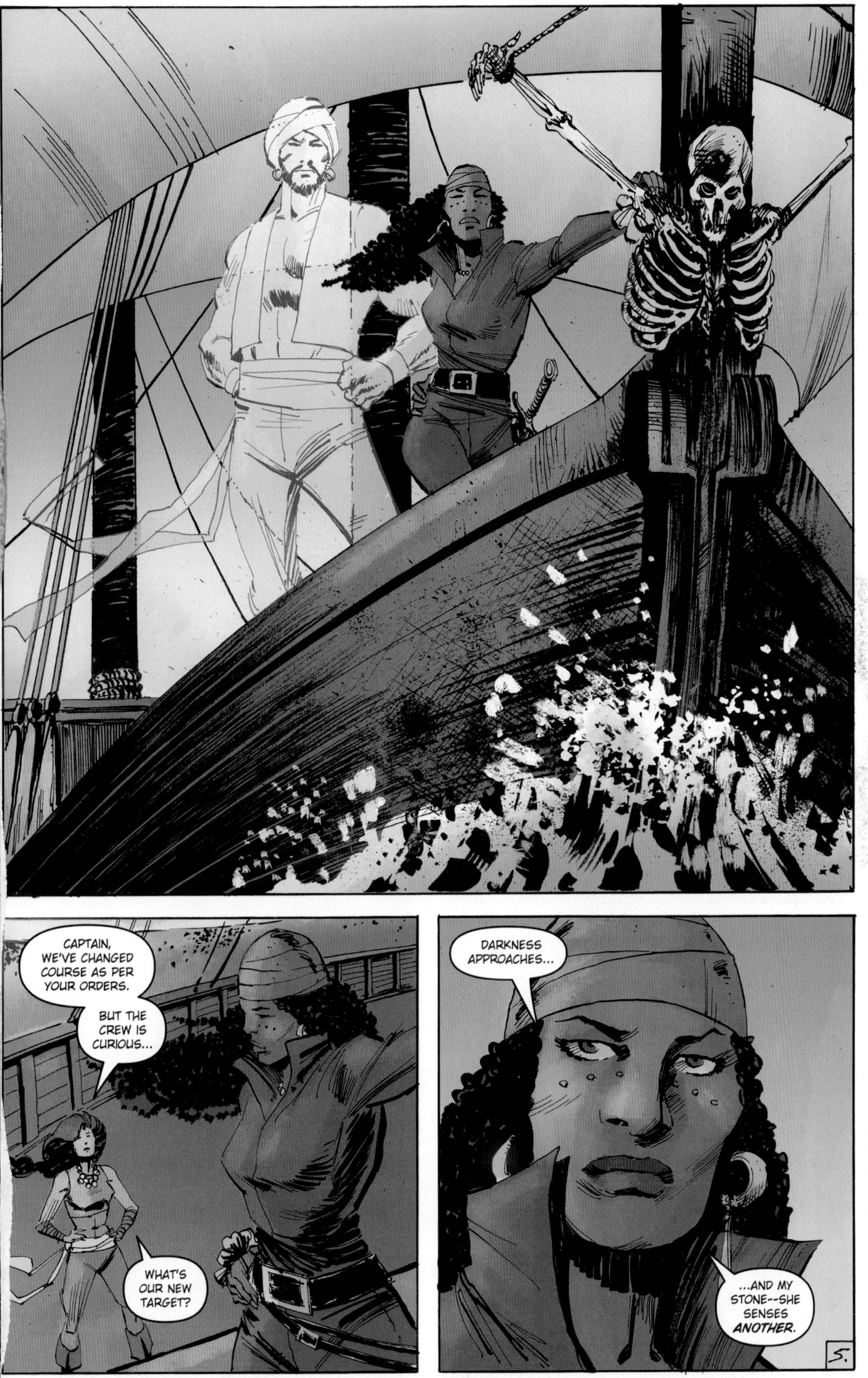
CAPTAIN, WE'VE CHANGED COURSE AS PER YOUR ORDERS.
BUT THE CREW IS CURIOUS...
WHAT'S OUR NEW TARGET?
DARKNESS APPROACHES...
...AND MY STONE--SHE SENSES *ANOTHER*.
5.

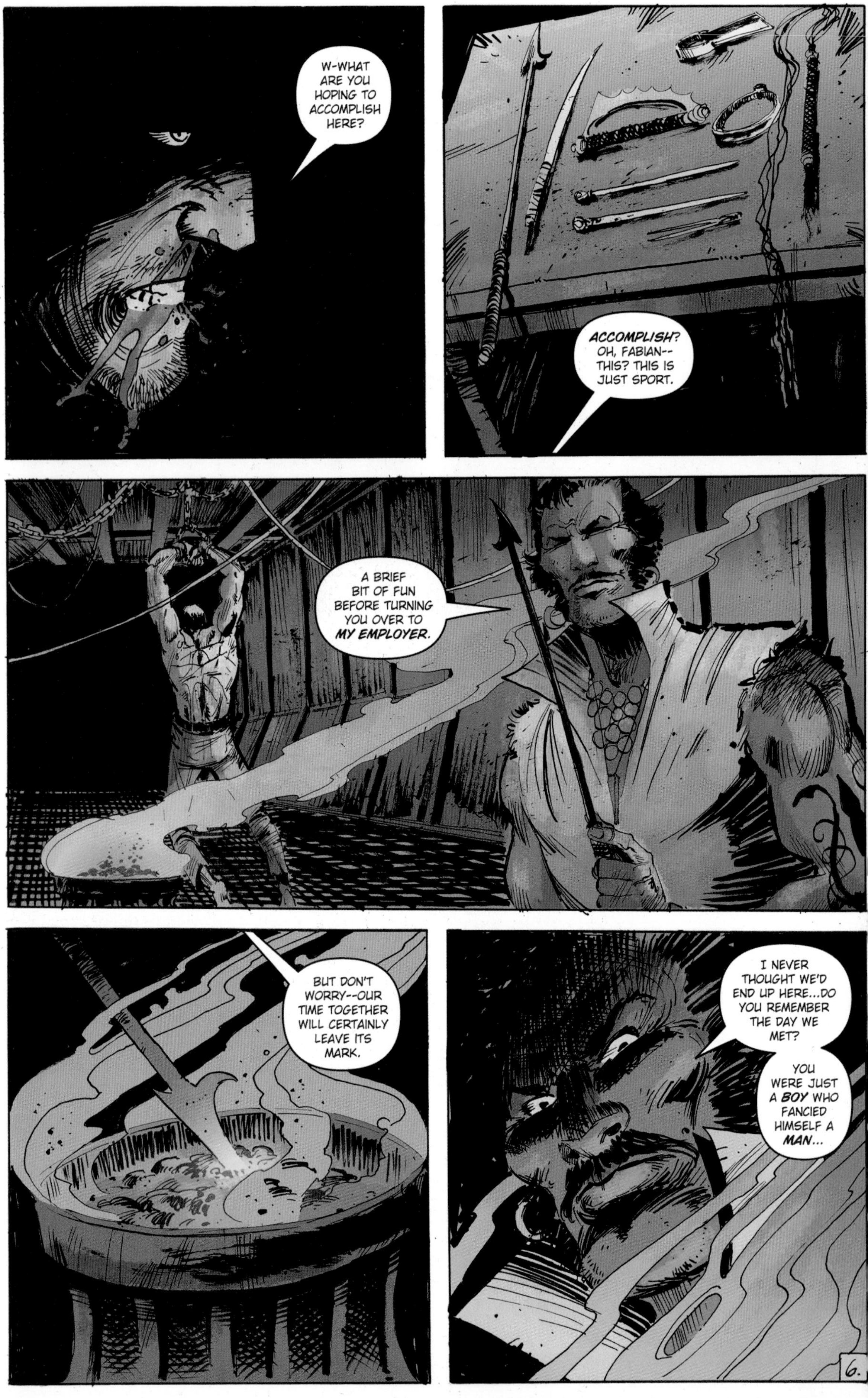
W-WHAT ARE YOU HOPING TO ACCOMPLISH HERE?
ACCOMPLISH? OH, FABIAN-- THIS? THIS IS JUST SPORT.
A BRIEF BIT OF FUN BEFORE TURNING YOU OVER TO MY EMPLOYER.
BUT DON'T WORRY--OUR TIME TOGETHER WILL CERTAINLY LEAVE ITS MARK.
I NEVER THOUGHT WE'D END UP HERE...DO YOU REMEMBER THE DAY WE MET?
YOU WERE JUST A BOY WHO FANCIED HIMSELF A MAN...
6.

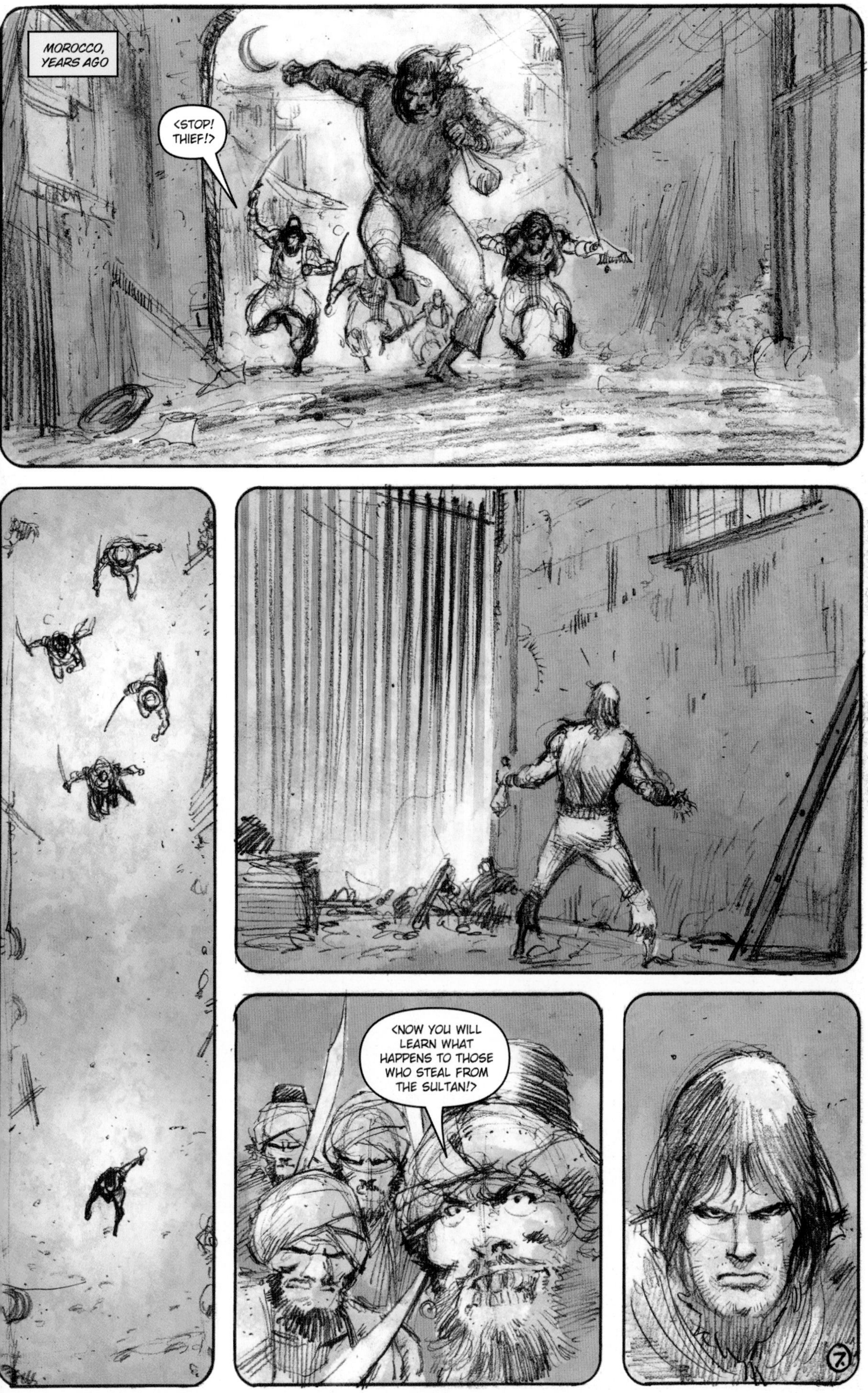
MOROCCO, YEARS AGO
<STOP! THIEF!>
<NOW YOU WILL LEARN WHAT HAPPENS TO THOSE WHO STEAL FROM THE SULTAN!>
7.

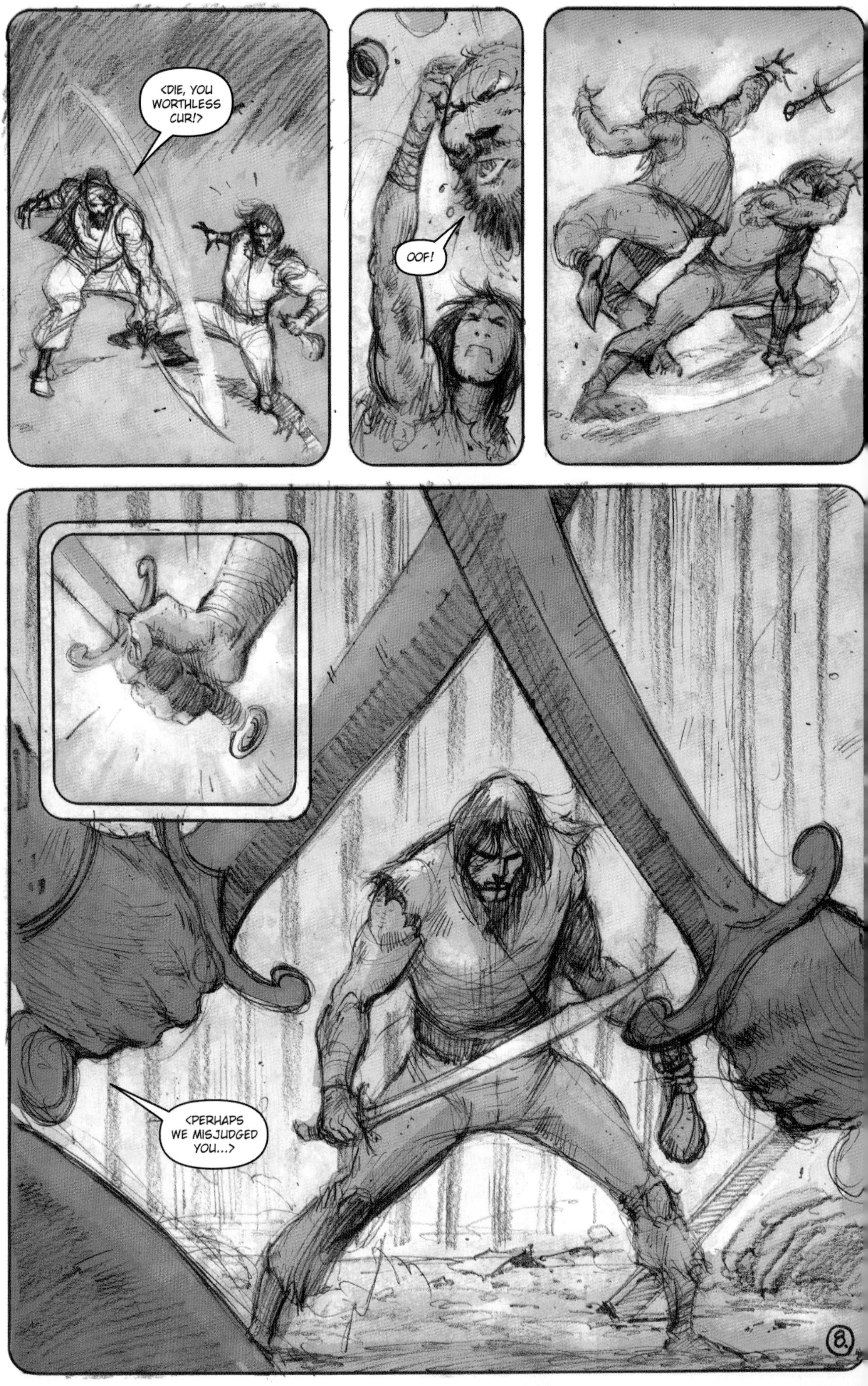

<DIE, YOU WORTHLESS CUR!>
OOF!
<PERHAPS WE MISJUDGED YOU...>

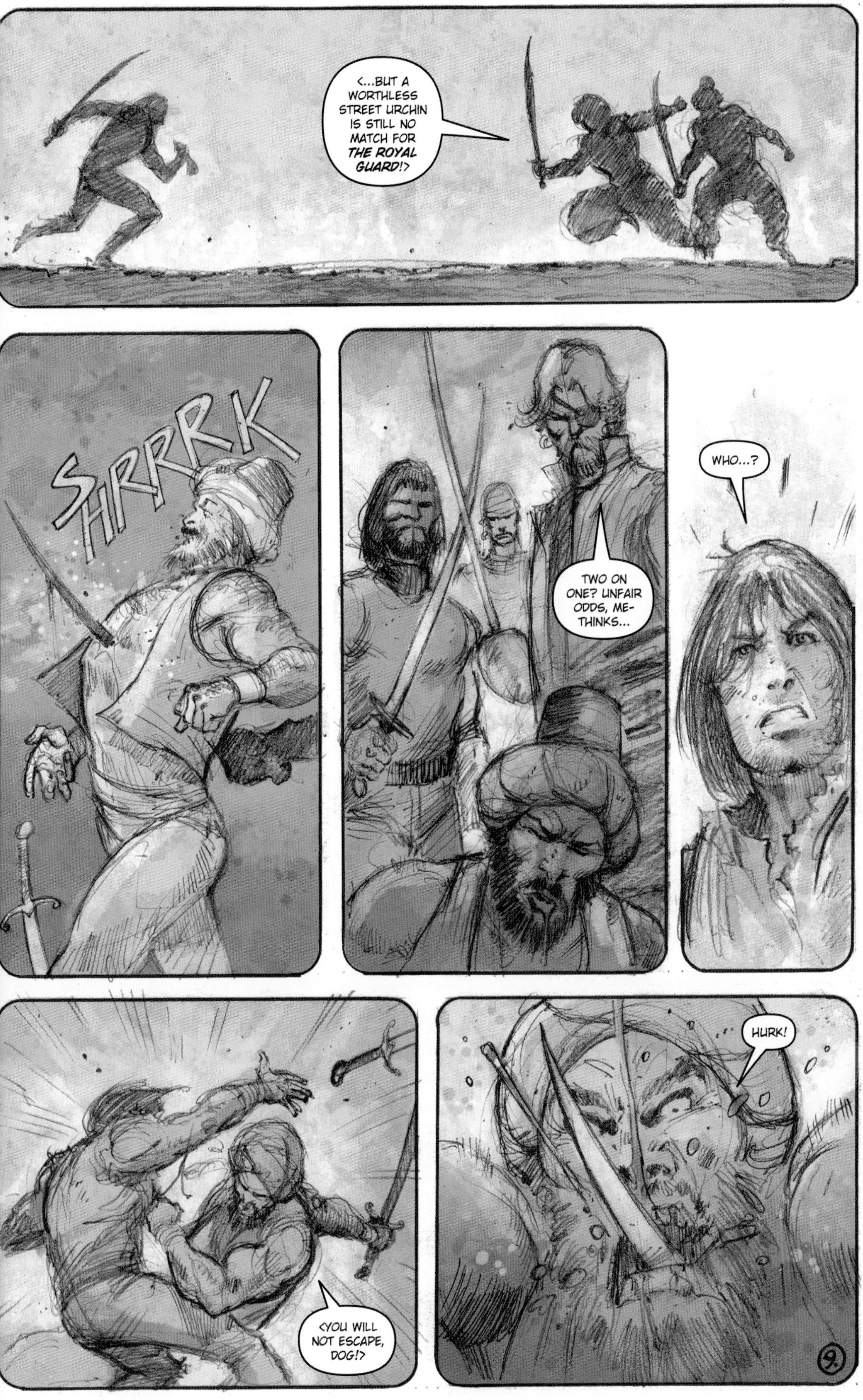

<...BUT A WORTHLESS STREET URCHIN IS STILL NO MATCH FOR THE ROYAL GUARD!>
SHRRRK
TWO ON ONE? UNFAIR ODDS, ME-THINKS...
WHO...?
<YOU WILL NOT ESCAPE, DOG!>
HURK!
9.

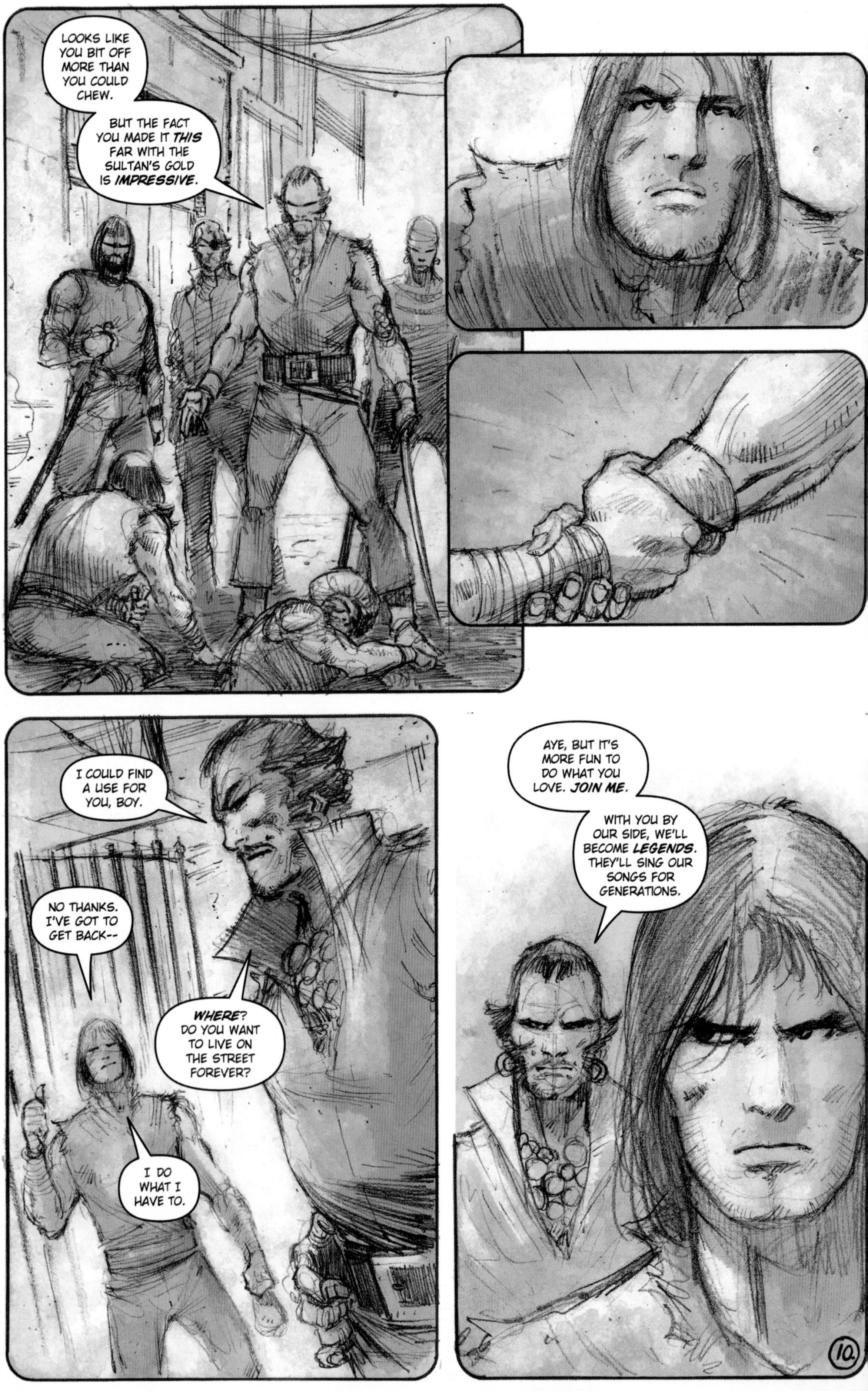
LOOKS LIKE YOU BIT OFF MORE THAN YOU COULD CHEW.
BUT THE FACT YOU MADE IT THIS FAR WITH THE SULTAN'S GOLD IS IMPRESSIVE.
I COULD FIND A USE FOR YOU, BOY.
NO THANKS. I'VE GOT TO GET BACK--
WHERE? DO YOU WANT TO LIVE ON THE STREET FOREVER?
I DO WHAT I HAVE TO.
AYE, BUT IT'S MORE FUN TO DO WHAT YOU LOVE. JOIN ME.
WITH YOU BY OUR SIDE, WE'LL BECOME LEGENDS. THEY'LL SING OUR SONGS FOR GENERATIONS.

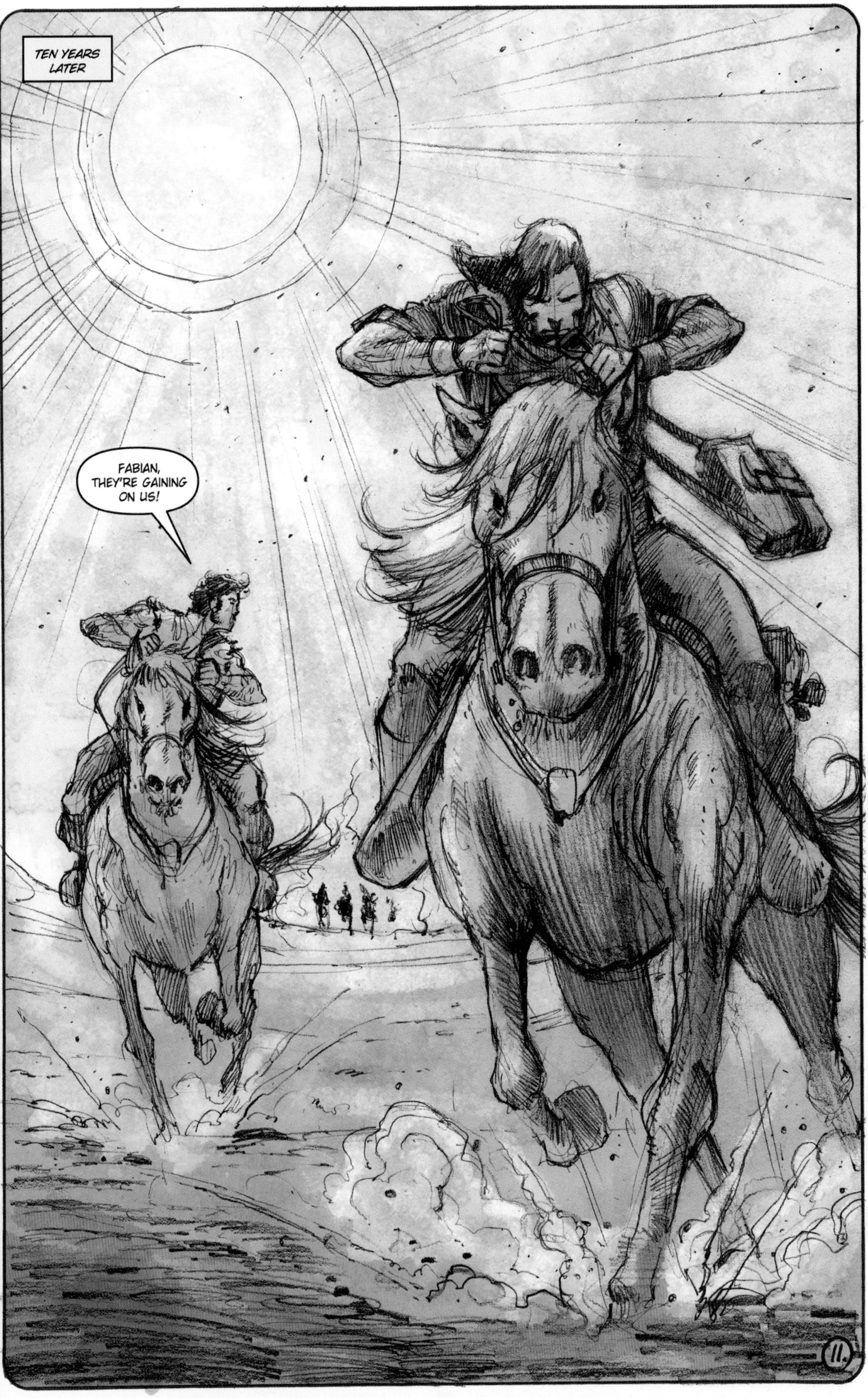
TEN YEARS LATER
FABIAN, THEY'RE GAINING ON US!
11.

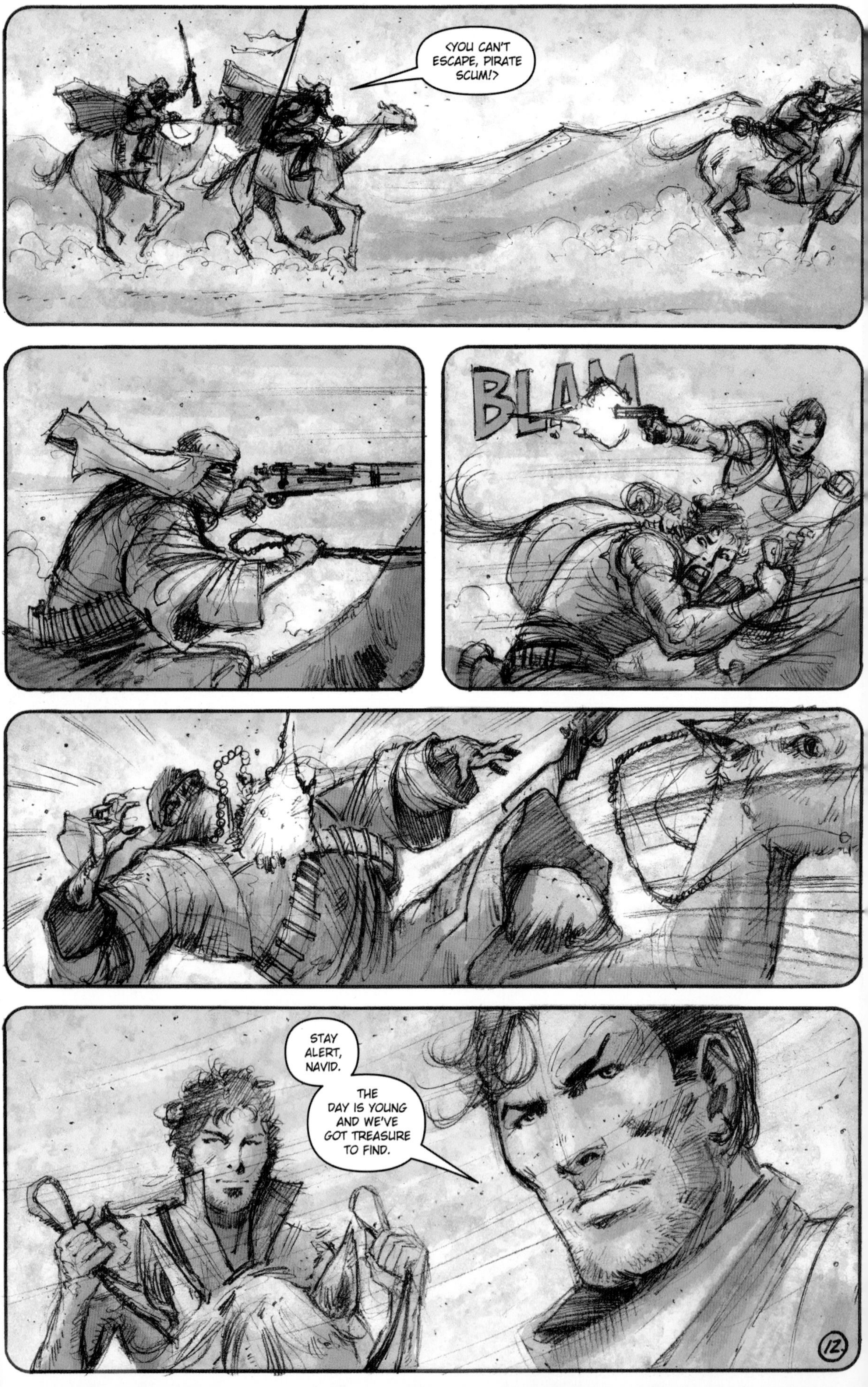
<YOU CAN'T ESCAPE, PIRATE SCUM!>
BLAM
STAY ALERT, NAVID.
THE DAY IS YOUNG AND WE'VE GOT TREASURE TO FIND.
12

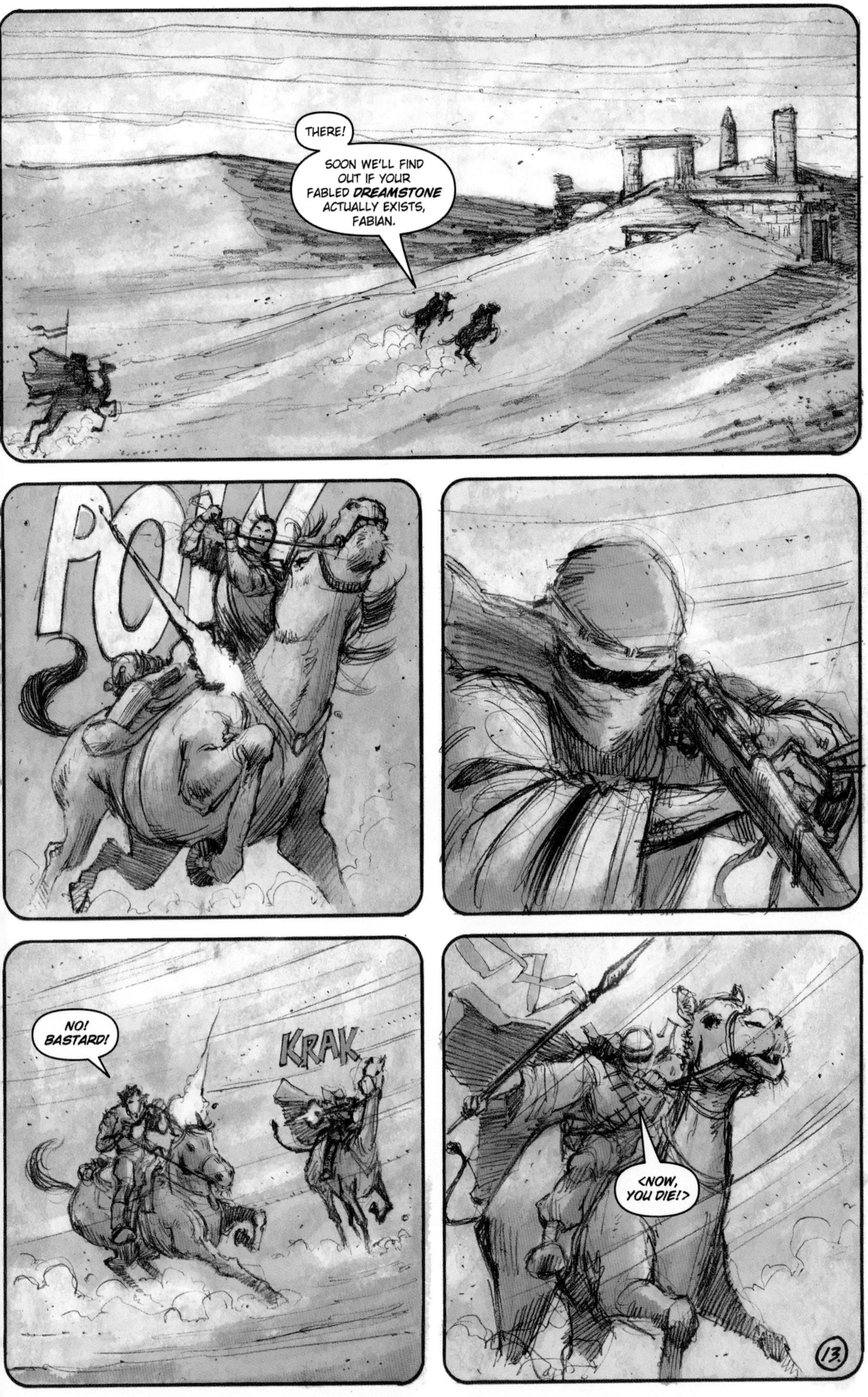
THERE!
SOON WE'LL FIND OUT IF YOUR FABLED ***DREAMSTONE*** ACTUALLY EXISTS, FABIAN.
NO! BASTARD!
KRAK
<NOW, YOU DIE!>

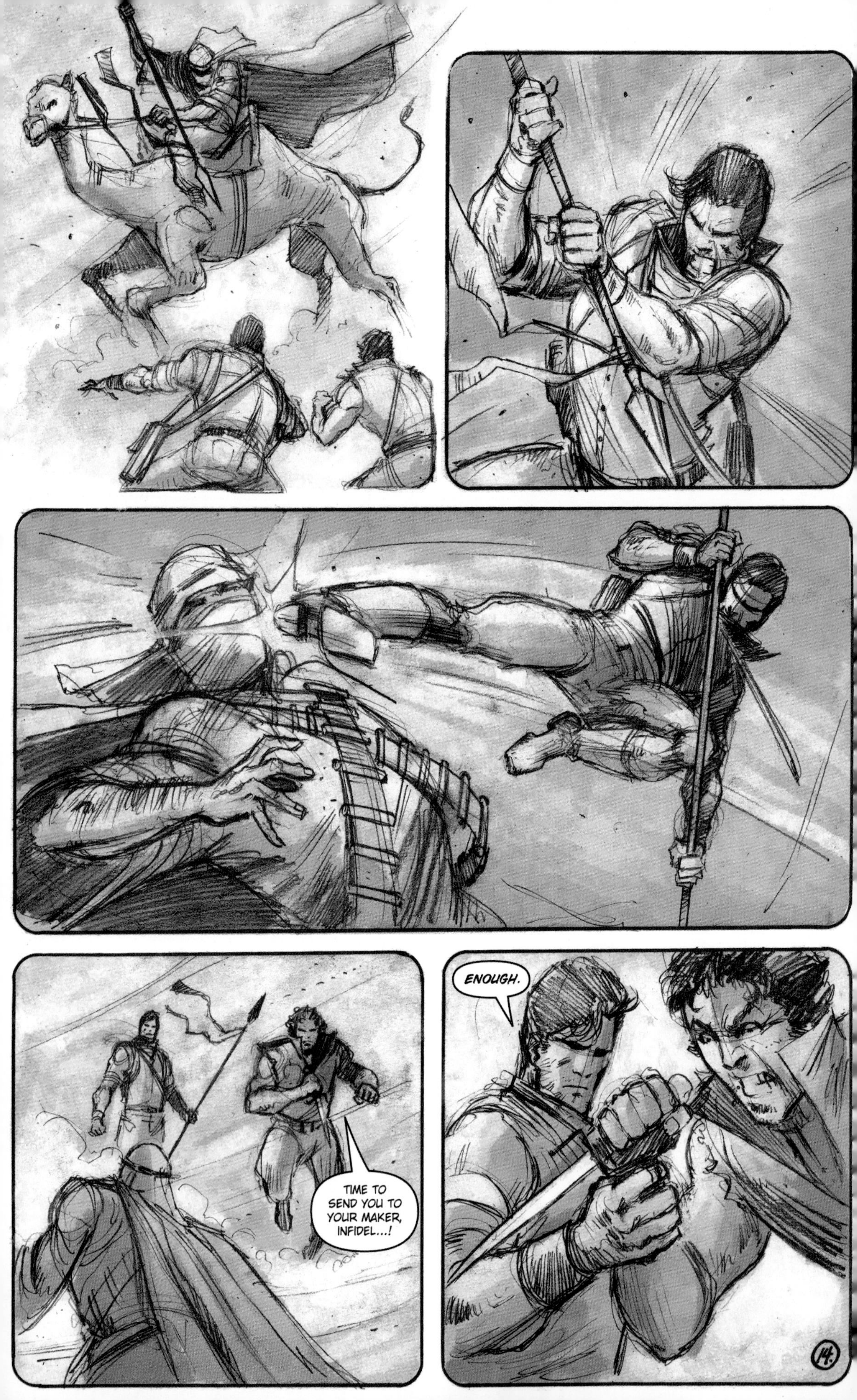
TIME TO SEND YOU TO YOUR MAKER, INFIDEL...!
ENOUGH.

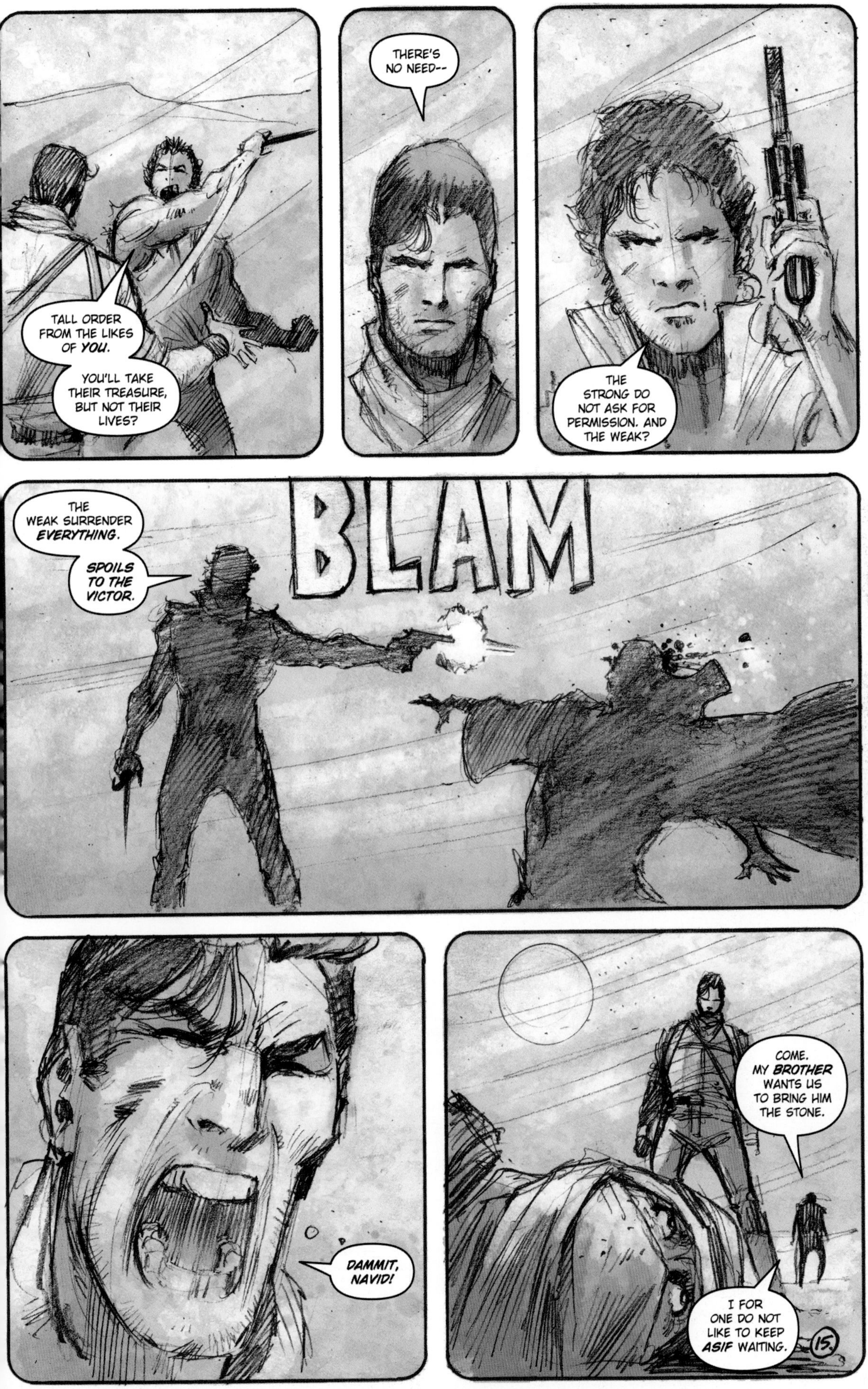
TALL ORDER FROM THE LIKES OF YOU.
YOU'LL TAKE THEIR TREASURE, BUT NOT THEIR LIVES?
THERE'S NO NEED--
THE STRONG DO NOT ASK FOR PERMISSION. AND THE WEAK?
BLAM
THE WEAK SURRENDER EVERYTHING.
SPOILS TO THE VICTOR.
DAMMIT, NAVID!
COME. MY BROTHER WANTS US TO BRING HIM THE STONE.
I FOR ONE DO NOT LIKE TO KEEP ASIF WAITING.
15.

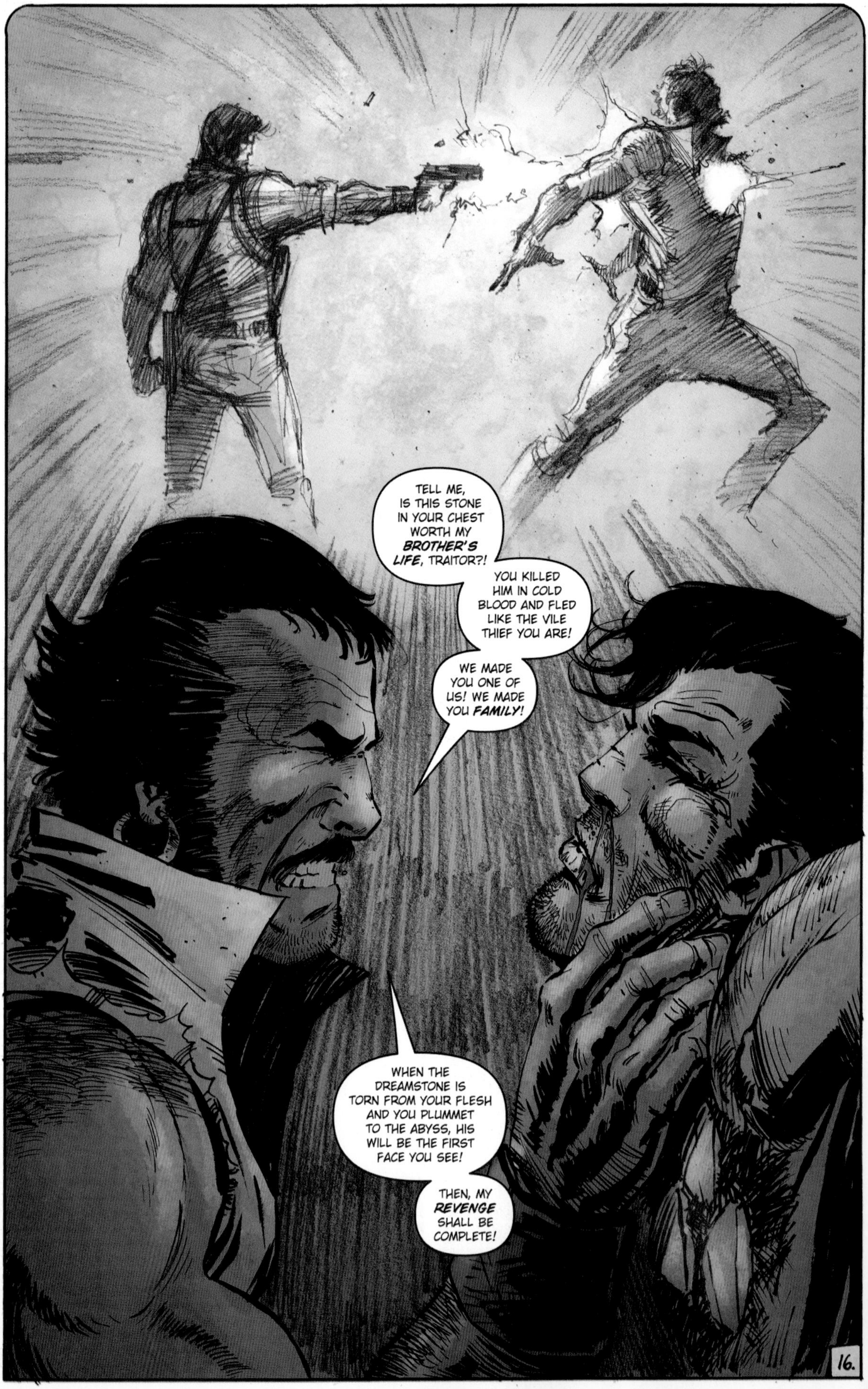
TELL ME, IS THIS STONE IN YOUR CHEST WORTH MY **BROTHER'S LIFE**, TRAITOR?!
YOU KILLED HIM IN COLD BLOOD AND FLED LIKE THE VILE THIEF YOU ARE!
WE MADE YOU ONE OF US! WE MADE YOU **FAMILY**!
WHEN THE DREAMSTONE IS TORN FROM YOUR FLESH AND YOU PLUMMET TO THE ABYSS, HIS WILL BE THE FIRST FACE YOU SEE!
THEN, MY **REVENGE** SHALL BE COMPLETE!

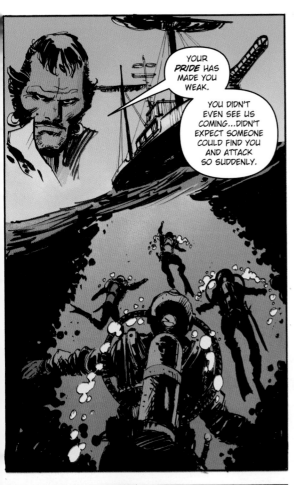

YOUR *PRIDE* HAS MADE YOU WEAK.

YOU DIDN'T EVEN SEE US COMING...DIDN'T EXPECT SOMEONE COULD FIND YOU AND ATTACK SO SUDDENLY.

"NOTHING BUT A RAGTAG CREW OF SECOND-RATE BEGGARS AND VILLAINS."

"YOU COULDN'T EVEN *DEFEND* YOURSELF PROPERLY."

"STRIPPED OF YOUR *ABILITIES* YOU'RE WORTHLESS."

"I THOUGHT BETTER OF YOU, FABIAN."

"DID YOU LEARN NOTHING IN THE TIME WE SPENT TOGETHER?"

"THEN AGAIN, WHAT ELSE COULD I EXPECT FROM A TRAITOR IN THE COMPANY OF THIEVES?"

17.

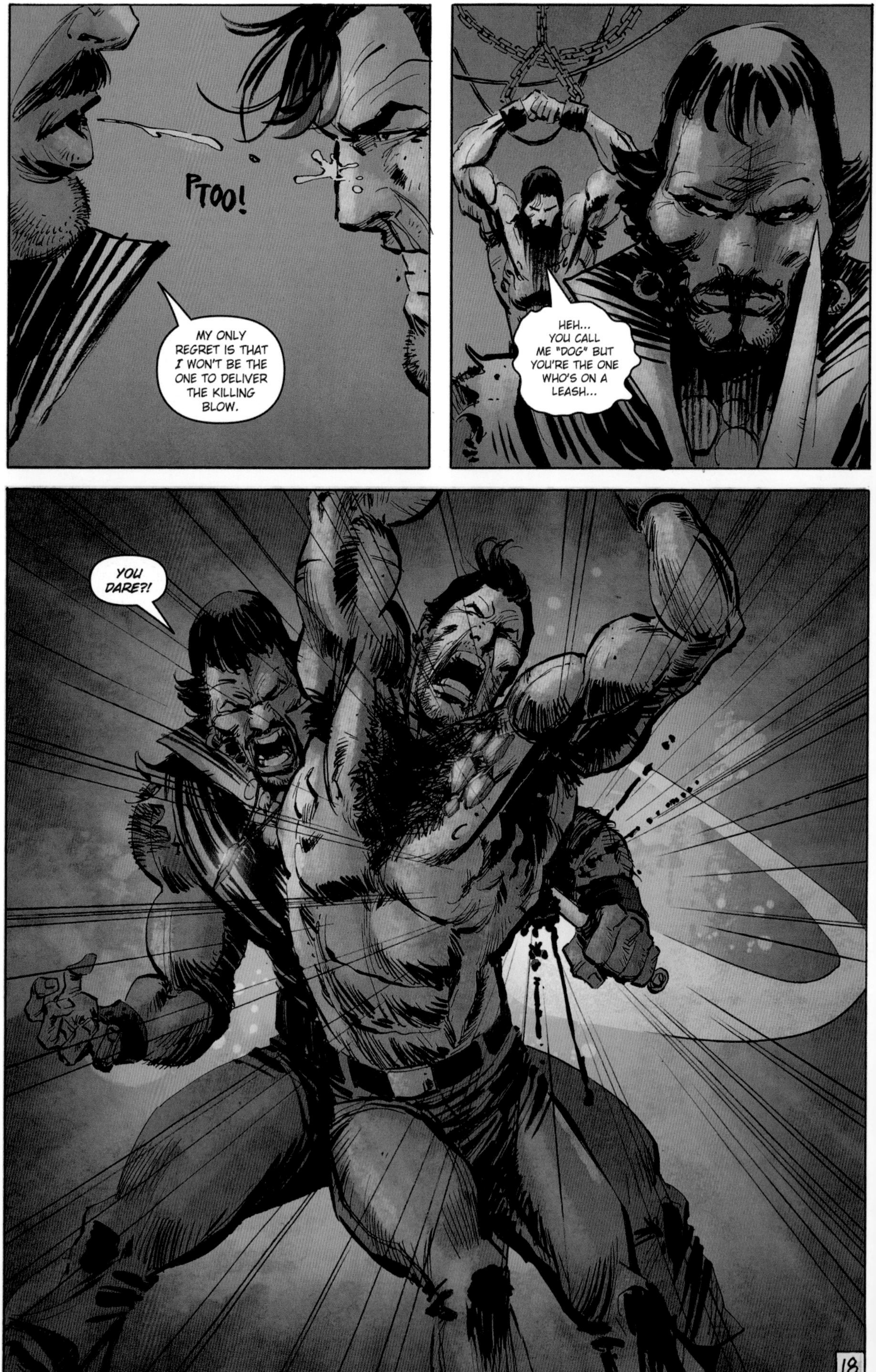
PTOO!
MY ONLY REGRET IS THAT I WON'T BE THE ONE TO DELIVER THE KILLING BLOW.
HEH... YOU CALL ME "DOG" BUT YOU'RE THE ONE WHO'S ON A LEASH...
YOU DARE?!

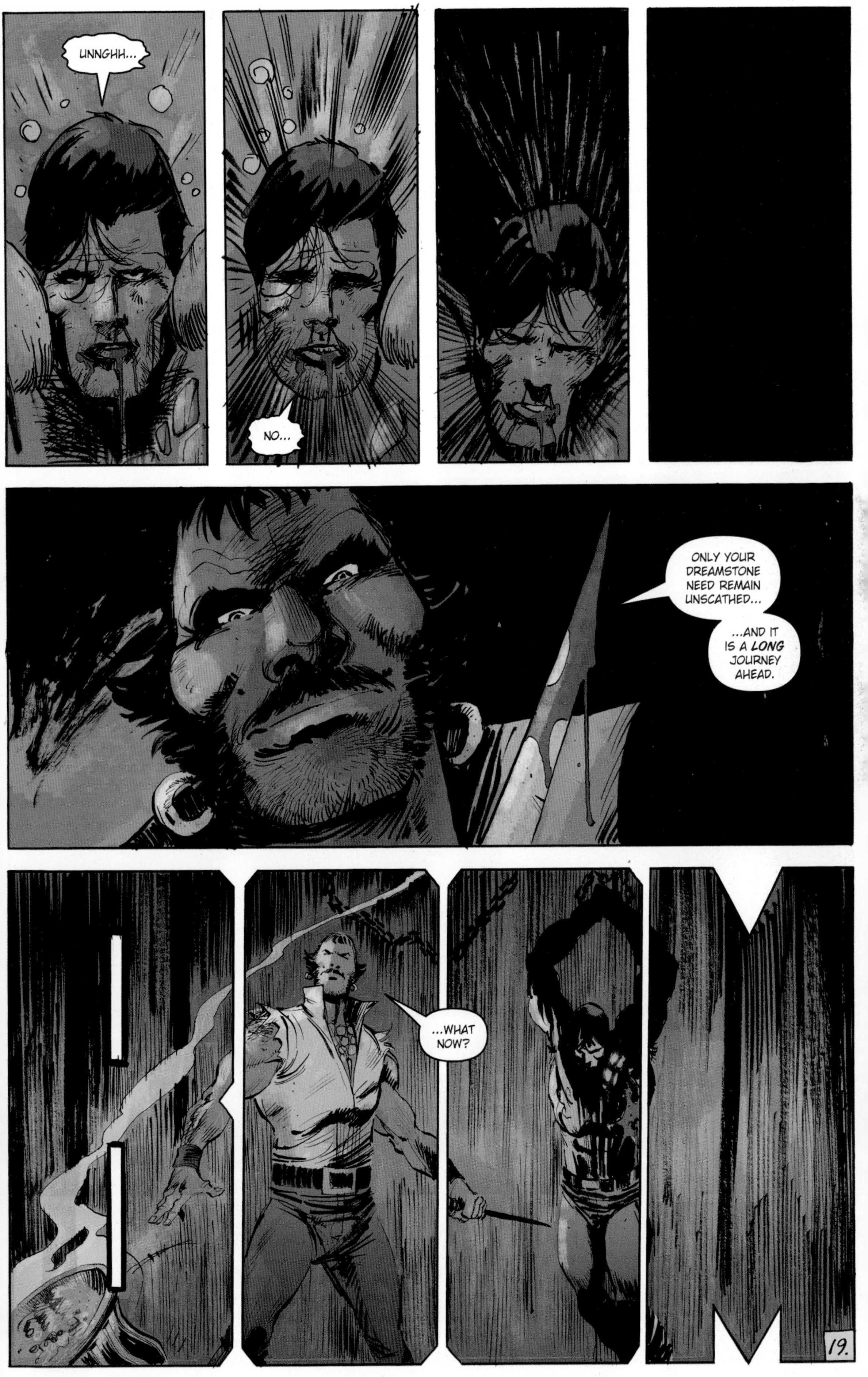
UNNGHH...
NO...
ONLY YOUR DREAMSTONE NEED REMAIN UNSCATHED...
...AND IT IS A LONG JOURNEY AHEAD.
DOOM
...WHAT NOW?

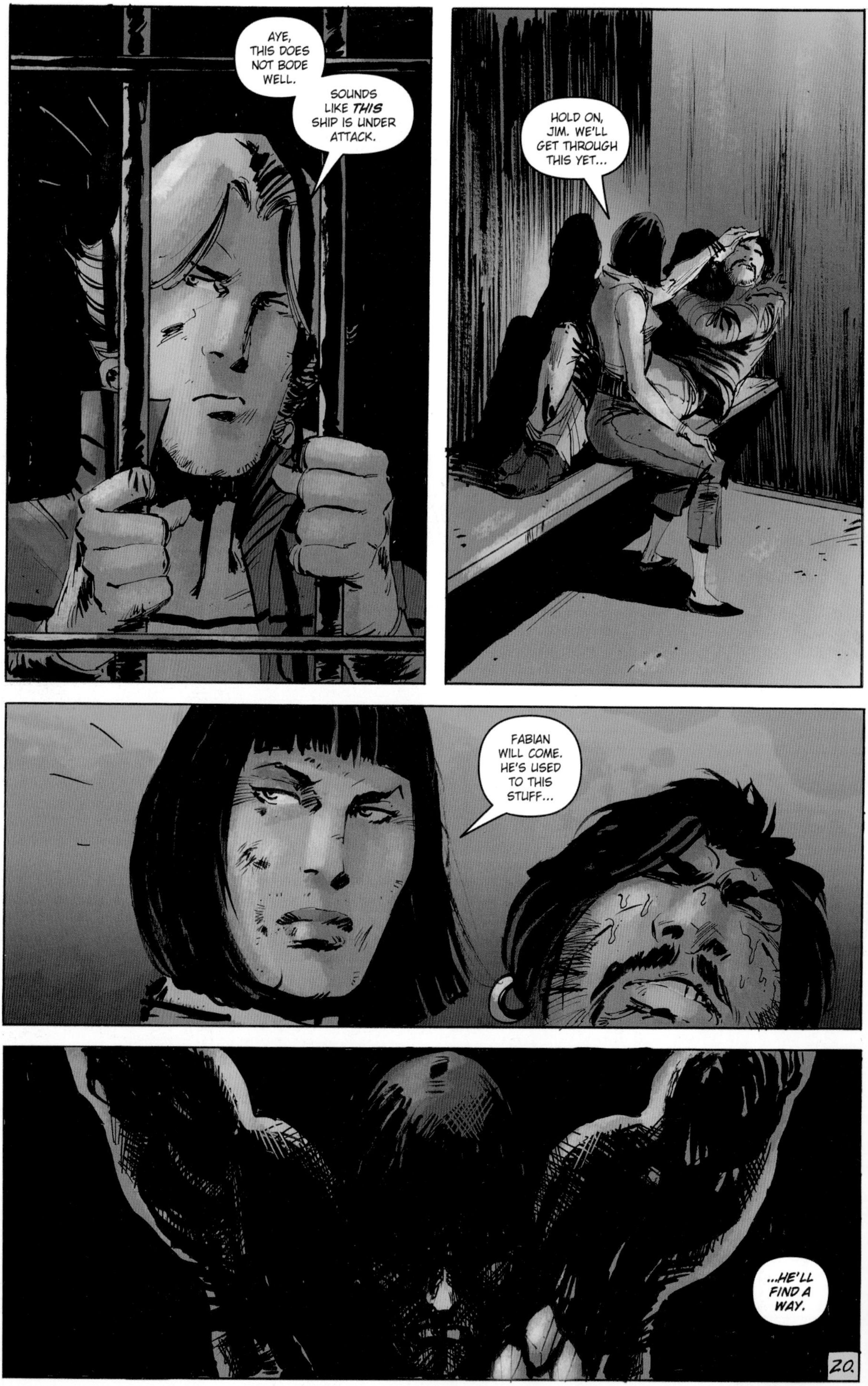
AYE, THIS DOES NOT BODE WELL.
SOUNDS LIKE *THIS* SHIP IS UNDER ATTACK.
HOLD ON, JIM. WE'LL GET THROUGH THIS YET...
FABIAN WILL COME. HE'S USED TO THIS STUFF...
...HE'LL FIND A WAY.

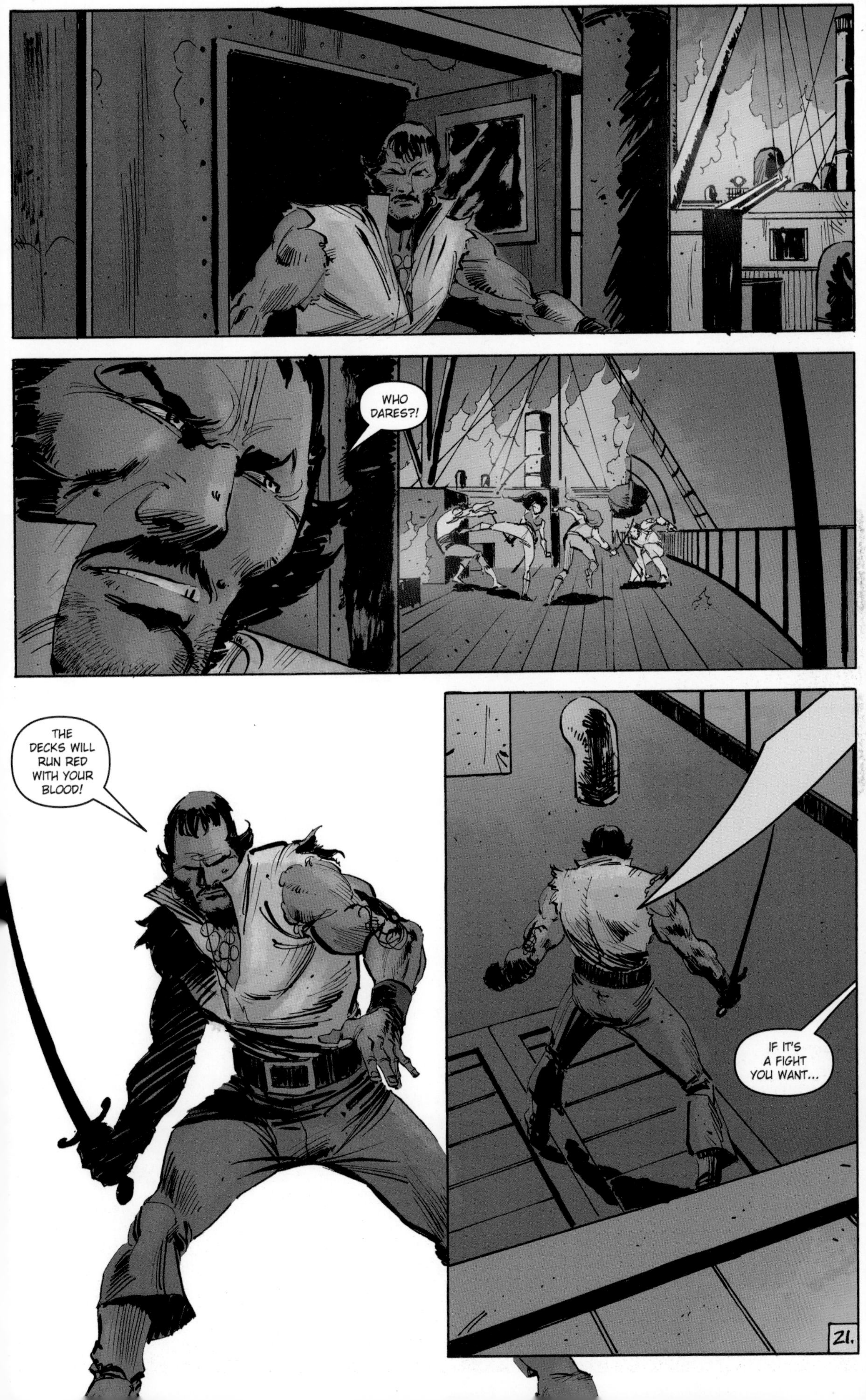

WHO DARES?!
THE DECKS WILL RUN RED WITH YOUR BLOOD!
IF IT'S A FIGHT YOU WANT...

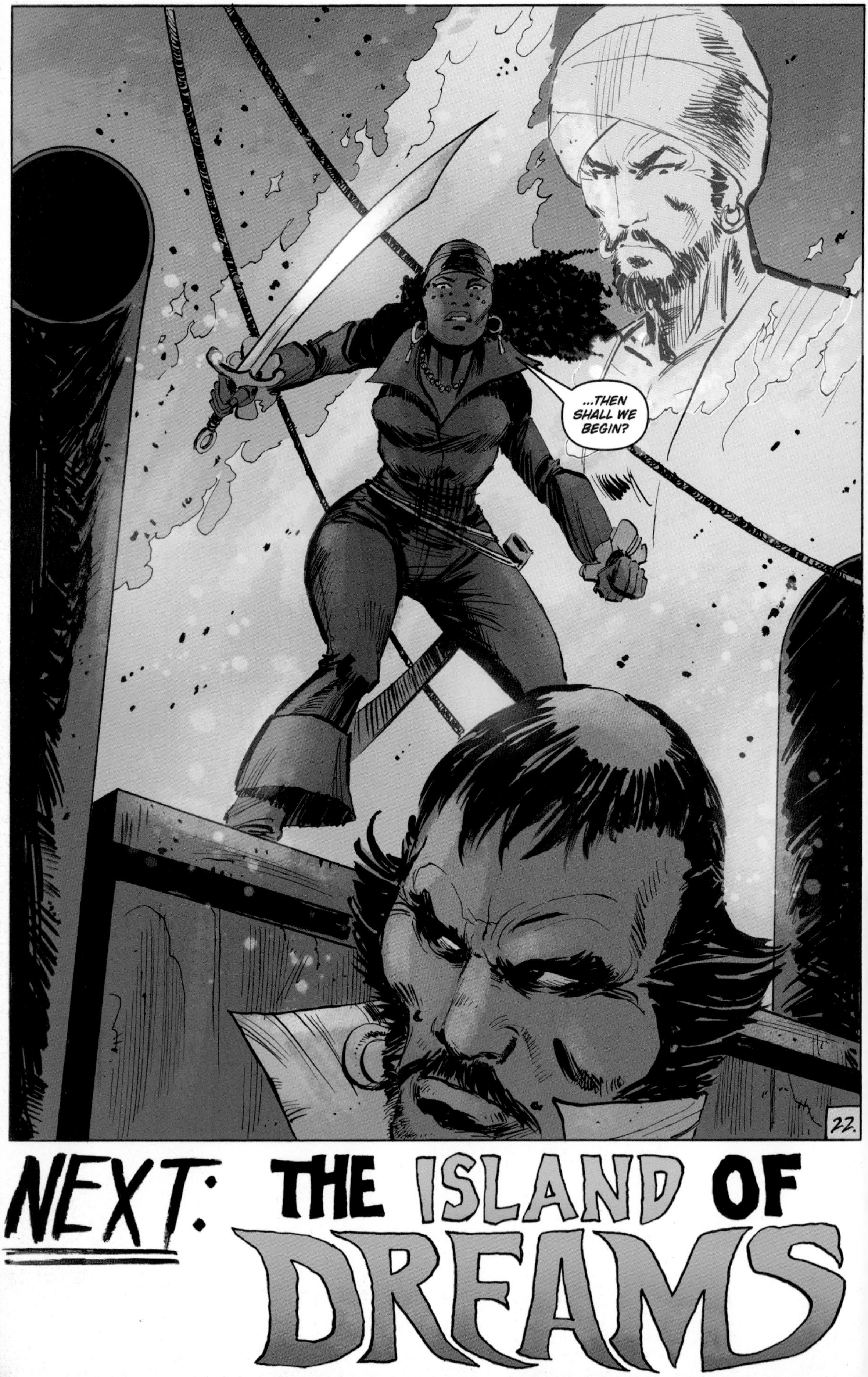
...THEN SHALL WE BEGIN?
22.

NEXT: THE ISLAND OF DREAMS

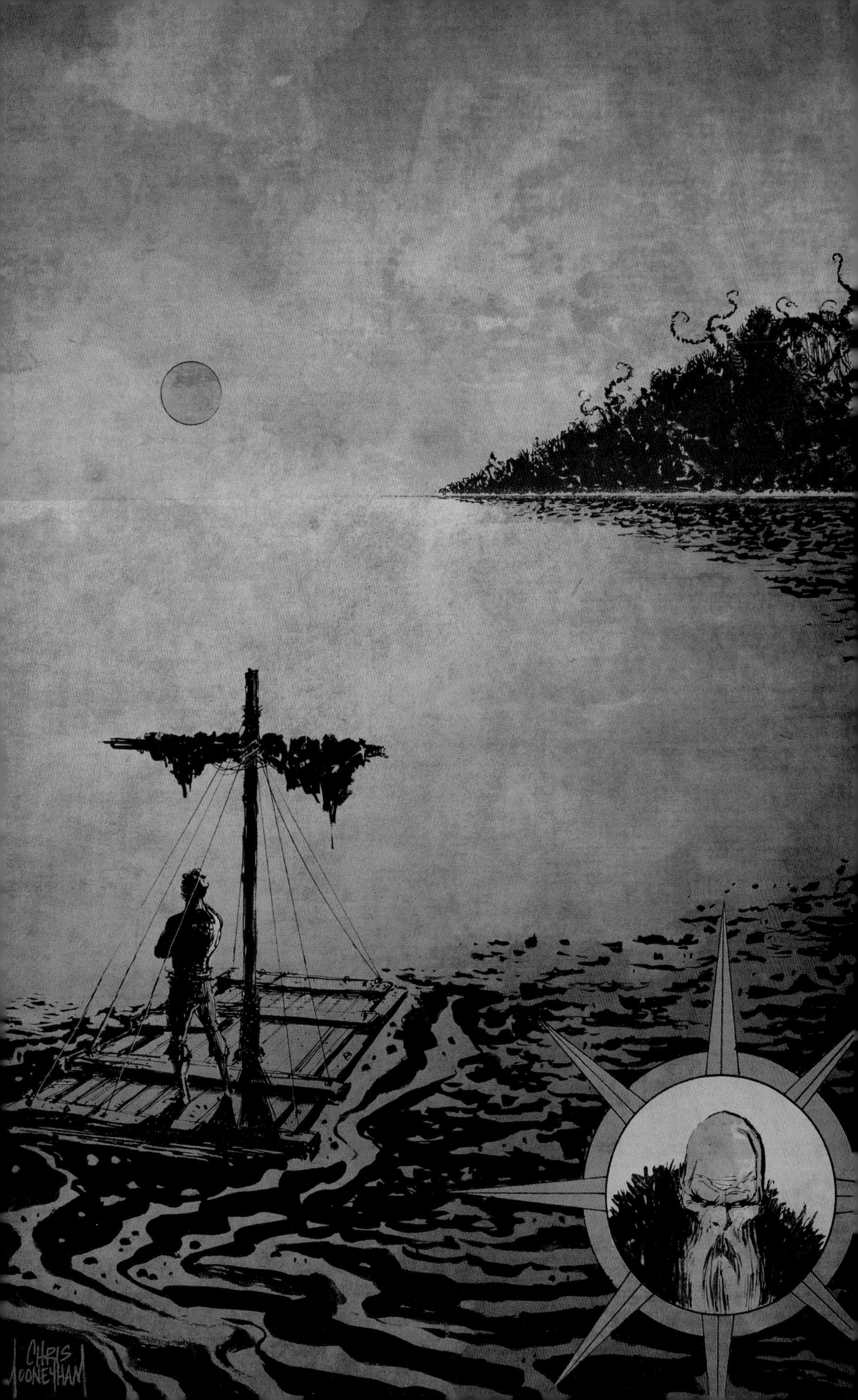
CHRIS
MOONEYHAM

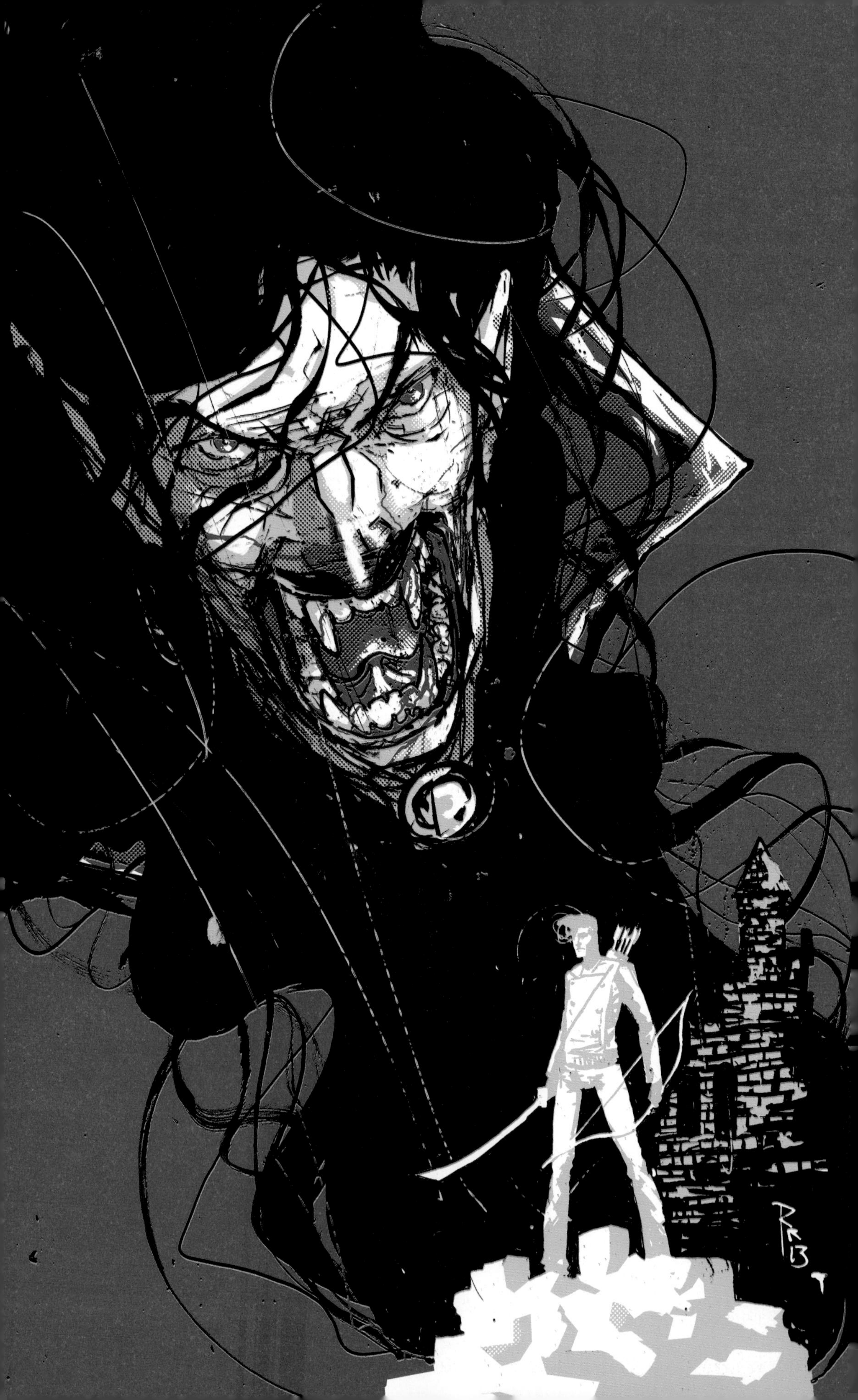

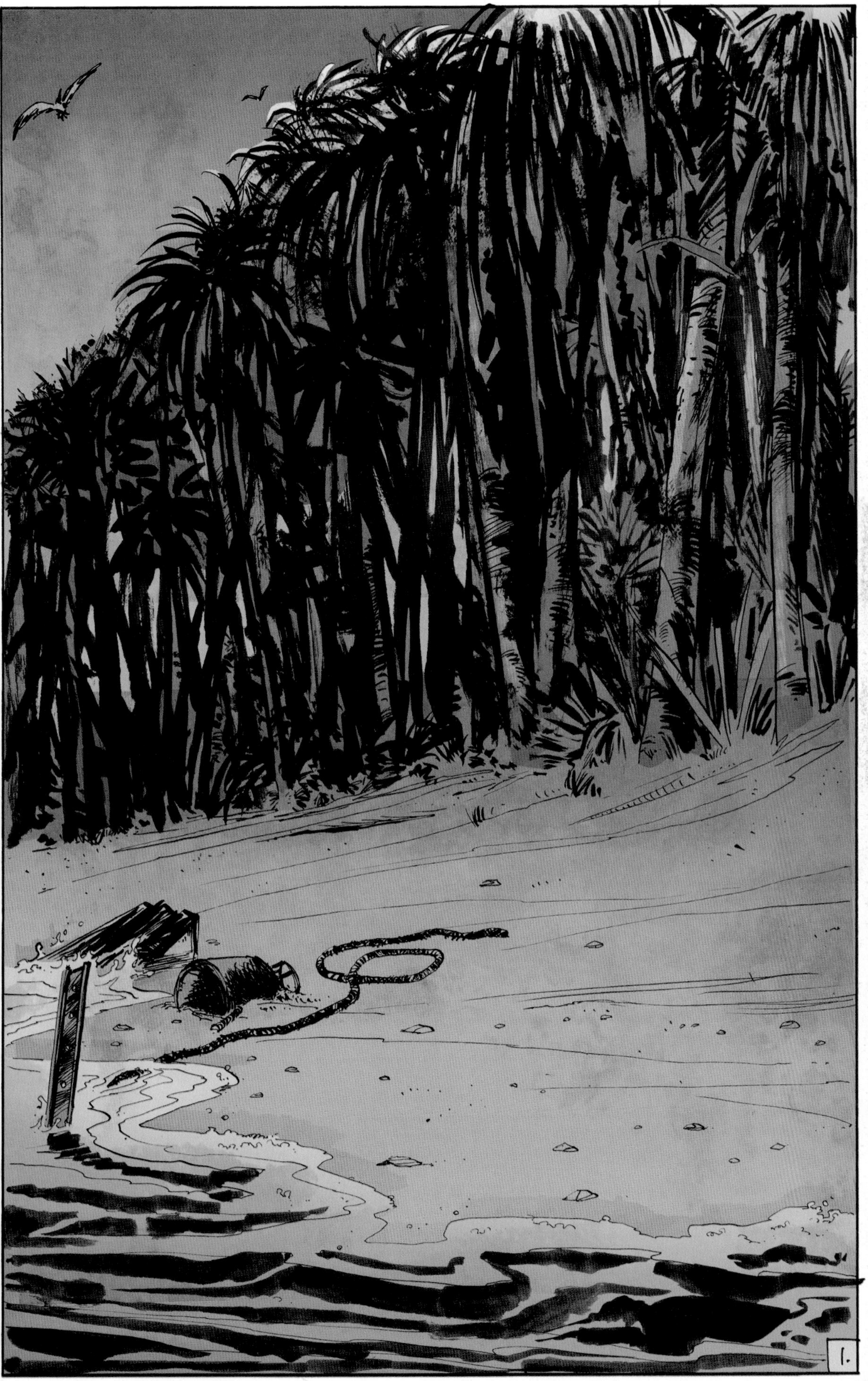

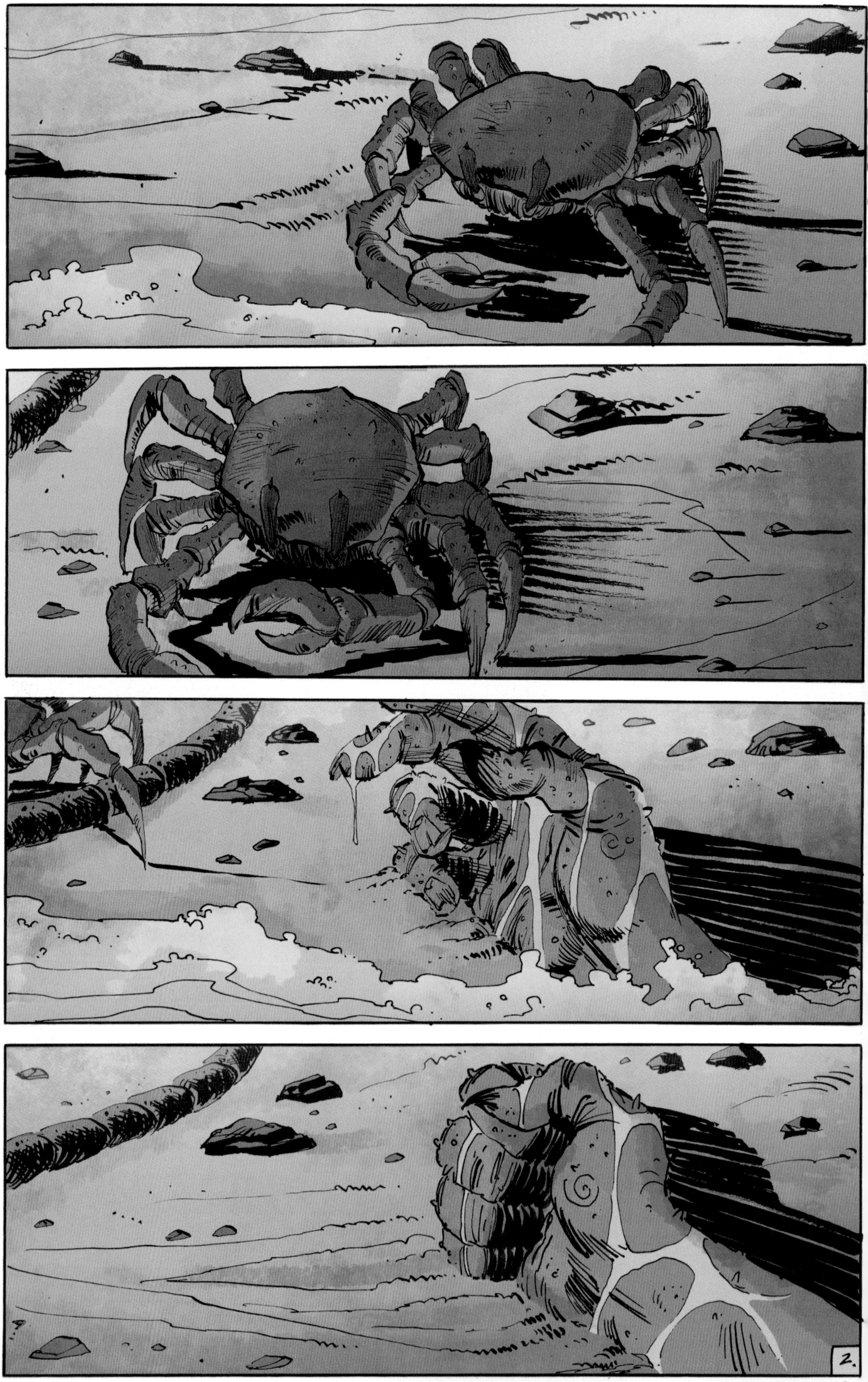

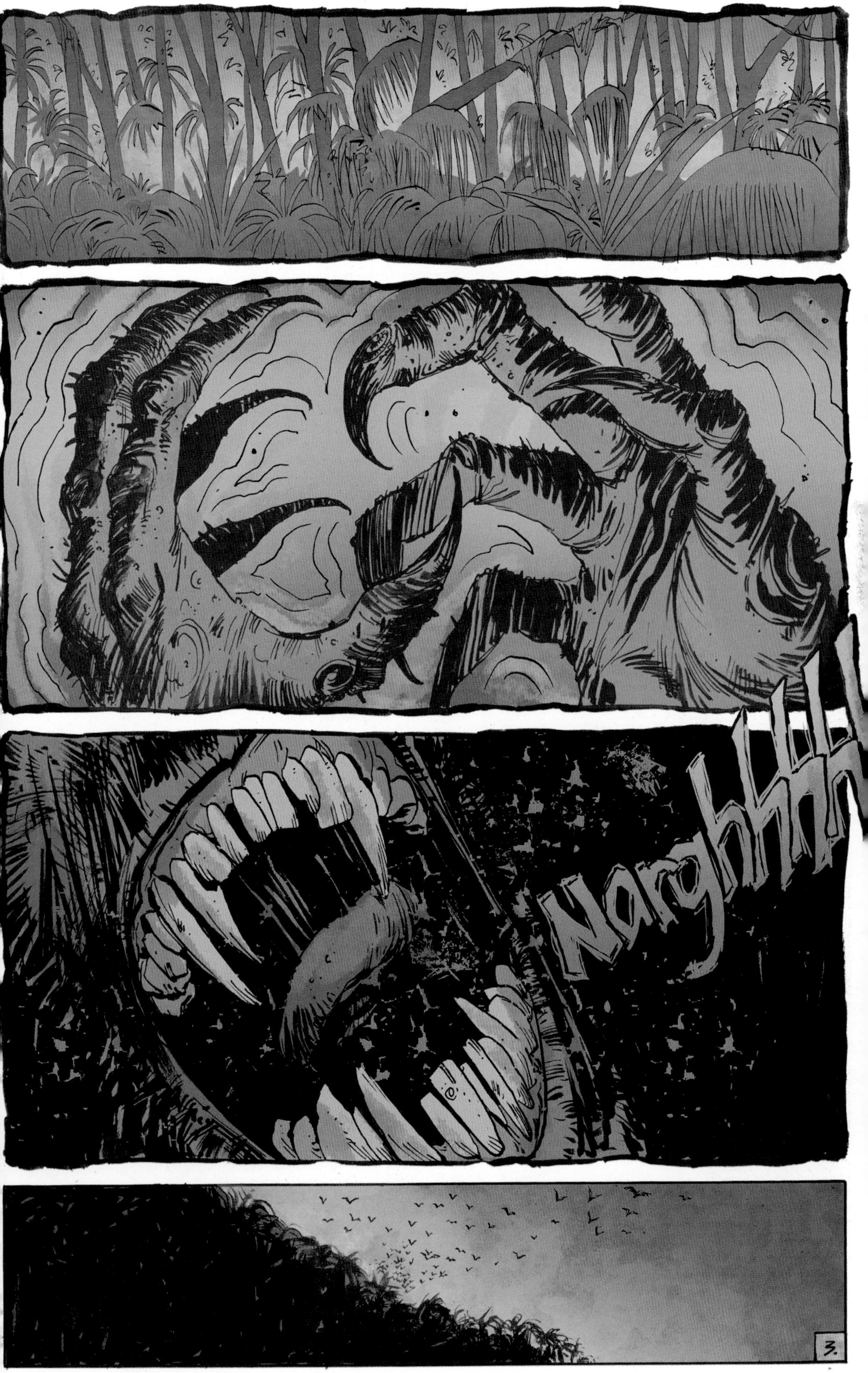
Narghhhh
3.

KRK
SORRY, LITTLE GUY...
...BUT I'M FINALLY GETTING THE HANG OF THIS.

PART IV "THE ISLAND OF DREAMS"

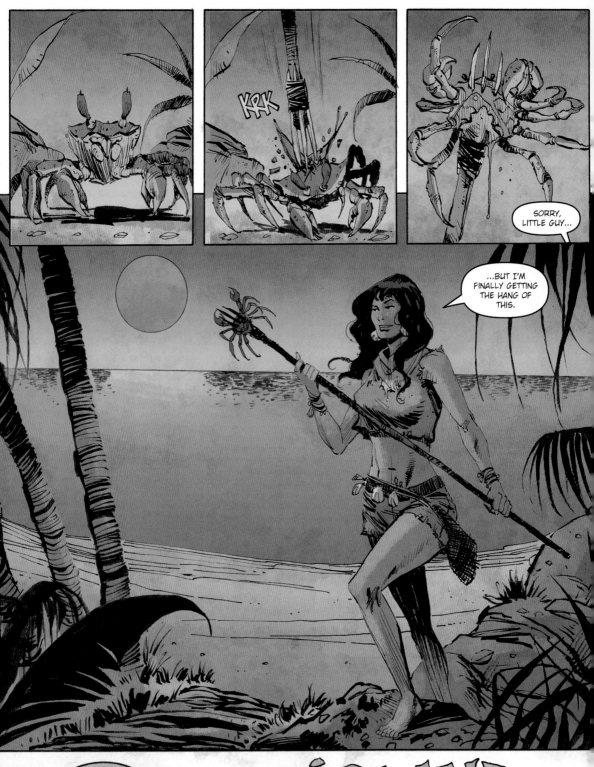

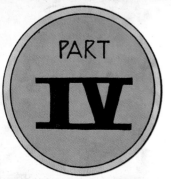

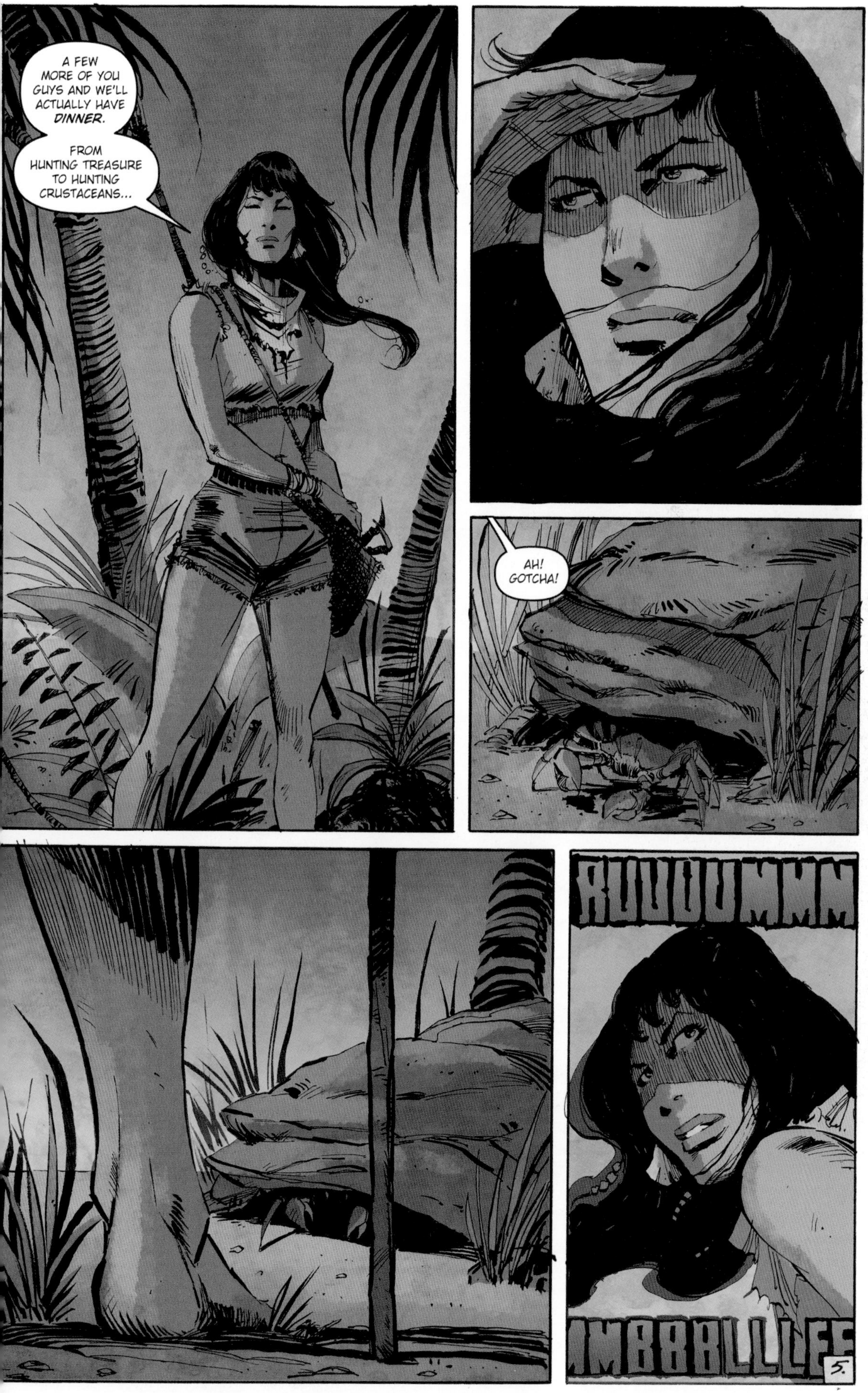
A FEW MORE OF YOU GUYS AND WE'LL ACTUALLY HAVE *DINNER*.
FROM HUNTING TREASURE TO HUNTING CRUSTACEANS...
AH! GOTCHA!
RUUUUMMM
MBBBALLLFF

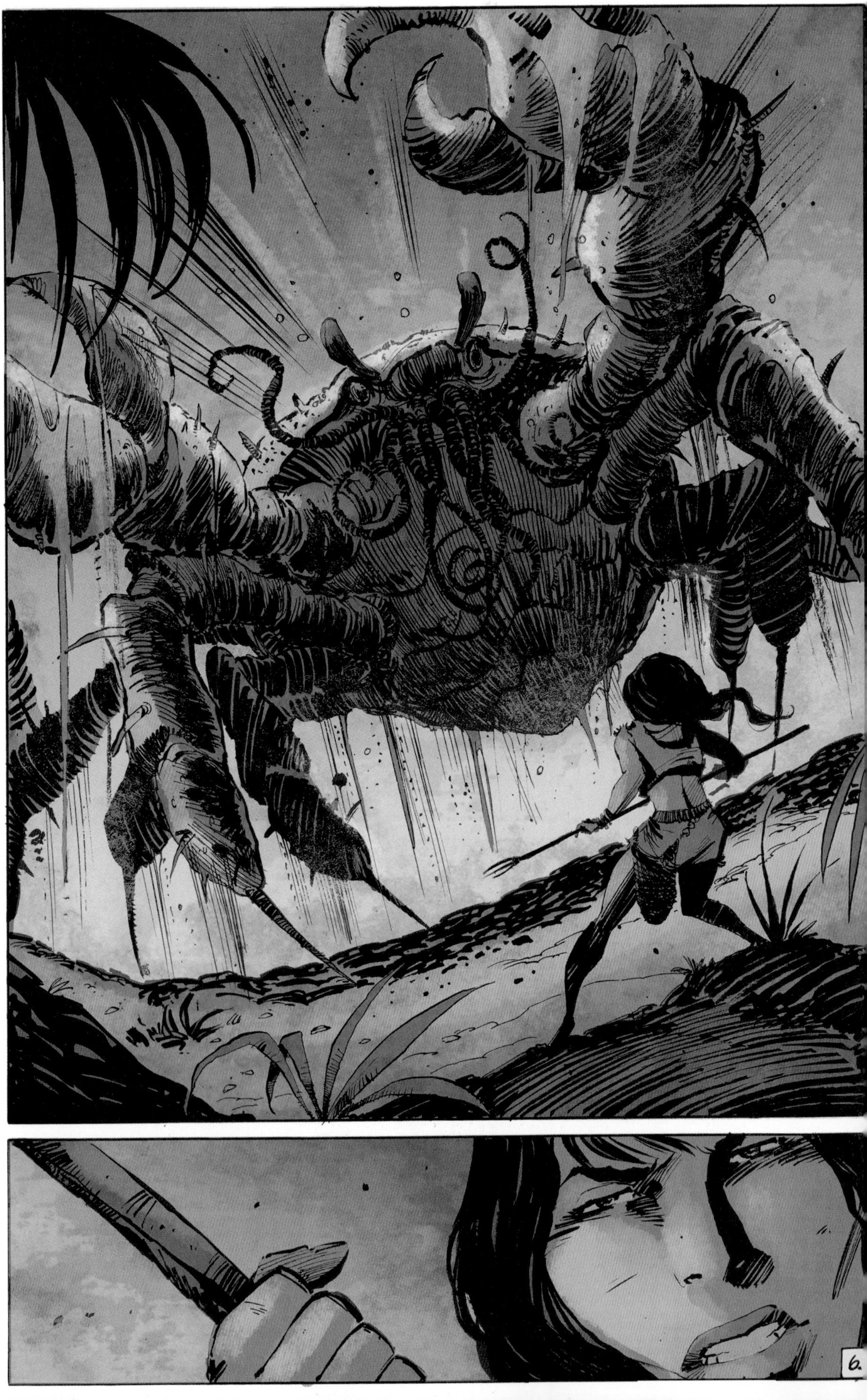

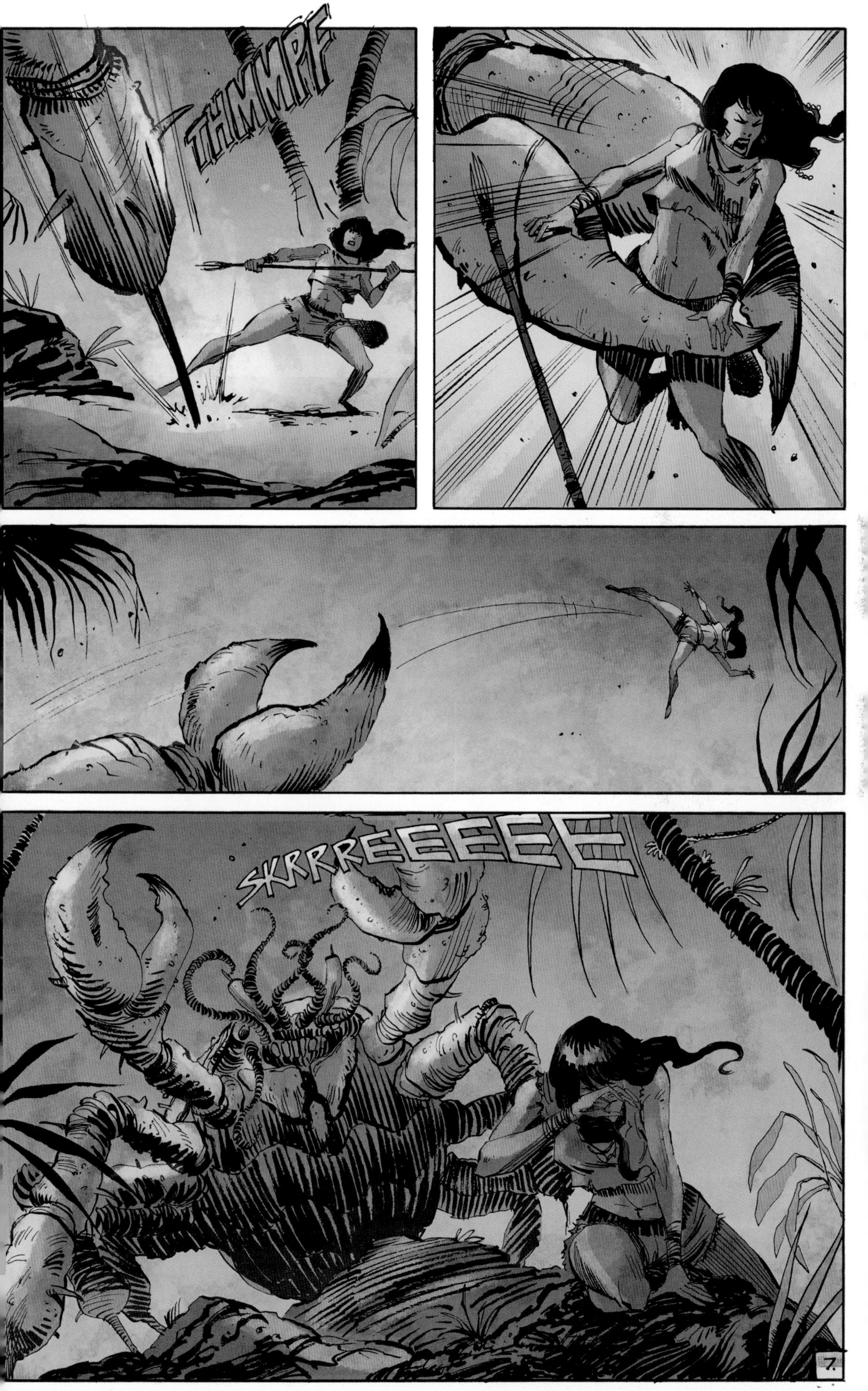
THMMPF
SKRRREEEEEE

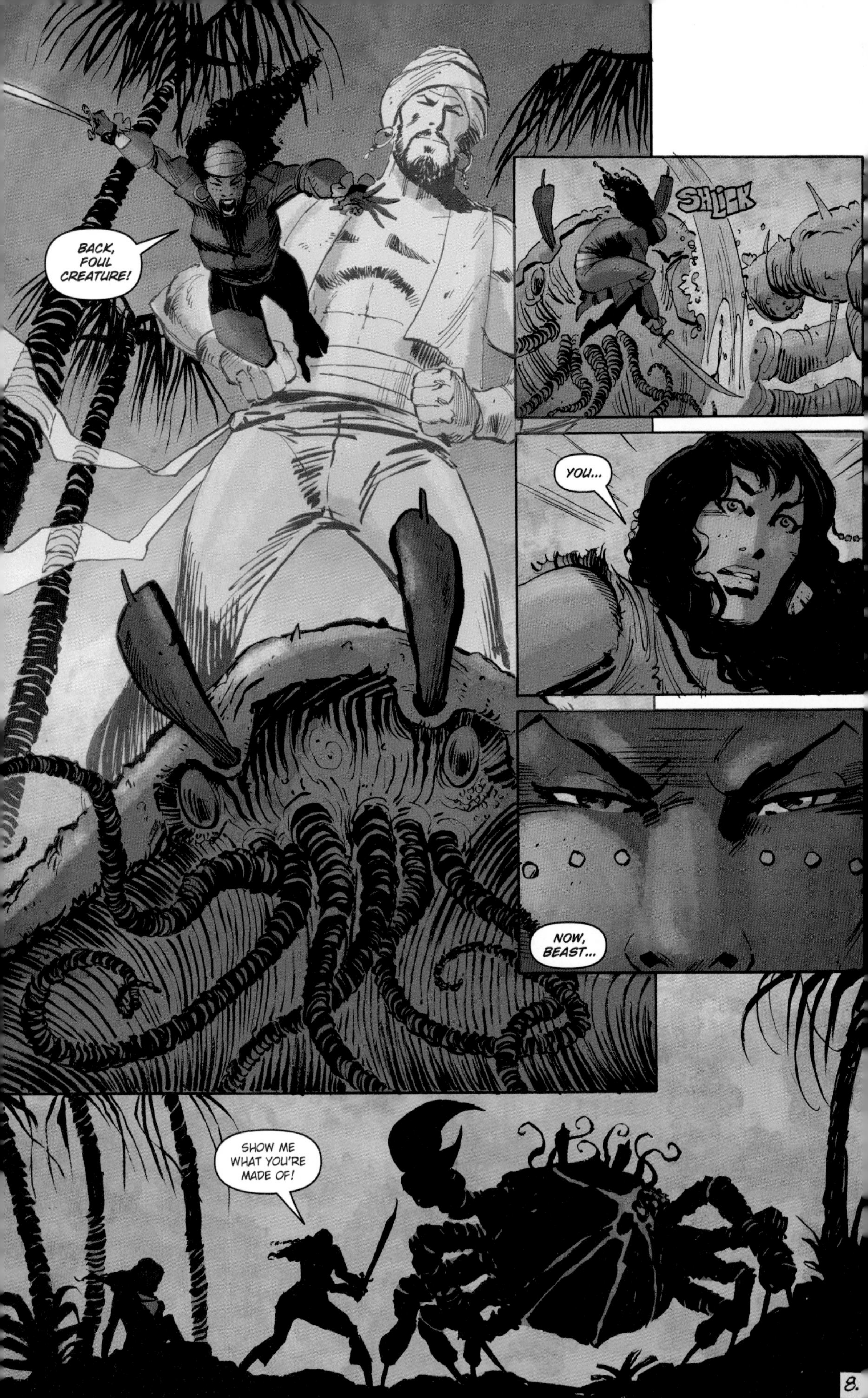
BACK, FOUL CREATURE!
SHLICK
YOU...
NOW, BEAST...
SHOW ME WHAT YOU'RE MADE OF!

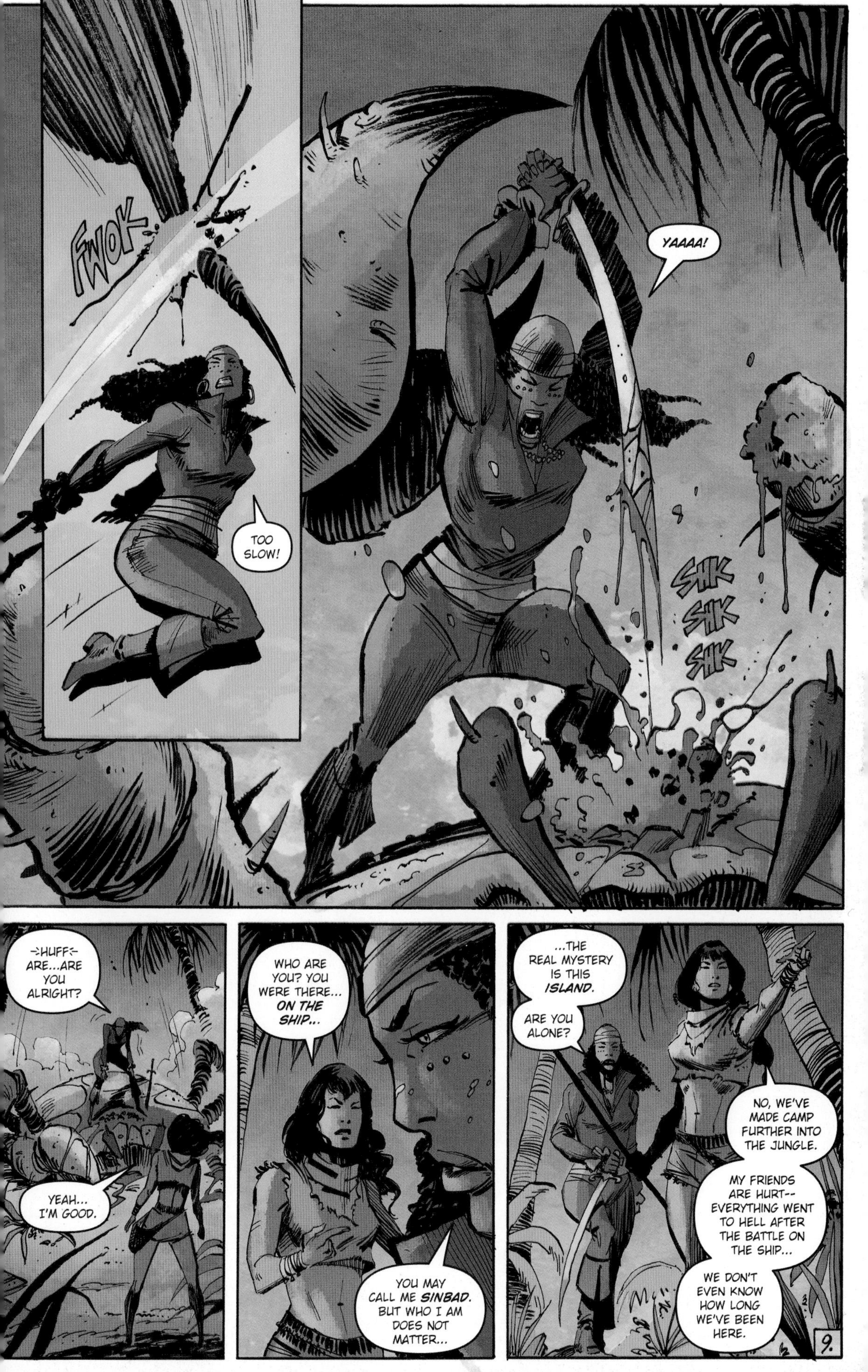
FWOK
TOO SLOW!
YAAAA!
SHK SHK SHK
-HUFF- ARE...ARE YOU ALRIGHT?
YEAH... I'M GOOD.
WHO ARE YOU? YOU WERE THERE... ON THE SHIP...
YOU MAY CALL ME SINBAD. BUT WHO I AM DOES NOT MATTER...
...THE REAL MYSTERY IS THIS ISLAND.
ARE YOU ALONE?
NO, WE'VE MADE CAMP FURTHER INTO THE JUNGLE.
MY FRIENDS ARE HURT-- EVERYTHING WENT TO HELL AFTER THE BATTLE ON THE SHIP...
WE DON'T EVEN KNOW HOW LONG WE'VE BEEN HERE.
9.

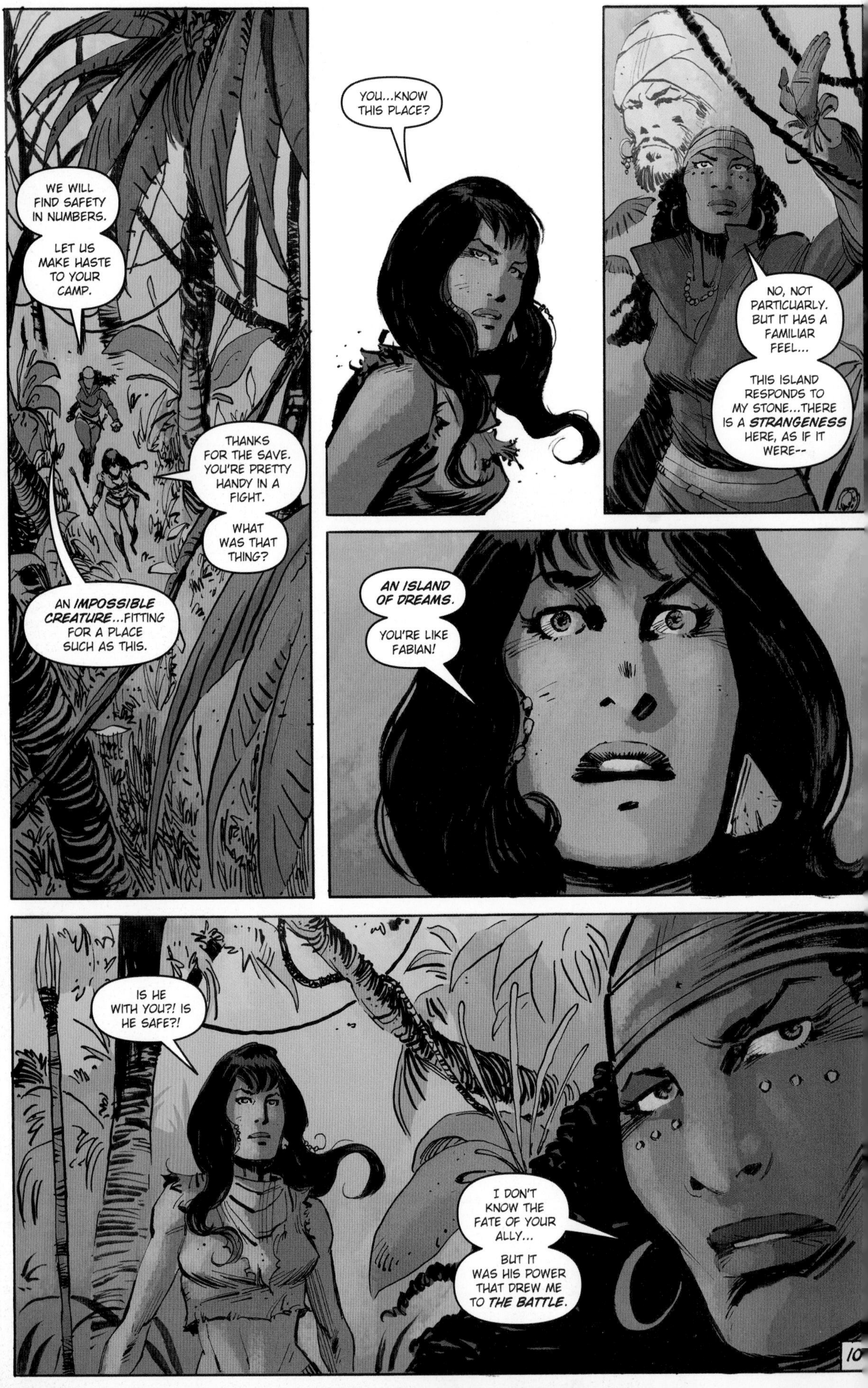
WE WILL FIND SAFETY IN NUMBERS.
LET US MAKE HASTE TO YOUR CAMP.
THANKS FOR THE SAVE. YOU'RE PRETTY HANDY IN A FIGHT.
WHAT WAS THAT THING?
AN *IMPOSSIBLE CREATURE*...FITTING FOR A PLACE SUCH AS THIS.
YOU...KNOW THIS PLACE?
NO, NOT PARTICULARLY. BUT IT HAS A FAMILIAR FEEL...
THIS ISLAND RESPONDS TO MY STONE...THERE IS A *STRANGENESS* HERE, AS IF IT WERE--
AN ISLAND OF DREAMS.
YOU'RE LIKE FABIAN!
IS HE WITH YOU?! IS HE SAFE?!
I DON'T KNOW THE FATE OF YOUR ALLY...
BUT IT WAS HIS POWER THAT DREW ME TO *THE BATTLE*.
10

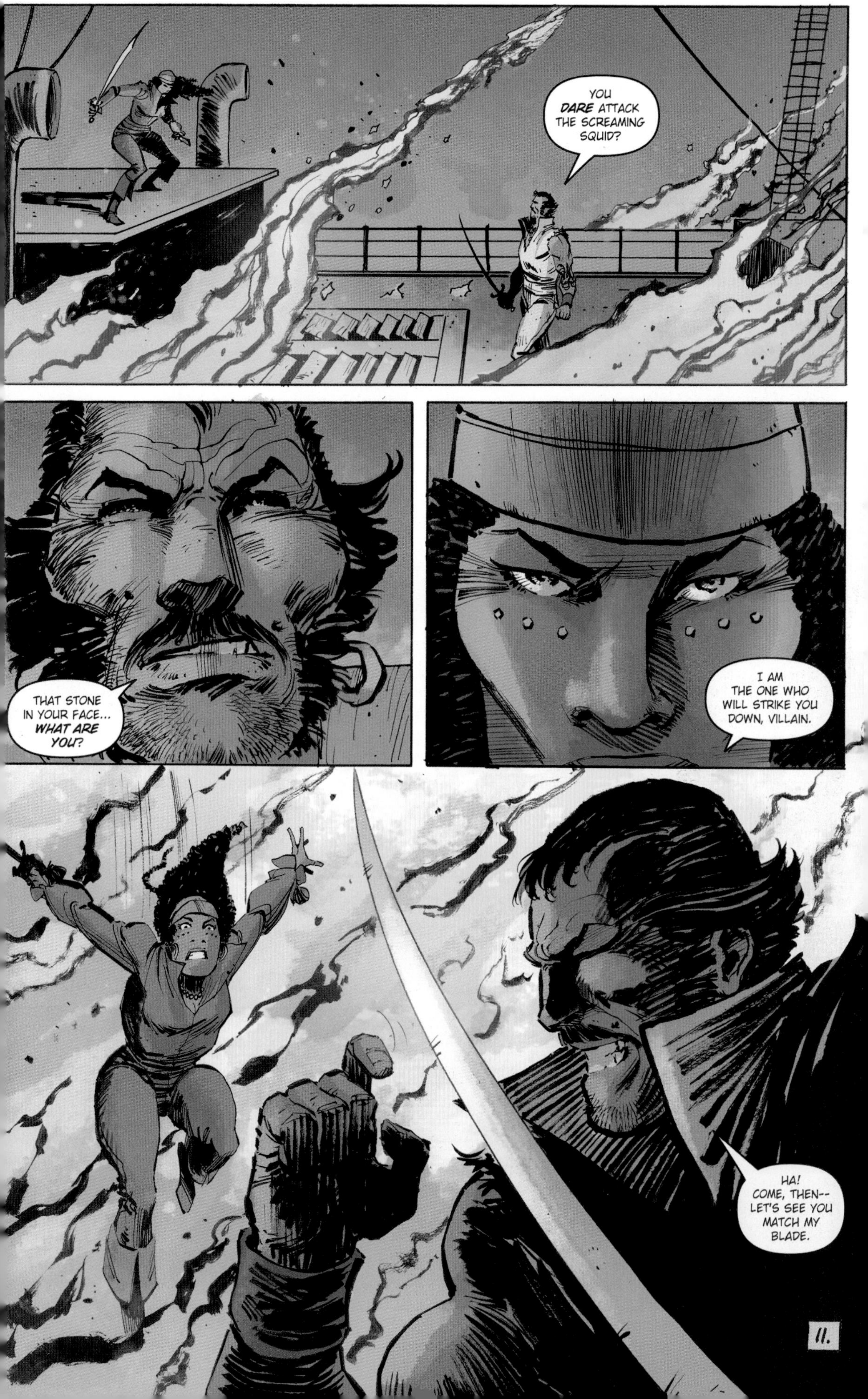
YOU DARE ATTACK THE SCREAMING SQUID?
THAT STONE IN YOUR FACE... WHAT ARE YOU?
I AM THE ONE WHO WILL STRIKE YOU DOWN, VILLAIN.
HA! COME, THEN-- LET'S SEE YOU MATCH MY BLADE.
11.

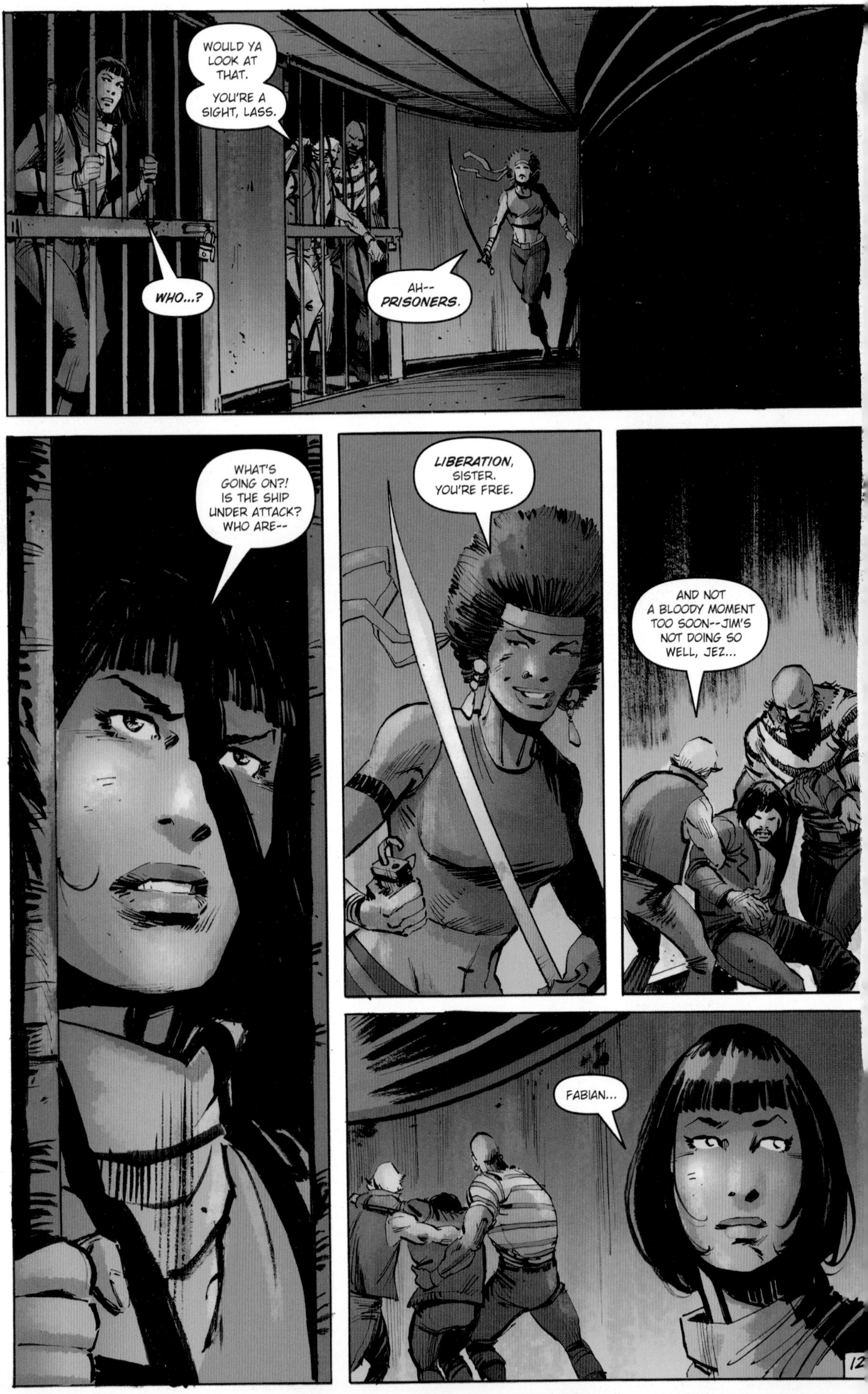
WOULD YA LOOK AT THAT.
YOU'RE A SIGHT, LASS.
WHO...?
AH-- PRISONERS.
WHAT'S GOING ON?! IS THE SHIP UNDER ATTACK? WHO ARE--
LIBERATION, SISTER. YOU'RE FREE.
AND NOT A BLOODY MOMENT TOO SOON--JIM'S NOT DOING SO WELL, JEZ...
FABIAN...
12

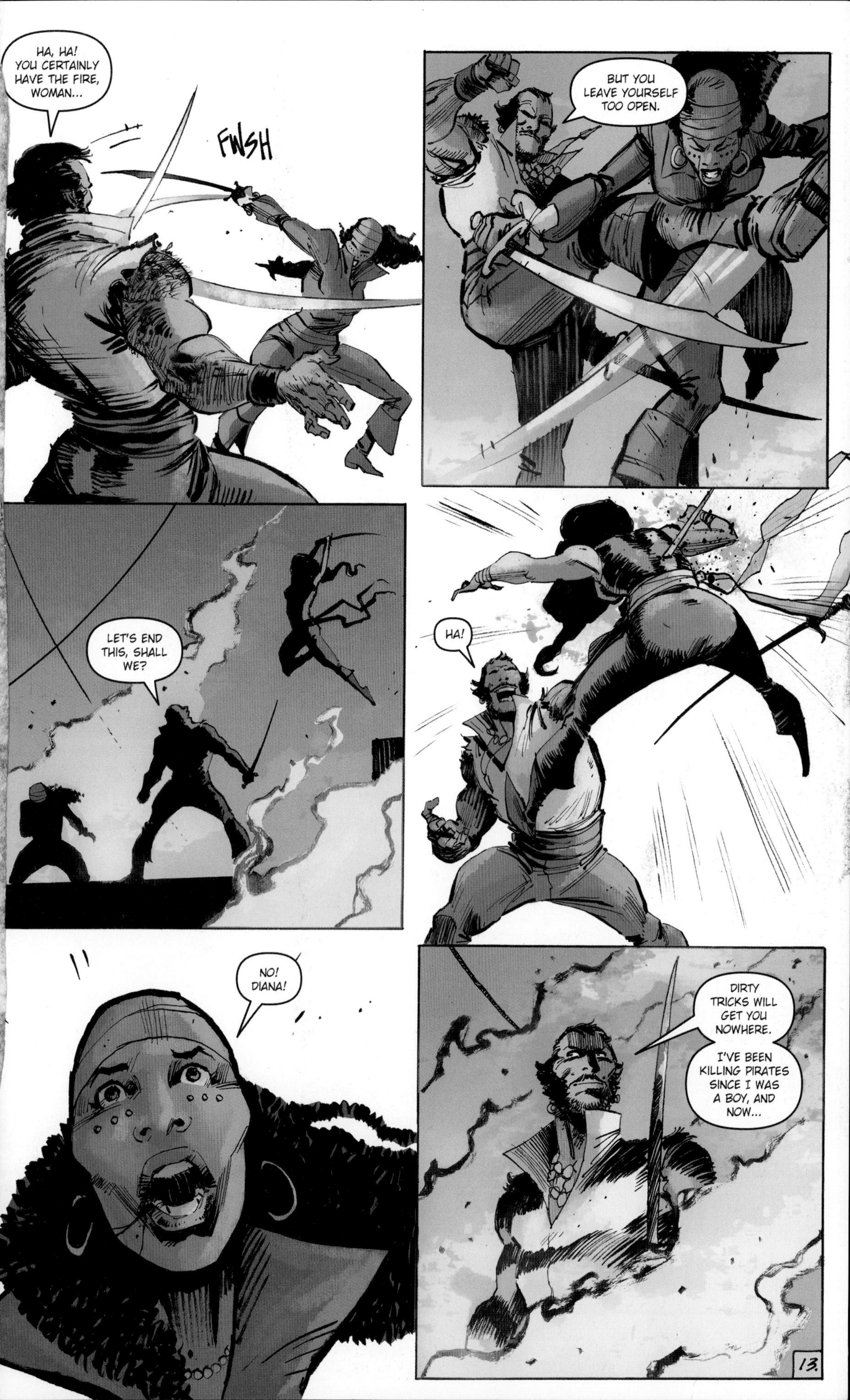
HA, HA! YOU CERTAINLY HAVE THE FIRE, WOMAN...
FWSH
BUT YOU LEAVE YOURSELF TOO OPEN.
LET'S END THIS, SHALL WE?
HA!
NO! DIANA!
DIRTY TRICKS WILL GET YOU NOWHERE.
I'VE BEEN KILLING PIRATES SINCE I WAS A BOY, AND NOW...
13.

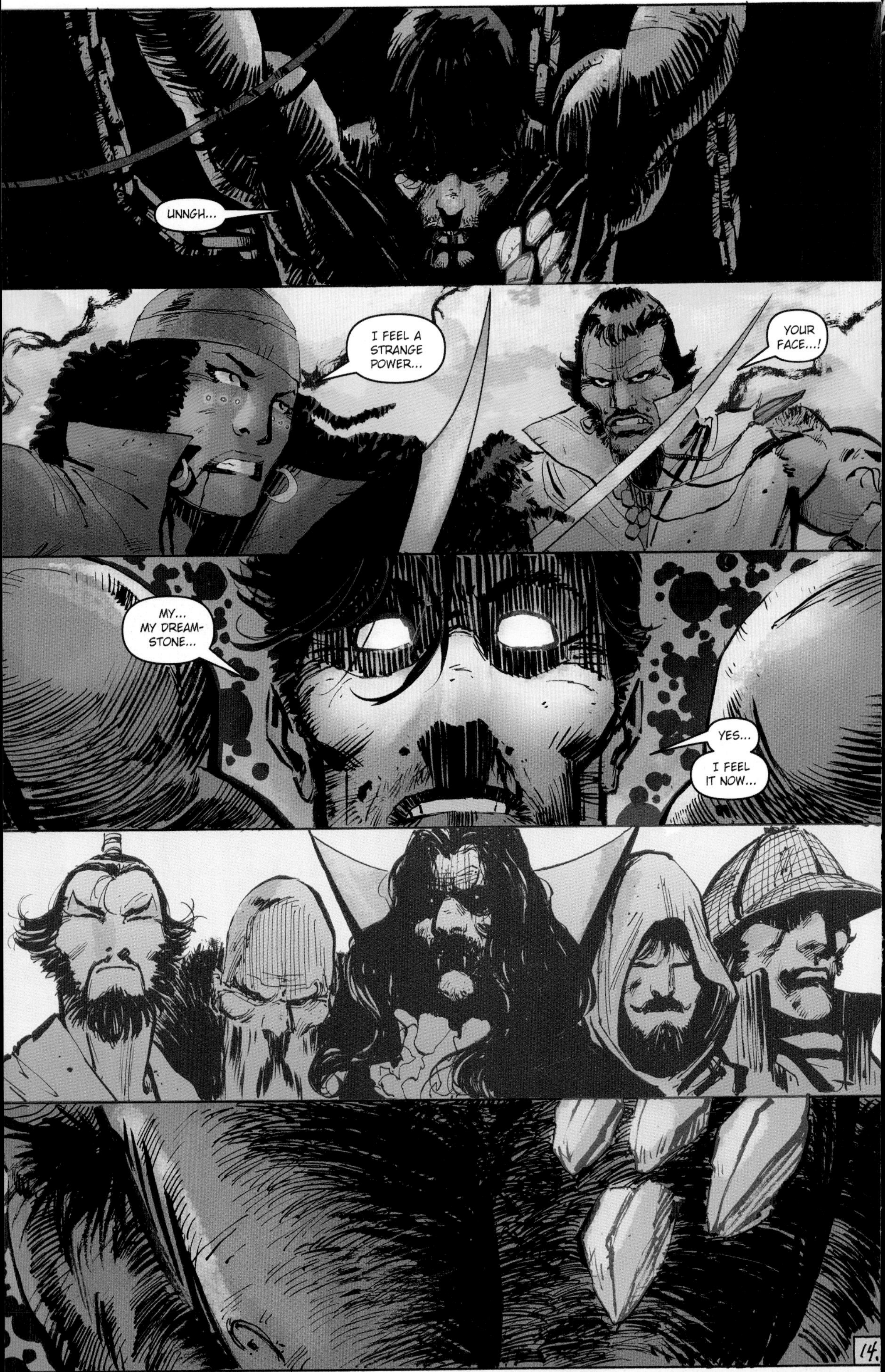
UNNGH...
I FEEL A STRANGE POWER...
YOUR FACE...!
MY... MY DREAM-STONE...
YES...
I FEEL IT NOW...
14.

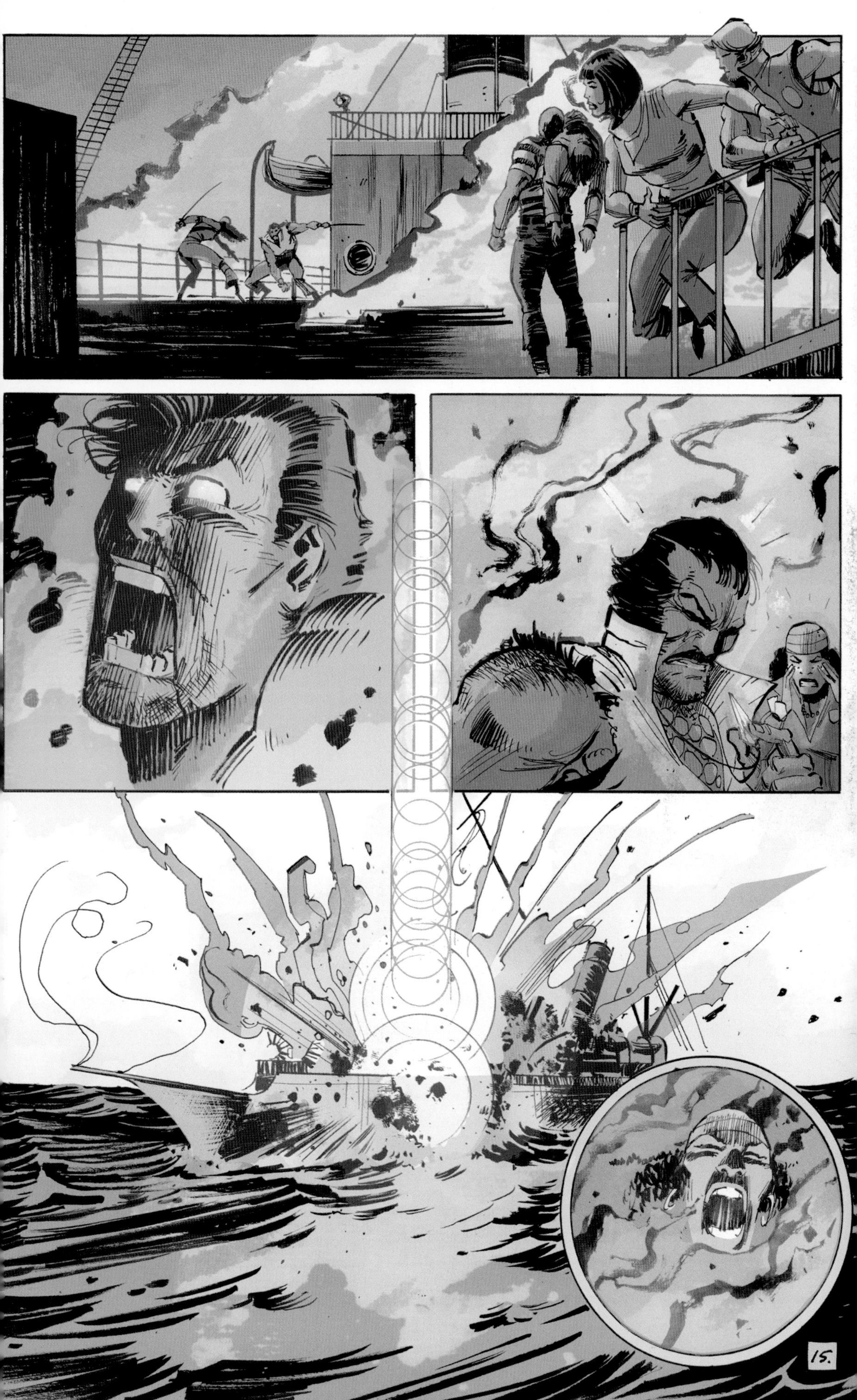

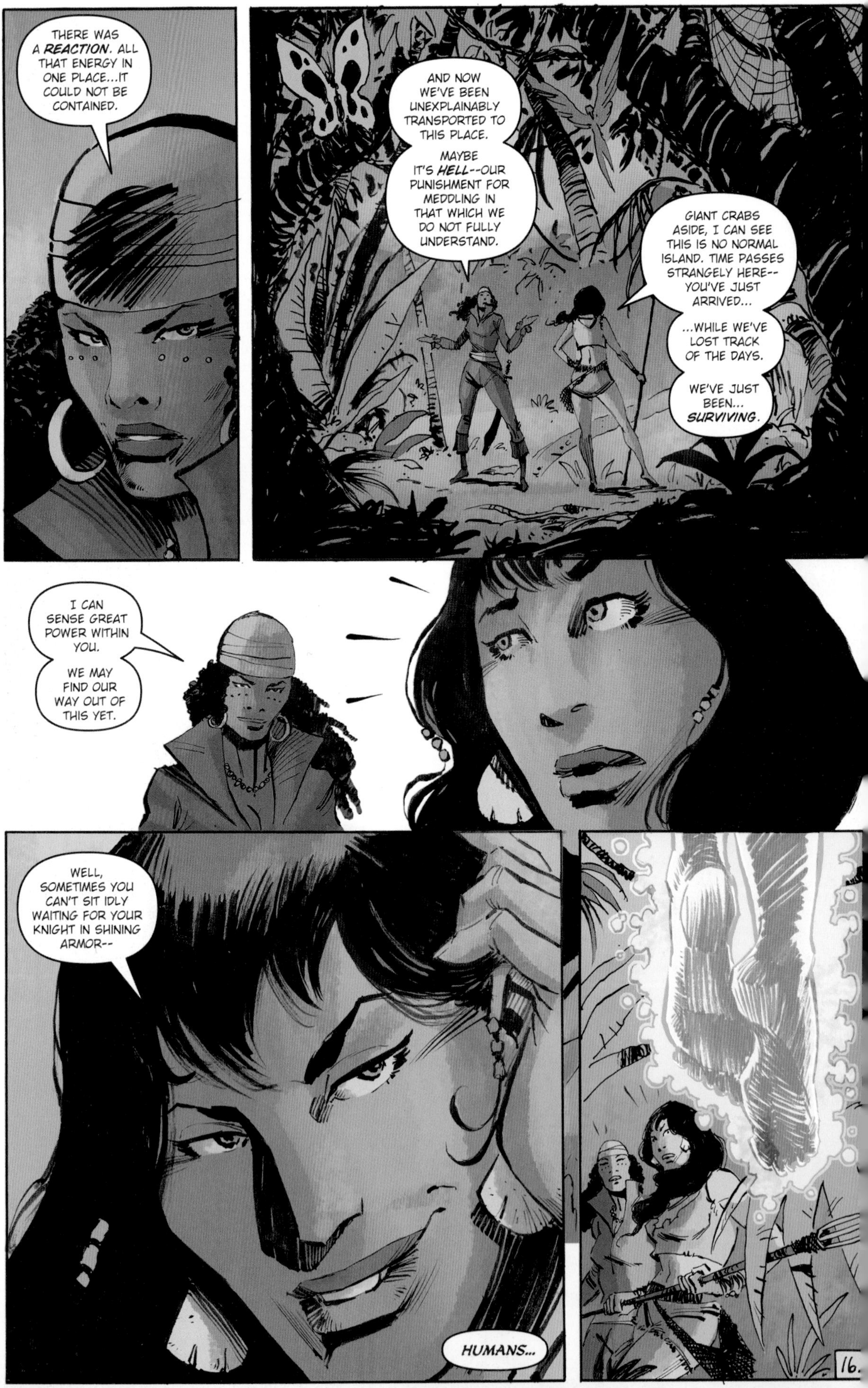

THERE WAS A **REACTION**. ALL THAT ENERGY IN ONE PLACE...IT COULD NOT BE CONTAINED.
AND NOW WE'VE BEEN UNEXPLAINABLY TRANSPORTED TO THIS PLACE.
MAYBE IT'S **HELL**--OUR PUNISHMENT FOR MEDDLING IN THAT WHICH WE DO NOT FULLY UNDERSTAND.
GIANT CRABS ASIDE, I CAN SEE THIS IS NO NORMAL ISLAND. TIME PASSES STRANGELY HERE--YOU'VE JUST ARRIVED...
...WHILE WE'VE LOST TRACK OF THE DAYS.
WE'VE JUST BEEN... **SURVIVING**.
I CAN SENSE GREAT POWER WITHIN YOU.
WE MAY FIND OUR WAY OUT OF THIS YET.
WELL, SOMETIMES YOU CAN'T SIT IDLY WAITING FOR YOUR KNIGHT IN SHINING ARMOR--
HUMANS...

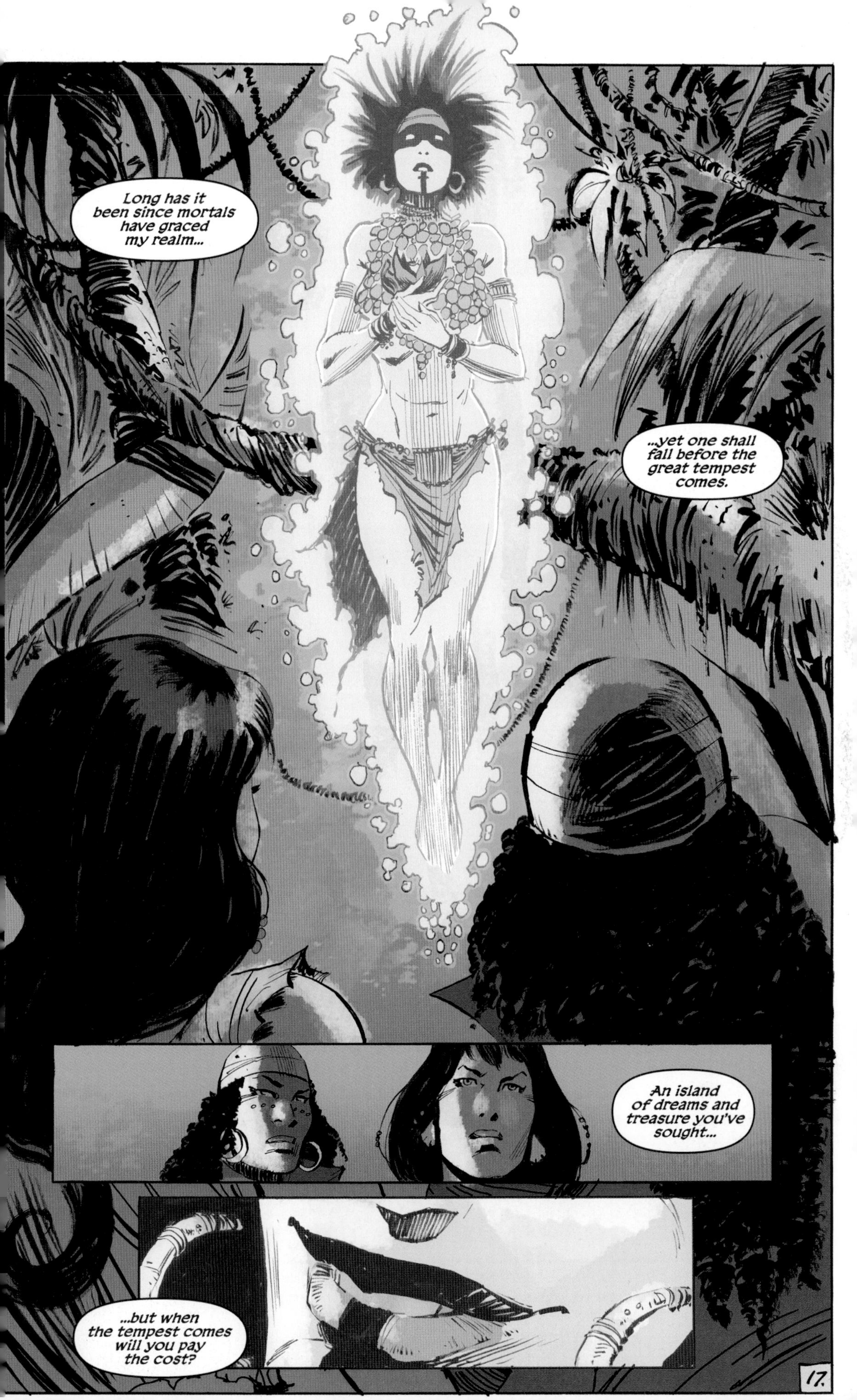
Long has it been since mortals have graced my realm...
...yet one shall fall before the great tempest comes.
An island of dreams and treasure you've sought...
...but when the tempest comes will you pay the cost?

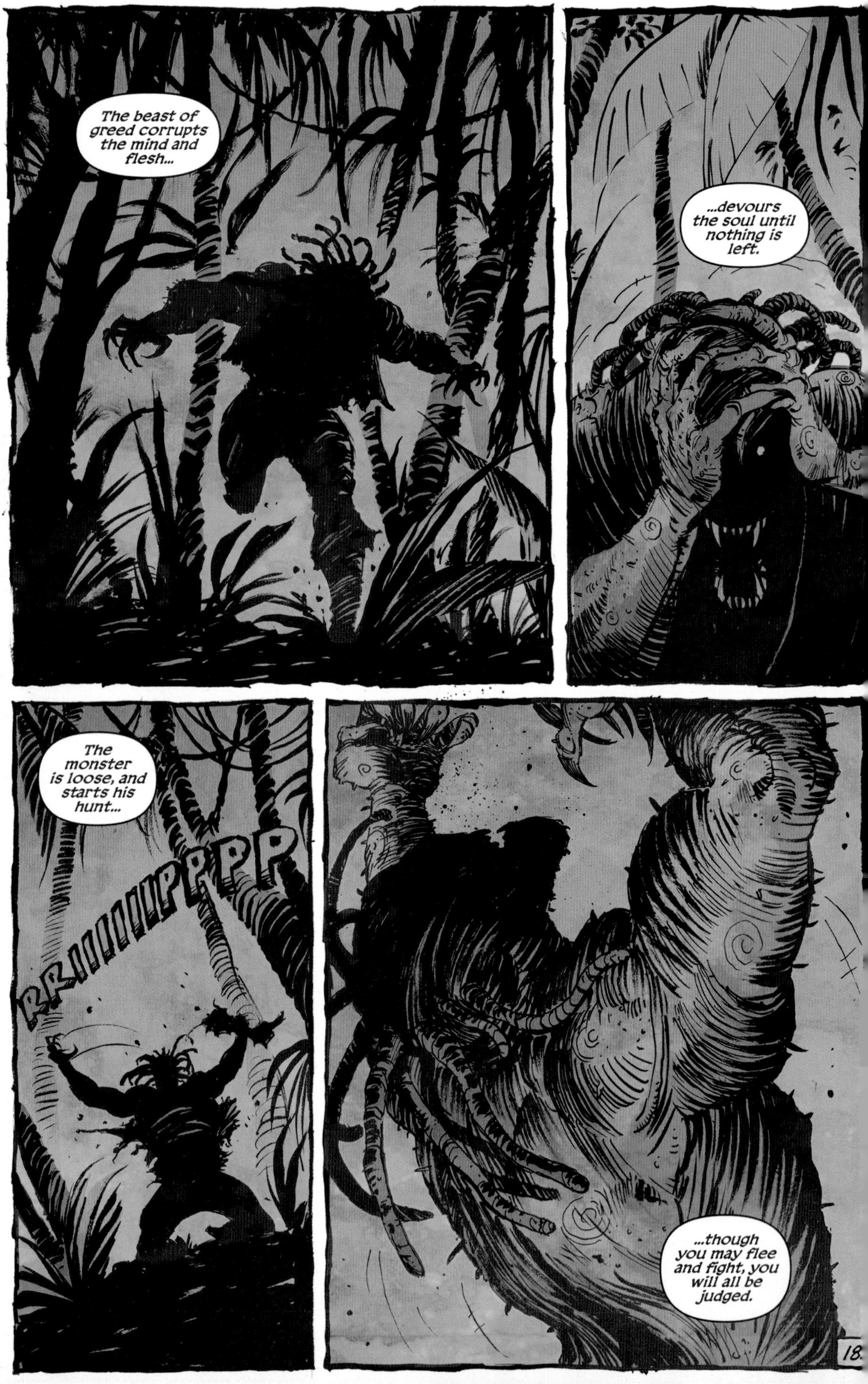
The beast of greed corrupts the mind and flesh...
...devours the soul until nothing is left.
The monster is loose, and starts his hunt...
RRIIIIIIIPPPPP
...though you may flee and fight, you will all be judged.

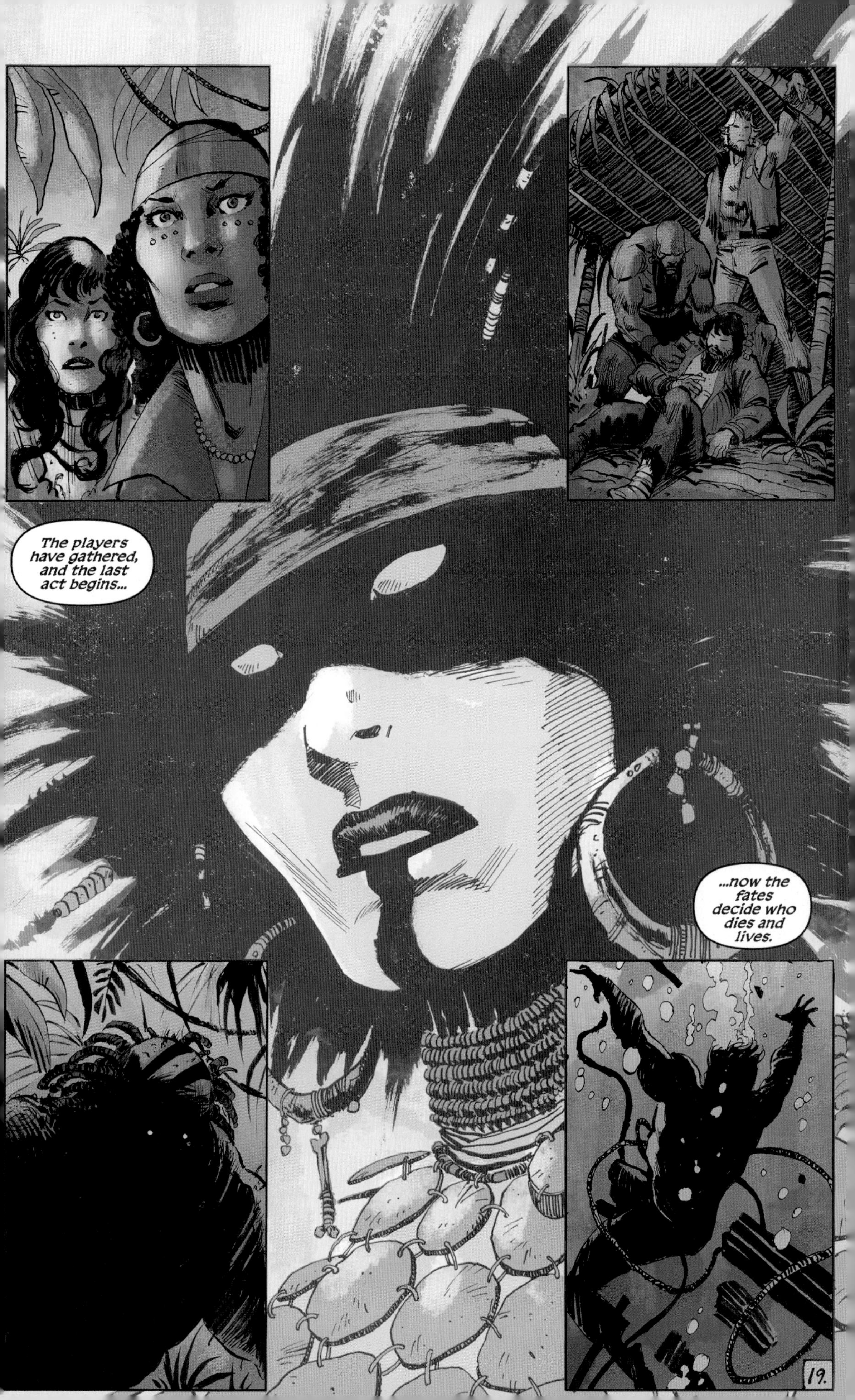
The players have gathered, and the last act begins...
...now the fates decide who dies and lives.

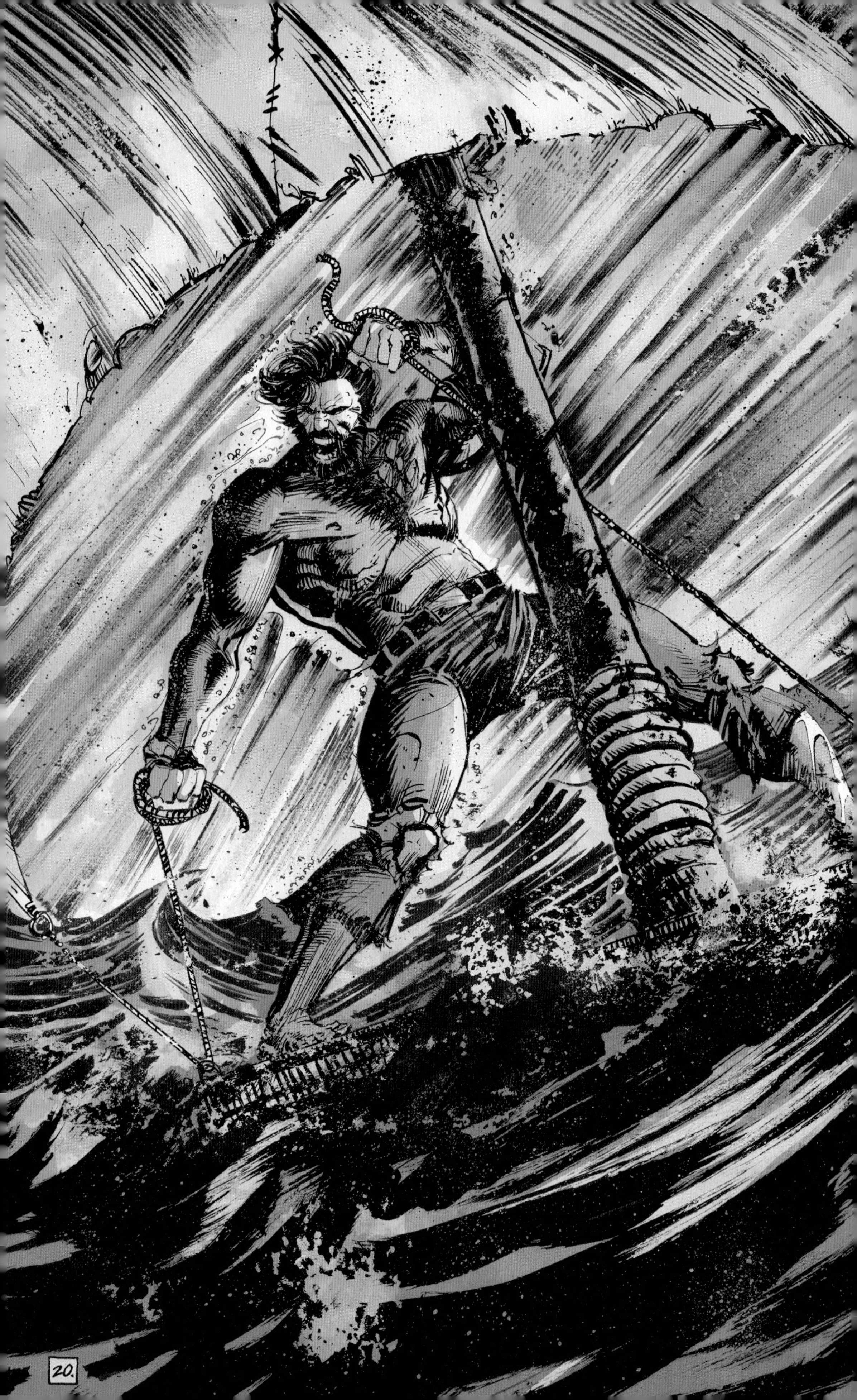

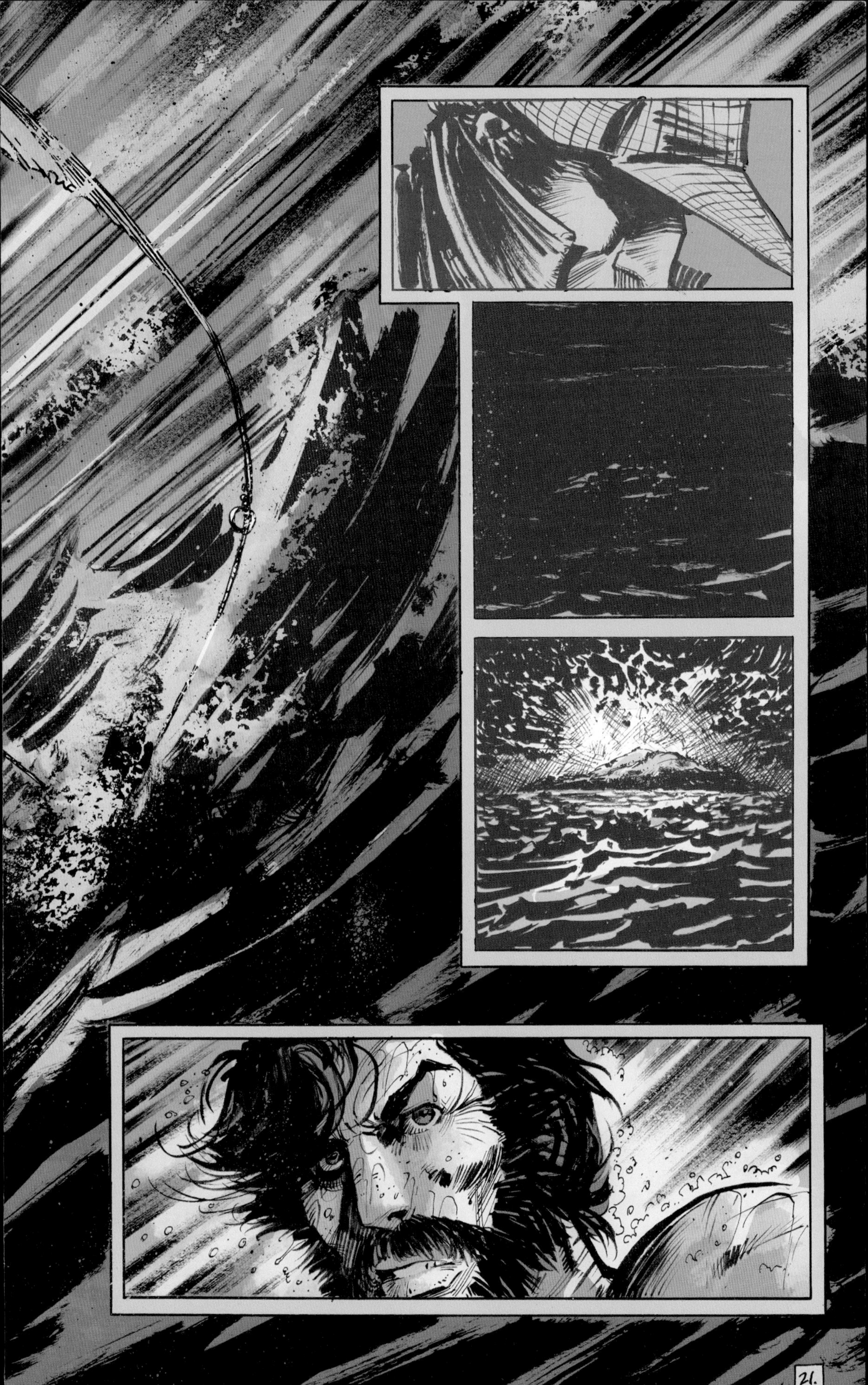

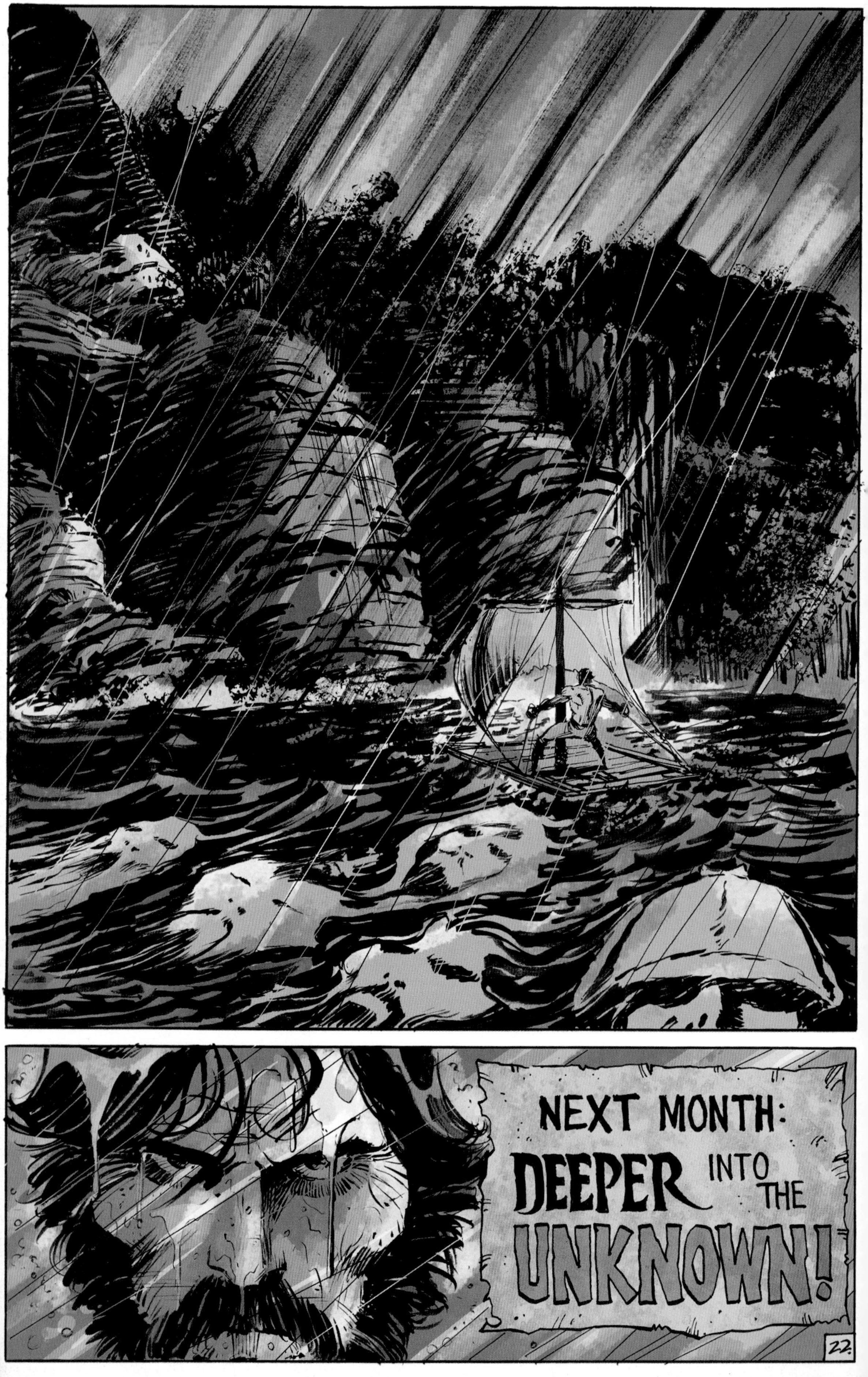
NEXT MONTH:
DEEPER INTO THE UNKNOWN!
22.

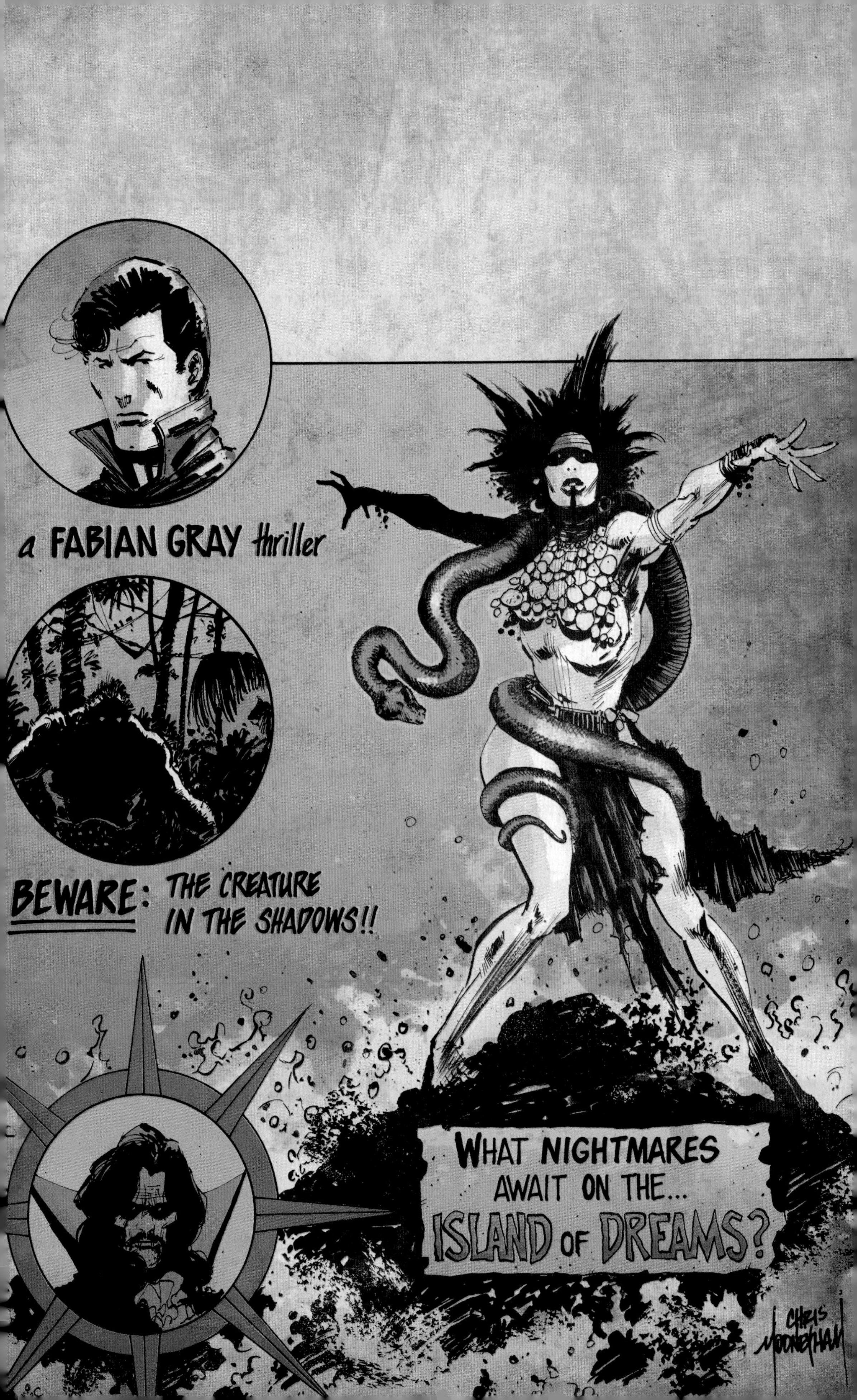
a FABIAN GRAY thriller
BEWARE: THE CREATURE IN THE SHADOWS!!
WHAT NIGHTMARES AWAIT ON THE... ISLAND OF DREAMS?
CHRIS MOONEYHAM

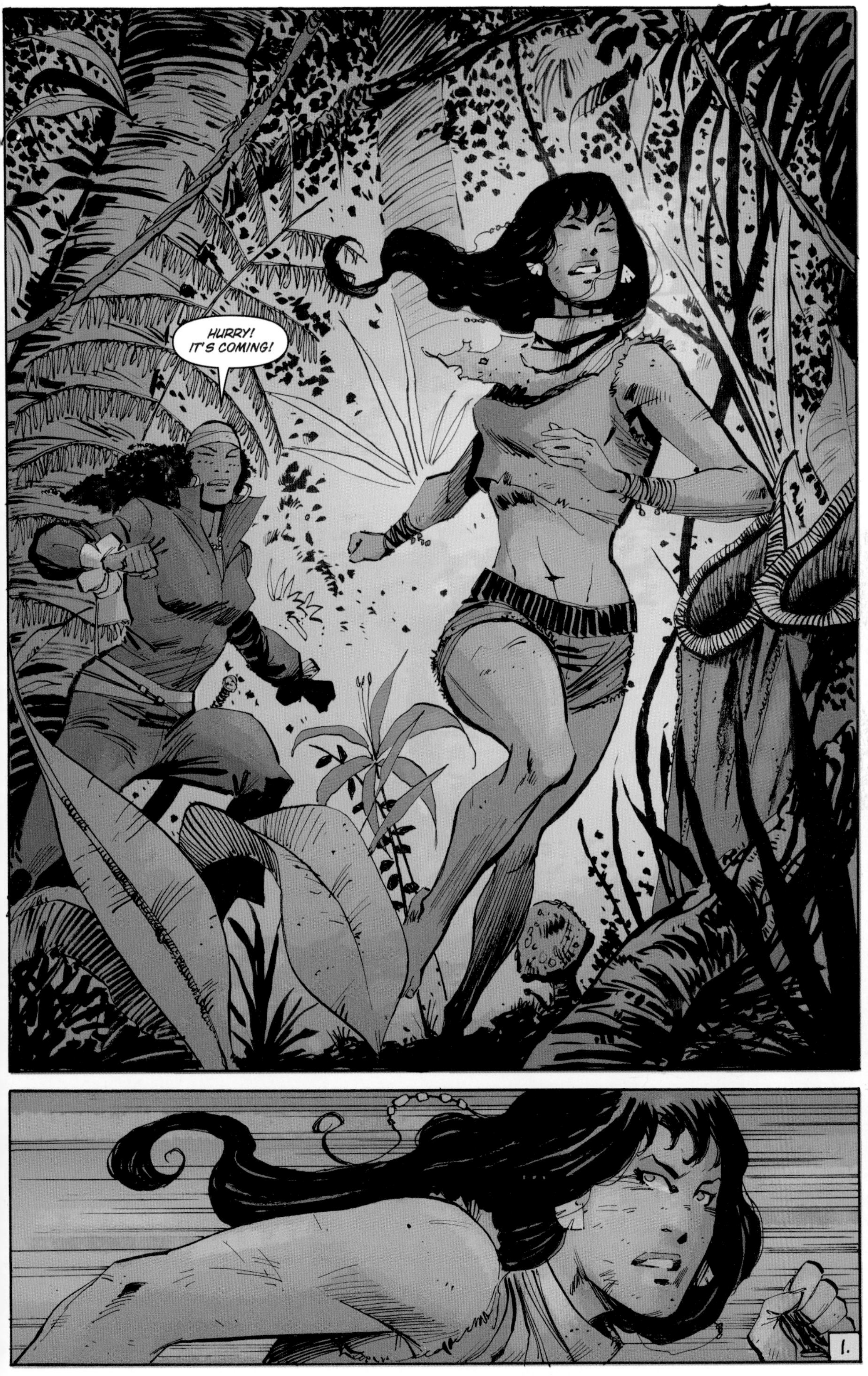
HURRY! IT'S COMING!

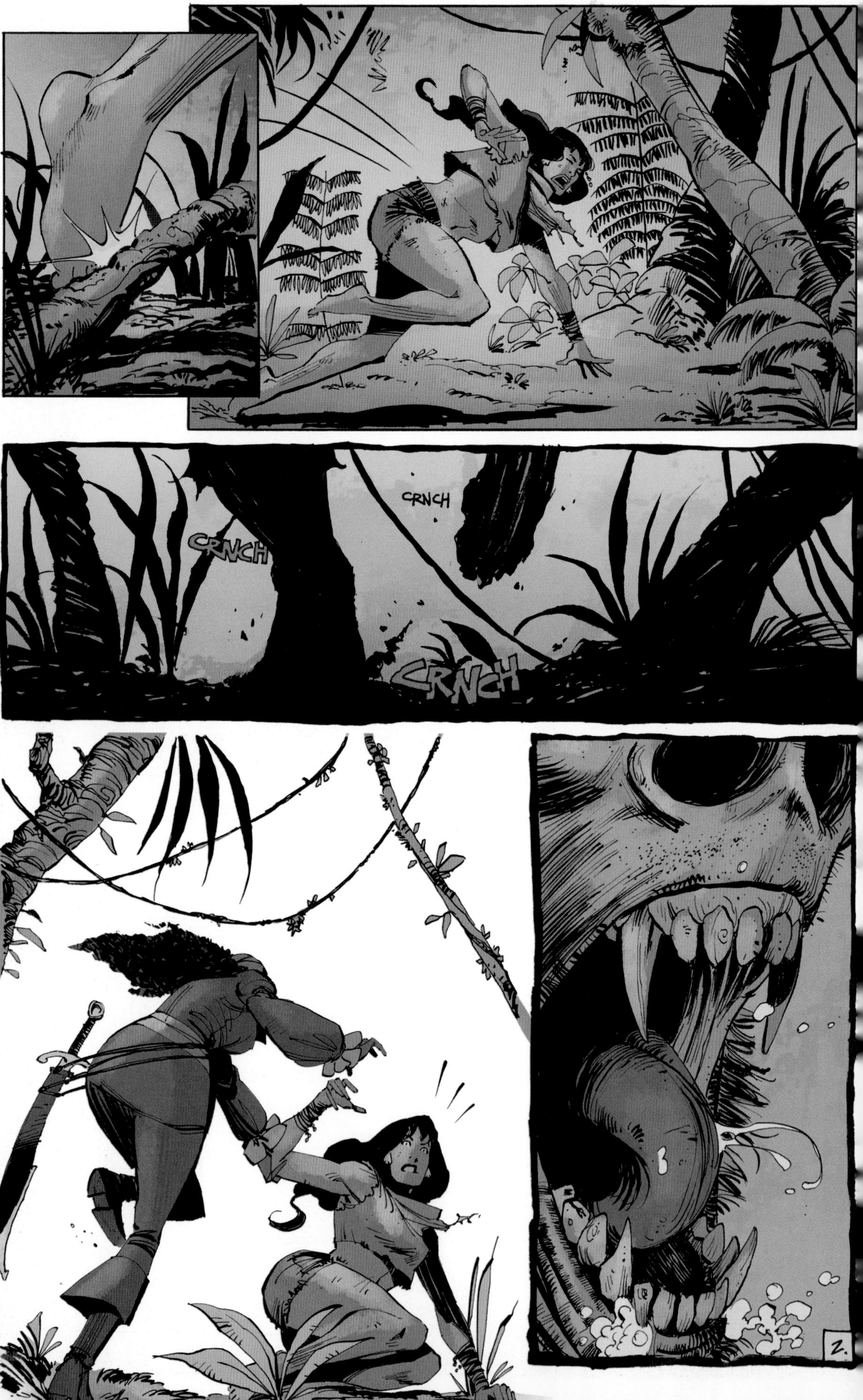

CRNCH
CRNCH
CRNCH

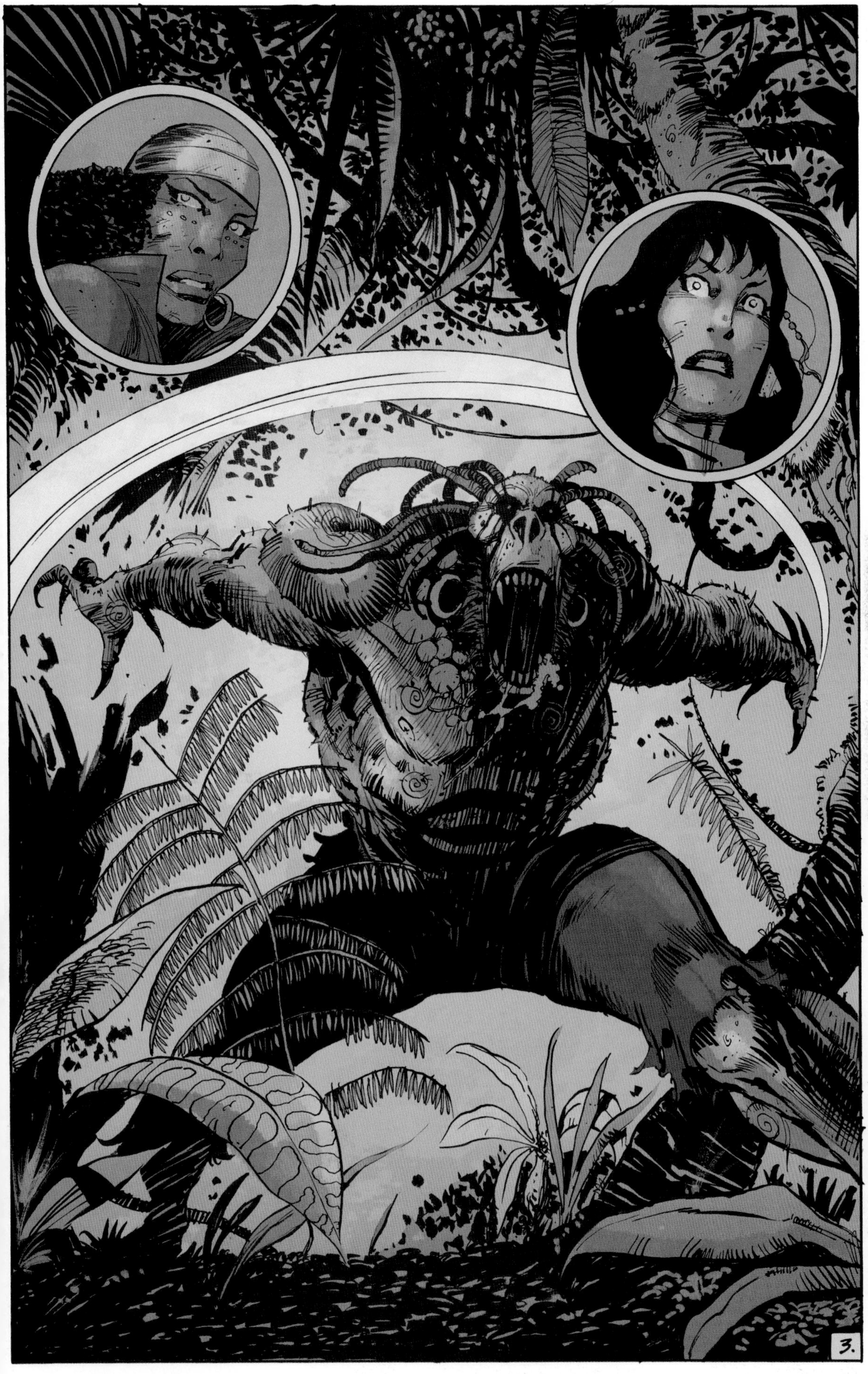

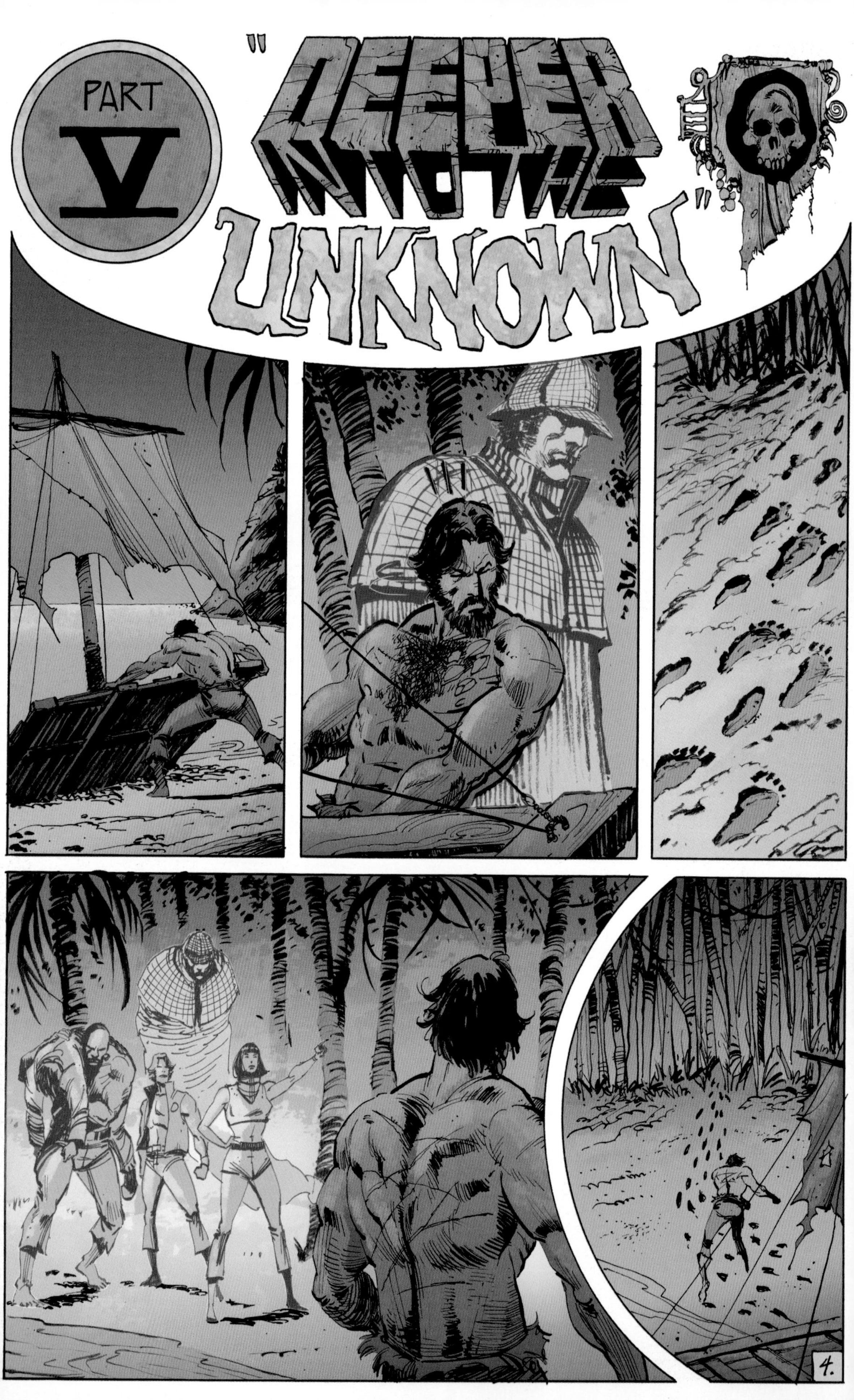
PART
V
"DEEPER INTO THE
UNKNOWN"
4.

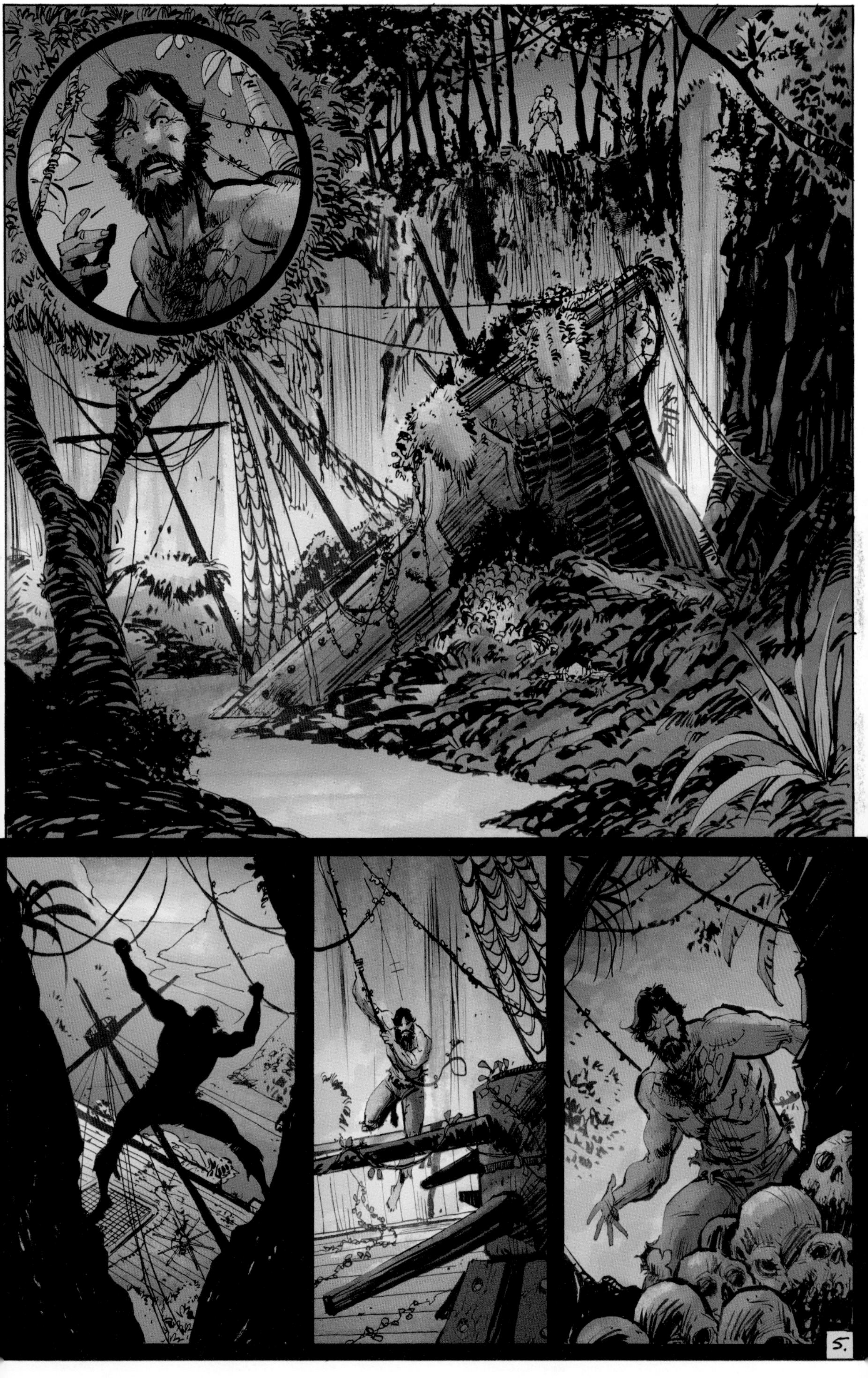

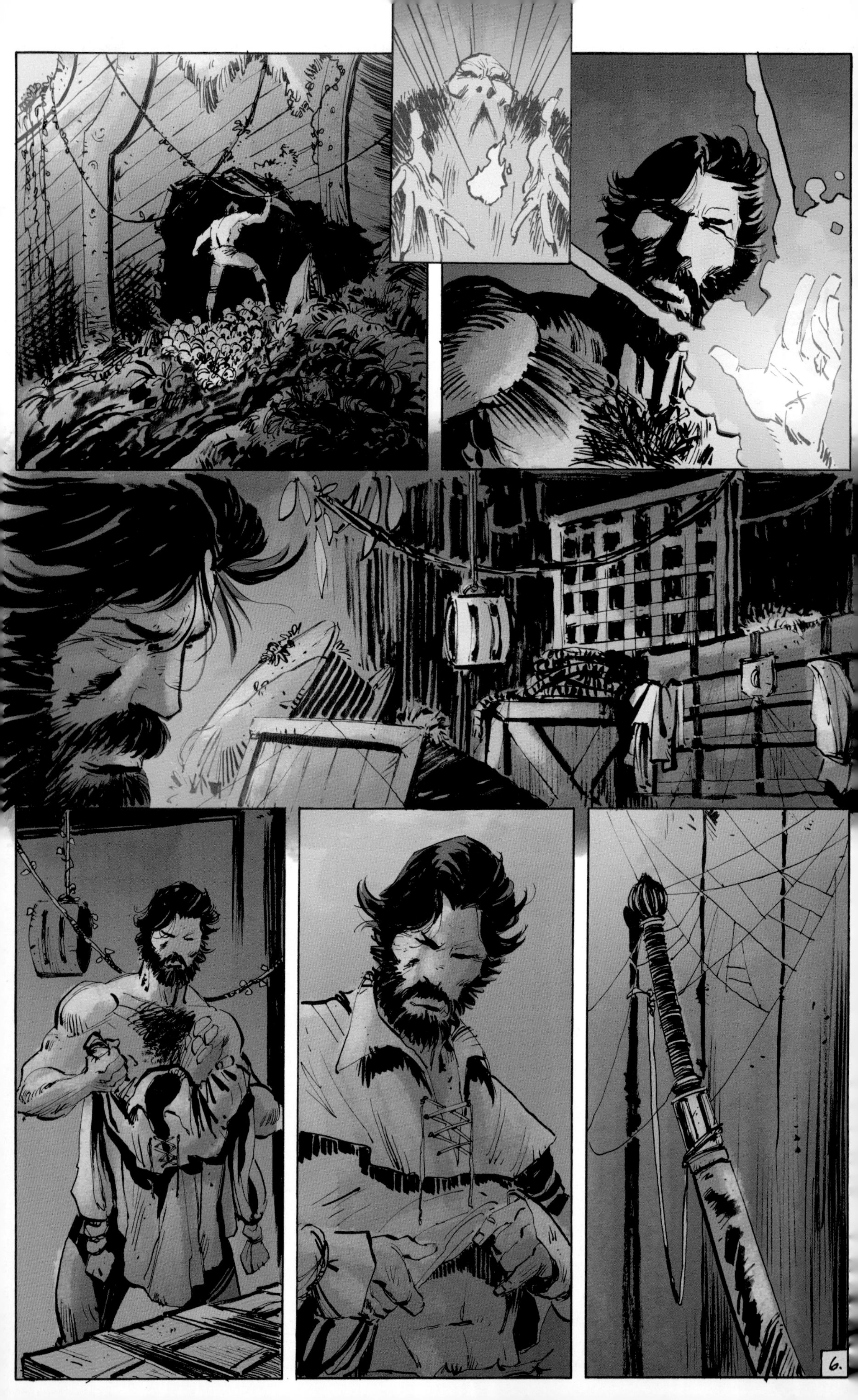
6.

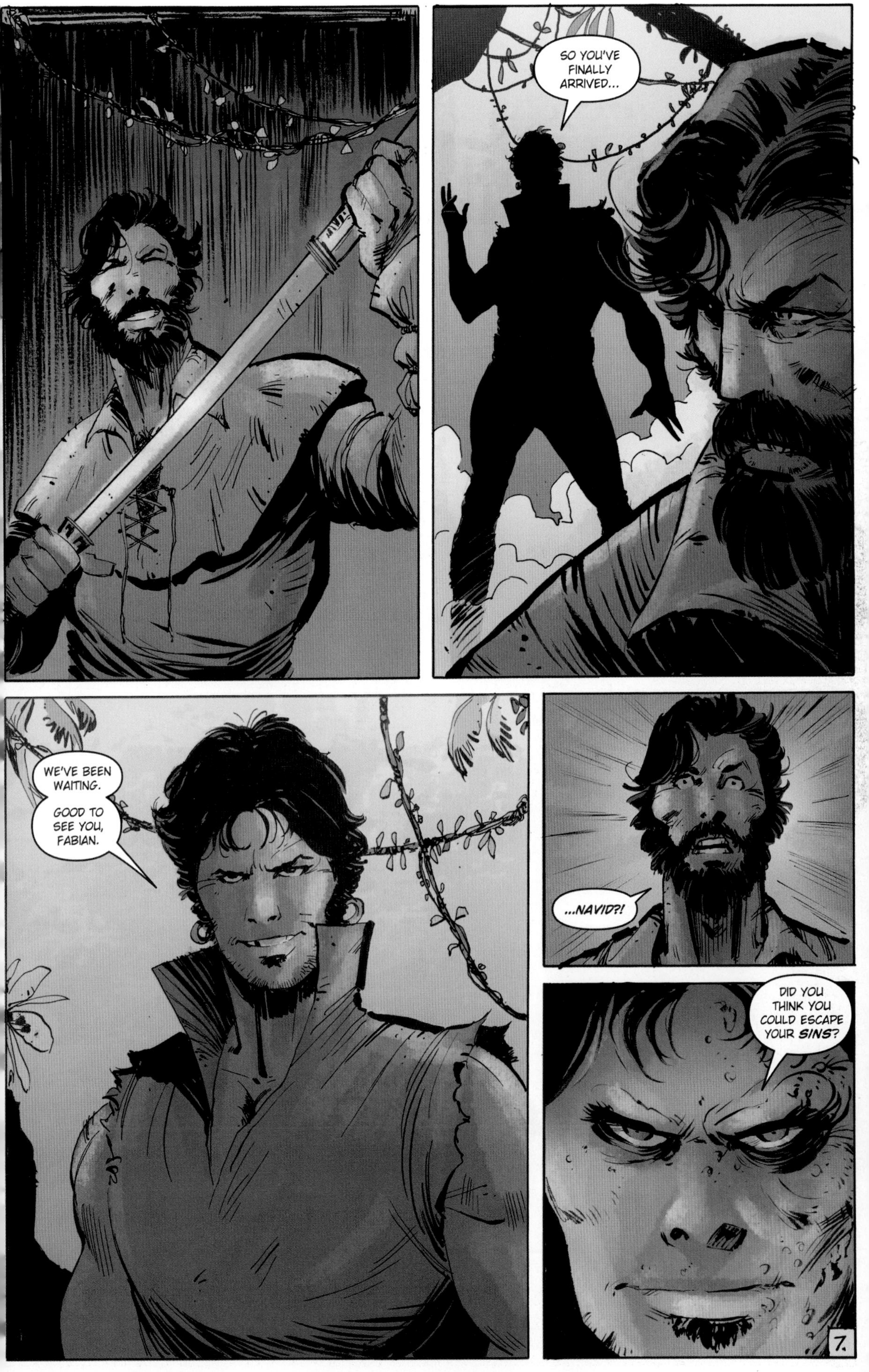

SO YOU'VE FINALLY ARRIVED...
WE'VE BEEN WAITING.
GOOD TO SEE YOU, FABIAN.
...NAVID?!
DID YOU THINK YOU COULD ESCAPE YOUR SINS?

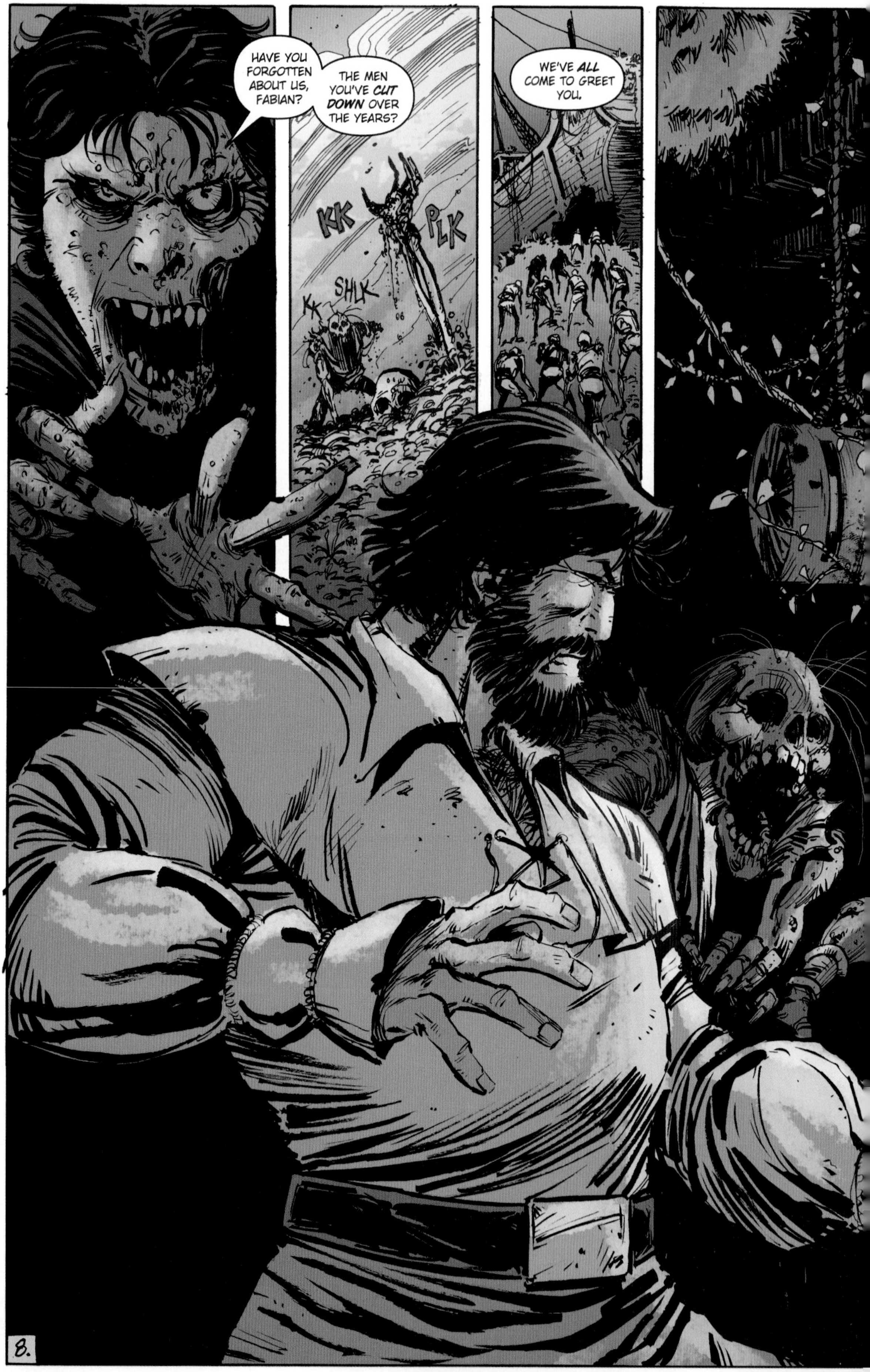
HAVE YOU FORGOTTEN ABOUT US, FABIAN?
THE MEN YOU'VE CUT DOWN OVER THE YEARS?
KK
PLK
SHLK
KK
WE'VE ALL COME TO GREET YOU.

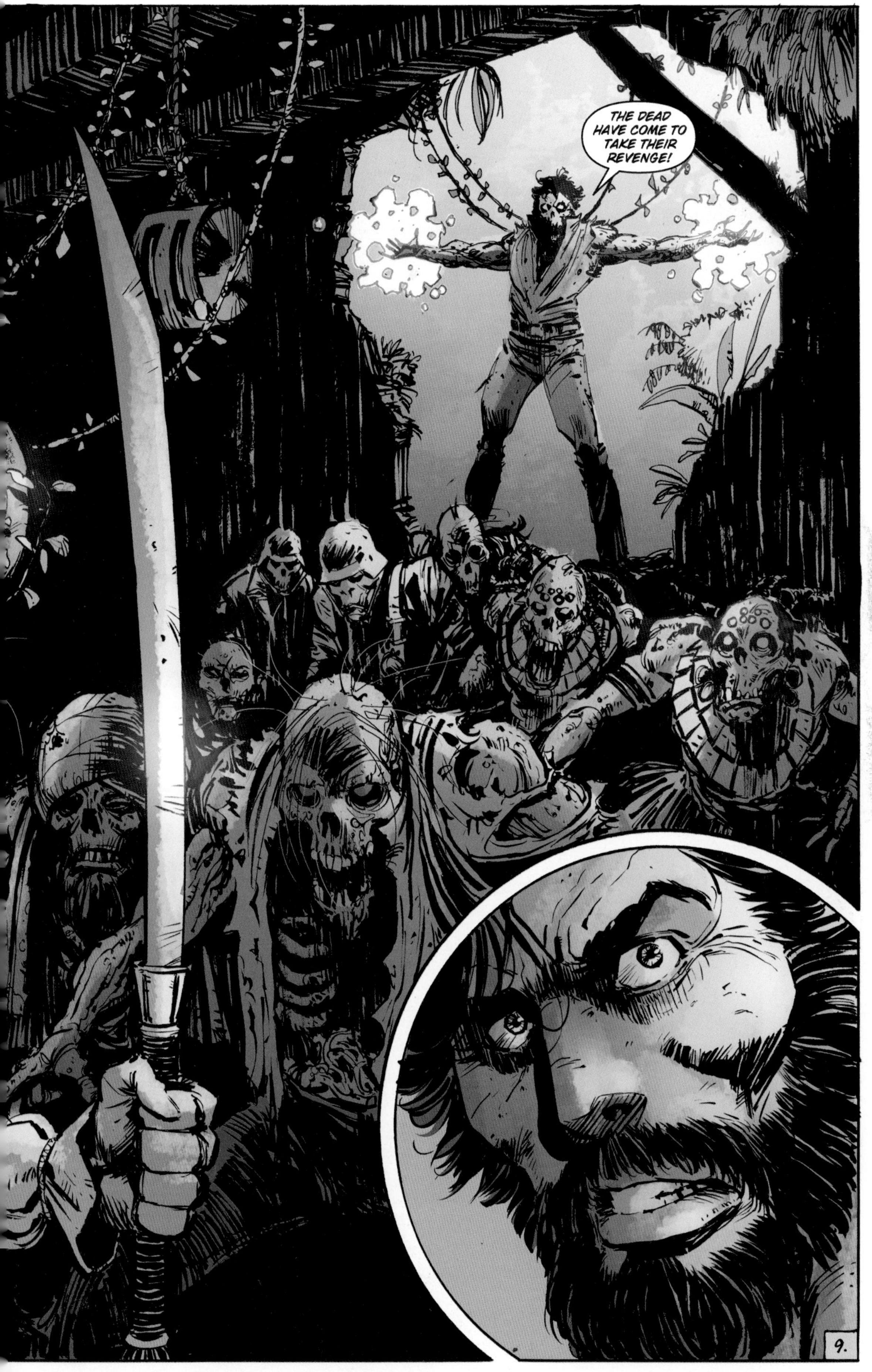
THE DEAD HAVE COME TO TAKE THEIR REVENGE!

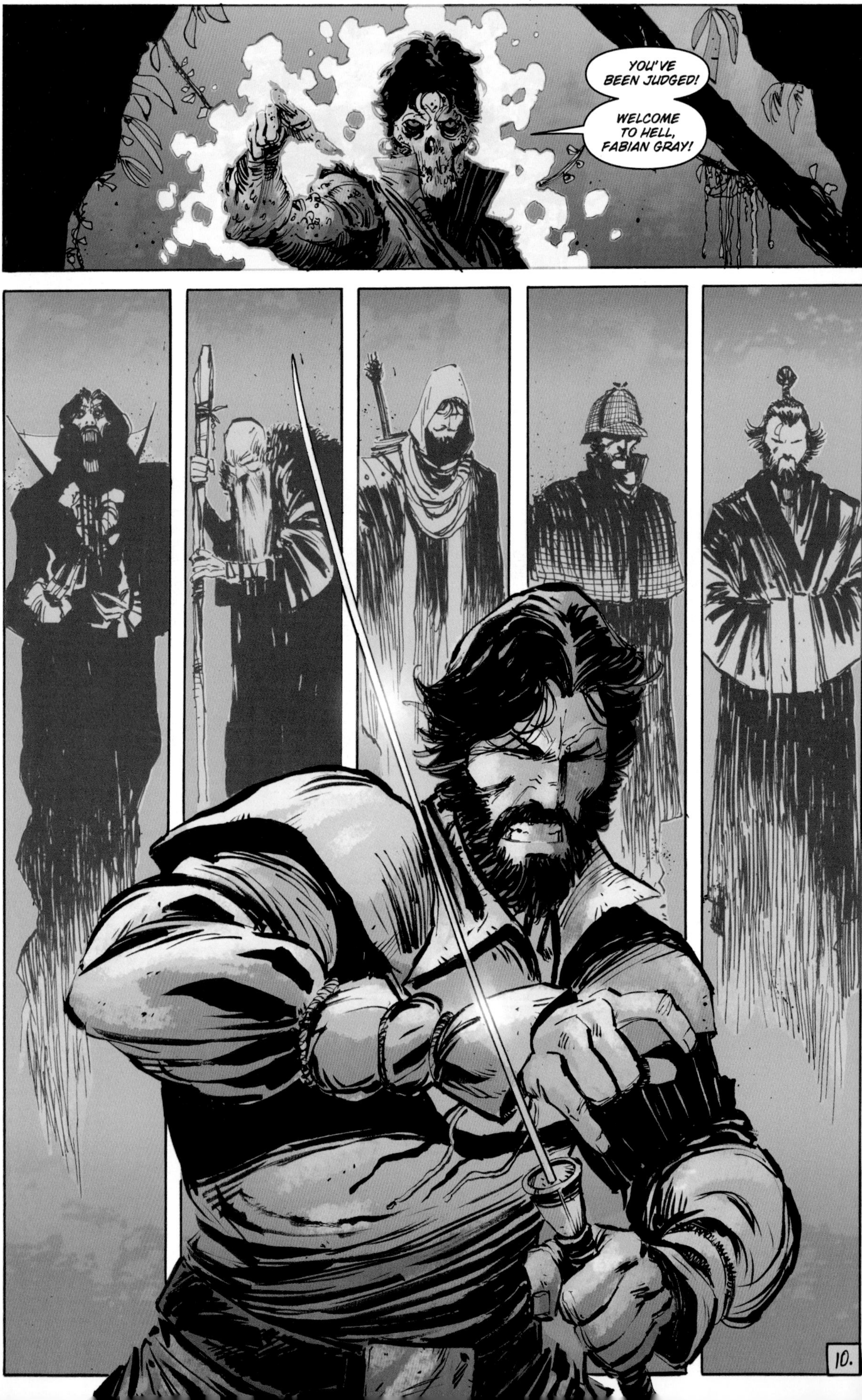
YOU'VE BEEN JUDGED!
WELCOME TO HELL, FABIAN GRAY!
10.

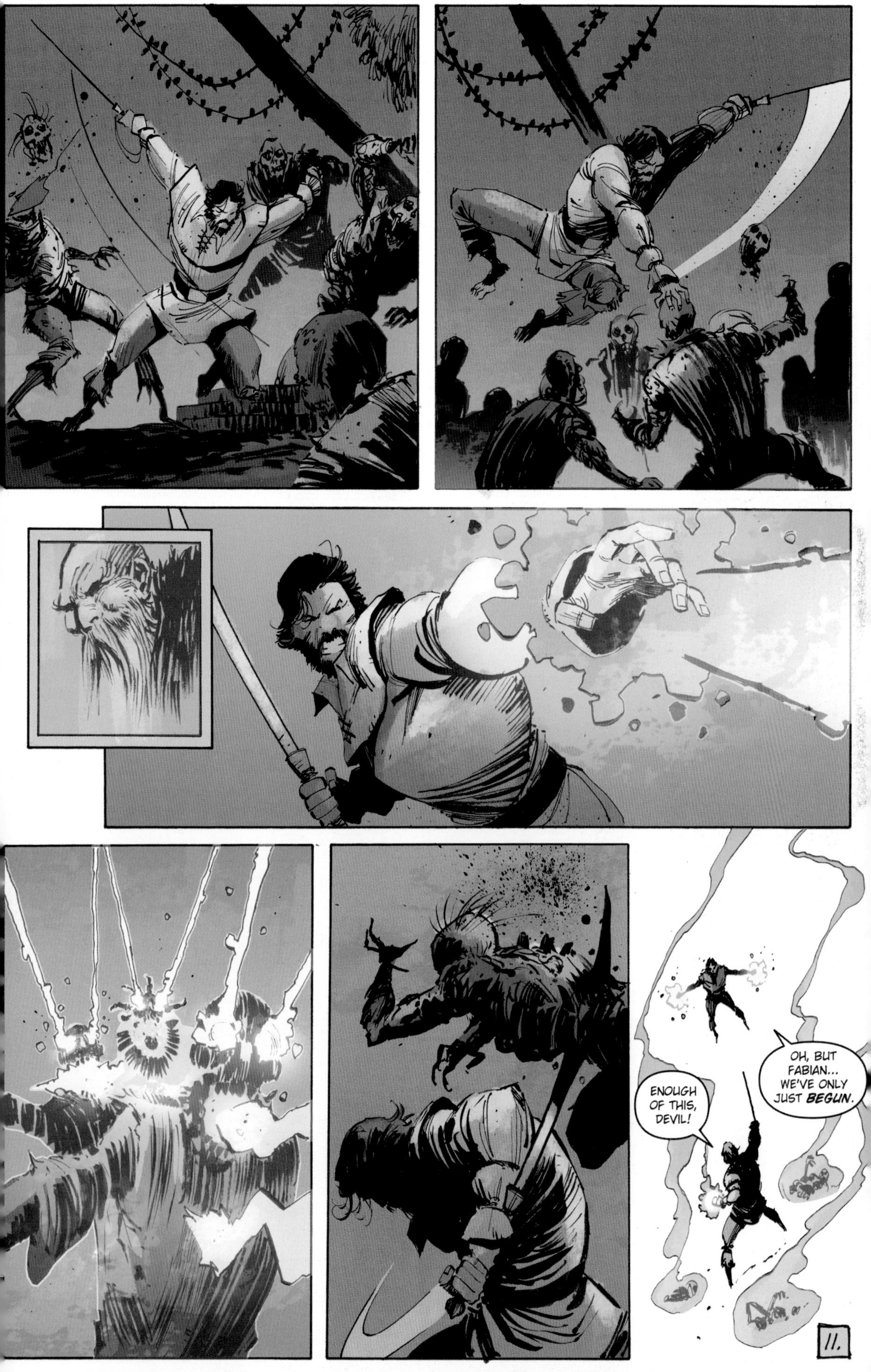

ENOUGH OF THIS, DEVIL!
OH, BUT FABIAN... WE'VE ONLY JUST BEGUN.

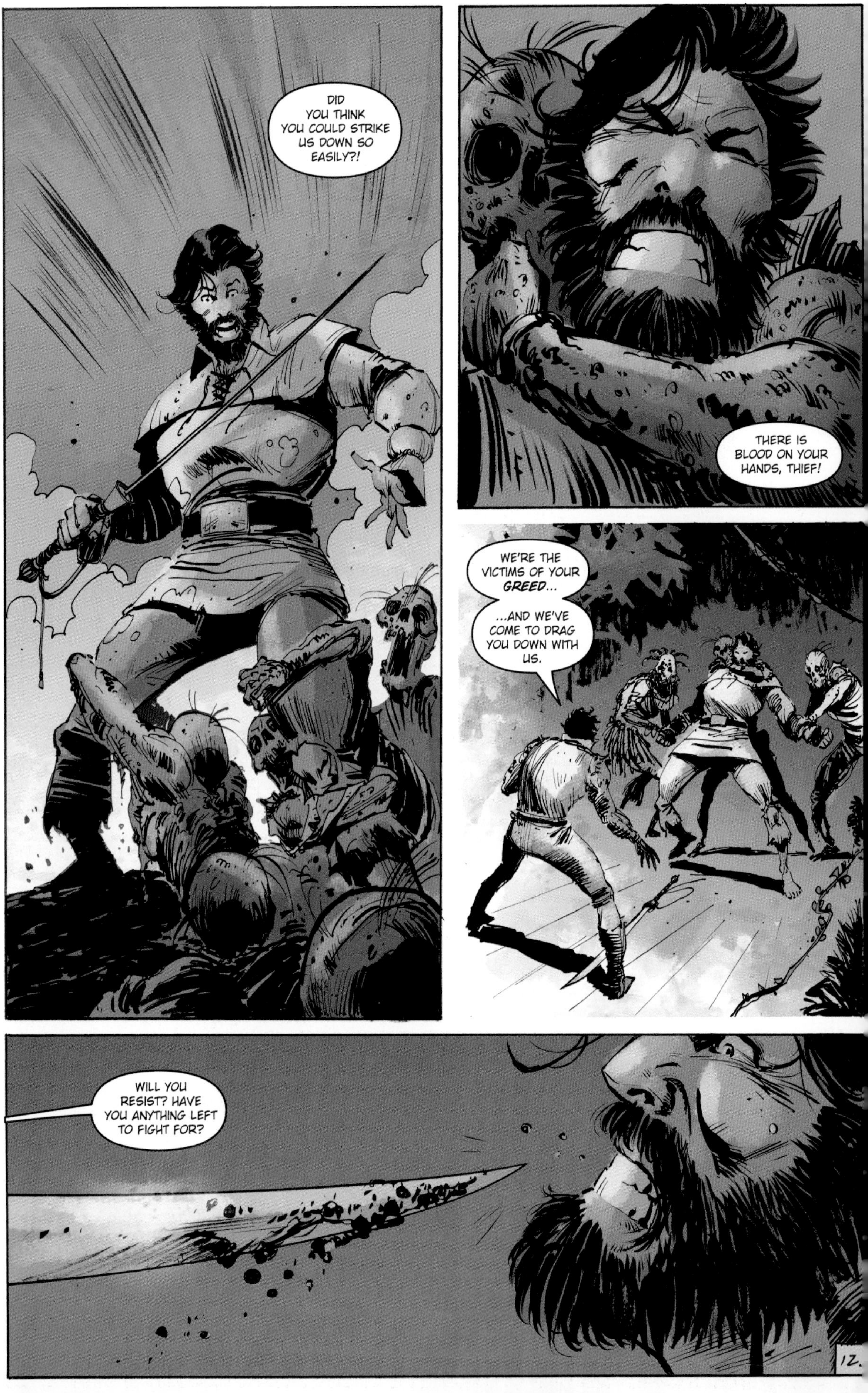
DID YOU THINK YOU COULD STRIKE US DOWN SO EASILY?!
THERE IS BLOOD ON YOUR HANDS, THIEF!
WE'RE THE VICTIMS OF YOUR **GREED**...
...AND WE'VE COME TO DRAG YOU DOWN WITH US.
WILL YOU RESIST? HAVE YOU ANYTHING LEFT TO FIGHT FOR?
12.

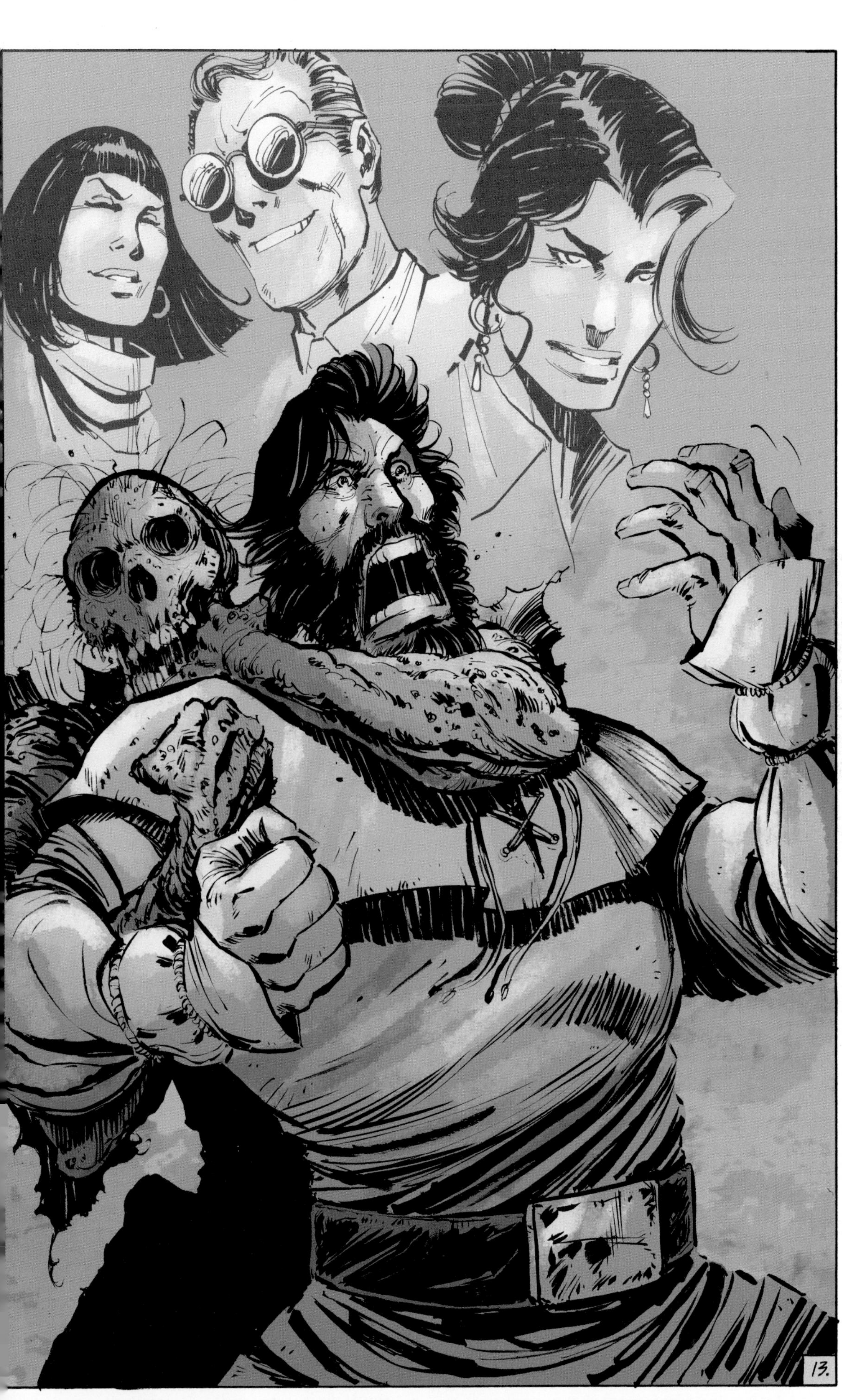

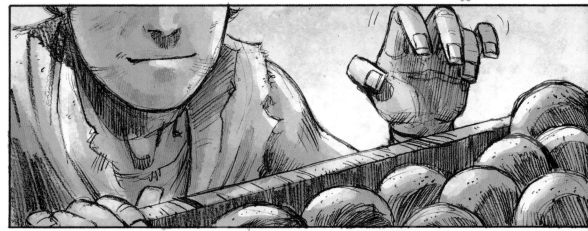

14

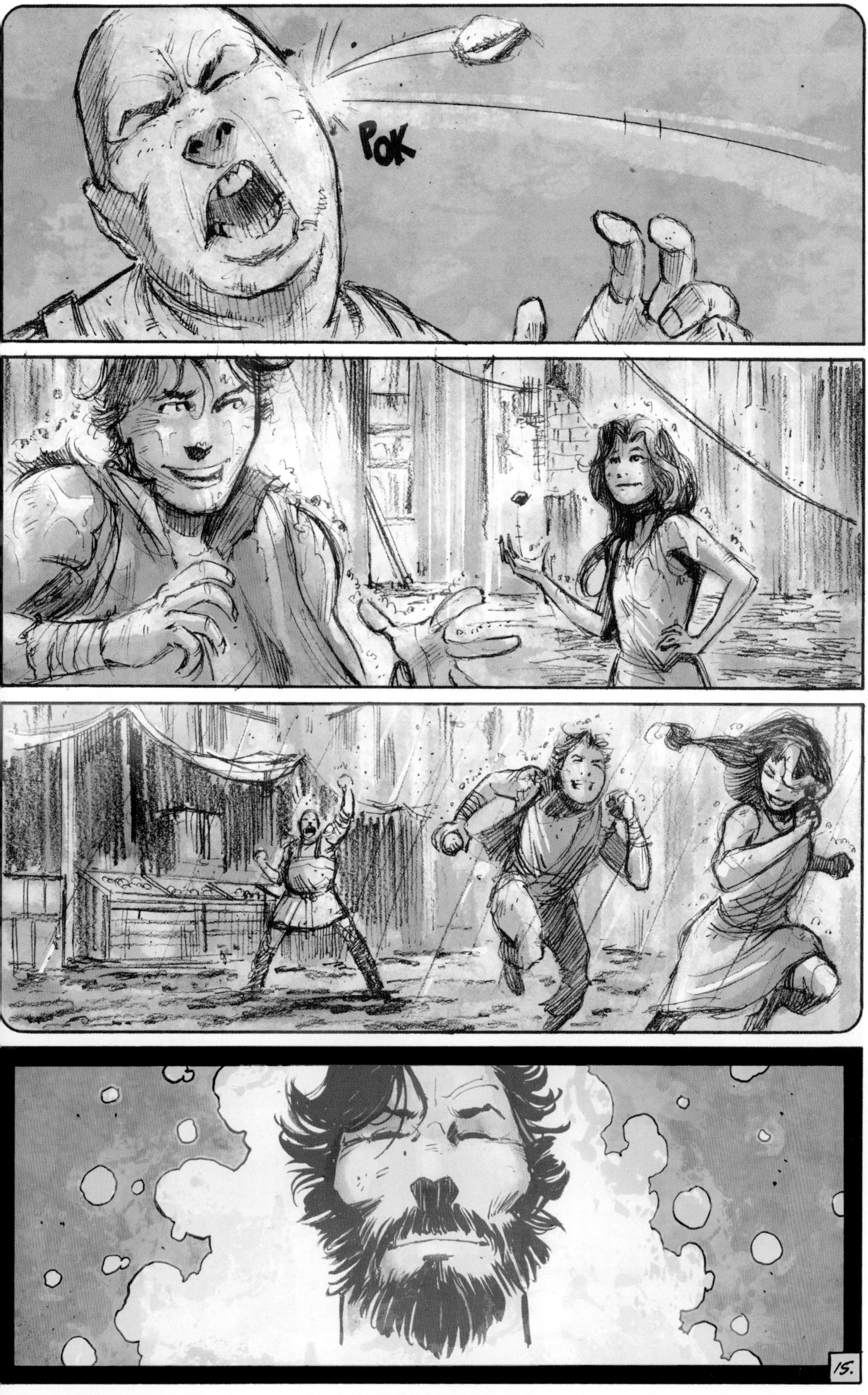
POK

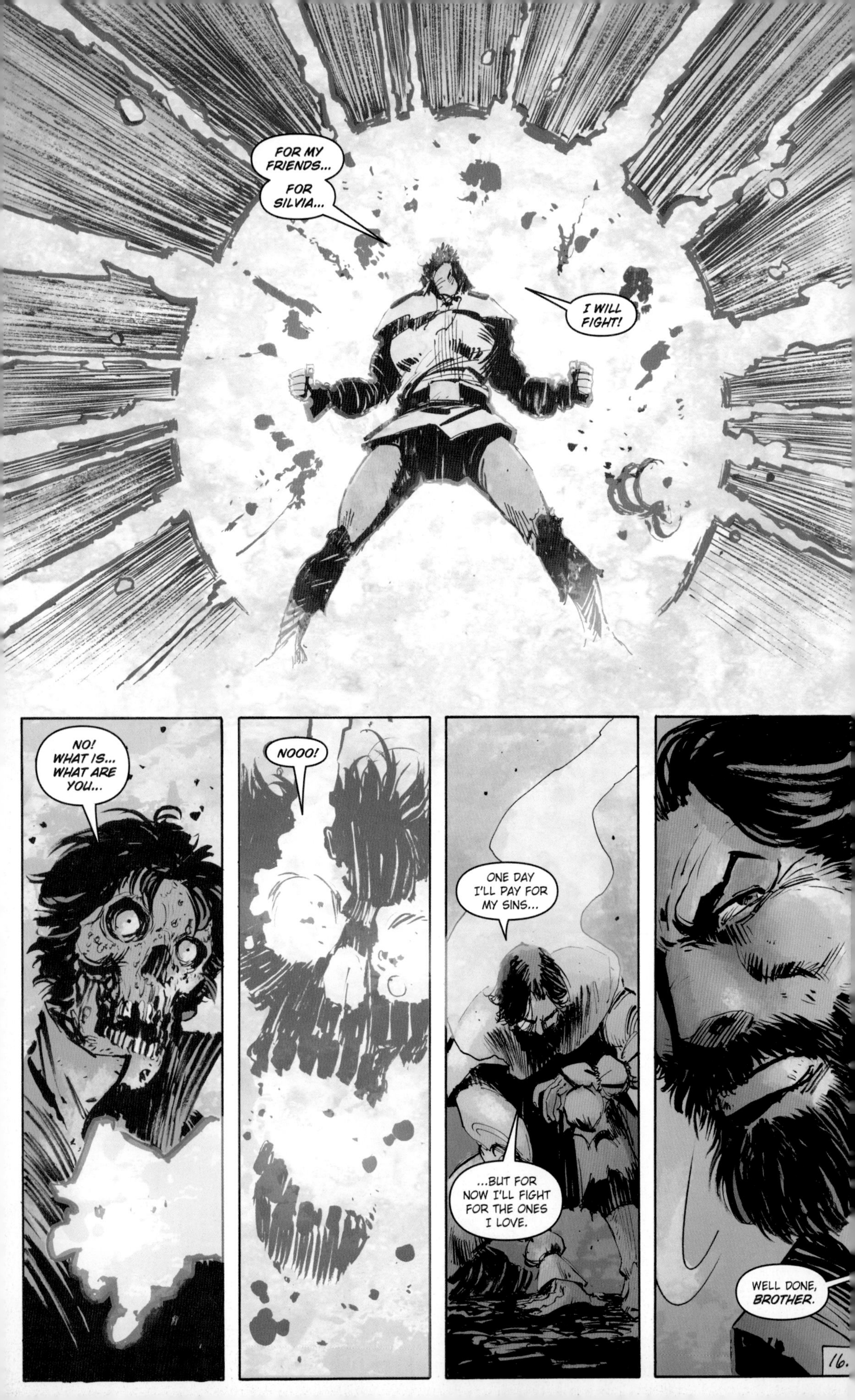
FOR MY FRIENDS...
FOR SILVIA...
I WILL FIGHT!
NO! WHAT IS... WHAT ARE YOU...
NOOO!
ONE DAY I'LL PAY FOR MY SINS...
...BUT FOR NOW I'LL FIGHT FOR THE ONES I LOVE.
WELL DONE, BROTHER.
16.

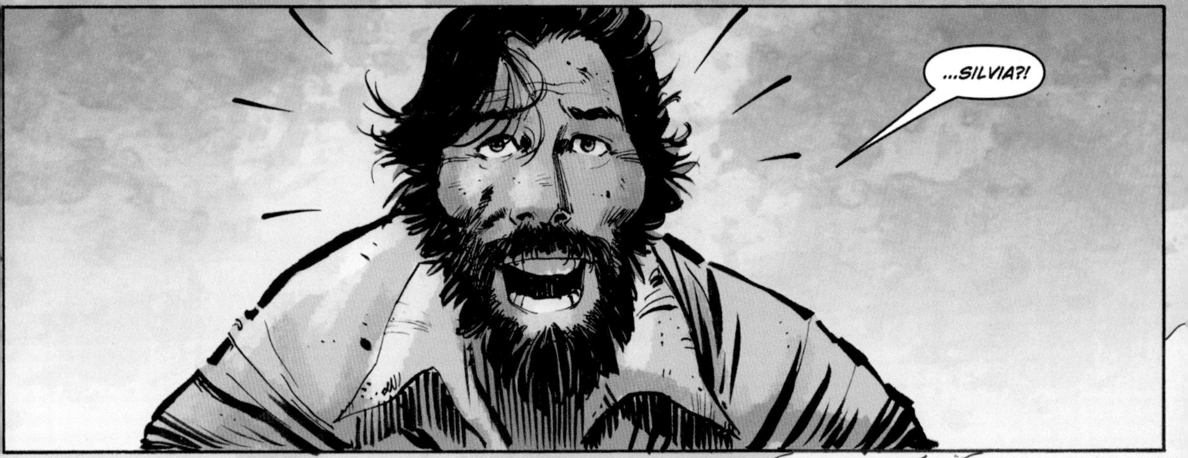
...SILVIA?!

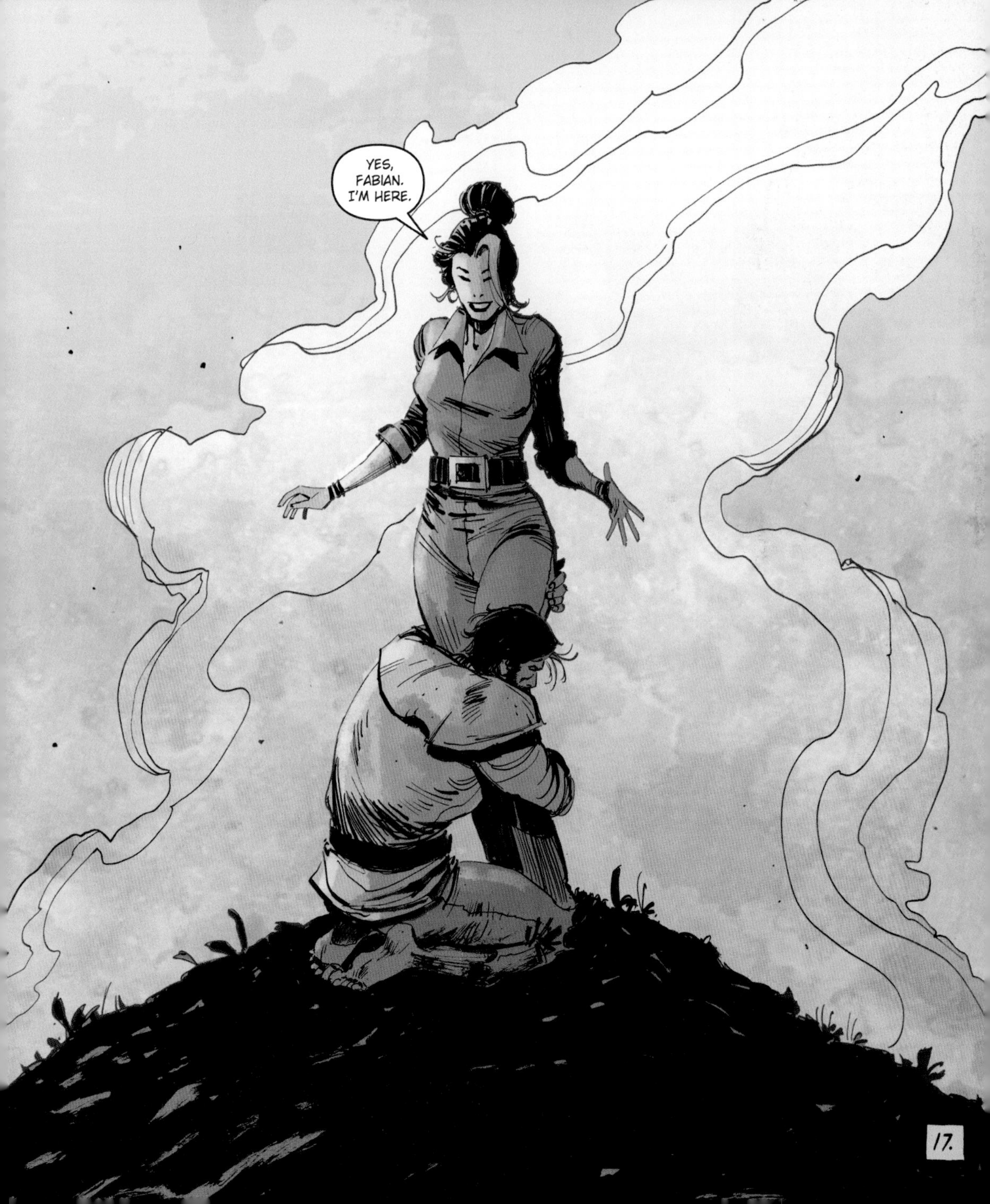
YES, FABIAN. I'M HERE.

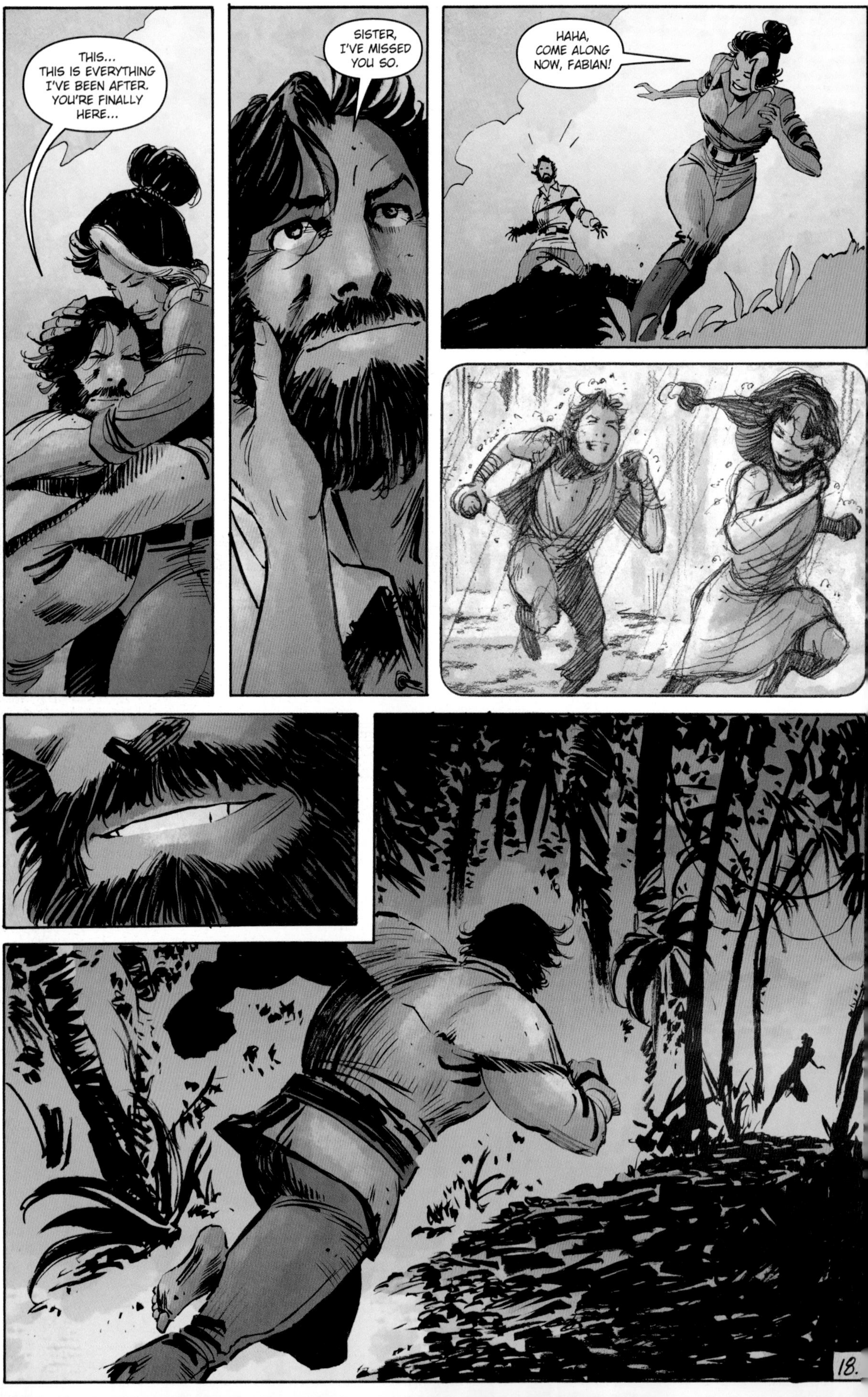
THIS... THIS IS EVERYTHING I'VE BEEN AFTER. YOU'RE FINALLY HERE...
SISTER, I'VE MISSED YOU SO.
HAHA, COME ALONG NOW, FABIAN!

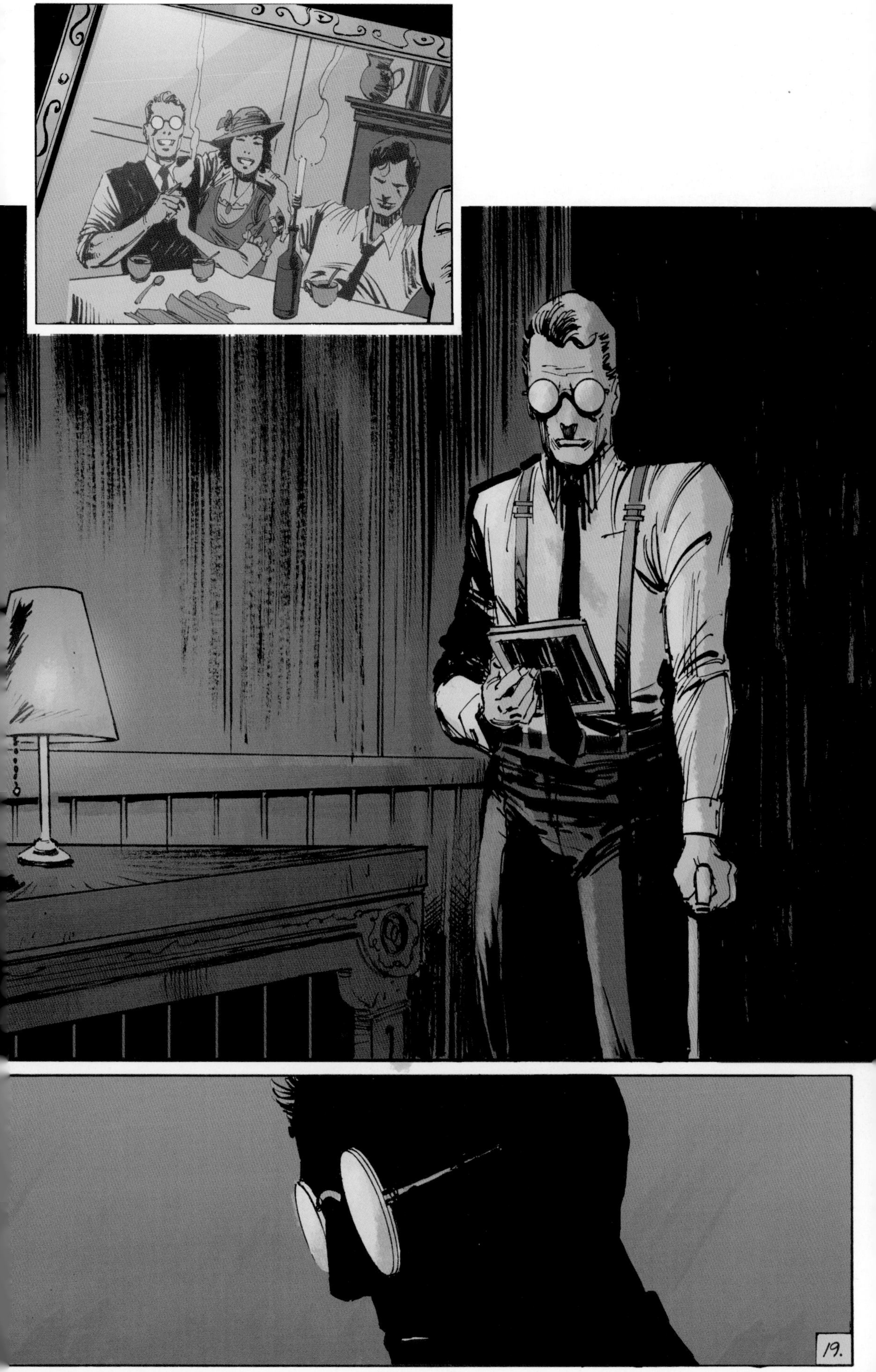

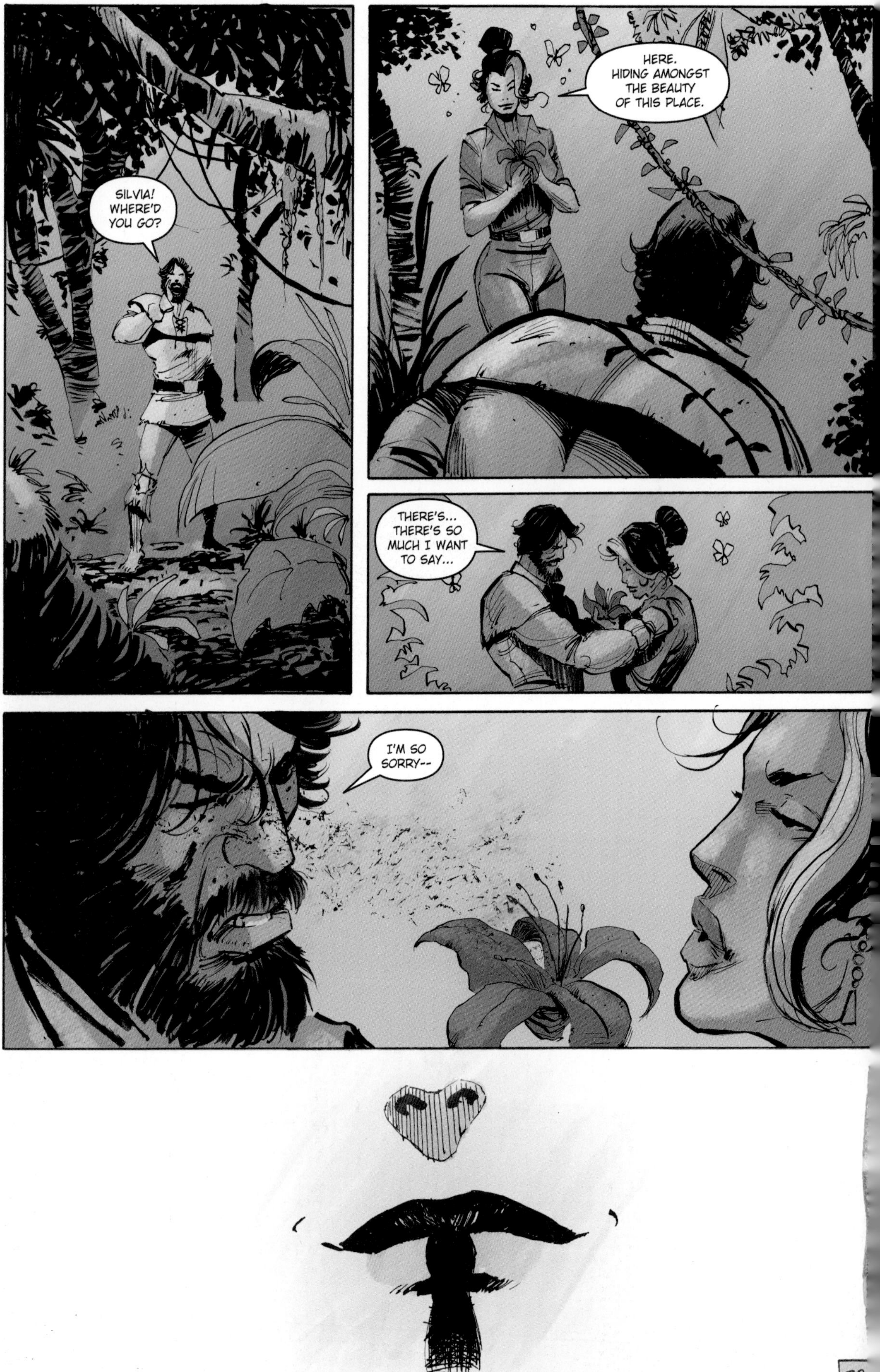
SILVIA! WHERE'D YOU GO?
HERE. HIDING AMONGST THE BEAUTY OF THIS PLACE.
THERE'S... THERE'S SO MUCH I WANT TO SAY...
I'M SO SORRY--

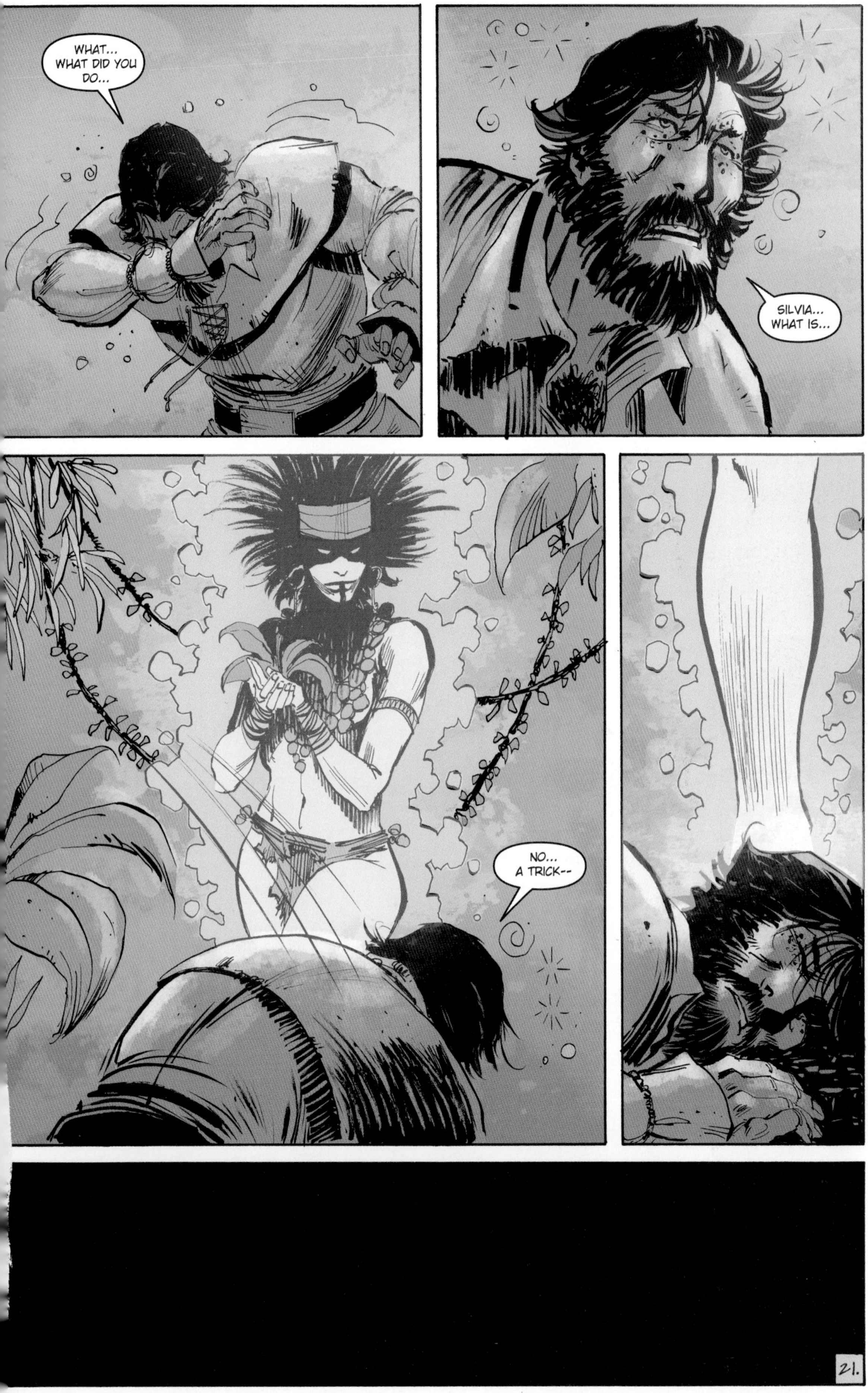
WHAT... WHAT DID YOU DO...
SILVIA... WHAT IS...
NO... A TRICK--

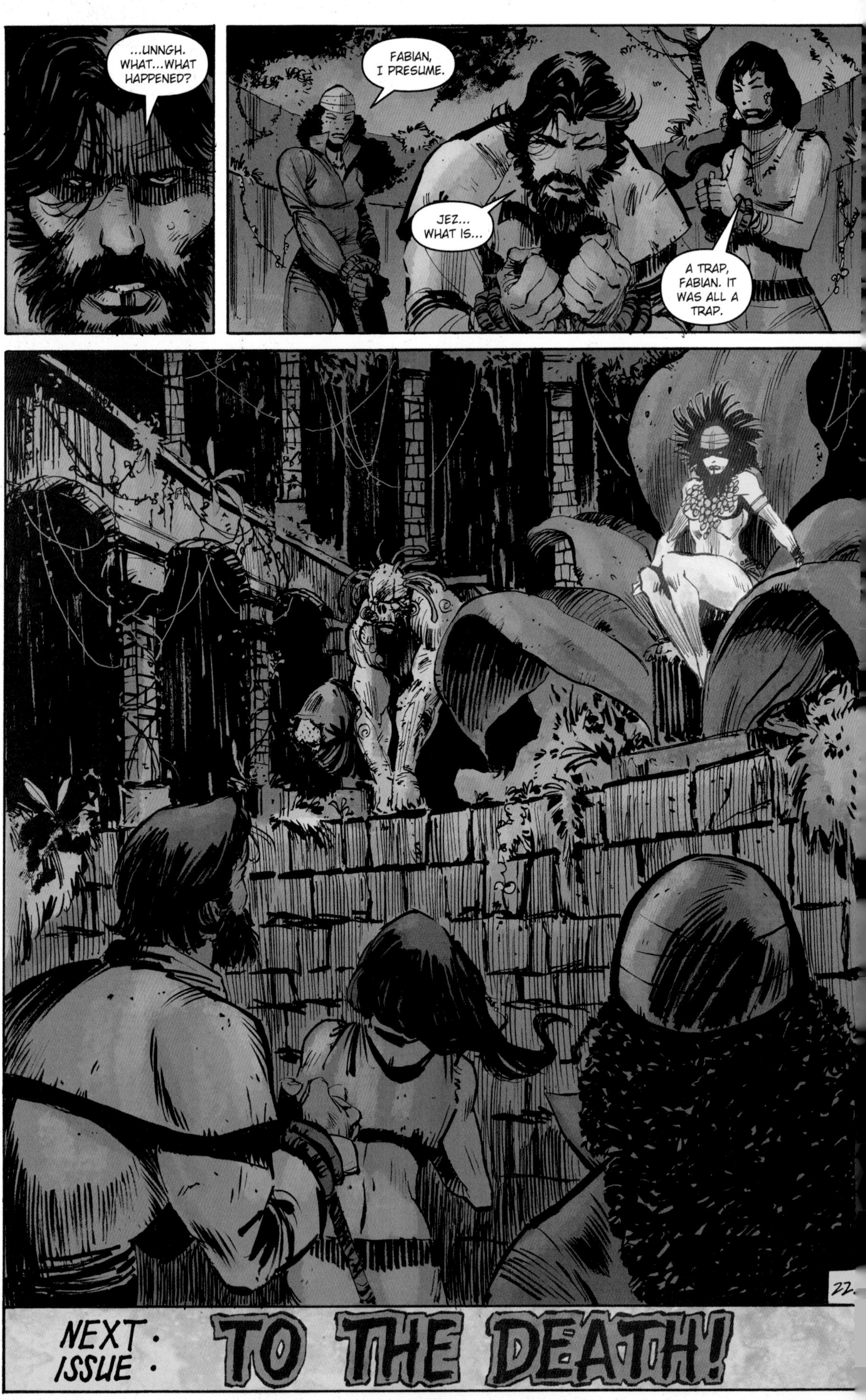
...UNNGH. WHAT...WHAT HAPPENED?
FABIAN, I PRESUME.
JEZ... WHAT IS...
A TRAP, FABIAN. IT WAS ALL A TRAP.
22.
NEXT ISSUE: TO THE DEATH!

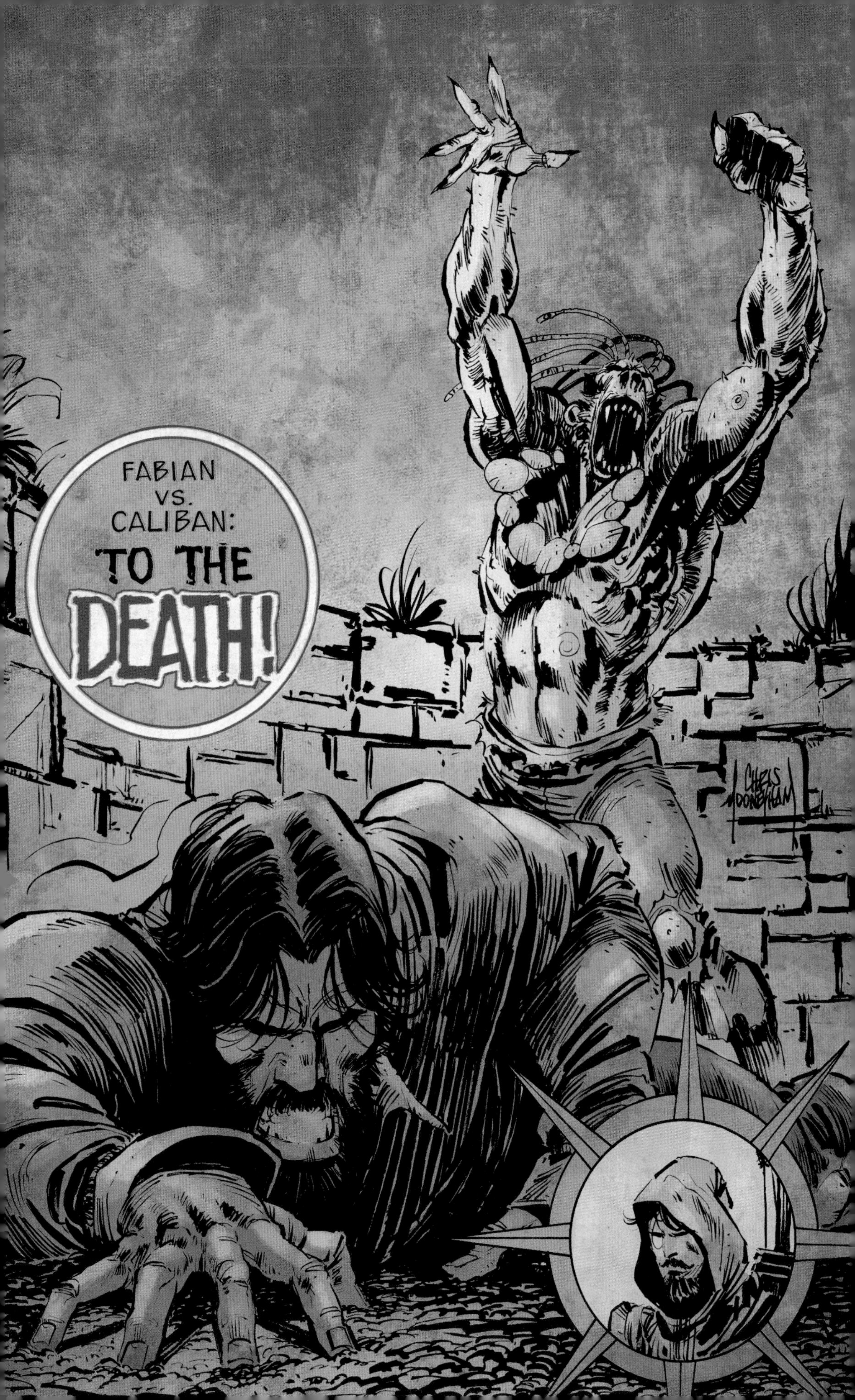
FABIAN
VS.
CALIBAN:
TO THE
DEATH!

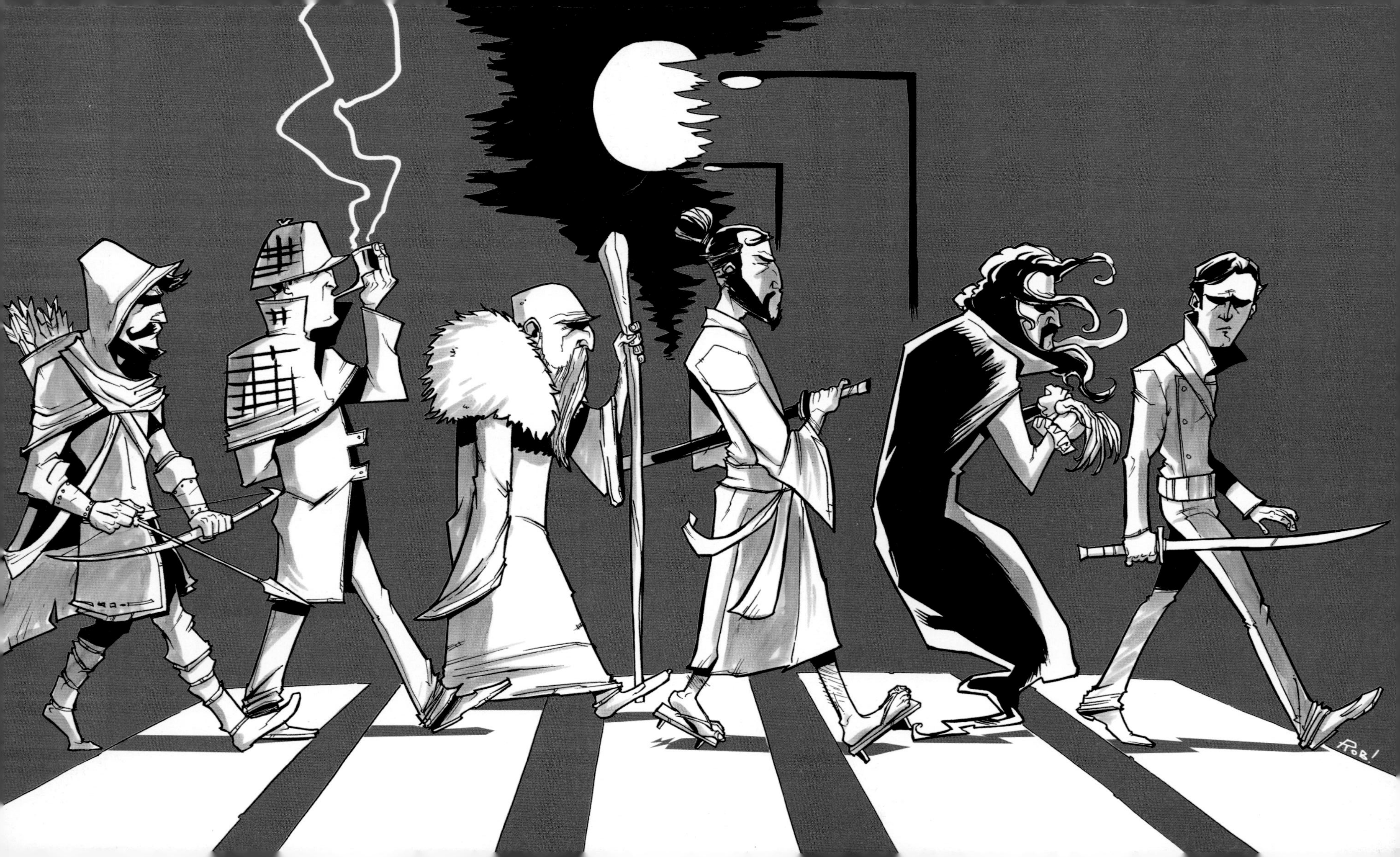
ROB!

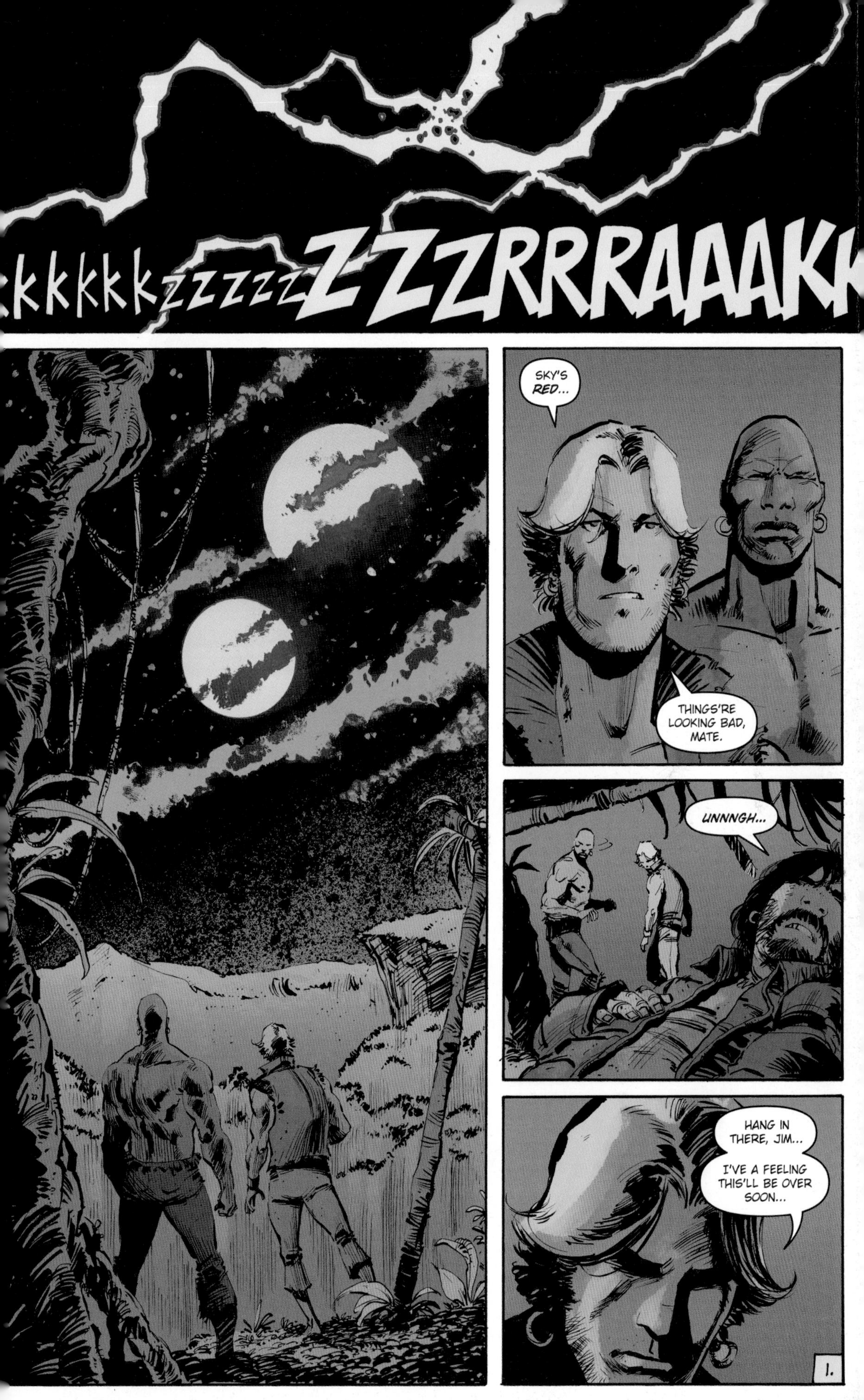
kkkkkzzzzzzZZZRRRAAAK
SKY'S *RED*...
THINGS'RE LOOKING BAD, MATE.
UNNNGH...
HANG IN THERE, JIM...
I'VE A FEELING THIS'LL BE OVER SOON...

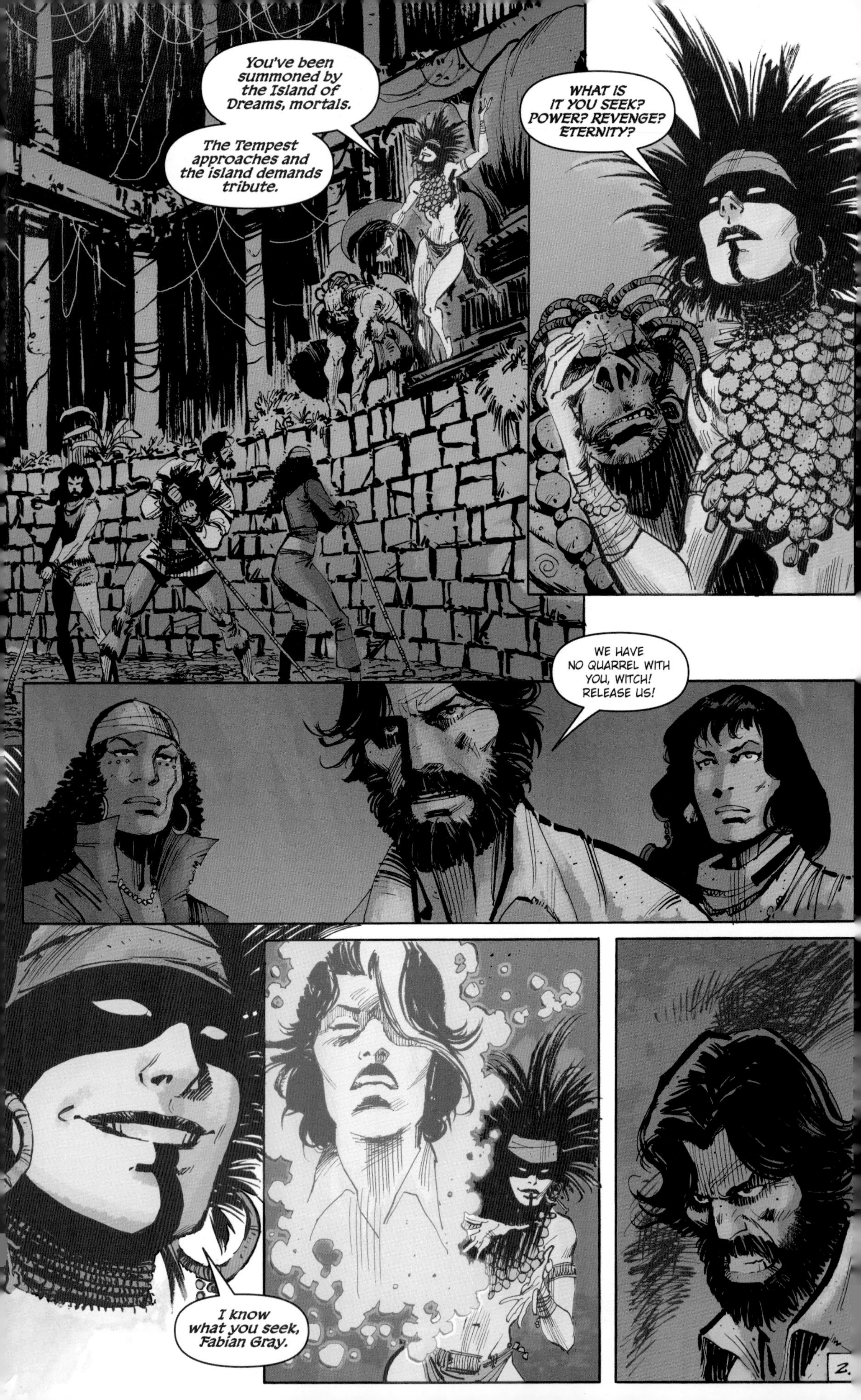
You've been summoned by the Island of Dreams, mortals.
The Tempest approaches and the island demands tribute.
WHAT IS IT YOU SEEK? POWER? REVENGE? ETERNITY?
WE HAVE NO QUARREL WITH YOU, WITCH! RELEASE US!
I know what you seek, Fabian Gray.
2.

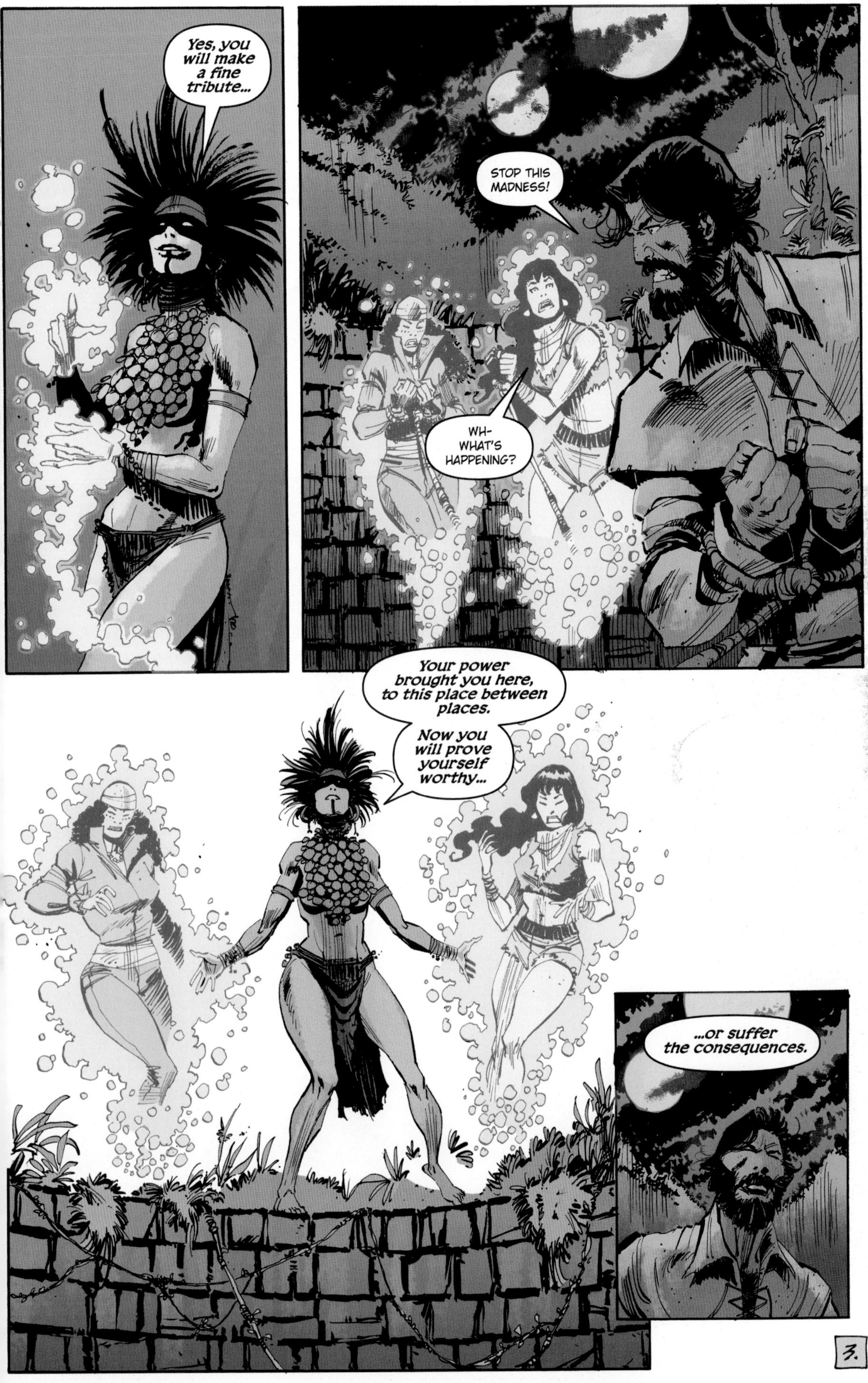
Yes, you will make a fine tribute...
STOP THIS MADNESS!
WH- WHAT'S HAPPENING?
Your power brought you here, to this place between places.
Now you will prove yourself worthy...
...or suffer the consequences.

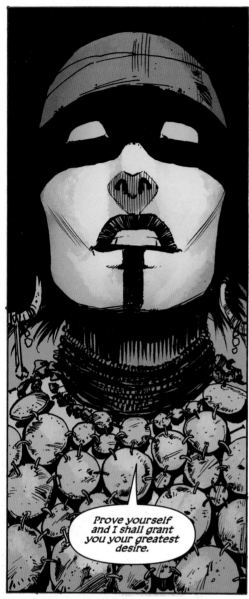

Prove yourself and I shall grant you your greatest desire.

PART
VI

"TO THE
DEATH"

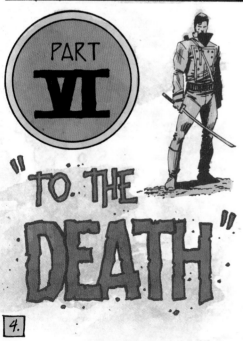

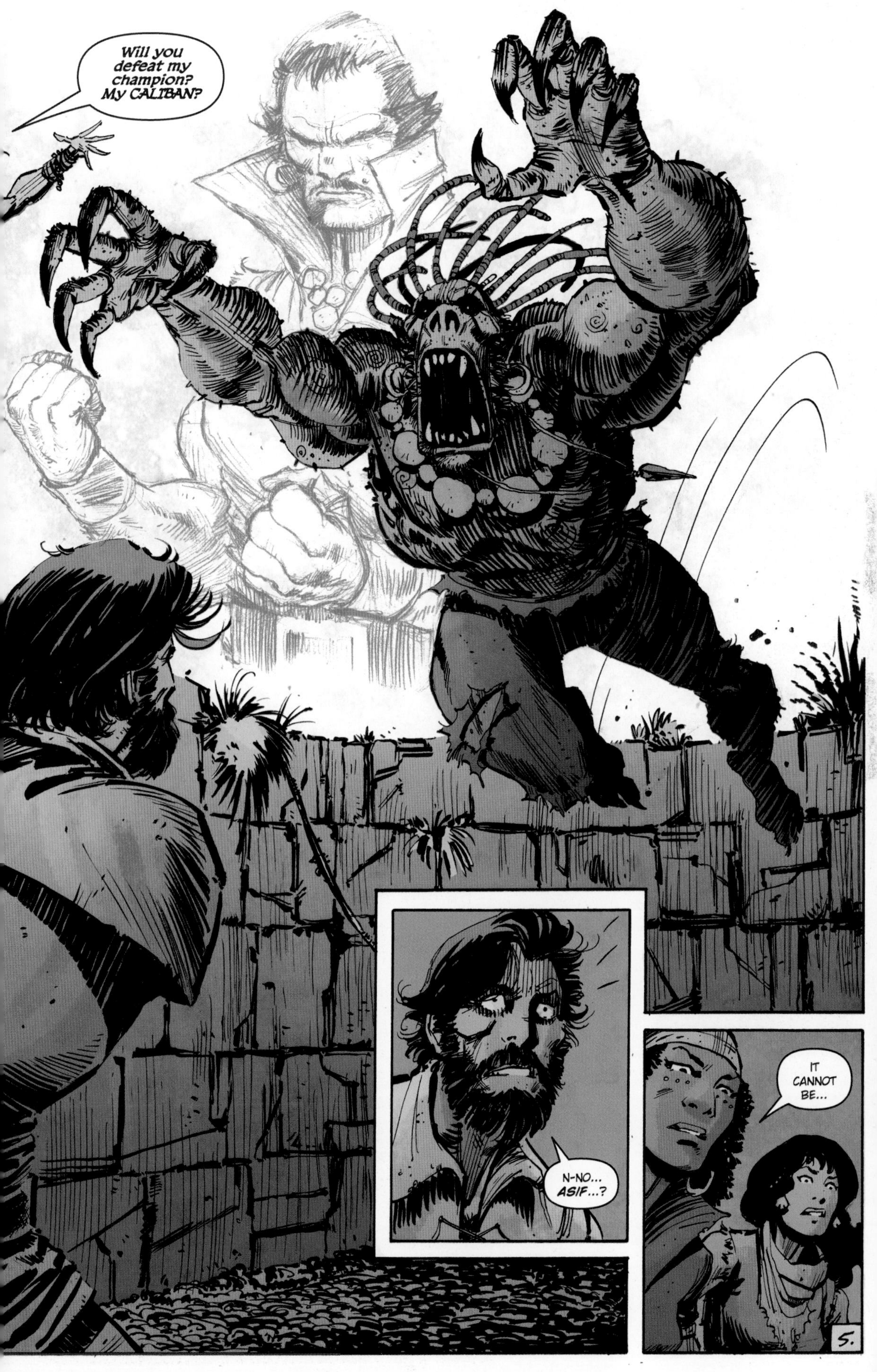
Will you defeat my champion? My CALIBAN?
N-NO... ASIF...?
IT CANNOT BE...
5.

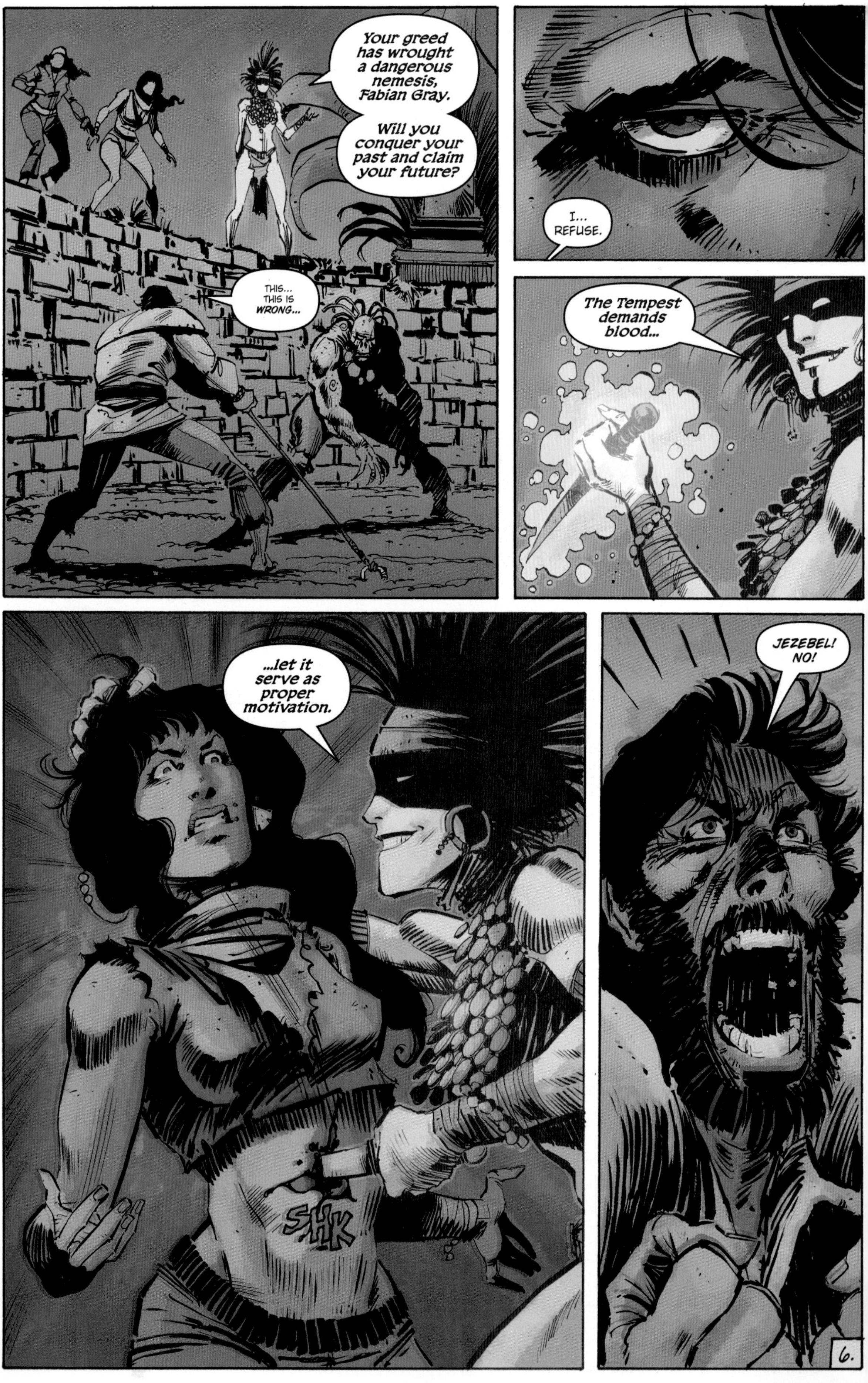
Your greed has wrought a dangerous nemesis, Fabian Gray.
Will you conquer your past and claim your future?
This... this is wrong...
I... Refuse.
The Tempest demands blood...
...let it serve as proper motivation.
SHK
Jezebel! No!
6.

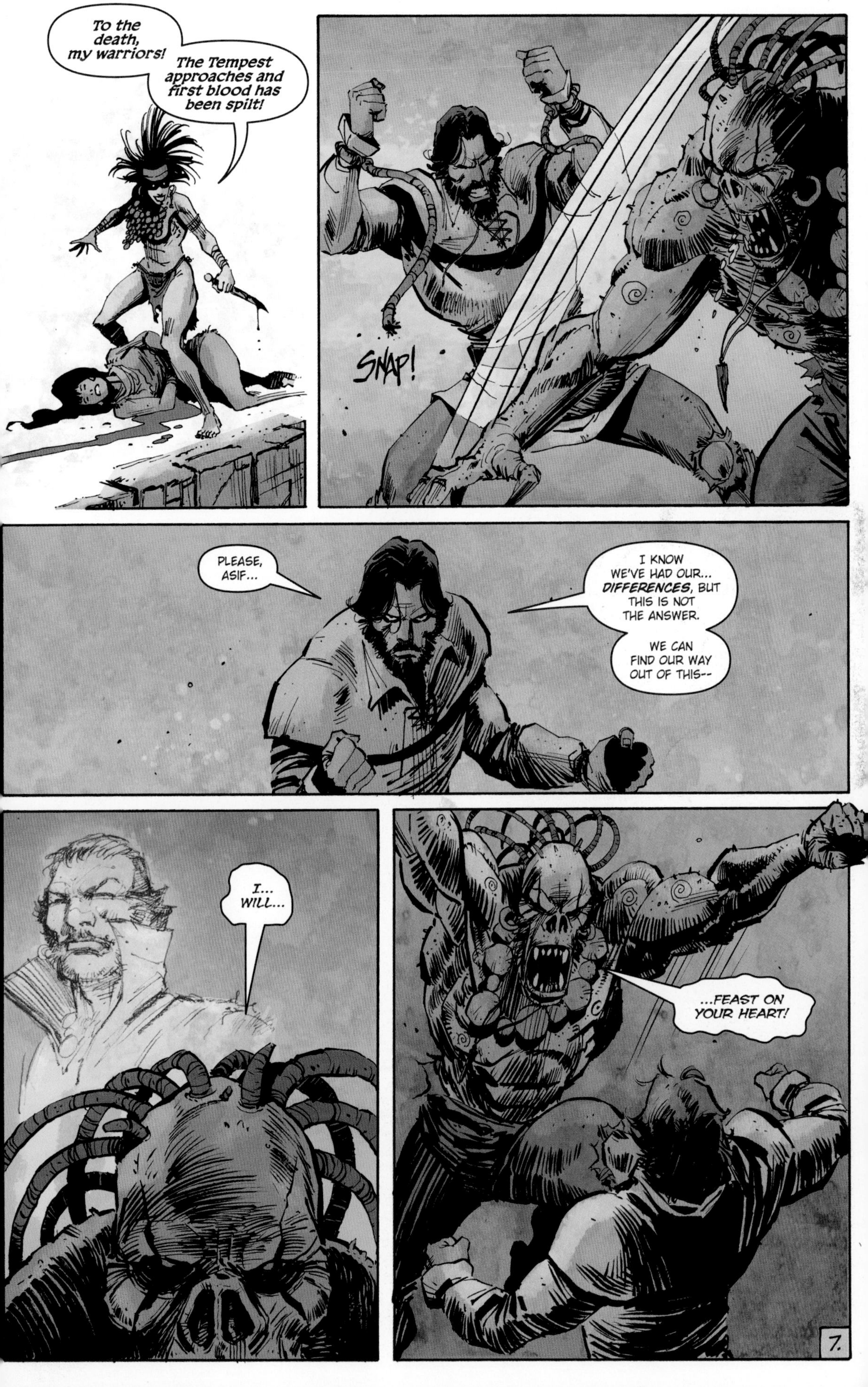
To the death, my warriors!
The Tempest approaches and first blood has been spilt!
SNAP!
PLEASE, ASIF...
I KNOW WE'VE HAD OUR... DIFFERENCES, BUT THIS IS NOT THE ANSWER.
WE CAN FIND OUR WAY OUT OF THIS--
I... WILL...
...FEAST ON YOUR HEART!
7.

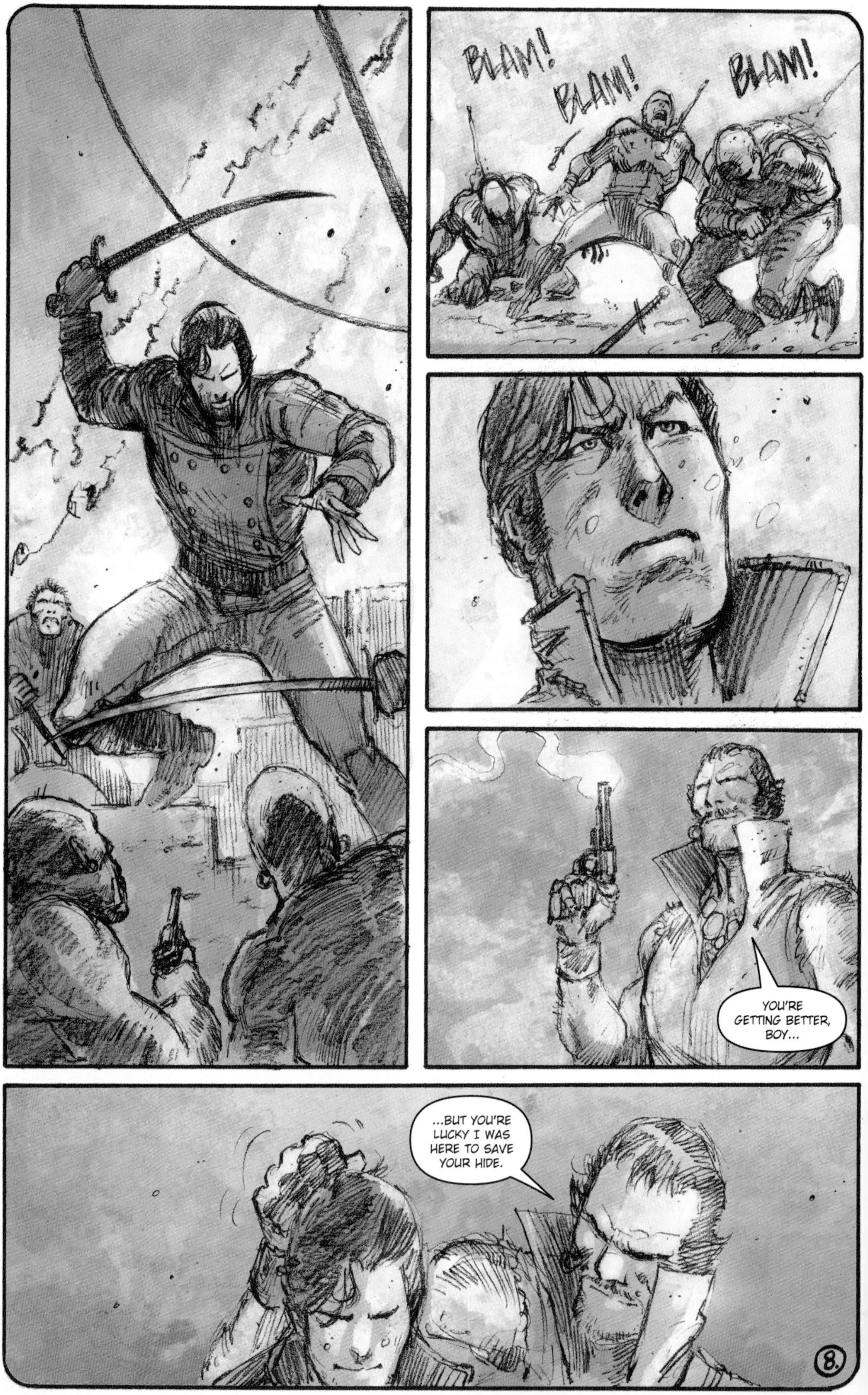
BLAM!
BLAM!
BLAM!
YOU'RE GETTING BETTER, BOY...
...BUT YOU'RE LUCKY I WAS HERE TO SAVE YOUR HIDE.

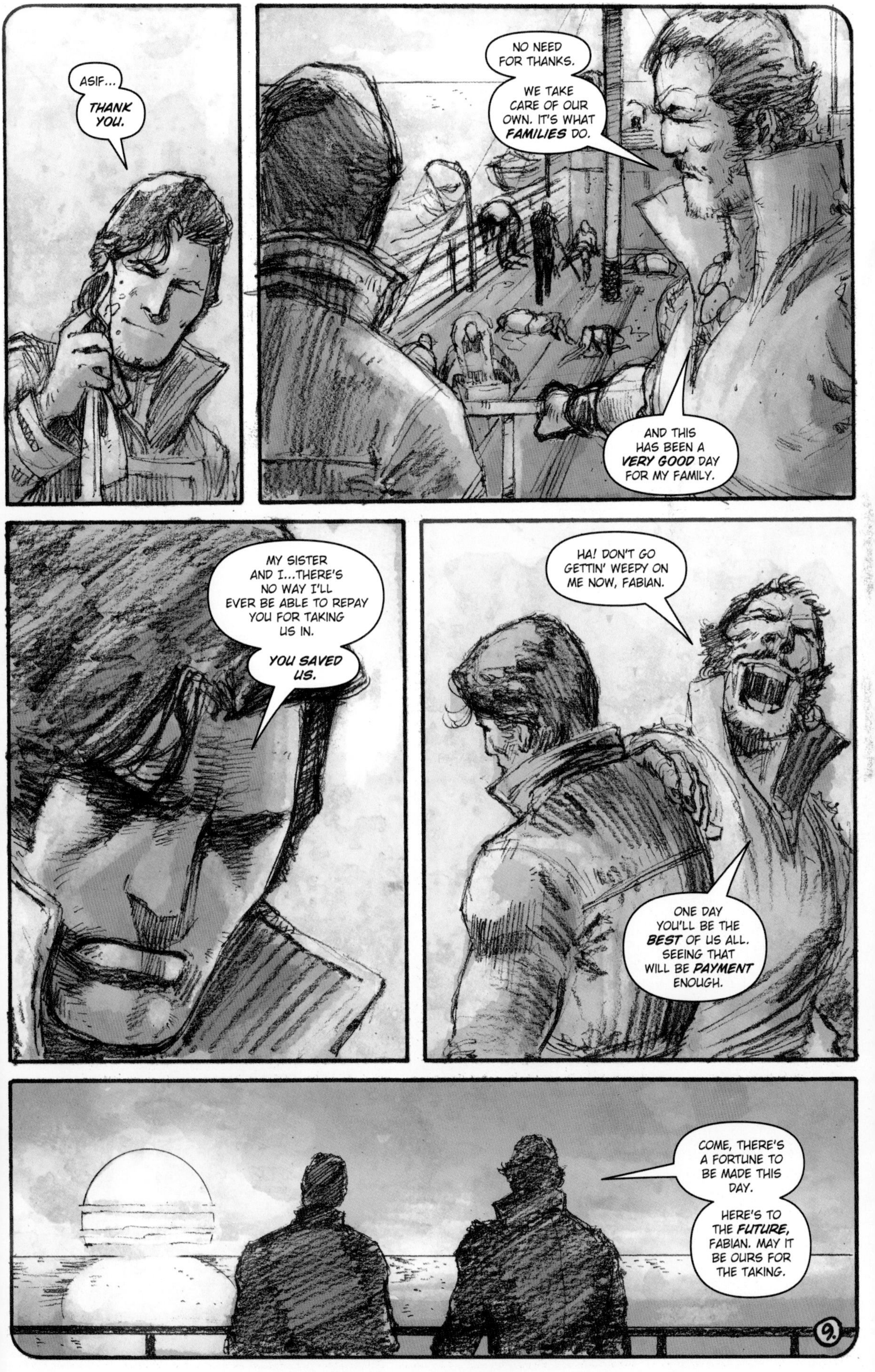

ASIF...
THANK YOU.
NO NEED FOR THANKS.
WE TAKE CARE OF OUR OWN. IT'S WHAT FAMILIES DO.
AND THIS HAS BEEN A VERY GOOD DAY FOR MY FAMILY.
MY SISTER AND I...THERE'S NO WAY I'LL EVER BE ABLE TO REPAY YOU FOR TAKING US IN.
YOU SAVED US.
HA! DON'T GO GETTIN' WEEPY ON ME NOW, FABIAN.
ONE DAY YOU'LL BE THE BEST OF US ALL. SEEING THAT WILL BE PAYMENT ENOUGH.
COME, THERE'S A FORTUNE TO BE MADE THIS DAY.
HERE'S TO THE FUTURE, FABIAN. MAY IT BE OURS FOR THE TAKING.

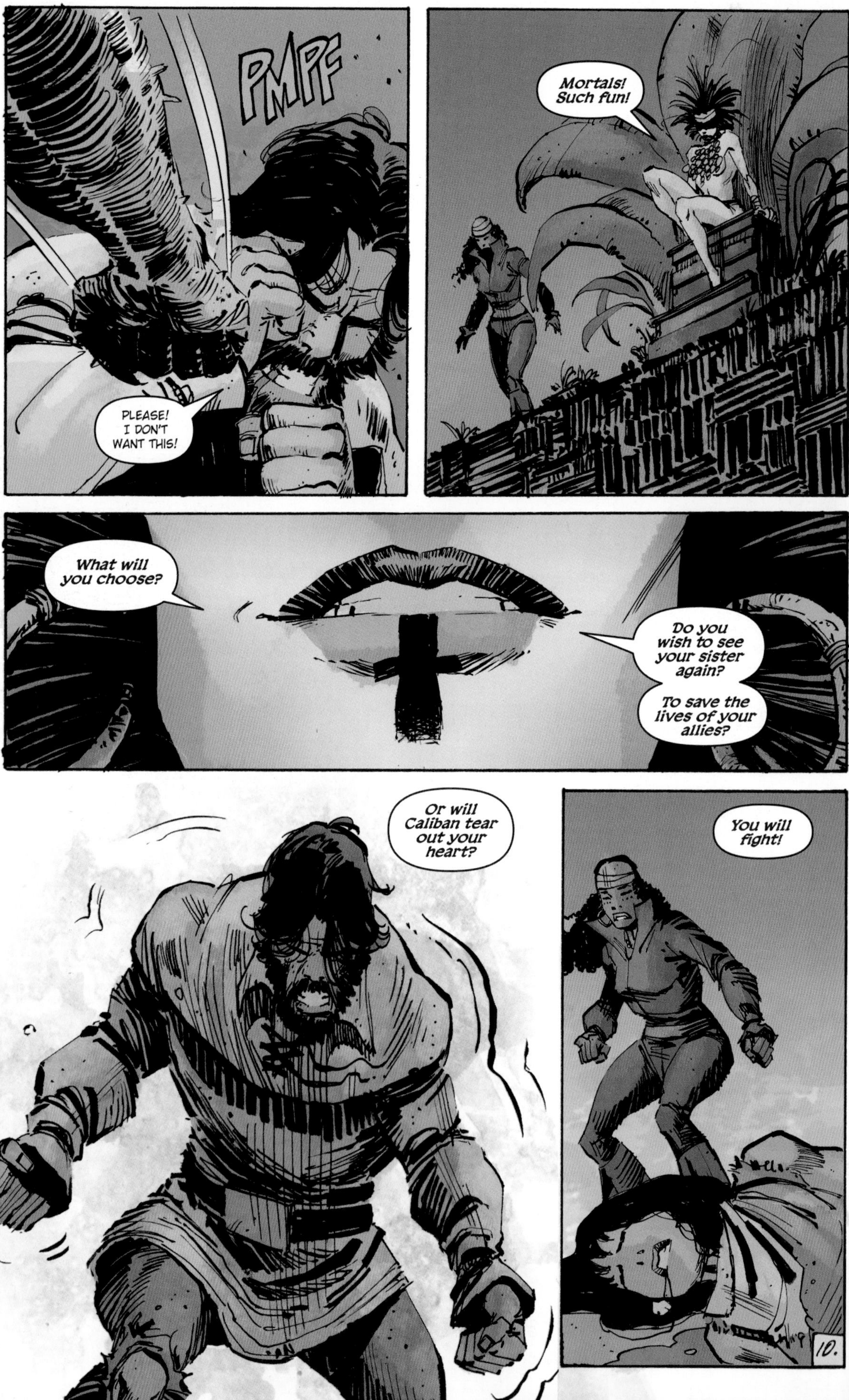
PMPF
PLEASE! I DON'T WANT THIS!
Mortals! Such fun!
What will you choose?
Do you wish to see your sister again?
To save the lives of your allies?
Or will Caliban tear out your heart?
You will fight!
10.

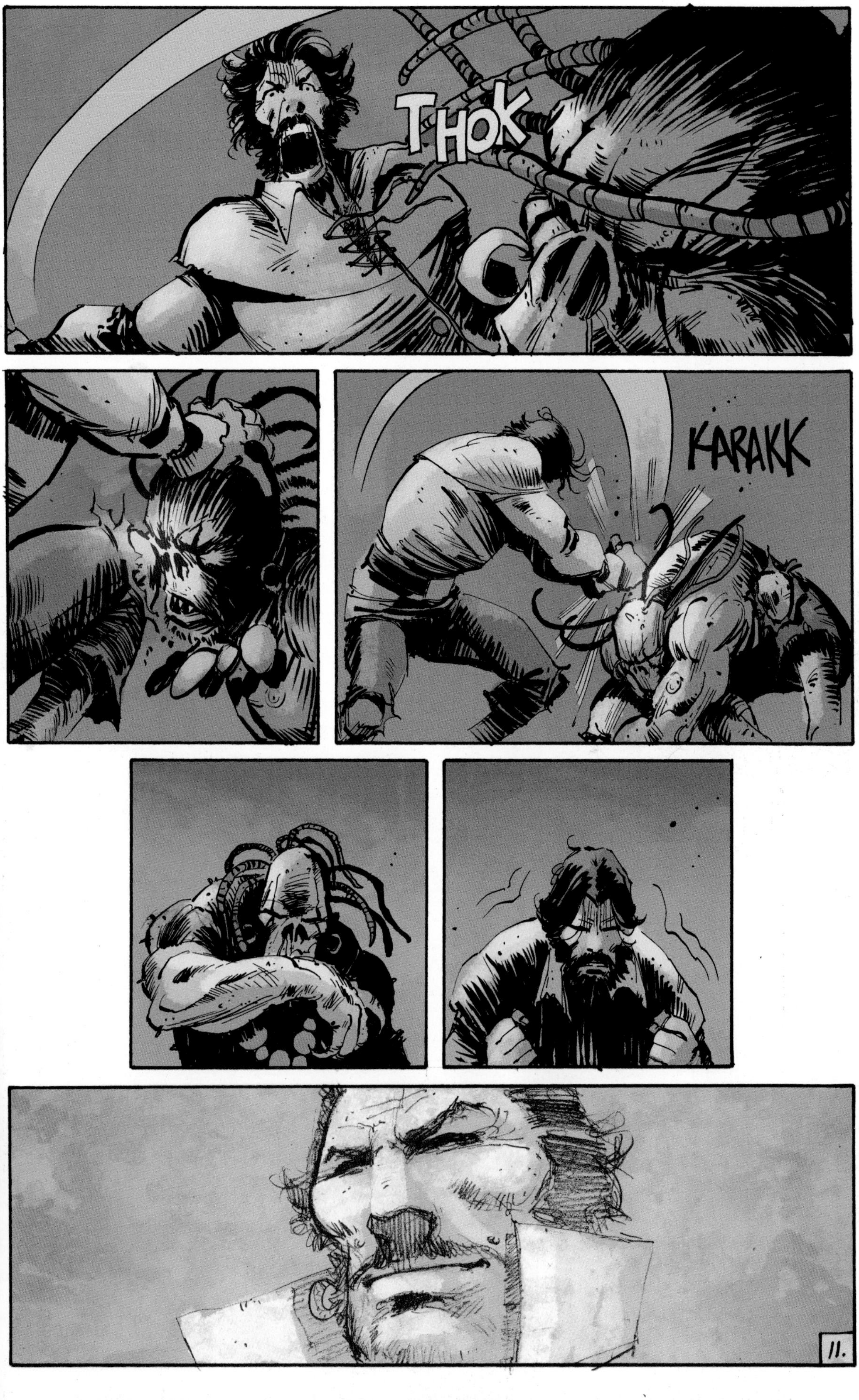
THOK
KARAKK
11.

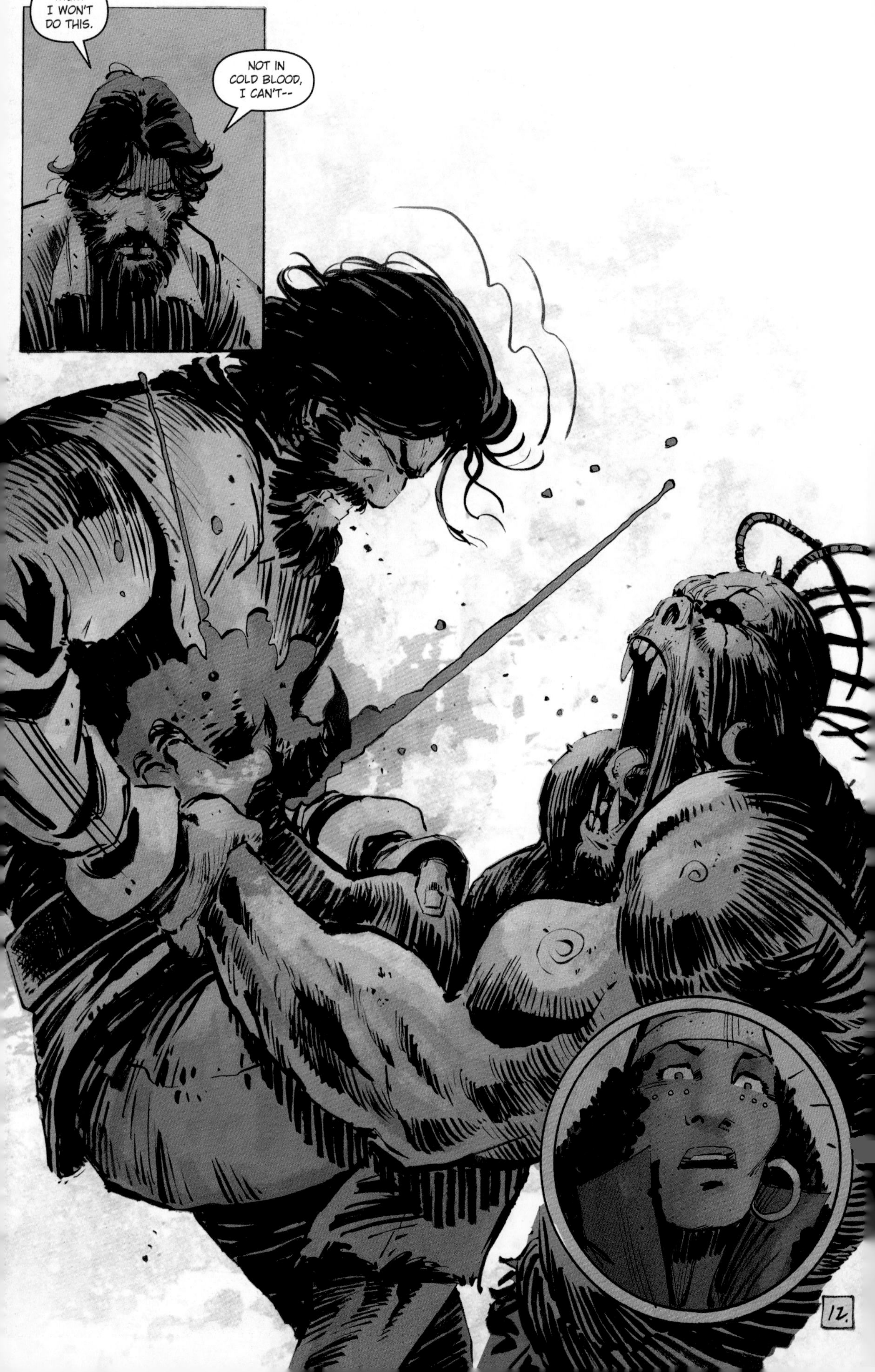
...I...
I WON'T
DO THIS.
NOT IN
COLD BLOOD,
I CAN'T--

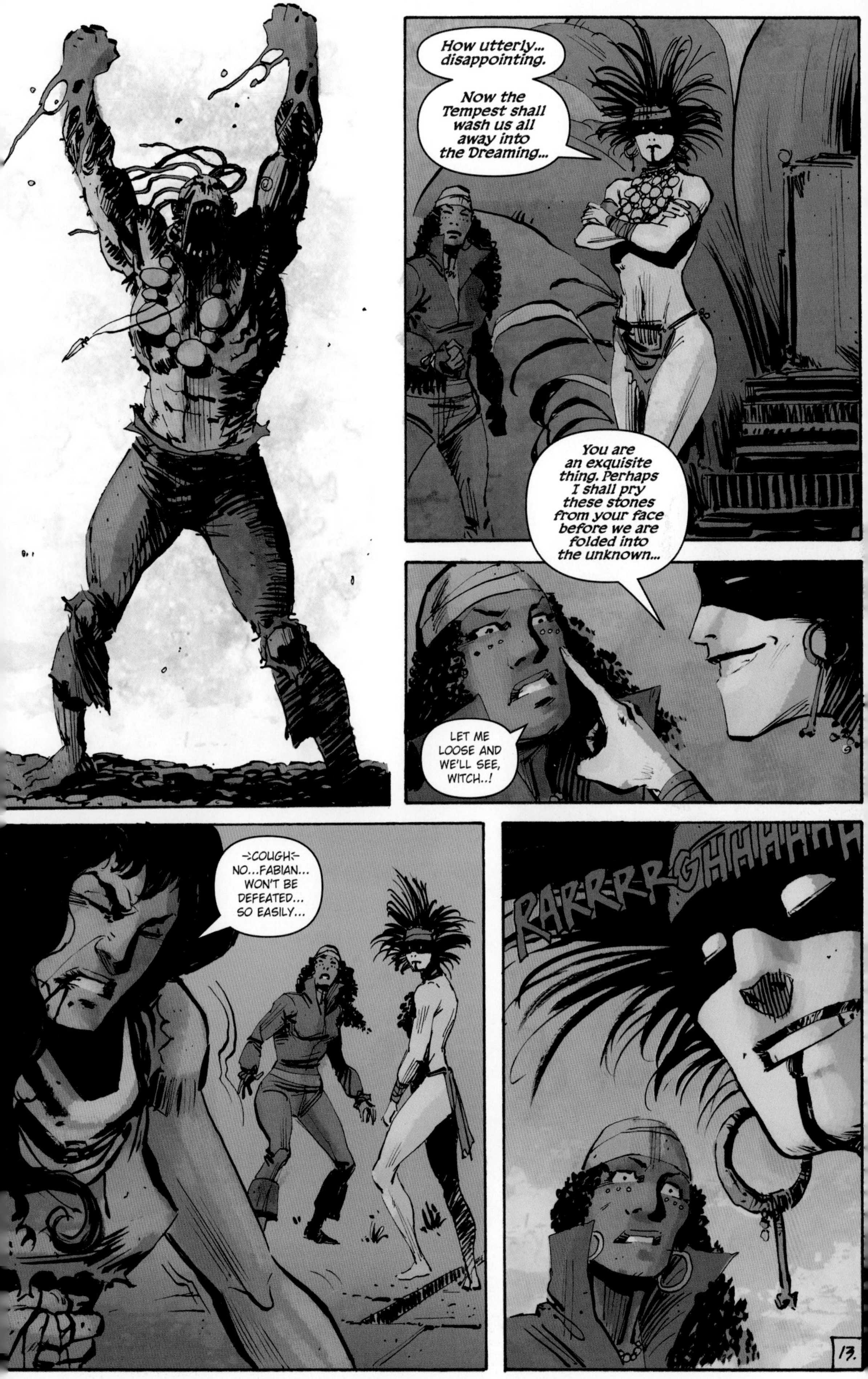
How utterly... disappointing.
Now the Tempest shall wash us all away into the Dreaming...
You are an exquisite thing. Perhaps I shall pry these stones from your face before we are folded into the unknown...
LET ME LOOSE AND WE'LL SEE, WITCH..!
-COUGH- NO...FABIAN... WON'T BE DEFEATED... SO EASILY...
RARRRRRGHHHHHH
13.

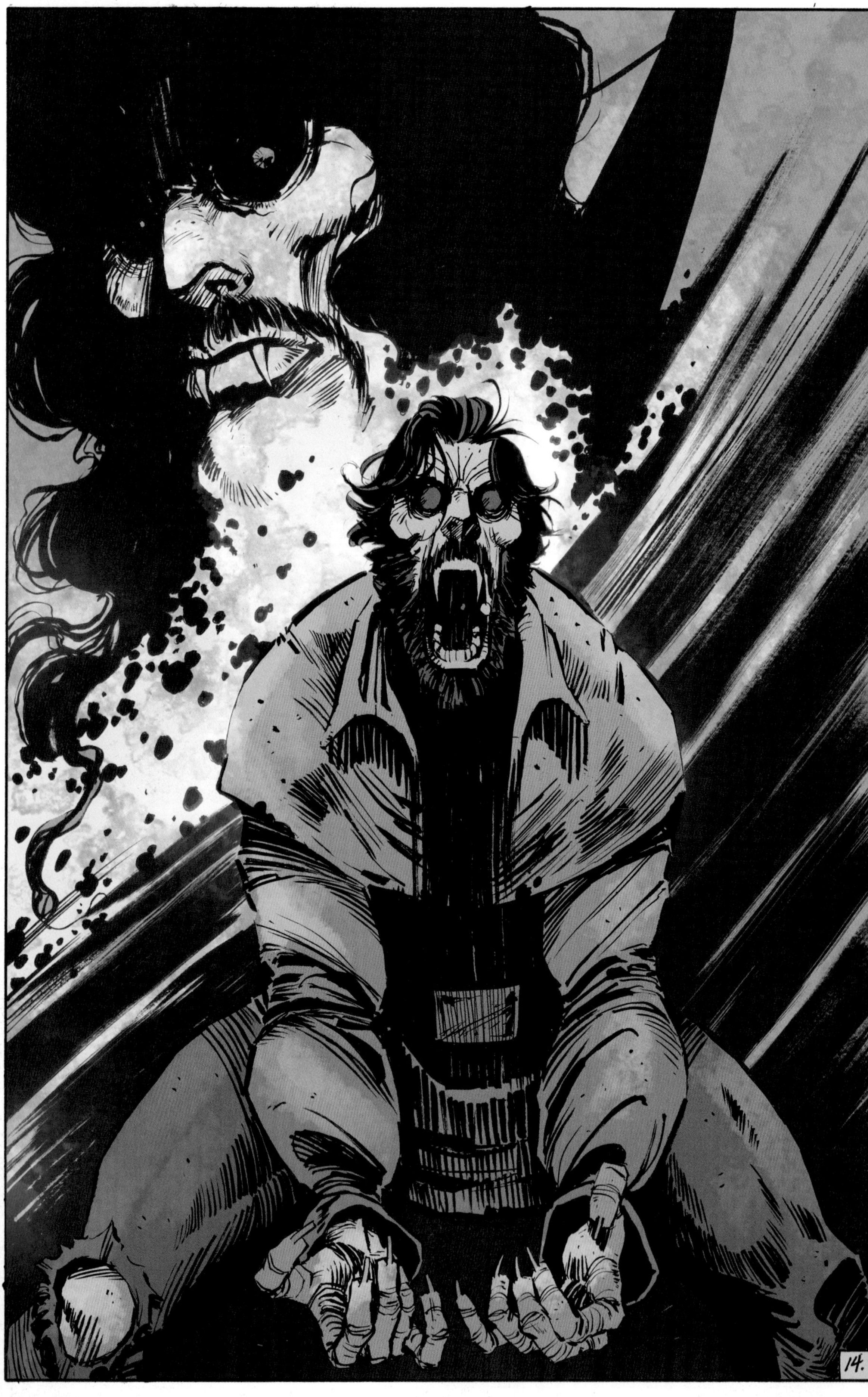

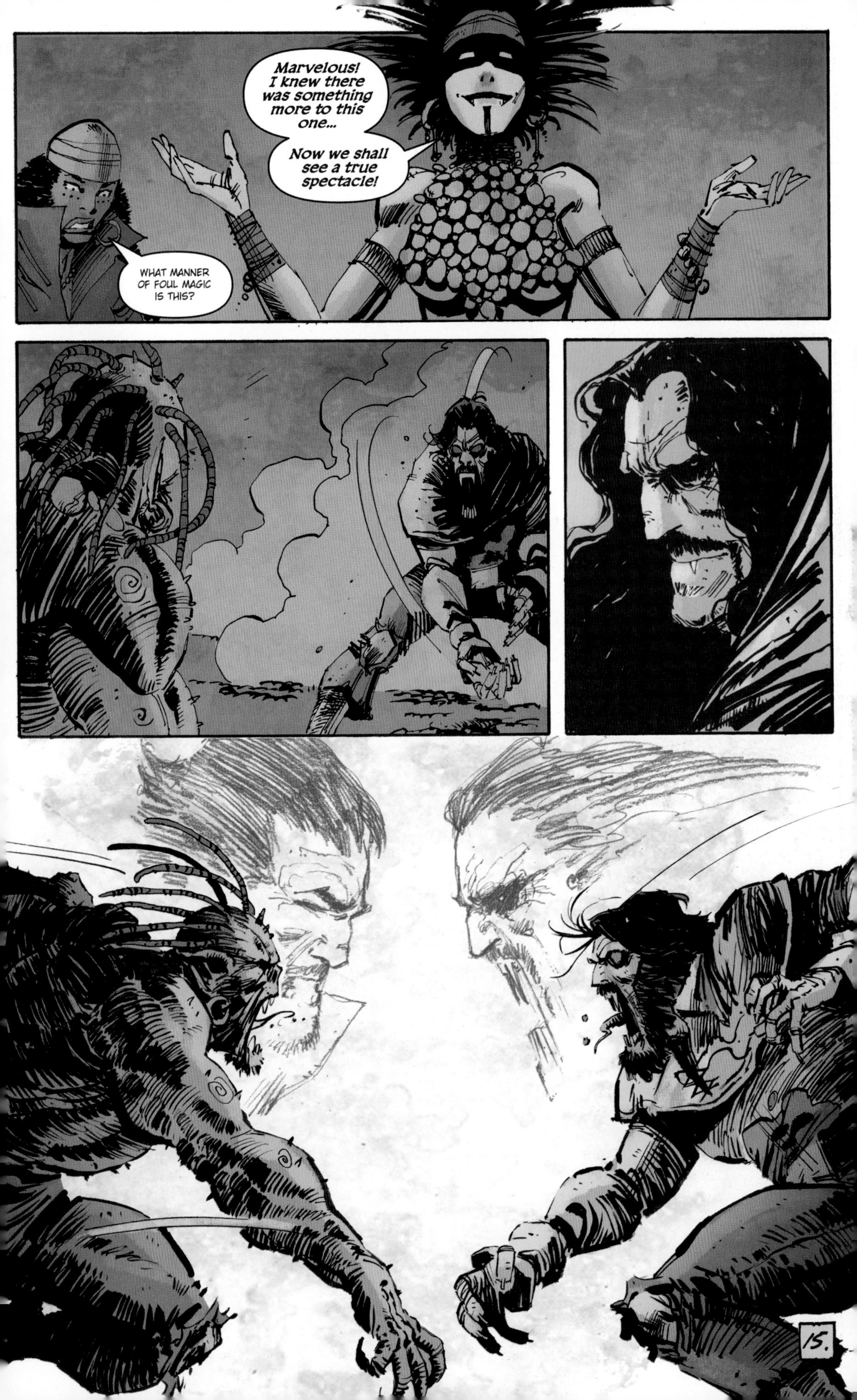
Marvelous! I knew there was something more to this one...
Now we shall see a true spectacle!
WHAT MANNER OF FOUL MAGIC IS THIS?

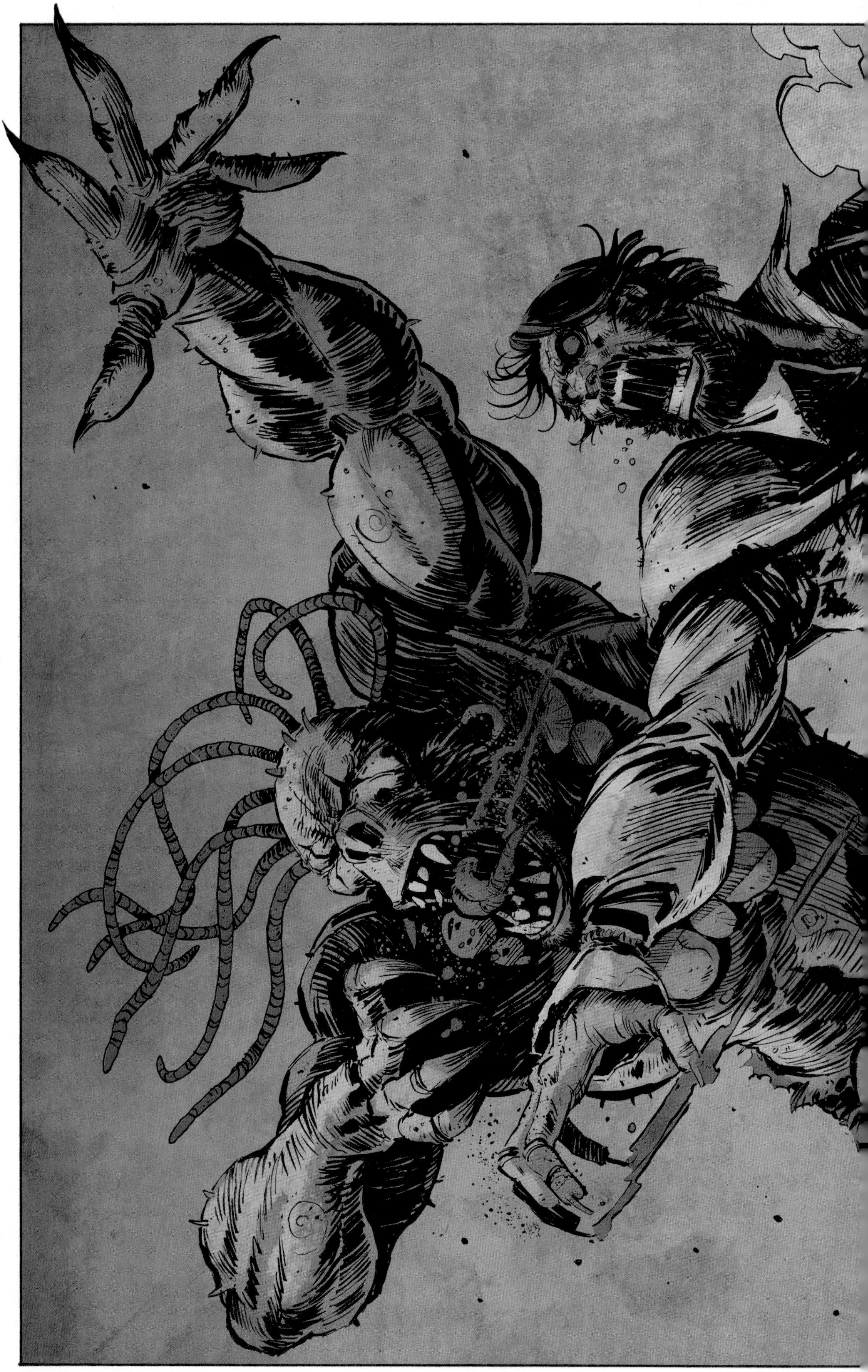

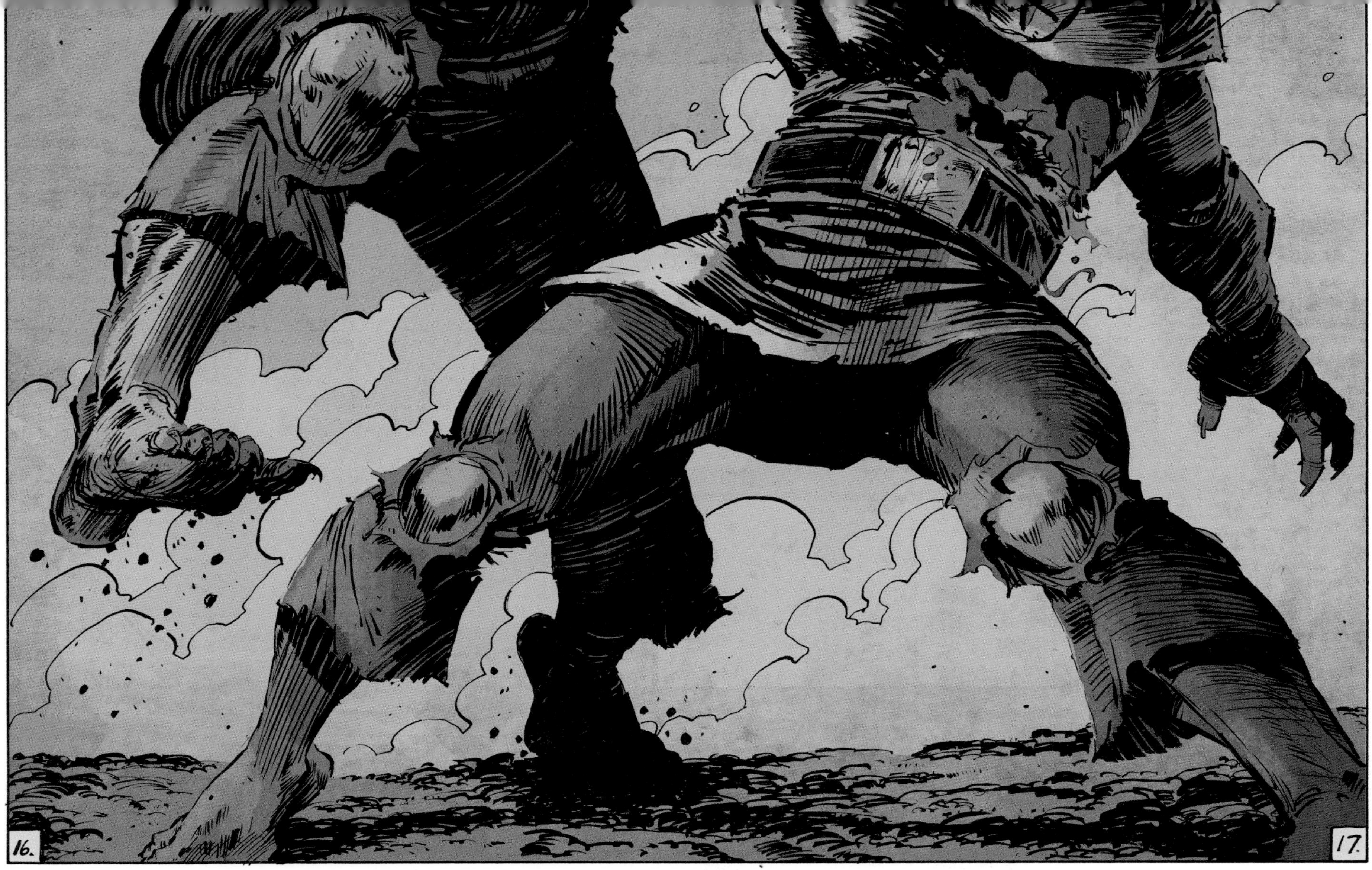
16.
17.

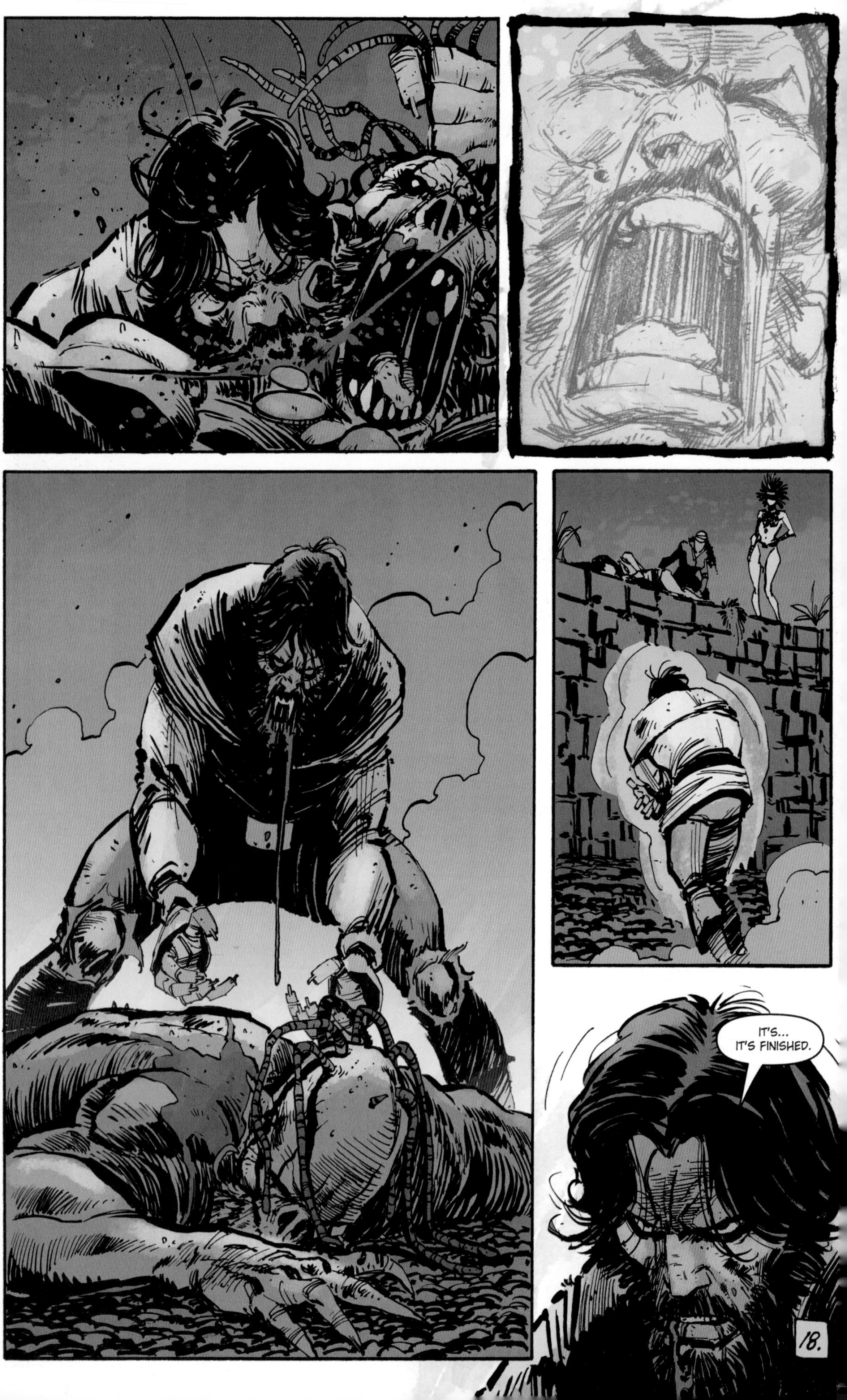
IT'S... IT'S FINISHED.
18.

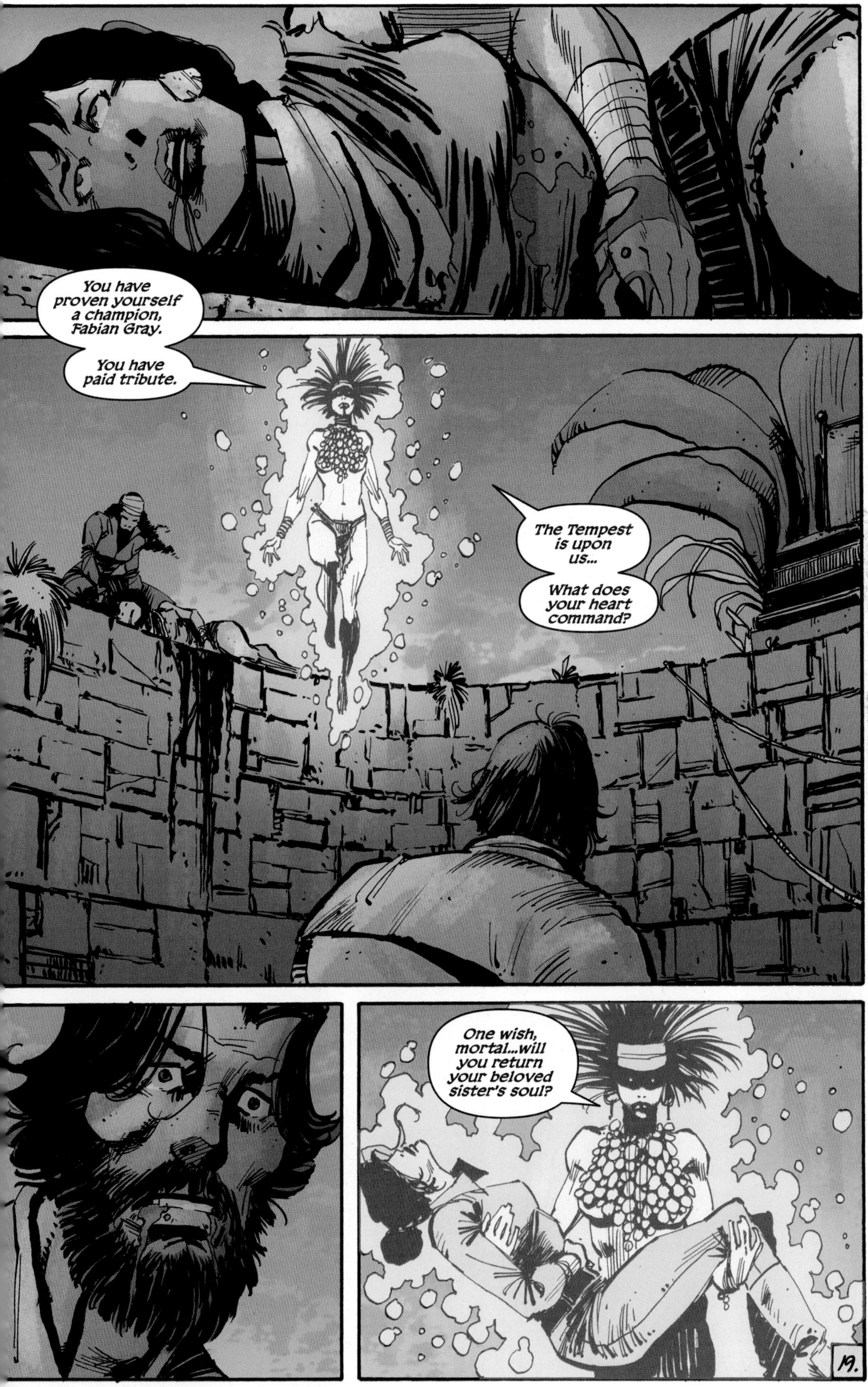
You have proven yourself a champion, Fabian Gray.
You have paid tribute.
The Tempest is upon us...
What does your heart command?
One wish, mortal...will you return your beloved sister's soul?
19.

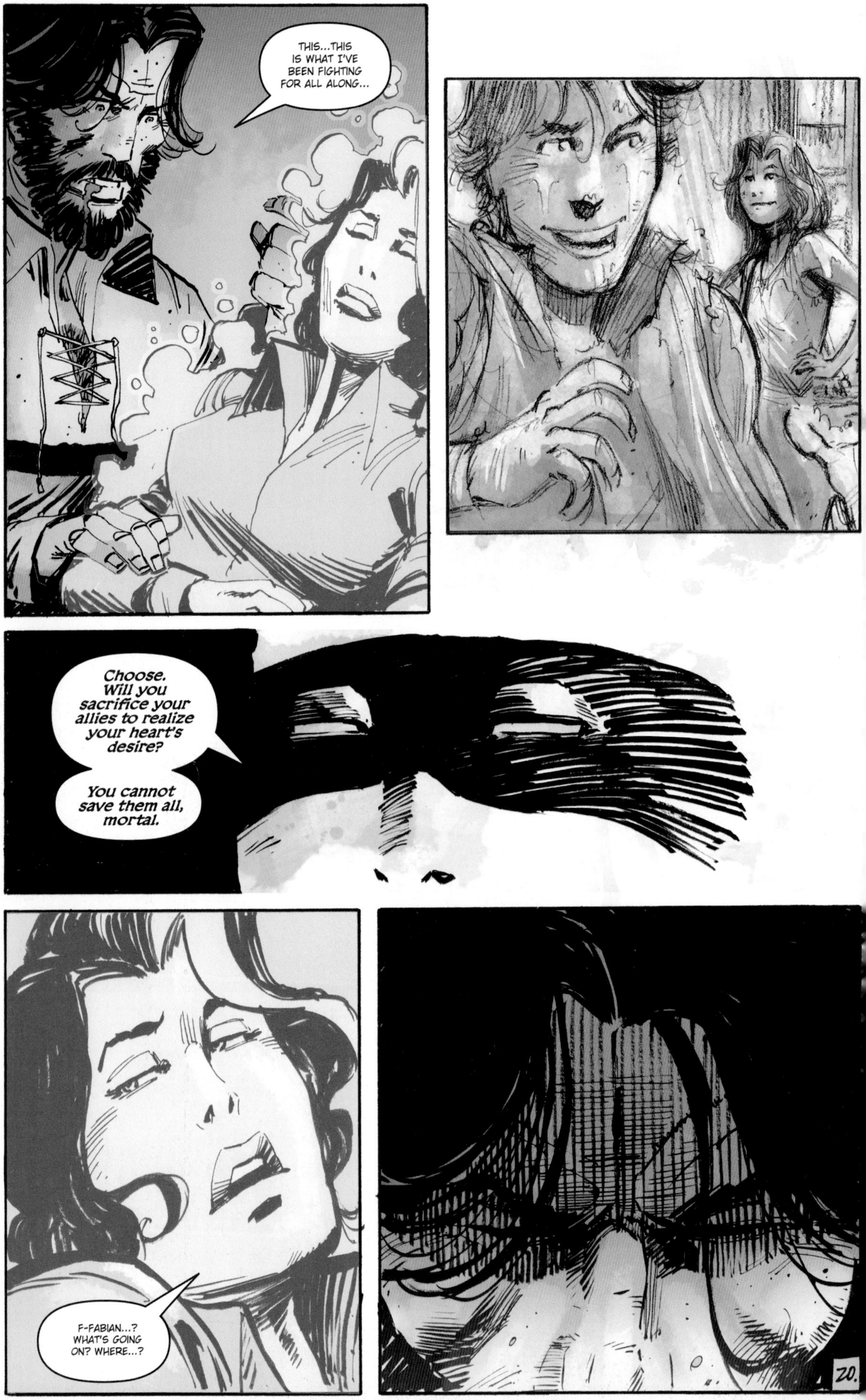
THIS...THIS IS WHAT I'VE BEEN FIGHTING FOR ALL ALONG...
Choose. Will you sacrifice your allies to realize your heart's desire?
You cannot save them all, mortal.
F-FABIAN...? WHAT'S GOING ON? WHERE...?
20.

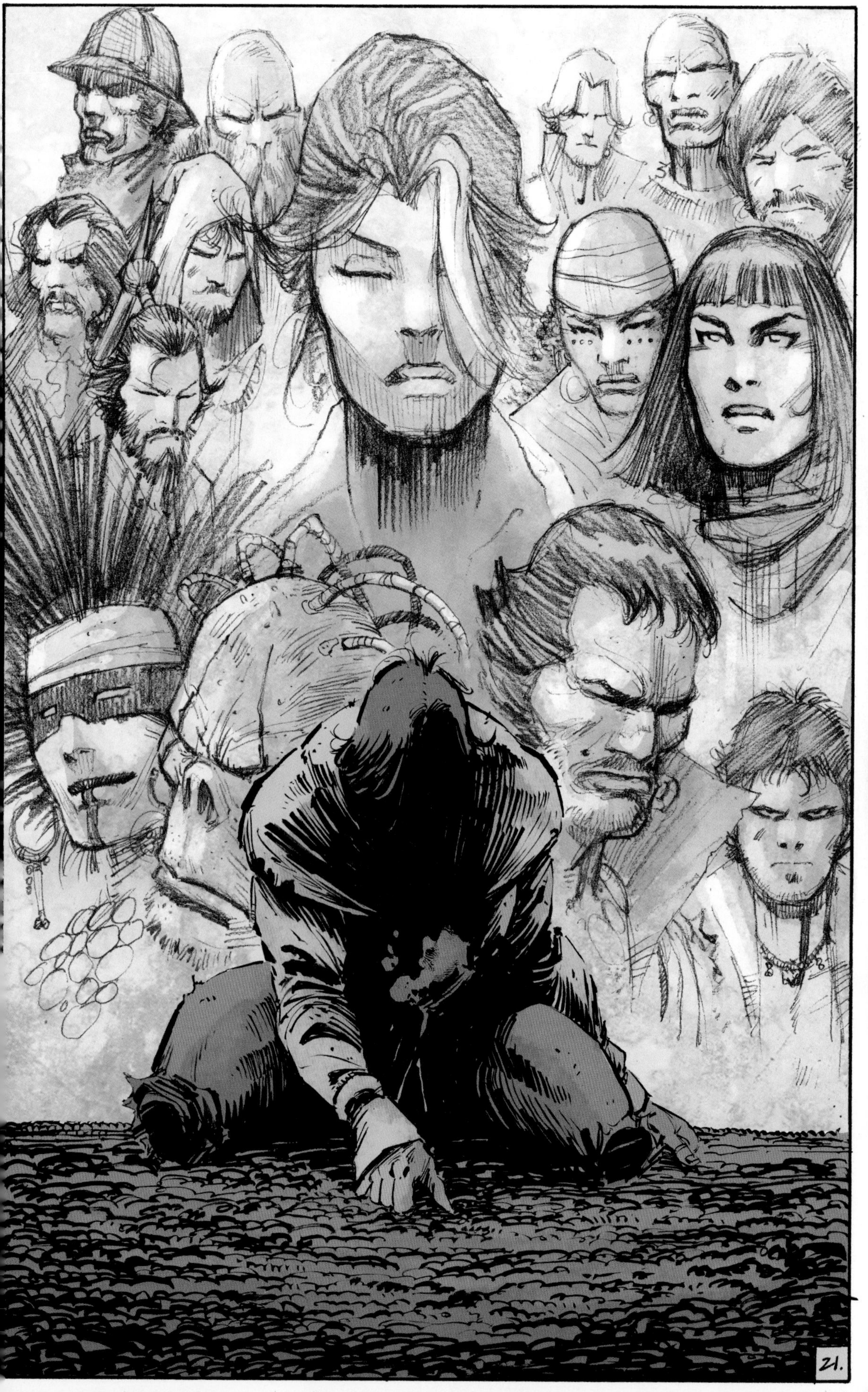

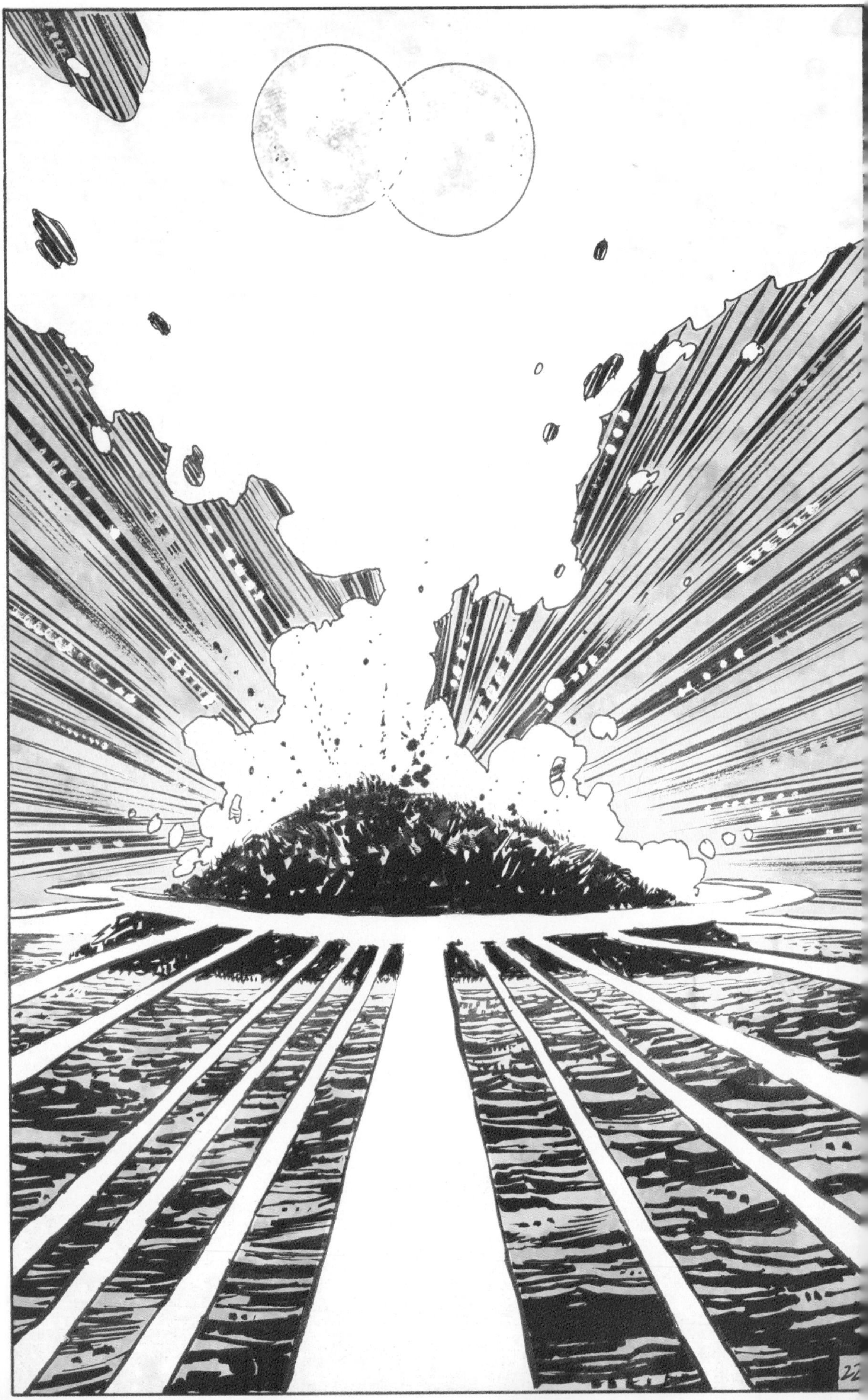

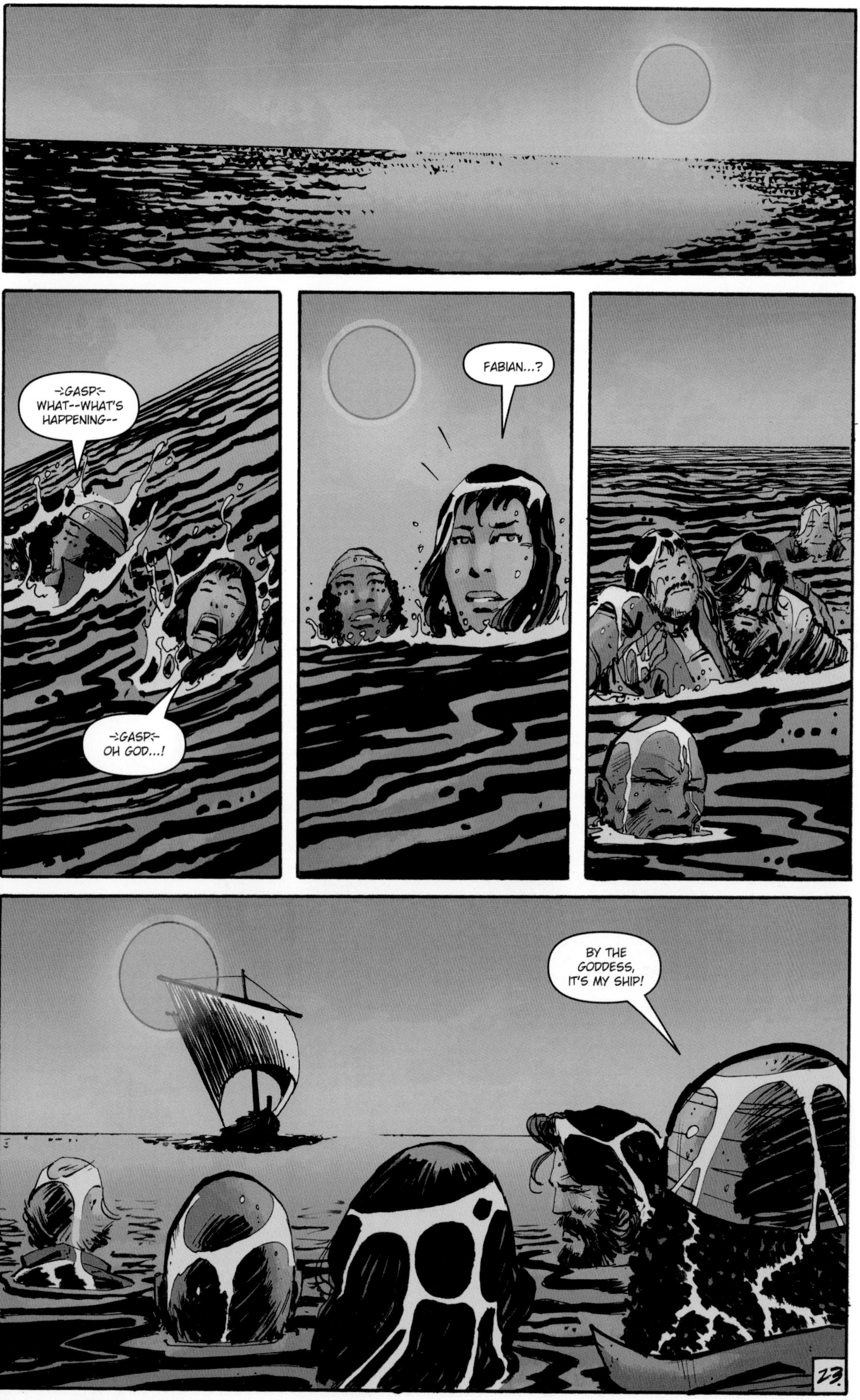

-GASP-
WHAT--WHAT'S HAPPENING--
-GASP-
OH GOD...!
FABIAN...?
BY THE GODDESS, IT'S MY SHIP!
23

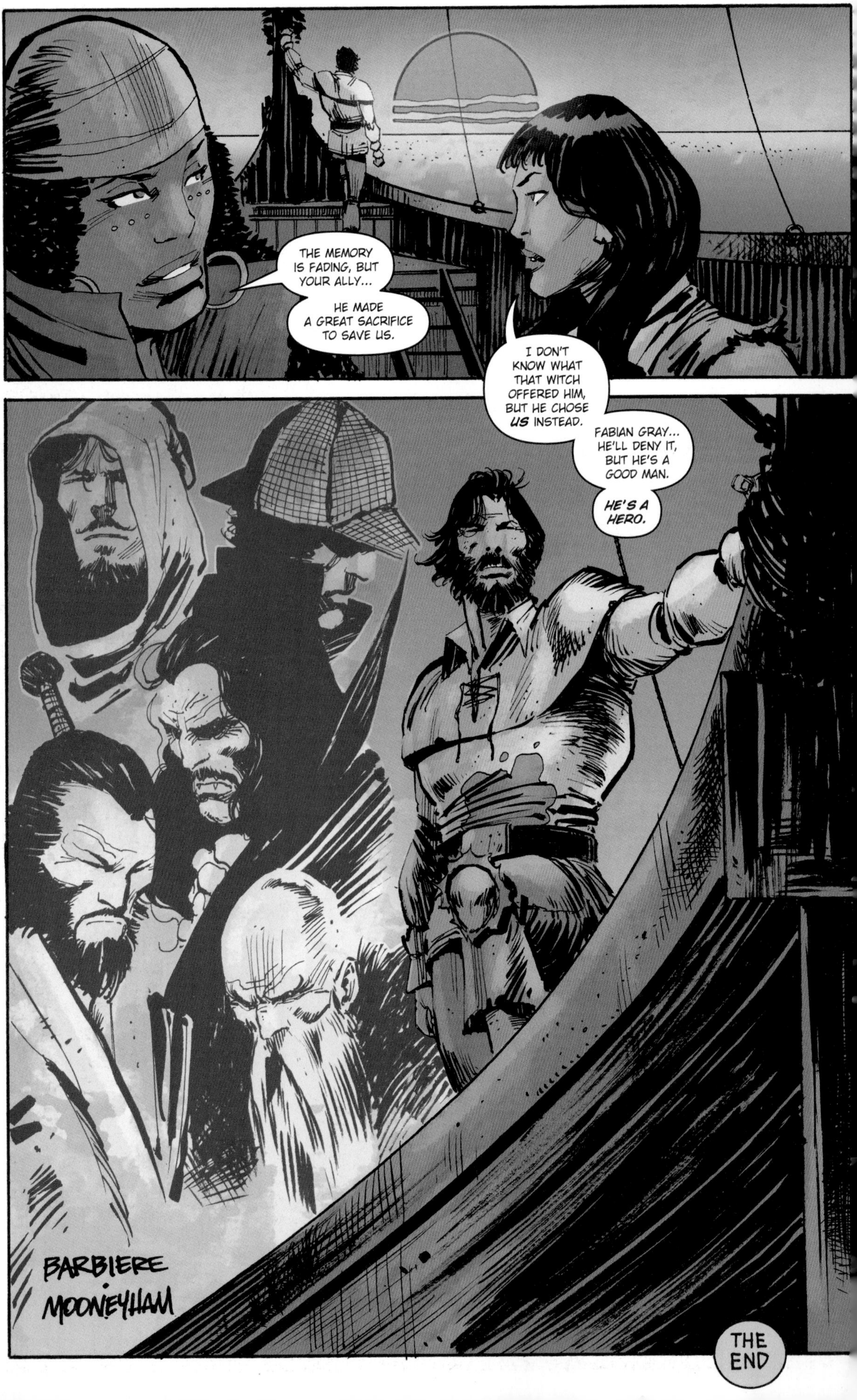
THE MEMORY IS FADING, BUT YOUR ALLY...
HE MADE A GREAT SACRIFICE TO SAVE US.
I DON'T KNOW WHAT THAT WITCH OFFERED HIM, BUT HE CHOSE *US* INSTEAD.
FABIAN GRAY... HE'LL DENY IT, BUT HE'S A GOOD MAN.
HE'S A HERO.
BARBIERE • MOONEYHAM
THE END

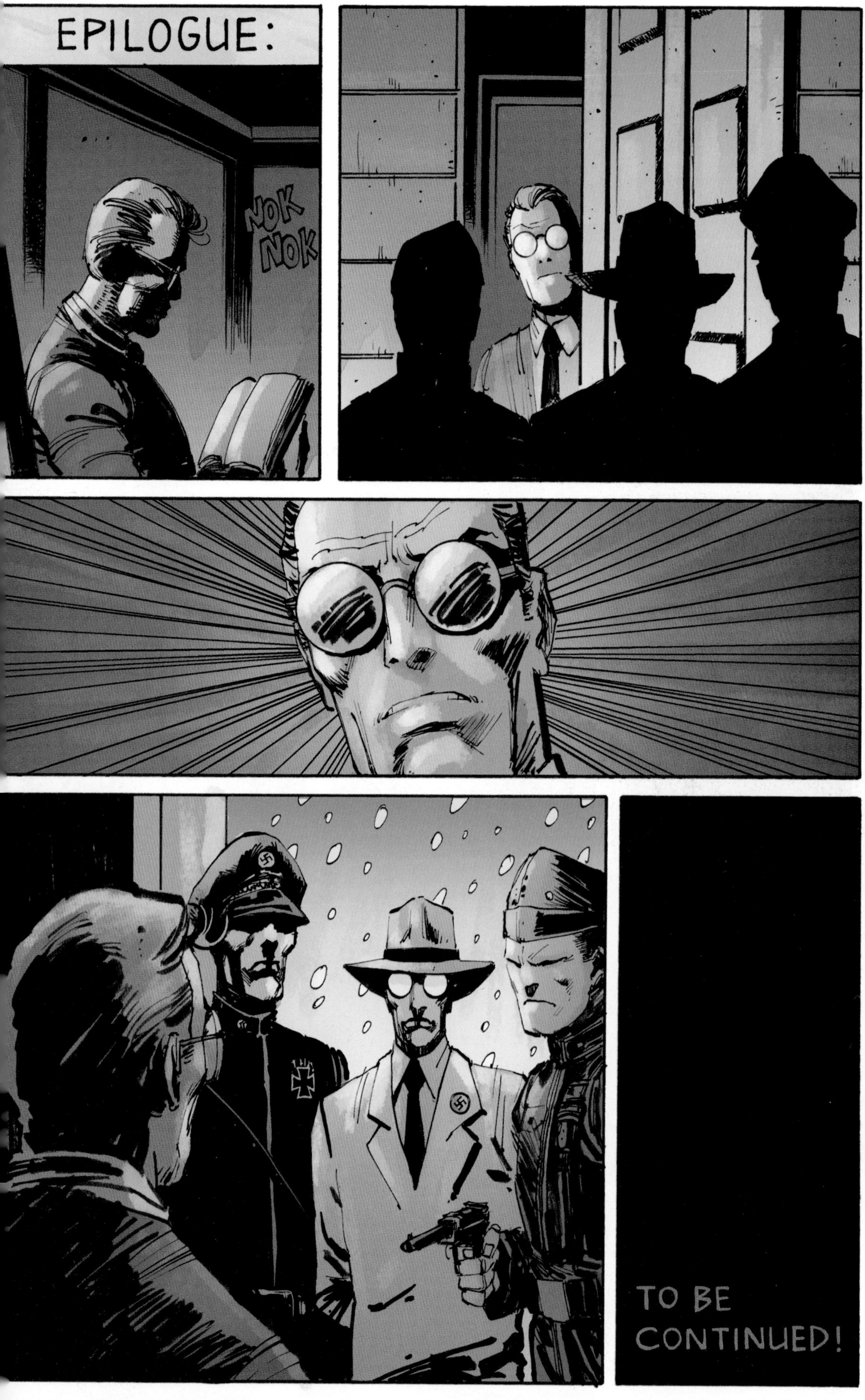
EPILOGUE:
NOK NOK
TO BE CONTINUED!

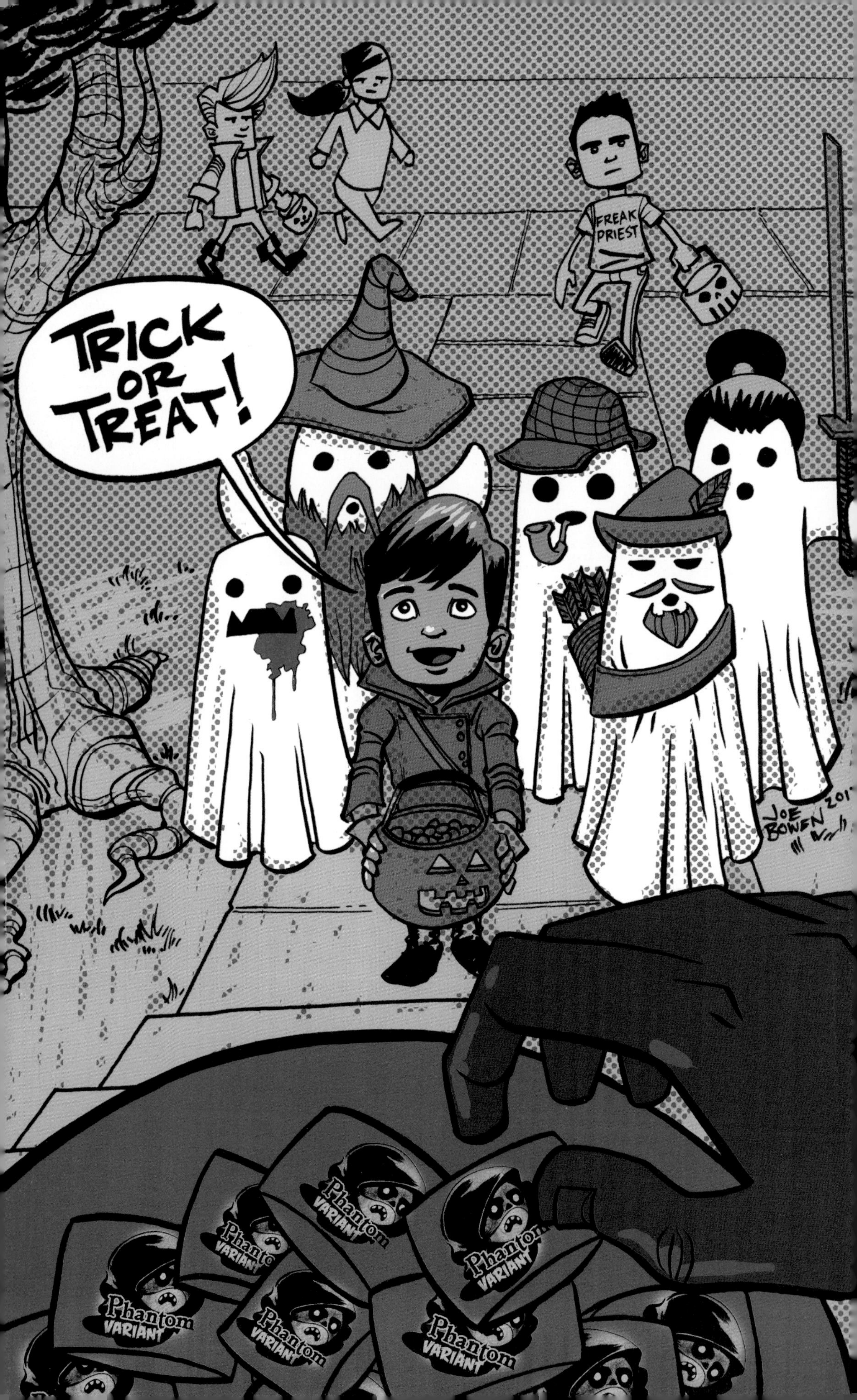
TRICK OR TREAT!
FREAK PRIEST
JOE BOWEN 201
Phantom VARIANT

FRANK J. BARBIERE *IS A WRITER LIVING
IN BROOKLYN. ORIGINALLY FROM NEW JERSEY,
HE IS A FORMER ENGLISH TEACHER WITH
DEGREES IN LITERATURE, CREATIVE WRITING,
AND ENGLISH EDUCATION.*

*IN HIS SHORT TIME IN THE INDUSTRY
FRANK HAS ALSO WORKED WITH MARVEL
COMICS, DC COMICS, DARK HORSE COMICS,
BOOM! STUDIOS, AND DYNAMITE
ENTERTAINMENT.*

*HTTP://WWW.ATLASINCOGNITA.COM
@ATLASINCOGNITA*

CHRIS MOONEYHAM *GRADUATED FROM THE
JOE KUBERT SCHOOL OF CARTOON AND
GRAPHIC ART IN 2010. IN ADDITION TO FIVE
GHOSTS, HE IS CURRENTLY WORKING ON
PREDATOR FOR DARK HORSE COMICS AND
HIS COVER WORK HAS BEEN FEATURED
AT BOOM! STUDIOS. HE CURRENTLY
RESIDES IN WISCONSIN.*

*HTTP://MOONEYHAM.TUMBLR.COM
@CTMOONEYHAM*

*ORIGINAL ART FOR SALE AT
HTTP://WWW.FELIXCOMICART.COM*

LAUREN AFFE *IS AN ARTIST AND COLORIST
LIVING IN NEW YORK CITY. HER WORK HAS
BEEN PUBLISHED BY DARK HORSE COMICS,
DYNAMITE ENTERTAINMENT, BOOM!
STUDIOS AND SLG.*

HTTP://LAURENAFFE.TUMBLR.COM